TRUTH
ABOUT
HEART
BREAK

B. CELESTE

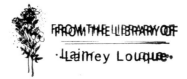

THE TRUTH ABOUT HEARTBREAK

He wasn't mine to love...

B. CELESTE

The Truth about Heartbreak

This is a work of fiction. Names, characters, businesses, places, events and incidents are either the products of the author's imagination or used in a fictitious manner. Any resemblance to actual persons, living or dead, or actual events is purely coincidental.

Cover Artist: RBA Designs

Editing by: K&B Editing

Formatting: Micalea Smeltzer

Published by:

B. Celeste

Hi, Mom.
You should probably skip the epilogues.

Playlist

"Wanted You More" - Lady Antebellum
"i hate you, i love you" - Gnash
"Lights Down Low" - Max
"Lips of an Angel" Hinder
"Mercy" - Brett Young
"Naked" - James Arthur
"Be Alright" - Dean Lewis
"Here Tonight" - Brett Young
"Yours" (wedding edition) - Russell Dickerson
"Ride" - Chase Rice (feat. Macy Maloy)

PROLOGUE

River / Present / 23

The velvet caress of silk sheets against my bare skin leaves me hyperaware of what I've done. Early morning sunlight slips through the cracked blinds and kisses my exposed back, coating the room in soft pinks and yellows.

Steady, rhythmic breathing sounds from behind me. In, out. In, out. It's a melody that makes my muscles lock, too afraid to reacquaint my eyes with every dip and curve of chiseled muscle displayed inches away.

His natural musky scent wraps around me, overwhelming my senses until my heart thumps wildly in my chest. It doesn't take away the memories of lingering touches, gentle kisses, and an overpowering sense of belonging. And less than twelve hours ago, I belonged to Everett Tucker in ways I never thought possible in the ten years of knowing him.

His touches scorched me.

His kisses burned me.

And his body...

The mattress dips with the shift of his weight. I hold my breath, waiting to see if he's awake. When his soft snores echo in the half-empty room, I release the breath and white knuckle the sheets against my breasts. Carefully, I sit up and squeeze my eyes closed like it'll soften the blow of reality.

I wait for the pounding headache or quake of unavoidable nausea to punish me, but my conscience reminds me of what I already know. I wasn't drunk last night. What I've done can't be blamed on alcohol.

My hand drags across my bare neck until my heart thunders in pure panic over my missing possession. I swallow my anxiety when I catch the silver chain resting on the night stand and remember the very moment he took it off me.

Nothing but skin. That's what he said he wanted between us. I've only taken this necklace off to shower and sleep. It goes everywhere with me, the silver paint palette and brush charm sweeping over my heartbeat as a reminder that he cares. But in the moment I had him as more than a wish, a hope, a dream, he didn't want it lingering.

Nothing but skin.

My fingertips touch the newest charm, a cracked heart, and I suck in a short breath when the contact shocks me. Clenching the sheets tighter to me, I turn slightly to peek through my peripheral and see a tussle of dirty blond hair against my starch white pillow case.

Look, my conscience taunts. *Look at him.*

Slivers of tan skin make their way into my sight as I shift, my gaze drifting up the mountain of hard muscles that form his toned biceps as they wrap around a pillow. Worrying my bottom lip, my heart somersaults in my chest when the curve of his square jaw comes into view. The sharp line of it is coated with early morning shadow that he'll shave despite preferring a thin layer of stubble.

He looks peaceful when he's sleeping; the hard edge he normally radiates eased to a laxed slumber. From this angle, I can see the faded white scar that stretches from the bottom of his left ear along the curve of his throat, landing just above his pulse. You wouldn't know it's there unless you know the story, and he doesn't tell just anyone.

But I'm not just anyone.

Especially not now.

My throat tightens from the emotions lodging in the back of it as I scope out his sculpted body. He works hard for every muscle, spends countless hours in the gym or training at the fire department, and it shows. The man sleeping beside me has been a figment of my imagination that I've conjured thousands of times, but his body is a masterpiece I never could have perfected unless I saw it in person.

I absorb the memory of his body spread on my mattress, bare to me. Every vulnerability laying in a mess of sheets, open to pull apart and dissect and regret when the sun fully rises.

Less than twelve hours ago I belonged to the minty

eyed boy I've loved since I was thirteen. But Everett Tucker isn't mine to love.

He stirs when I rise from bed.

"Everett," I whisper brokenly, my heart shattering inside my chest. I can feel the pieces splintering apart as I choke out my final words. "We made a mistake."

BEFORE

ONE

Everett / 17

Thud. Thud. Thud.

The loud echo of hard rubber dribbling against wood fills the gymnasium, paired with the piercing squeal of sneakers against the freshly polished floor as they run at me to block my shot. I focus on the basket and side-step Zach, some freshman who wanted in on our private game, and make the basket without much hassle.

My buddies hoot at me as I jog after the basketball, tossing it at Oliver who catches it easily. Tucking it under his arm and brushing the back of his wrist across his forehead, he nudges my arm.

"How many points is that for you?"

"Like we could keep count," the freshie scoffs. He's bitter because I wouldn't pass it to him, but the asshole wouldn't even change out of his work boots before joining in. If I were Coach, I'd throw a shit fit for fucking up the floor.

Freemont is scrawled in big blue and white block letters across the red outline of the polished court. Patriotic, since we're the Freemont Patriots. The mats lining the walls are the same blue as the letters, with some creepy sketch of our first mascot on the end mat since we can't have an actual mascot anymore. Who knows why? I don't really care enough to ask Coach.

I grunt when the ball smacks into my chest, and glare at Oliver when he feigns innocence. The fucker loves getting on my nerves.

I toss the ball back and we do that a few more times before we go one-on-one like we usually do right before lunch ends. "I'm trying to talk to you, and you keep spacing out. What's your deal?"

Shit.

Oliver's parents have been in the long process of adoption. For about two years, they've talked about adding on to their family. I know this because I spend ninety percent of my time at the James' residence. Bridgette and Robert are practically parents to me, so I know how big today is for them because they're finally signing papers to get some pre-teen they've spent time with for a while now.

He tries tricking me by darting left, but my reflexes are better. I easily block him and steal the ball. "Why aren't you with them right now?"

Managing to get the ball back, we battle it out until he gets a shot in on me. "It's not like I haven't met the girl before. They tried fostering her once before, remember? But something fell through on their application, so they settled for us meeting her in stages."

I grunt. "Still think you should be there."

He shrugs, glancing at the clock. "I've got a bio test today that I actually studied for. They understand."

Coach has been on his ass about keeping his grades up, because the ten-week progress reports showed a less than stellar grade point average. Anyone getting a sixty-five or lower in any class has to sit out on games. It's school policy.

When we realize the bell is going to ring in less than five minutes, we head to the storage room and toss the ball back on the rack. "What's she like anyway?"

"Quiet."

My brow quirks.

He shoves the locker room door open. "I don't know, Rhett. She's not very talkative, even when my parents asked her questions about herself. Her social worker had to fill us in any time we met."

Sounds normal given the circumstances. I'm not keen on opening up to strangers about my personal life either.

"What's her story?"

He splashes water on his face. "Not sure. Mom and Dad didn't really fill me in on why she's in foster care, just that she doesn't have anybody else to take care of her."

I just nod and wait until he has his books before we walk out into the hall as the bell rings. Crowds of high schoolers swarm the narrow hallways leading to the different wings of Freemont High. It's not a big school by physical size or number of enrollees considering we're smack dab in the middle of Bridgeport. Then again, the city has two different private academies across town that battle it out for kids.

I'm surprised some of the students aren't enrolled in Bridgeport or Rousseau Academy. Oliver being one of them. He comes from money, since his parents are both big players in the business world here in Bridgeport. His dad helped found a multi-million-dollar company with my late father that employs a good portion of the city's residents. If not in their main building on the outskirts of the business district, then in one of the different branches across New York State.

But Bridgette and Robert thought he would do better in a public setting. If Oliver wanted to switch, they probably would have let him. But he seems to do just fine blending in with the rest of us.

"You coming over to meet her later?"

His question catches me off guard. "Why? It seems like that's a family thing."

He smacks my chest when we stop outside my history class. "You're family, dude. She might as well get used to seeing you around. You practically live with us."

He's exaggerating, even if there's a room with some of my shit in it. Spare clothes, a toothbrush, the basics. It's mostly if I crash after a game or just don't feel like going home.

"She'll have enough people to meet." I wave him off, backing into the classroom. "Let me know how it goes though."

He shakes his head but doesn't say anything, disappearing in the crowd of lingering kids getting to their classes.

Mr. Hall tips his head as I pass his desk to my seat. "Mr. Tucker. Good of you to join us. See me after class about the work you missed."

He's referring to my habit of skipping afternoon classes. Not enough to fail, just to catch notice. Most of my teachers have mentioned it to me, even to my grandfather. But since I'm usually *with* my grandfather in the afternoon, he doesn't scold me for it. He knows I'm trying to help, even if he prefers I stick out the school day.

Fact of the matter is, I don't care for school or my grades. It's a waste of time to sit in class and hear about how the Industrial Revolution transformed America. The only thing worth sitting through is English, which most people dread. Not just because Ms. Perkins is a hard ass, but because the material is usually dry. Me? I prefer the subject. I'm one of the few.

I respond with a tip of my head, which he takes as a confirmation of his request. He leaves me be as the rest of the class pours in.

Peter York saunters into the room and drops into the seat next to mine, absentmindedly waving toward the group of girls who greet him in shrill voices.

My chin tips in their direction. "Don't want to sit by your fan club? Seems like they'd be good company to keep during the lecture."

He snorts and smacks his notebook and pen down on

the desk. Images of genitalia are carved into the green cardboard cover. "Aw, don't want me around, Tuck? That shit hurts my feelings."

I ignore him. He knows I hate when he calls me Tuck. My last name is Tucker, which plenty of people refer to me as. But he feels justified to call me anything he wants.

He nudges my arm. "I know I'm not James, but I think I'm pretty awesome company."

York is the point guard of Freemont's basketball team. He's up against Oliver to make captain since our last one got expelled, but Coach told them both they'd have to prove to him who wants it more. They're both good players—great, even. But York's arrogance will get in the way of Coach choosing him if he's not careful.

"You're all right."

Peter snorts. "Whatever, man."

He used to be tight with Oliver until they both made the team. Then York's competitive side came out and screwed things up. He's always given me shit for being close with the James'. Not just because of my friendship with Oliver, but because their family took me in. He knows the circumstances, the reason I need a set of parents like Bridgette and Robert. But he doesn't see it like that. He just wants to be in with Bridgeport's biggest names.

That's why I'll never respect Peter. Doesn't mean I'll willingly be an ass. I'm a lot of things, but nothing like him. Stooping to his level is below me.

When Mr. Hall starts class, nobody tries talking to me. It gives me time to soak in the pointless information, jotting down a few notes but mostly drifting off and wondering about the newest James member.

Freemont isn't a bad school, and the people are better than the ones in the ritzy academies. But that won't stop people like York trying to get in with the family using any means necessary. And this girl is young, twelve or thirteen if I remember correctly. I wonder if Oliver thought of that before, if he'll make sure she's protected from the gold diggers disguised with friendly smiles.

For her sake, I hope so.

TWO

River / 13

The exterior of the house that the car rolls up to is made of pristine red brick with large white pillars lining the front. It's a mansion, nothing like I've ever been to before. From my view through the tinted car window, I'd guess three stories if not four. That doesn't include the full basement and attic they probably have.

Considering the James family's wealth, I expected there to be a gate protecting the property. Instead, it's surrounded by similar, less extravagant houses in the residential side of town.

They told me about their home. *My* home now, I guess. It's no surprise that Bridgette and Robert James are made of money. I could see that the second they stepped into the small room Jill, my social worker, had us meet in. Robert's gray suit was pressed, and Bridgette's plum dress was ironed and tailored to fit perfectly to her body.

But *seeing* their home is different than trying to picture it. It didn't matter how many times they told me about the seven bedrooms and who knows how many baths, my imagination did it no justice. I take it all in as Robert parks just in front of the cement steps that lead to the wrap around porch and entrance. Trimmed flower bushes line either side of the cobblestone walkway leading to the stairs, giving a little color to the monotone exterior.

Sucking in a breath when Bridgette brushes my arm, I snap my eyes from their house to her. I'm greeted with a soft, white smile. The curve of her painted lips is a friendly gesture, and there's sympathy mixed in the hues of her hazel eyes.

"We're home, River."

Home.

They've used that word nine times today. First when they told me they couldn't wait to take me here, and again not even seconds later when they told Jill that everybody was more than ready to have me. No matter their insistence on referring to the mansion positioned next to us as my home, it's a concept that tastes bitter in my mouth.

Jill called the single-wide trailer I lived at for the past eight months my home. I shared a tiny bedroom and a full-size bed with a three and ten-year-old. Before that, Jill referred to my home as the two-story blue house on Maple Avenue in Exeter. I lived with a middle-aged couple and another foster, a boy named Trevor.

Home is relative. It's a place of residence, no matter how temporary. So, I suppose they're right. This is my new home. It's a roof over my head until something happens, and something *always* happens.

"River?" Robert speaks this time, his baritone voice locking my muscles in the back seat. Bridgette takes notice and gives me a comforting gaze, her hand itching to touch mine but keeping a distance.

Jill told them about me. Not everything, but enough. They know I don't like to be touched, or to be left alone with men. But they don't know the gruesome details behind my fear. I asked Jill not to say anything, and she promised it was my story to tell.

My lips are sealed.

"It's … large." My voice is an audible whisper, barely loud enough for me to hear. Gazing back at the mansion, I note the flowerpots in the lower level windows, with green leafy plants waterfalling over the sides. They're pretty. Serene.

I catch a light flickering on in one of the rooms, and Robert must notice too. "Ah, Oliver must be home."

Bridgette smiles at me. "You remember Oliver, right? We took you both out for frozen yogurt at the strip mall a few months ago."

Oliver is their biological son. Before bringing him on the meet-up she refers to, they told me all about him. Pride always radiates from their stories when Robert mentions his spot on the school basketball team or when Bridgette mentions his role in student council. They love their son, they're proud of him. And why shouldn't they be? He sounds like the type of person who will achieve big things. And from what I hear about the James family, it's a good thing he's so involved in school. He's got a lot to live up to.

Which makes me all the more anxious. What role do I play here? I've never been in one school long enough to join a sports team or club, which leaves me at a disadvantage. I stand no chance in a family the public loves, and I don't want to compete for their attention. In fact, I don't want any of it. I've been in ten different homes that I can remember, thirteen including the ones from long before I could recall making memories.

The James' adopted me, but who's to say it won't fall through? This could just be house number fourteen. I've learned not to get my hopes up, because when things come crashing down I'm the one left suffering while everyone else walks away unscathed.

"Are you ready, sweetheart?"

Sweetheart. I'm not used to the gentle term of endearment. I've been called a lot of things, a lot of names I want to forget. *Brat. Bitch. Slut.* But the way Bridgette ushers me with a hopeful smile makes me absorb the pet name, even if for just a second. I want to pretend I'm a normal girl and this is the only normal I've ever known.

I open the backdoor and step out, my torn sneakers hitting the flawless pavement. Wiggling my toes, my eyes capture the frayed cloth that reveals my white socks underneath.

The soft *click* of Bridgette's heels contacting the driveway peel my eyes from my unfortunate state of dress. Jill told me to wear the nicest outfit I have because it's a big day. But the nicest clothes I own are jeans that are both too big and too long and a long sleeve shirt with a bleach stain mixed in with the floral pattern. My white shoes used to match it, but they're turning gray from the years of wear.

Bridgette is in one of her normal dresses, this one light gray and ending just above her knees. It's warm out, almost seventy degrees, so she forgoes any type of sweater. The clunky jewelry she usually sports comes in the form of a necklace and large dangly earrings that look uncomfortable. But she's beautiful like always.

Robert opens the back of their Escalade and pulls out the black duffle bag Jill bought for me. She said it was for good luck, because one day I'd use it to move to my forever home. The papers signed this morning indicate this is it, but I'm still not sure. You learn after a while not to trust the good things, because eventually they'll inevitably end.

Bridgette gestures for me to follow her in, with Robert trailing behind us silently. He doesn't talk much, mostly because Bridgette fills the silence with her chatter. She always asks me questions, though I rarely answer them. When Robert does talk, it's nothing particularly important. Mostly just small acknowledgments when Bridgette says something about their history. I'm not sure if it's me who makes him quiet or if that's how he naturally is.

As soon as we enter the front door, the smell of

something sweet hits me. I'm familiar with the cinnamon scent but can't figure out what it's mixed with.

"Darlene must have made her famous cinnamon rolls," Robert notes, setting my bag down on the floor in the foyer. It's an open space that stretches out into three different rooms, with archways separating them. There's a large staircase leading upstairs not even ten feet from us, and from my peripheral I can see a big brown couch in the room to the right and an expensive looking wooden dining set to my left.

Bridgette gestures toward the left, guiding me into a dining room that offsets a large looking kitchen area. The smell is stronger the closer we get, until an older woman with white hair and glasses wearing an apron turns toward us.

Bridgette smiles at the woman. "Hi, Darlene. I thought you'd be home by now."

Her tone is soft, friendly, just as her smile is. She doesn't say it like she prefers the woman to be gone, just states it in pleasant surprise.

The woman slides off the oven mitts and sets them next to a pan of doughy dessert. "I wanted to make sure there was something special for when you got home, but I lost track of time." Her eyes drift to me, looking me up and down with a big smile on her face. "You must be River. I'm Darlene. I've worked for the James' for over twelve years now."

She works for them?

It shouldn't surprise me that they have a cook. They

probably have a housekeeper too. I've read plenty of books that I've snuck out of private libraries over the years. People with money use it in ways I'll never understand.

My throat is dry, but I remember what Jill taught me about manners. "It's nice to meet you."

I wait for her to tell me to speak up and stop mumbling but the scolding never comes. She just keeps smiling and asks Robert and Bridgette if they're relieved to have me home.

"By the looks of you," Darlene notes, gesturing toward my midsection, "you could stand a few of these rolls. There are leftover muffins over on the island. Chocolate chip, if you like that sort of thing. We need to get some meat on those bones."

Heat creeps up the back of my neck and settles into my cheeks. The same cheeks that Jill said reminded her of my mother's when she first dropped me off. The only picture I have of my biological mother is of us when I was an infant. Mom was all skin and bones and her hair was blonde instead of the red that apparently runs in the family. Jill's words, not mine. I don't remember my mother.

But Jill mentioned that the woman who gave me up was struggling with addiction. Cocaine. Meth. Anything she could get her hands on. I'm lucky, according to Jill. So why don't I feel like it?

Before anyone says anything else, a teenager that I recognize as their son walks into the kitchen from the back hallway. He pauses when he sees us, his eyes darting to me, then Darlene and his parents.

"Uh ... sorry."

Robert chuckles. "No need to apologize, Oliver. We're just showing River around. River, you remember Oliver, right?"

Oliver stuffs his hands in the pockets of his expensive looking jeans. My bootcut jeans are from a thrift store, second hand. Or third or fourth hand, if I'm being honest. They're worn out and frayed at the ends, stained with muck and who knows what else from over the past year I've had them. He doesn't dress like his parents, but casually. Kind of like my old foster siblings used to. And it's weird, realizing that he's not just another foster brother. He's my adopted brother. Or, I suppose, *I'm* his adopted sister. I don't know how he feels about that, but he offers me a small smile like the one he gave me the first time we met.

"H-Hi," I offer, wetting my bottom lip. The tip of my tongue grazes the slightly jutted scar lingering on the corner of it. I know it's there and visible, a pinkish-white against my pale lips.

"Sup?"

Sup? How am I supposed to answer that? It's rhetorical, I realize, because he doesn't look like he's expecting an answer.

While Oliver James doesn't dress like his parents, he's their perfect replica. More so of Robert than Bridgette in his squared, tapered jaw, but I see the warmth of his hazel eyes that Bridgette has too. His hair is cut short and the kind of dark brown that almost looks black, but it looks good against his olive skin tone. If I had black hair, I'd look like a walking corpse. I'm sure of it.

Bridgette claps her hands abruptly, startling me. I flinch and try recovering, hoping nobody saw. But Oliver did. His brows draw in for a split second until he sees my frantic expression, then goes back to neutral when his mom starts speaking.

"Ollie, how about you take River's bag up to her room? We'll finish showing her around and then maybe we can all go out to dinner."

She sounds excited, and I assume that's her normal setting. Every time Bridgette would come to see me, she was all smiles and optimism. I like that about her, but this instance makes me uncomfortable because the types of places they probably eat are fancy. I don't own fancy clothes.

Oliver glances at my wide eyes and parted lips and shifts slightly on his feet. "Why don't we stay in for dinner? It might be nice to do a homecooked meal for River's first night here."

Letting out a small breath of relief, I watch him with a grateful look on my face. Or, I think I do.

Bridgette beams the same time my shoulders ease from their tense position. I can't force myself to thank him, but he tips his head a fraction when we lock eyes as if he knows what I'm thinking. The drum of my anxious heartbeat settles back to normal as Bridgette and Robert nod and tell Oliver what a good idea that is.

Darlene offers to stay and cook, but Robert tells her they have it handled. She finishes coating the cinnamon rolls with homemade white frosting as Bridgette guides me around the first floor of their home.

Robert parts ways with us when we make it to his office-slash-study in the back of the first floor, just past the stairs. He says he'll get started on dinner once he checks in at work, leaving Bridgette as my tour guide.

I'm right. Their house is three stories, not including the full basement-turned-media room, whatever that is. We don't go down there, but Bridgette tells me Oliver and his friends usually hangout there, watch movies, and play *one of those silly violent video games* on the flat screen. I make a personal note not to go down there, if that's his domain. I know better than to step on people's toes and go where I don't belong.

My tongue touches the scar again.

The second floor is where Bridgette and Robert's room is, along with Bridgette's office, one of the guest rooms, and a guest bathroom down the hall. The third floor is where Oliver's and my rooms are, as well as two guest bedrooms. She mentions one of the bedrooms being claimed by Oliver's friend, who hangs around here a lot. His name starts with E, I think. My anxiety builds in the pit of my stomach over that news, because the stranger's room is right between Oliver's and mine.

When we make it to my room, Bridgette's smile

widens to the biggest I've ever seen. The room is painted a pale cream, and the ceiling, moulding, and windows are all white. My jaw drops slightly when I see the large wooden bed against the middle of the back wall, covered in a green and blue bed set that matches the rug, chair, and lamp in the corner. There are night-stands on both sides of the bed that match the beaded headboard, as well as a matching desk positioned on the opposite wall. Two doors are offset on the wall closest to us, which Bridgette explains leads to the closet and bathroom.

Oliver put my duffle bag on the edge of the bed, wrinkling the geometric patterned comforter. There's no way my clothes need the amount of space a walk-in closet has.

"What do you think?" Bridgette turns to me after fluffing one of the pillows.

It's hard to swallow, hard to think. I've never had so much space to myself before. It seems almost unfair, knowing there are kids I grew up with who won't have this. It makes me wonder why they chose me, the girl who barely spoke to them whenever they saw me. What makes me so special?

"It's ..." My voice cracks.

"It's a lot to take in," Bridgette says lightly, walking toward me. She doesn't reach out. "I know it'll take some time to get used to, but we're so happy you're here, River. Truly."

I itch to ask, *why?* But I don't. I don't say anything, like usual. Instead, my eyes drift back to the items that are now mine. It's surreal and I wonder when I'll be elbowed awake by a toddler and realize it's all a dream.

Bridgette clears her throat, snapping me back to reality. Because this *is* reality. One I don't quite fully grasp or understand but have to if I'm going to make this work.

"I thought we could go shopping tomorrow," she tells me, eying the duffle bag. "Jillian told me you don't have a lot of clothes, so I thought we could have some bonding time and get you the essentials. Do you like shopping?"

I've never been. I shrug.

Her smile softens. "Well, you don't start at Freemont until Monday, so that gives us all weekend. If you prefer to settle in, we can wait until Saturday to go into town. I don't know if you've been to the mall, but there are plenty of stores to go through. We can even get you decorations for your room. We want you to make it your own."

My room. I've never had one of my own before. Once, I had a pullout sofa to myself before the couple fostered another kid. They made us share, like usual, because they only had one bedroom.

"I would like that," I murmur, staring down at my shoes. The tips of her clean heels are in my eyeline, making me frown. Their whole family is put together, presentable. Then there's me. It's embarrassing because I haven't looked at myself in the mirror today. Is my auburn hair frizzy like normal? Are my brown eyes too hollow, the bags under them dark again my pale skin?

Does the shirt look as loose as it feels? I can only imagine what Bridgette thinks of me right now.

"River?"

My eyes slowly lift.

"Thank you," she whispers, emotion coating her words like tears do her eyes. What could she be thanking me for? "Thank you for letting us take you in, for being part of our family. We've ... we've waited a long time for this moment, and we're so happy."

Her voice cracks when she says *happy* and I realize that they may look put together, but they've struggled just as much as I have. And this arrangement, my adoption, isn't just benefitting me.

They get a daughter, one they want to be proud of. And I'm not familiar with the look, but somehow my presence is already making them proud of me.

And I wonder if I can keep it.

I'm not like Oliver, who fits in with people and has tons of friends. I close myself off to protect myself, waiting for the day Jill shows up to take me away. It always happens, even when I finally get used to a routine. The James are different. They want me here, and for the first time ever, I start to think I want to be here too.

I just hope they'll let me stay when they realize how deep my scars really go.

THREE

Everett / 17

The steps creak under my weight leading to the media room where Oliver tells me to meet him. Sundays are our game days, where we kick back and yell at whoever's playing. Usually, it's a weekly get-together between me, Oliver, and a few other guys in our small circle of friends. But with Oliver's new sister around, none of us were sure we'd be invited over.

Yesterday, Oliver called and told me to bring pizza and wings from the pizzeria near my grandfather's house. Southside Pizza is some of the best Bridgeport has to offer, and we can wipe out two full pies ourselves easily. After making sure Grandad was all right, I picked up the food and hauled it over.

Fact is, I'm not sure I should be here. If Bridgette and Robert weren't okay with it, Oliver would have shut it down. But it still seems like an invasion of privacy on his sister's behalf, especially with the group of rowdy assholes we surround ourselves with.

"O, you down here?" I call out, setting the steaming

cardboard onto the glass table positioned in front of the brown leather sectional.

A short gasp pulls my attention over to the corner of the room, where a short redheaded girl stands in the corner. Her eyes are wide as she drops what she's holding, a paperback book. *My* book that I lost last time I was here.

She draws her body into the corner, putting the matching leather Lazy Boy between her and me despite there being at least twenty feet separating us. My eyes trail downward at her shaking hand, which she tries controlling by grasping it with her other palm.

"Uh … sorry." My thumb stabs the air behind me in a pointless gesture. "Oliver told me to meet him down here."

The girl doesn't say anything. In fact, her lips are pressed in a tight line as she watches me like she's facing a firing squad. Clearing my throat, I bury my hands in my jeans pockets. She's terrified. Whether of me or just in general, I don't know. But if she doesn't like being surrounded by people, she won't like sticking down here when Tommy and Quinn arrive. They're not bad guys, they're just loud.

"You're River, right?"

Again. Silence.

I want to offer her pizza because there's nothing to the girl. She's lean and lanky and the clothes, although new by the looks of them, eat her small frame alive.

Frankly, she looks sick. I wonder if there's something wrong with her that made the James want to take her under their wing. After all, they like charity cases. It's why they embraced me.

Her eyes are dark, but I can't tell what color. Probably brown, though the few redheads I know sport green eyes and freckles that cover their cheeks and nose. This girl doesn't look like she has any, but I can't tell from where I'm standing. Walking over to her is out of the question, because she's literally shaking despite trying to force herself not to.

My eyes catch the fallen paperback copy of Hawthorne's *The Scarlet Letter*. It's a free read for class that Perkins said will get me out of the final if I write a paper on it. I thought I'd hate it, but it's not so bad.

"Did you read that? It's cool if you did."

Her lips part a fraction. "Y-Yes."

She's unsure. Scared. Hesitant. I get it. So, I don't hound her. She doesn't want to talk to me, to trust me. And why would she? We're strangers.

I tilt my chin toward the pizza. "Well, Oliver has some people coming over to watch the big game today. Basketball, if you're interested. If not, you can grab some food and head out. They'll be here any minute."

On cue, the front door slams shut upstairs, and two different voices call out Oliver's name. I cuss silently, seeing River's face pale at their obnoxious laughing.

Quickly, I grab a paper plate and slap a slice of cheese

pizza onto it. She flinches when I advance her, holding out the plate. "There's a second set of stairs over there," I point toward the back end of the room, "that lead just outside of Robert's study. The guys won't come down here that way."

Her small fingers wrap around the edge of the plate. When the door to the room opens and footsteps plow down them, I go to stall the idiots only to see River has already bolted in the direction I pointed her to.

Damn, she's fast.

Quinn is the first one down, nearly tripping over Tommy's foot when he tries passing him to get to the pizza first. Tommy's carrying two different kinds of chips and dip, and Quinn has Pepsi, Mountain Dew, and something shoved in a brown paper bag. I have a pretty good guess as to what.

"Look what I scored, fuckers." He yanks the bottle of rum out of the bag and waves it in the air, setting it down next to the soda and pizza.

Tommy smacks him upside the head. "It's rum and *Coke* not Pepsi, moron."

The distinction won't stop Tommy from drinking it. By the time they have to leave, they'll be on the verge of drunk, making excuses about why they should stay the night. It has happened before, but I hope Oliver doesn't let it happen again.

Oliver comes down last, followed by the last person I expect. Peter York.

B. CELESTE

Tommy and Quinn share my distaste. It's Quinn who asks, "Who the fuck invited York?"

Oliver shoves him and sets down some napkins and glasses. "I did. We going to complain about it or start eating?"

Halfway through the game, we're all spread out across the room with three quarters of the food consumed. Between Tommy, Quinn, and Peter, the rum is nearly gone. Oliver had a partial glass and I didn't have any.

When the game switches to a commercial, Peter glances around the room. "Yo, James? Where's your new sister at?"

Oliver shrugs. "I don't know. In her room probably, why?"

A sleezy smirk spreads across his face. "I just want to see the chick. Must be some hot shit for the James' to want her."

"She's thirteen," Oliver growls defensively.

My fists tighten on my sides. "The fuck, man?"

Tommy cackles and tosses a balled-up napkin at Peter. "Jailbait, bro. Not worth it, trust me."

Oliver and I both scowl at Tommy, who holds his hands up in surrender. My eyes shoot back to Peter, who doesn't seem phased by our death glares. It could be the alcohol, but they say liquor is a truth serum. It just shows how screwed up York really is.

Quinn doesn't say anything during any of this, just keeps eating his chips. I'm ninety percent sure he came here stoned, which would explain all the food he's consumed. Normally, he can't out-eat any of us.

"I'm just saying," York presses, "she's been the big topic of conversation for months. We shouldn't have to meet her the same time everybody else does."

My knuckles crack. "Why not?"

"Because we're Oliver's friends."

One of my brows arches. "Are you now?"

Quinn snorts. "York wishes."

Peter flips Quinn off.

"None of us are obligated to meet her," I inform York. Hell, all of them. "And it's probably best if we don't make a scene at school. She'll have enough shit to deal with."

Oliver tips his head. "He's right. River is off limits to you assholes. I don't want you messing with her. She's going to need time to adjust, and you won't help." The last jab is at York, but he doesn't seem to notice.

"Hey, I don't care if I meet her or not," Tommy tells us. He winces. "No offense, bro. Maybe thirteen-year-olds do it for York, but I like my women developed. If you get my drift." His hands fondle his chest like they're boobs, making Quinn laugh and the rest of us groan.

Peter scoffs. "You're all sick. I didn't mean anything by it."

Nobody says anything because no one believes him. York will do anything to get in with Oliver and the fact Oliver invited him should make him chill. It'll probably just fuel him to stay in our circle, despite everyone hating him.

"Cool it, douches," Oliver declares. "The game is back on."

Nobody mentions River again.

MONDAY COMES AROUND TOO QUICKLY, AND I'M almost late to first period because my grandfather had another fit. It took him an hour to convince me he didn't need to go to the hospital, and I only left because our neighbor Margaret came over and told me she'd look after him as usual when I'm gone.

Grandad has been getting sick more often since he beat cancer two years ago. His body isn't strong enough to fight off simple colds, so they always wind up turning into something worse. His latest one left him with walking pneumonia, and he's on the last few days of antibiotics for it.

Oliver is standing by my locker holding the usual white bag of pastries from the Quick Stop in town. The donuts are pretty good considering they're from a gas station, but Eddy's, the small bakery inside, makes them fresh every morning. I'm pretty sure Oliver is their prime customer.

I toss my books in my locker before taking only what I need for morning classes. It's day two, which means I've only got math and English along with a study hall and gym before lunch. On day ones, I'm stuck with more downtime than I like. So sometimes I'll use the extra study halls to go to the library or gym until lunch hits.

"Mind being a few minutes late to calc?" He hooks a sudden right that leads to the middle school wing, so I follow him. I hate calculus anyway.

"Where to?"

"It's River's first day." He shoots a few smiles to the passing teachers who pay us no attention. "Mom and Dad are worried about her and when some guy came by the office to show her around she looked like she was about to pass out."

Some guy? "Another student?"

He nods.

I blow out a breath. "I'm sure she's fine."

There's no way to know that for sure, so I get the need to check on her. I spent less than three minutes with her, and she looked like she wanted to vomit the entire time. She doesn't like being near strangers, it doesn't take a rocket scientist to see it.

My face screws at the thought. "Do you think it's a good idea for me to tag along?"

He gives me a pointed look. "Would you rather be in calc right now? Whitman hates tardiness."

He has a point. And it isn't like I'm not curious about his new sister. I am. I remember what it's like being the new kid when I moved in with my grandparents. It sucks.

"Nah. Just thought she'd do better with you."

Oliver's lips quirk as he nudges me. "I appreciate it,

Rhett. But honestly, she's still nervous around me too. The only person she seems to be okay with is Mom."

Interesting. Maybe it's not all strangers. I wonder what happened to her that makes her twitchy around men. But the more I think about it, the worse the possibilities that cross my mind get. I've heard some rough shit about the foster system, and from what I remember the James' saying, River has been in it her whole life.

We stop in front of a classroom already full of students. There's chatter inside that makes me assume class hasn't started yet.

River is sitting in the back corner of the room, hunkered down in the desk like she's trying to melt away. Oliver notices too, his lips twitching downward as his gaze drifts at the other kids who are talking to each other and paying River no attention. She probably likes that, but I can tell Oliver doesn't.

Before I can say anything about it, Oliver reaches for the door and walks in. I have no choice but to follow, walking over to the middle-aged teacher who's writing something on the chalkboard.

She startles for a moment over seeing us, and then composes herself. "Can I help you boys with something?"

From the corner of my eye, I see River staring in our direction. When I shift my head to look at her straight-on, she quickly looks away. Her hands are tucked in her lap underneath the desk, eerily still like if she doesn't move we won't see her.

I see you, River.

I'm only partially aware of Oliver talking in soft murmurs to the teacher, Mrs. Ortiz according to the name plaque on her desk. "...and I think it would be good to give her a little pep talk, you know? Brother to sister."

Mrs. Ortiz beams at him and agrees, letting Oliver head over to River's desk. Kids watch him approach her in curiosity, leaning in when he kneels next to her. She stiffens at his closeness but whatever he says makes her ease. Her eyes sneak a peek my way before darting back to Oliver. She nods, but keeps her lips pressed together.

After a long moment, Oliver stands and points to me. River's eyes meet mine, but this time she doesn't break the contact. I give her a small smile and wave to show that I may look like a giant, but I'm not a threat.

"She seems quiet," Mrs. Ortiz observes from next to me. Her voice is low enough for only me to hear. "The office mentioned she might struggle in this transition period, so I'm glad she has brothers like you."

Instead of correcting her on the matter, I give a short nod. "We just want to make sure she settles in okay. Being the new kid isn't fun."

Her smile softens. "No, it's not. But I can tell your family cares a great deal for River. And after being informed of her past, it's good to finally have people who will take care of her."

She knows about what happened to River? I suppose certain people are obligated to know, but it seems like an invasion of privacy.

Mrs. Ortiz gestures toward Oliver. "You don't want to

go say something to her too? I'm sure she could use all the encouragement."

"Oh, ah—" I wet my bottom lip. "Oliver is the one who has a way with words."

It's not a lie. Oliver has always been the pep-talker. People expect him to give them advice, especially before games. It's tradition.

Mrs. Ortiz nods in understanding and her smile widens when Oliver saunters back over to us. Glancing at River, I note her shoulders aren't as tense. But her lips are still pressed tight together, and her eyes don't look back at me.

Ortiz tells us to have a good day when we walk out.

"So?"

Oliver shrugs. "Her lunch is right before ours, so I'm going to cut study hall and check in on her. You in?"

He wants to eat with River? "Uh, sure."

Less time in my head is a good thing. It shouldn't surprise me that Oliver is living up to the big brother role. He's a natural protector, a decent human being. But he never admitted how he felt about his parents adopting a child, just went along with it because he knew that's what they wanted. Now that she's here, it's nice to see him looking out for her.

"Do you think she'll be okay here?" I ask, mostly because I worry about York. The guy is all talk and no show, but that doesn't mean he isn't a threat. His big mouth will get him into deep shit, especially if it involves River.

Oliver blows out a breath. "I hope so. Mom and Dad filled me in on some stuff she's gone through. It's ... yeah, it's fucked, bro. But she's a fighter. I can sense it about her."

"Must be what drew your parents to her."

His grin is prideful. "I think so, too."

Instead of heading to calculus twenty minutes late, we spend the last thirty minutes in the gym tossing around the basketball. Coach usually bites our heads off if he sees we're skipping class, but by this time he's normally in the elementary wing teaching kids how to kick a soccer ball with the other Phys Ed teacher.

When second period rolls around, we head our separate ways with plans to meet outside the cafeteria during fourth. Walking into Perkins's room, I drop into my seat and remember I never grabbed my book from Oliver's house. Then again, I wasn't sure if River was finished with it yet. I doubt it. It's not a long book, but not an easy one either. She's only been around for a few days.

Most of the people in here aren't my usual crowd, and I like it. Nothing against Oliver, but the rest of the idiots who hang around us would give me crap for wanting to participate in reading discussions. I could have been in AP English this year getting college credits, but I chose the easy way out because I had no clue if I was even going to college.

Our discussion on Orwell's *1984* turns into an argument over the film adaptation, which Perkins tries to reign in but can't. It leaves me bored because, yeah, the movie sucks. But this isn't a film class, it's an English one. These morons admitting they watched the movie instead of reading the book says a lot about their intelligence level.

When the bell rings, Perkins calls me over to her desk. Gripping my notebook in my palm, I stand in front of her and glance at the busy halls.

"How are you coming on the paper?"

My attention is pulled back to her. "Uh, good. I let a friend borrow the book, but I'm getting it back tonight."

I'm not, but whatever.

One of her blonde brows quirk. "It must be a pretty special friend for them to get a book out of your hand."

The amusement in her tone has my lips tilting slightly. She's not wrong, I don't like letting people take my books before I'm done with them. Then again, River didn't take it from me. I lost it. Not really great book-owning skills.

She grabs a stack of papers and straightens them out. "Just remember that I expect the paper by Friday. Your friend can always read it after you're done."

I just nod and walk out. The paper is nearly done; I just need to add a few quotes for evidence on my claim. Oliver told me he'd bring me the book today but forgot, which means I'll grab it tomorrow when we swing by after practice. Tuesdays are taco night at the James household. I never miss them.

When fourth period comes around, Oliver is right where he told me he'd be in front of the cafeteria entrance. The room is full of loud, echoing voices from the middle school occupying the space. It doesn't take us long to spot River because of her red hair and lone position in the corner of the room. The black sweater she's wearing is at least one size too big and she wraps it around herself like a blanket.

A security blanket, I realize. She obviously wishes she could disappear, but somehow she's all I see in the massive space.

Oliver walks over to her and waves, causing her to straighten up. Her eyes go from him to me, her lips twitching before pressing into a firm line again. I can't tell if I scare her or not, so I keep quiet and let Ollie do the talking.

"Hey." He jabs a finger at me. "This is Everett. I mentioned him before, remember?"

She blinks then nods, glancing over at me. Neither one of us mentions that we've technically met before, so we both play it off. It wasn't a formal meeting anyway.

"Anyway, I promised we'd eat with you, so here we are. Are they serving anything worth eating today? Should have probably warned you about bringing your own lunch. Darlene can whip something up for you ..."

Oliver keeps talking and River nods along, but I wonder what's going through her head. She doesn't seem upset we're here, I can tell by the way her arms rest easily at her sides. There's no indication of nervousness or skepticism like before.

"Spaghetti." Her voice is so quiet it almost drowns in

the sea of other conversations. But I hear it. The lull of her soft tone is woven with uncertainty and something else. Can't be sure what, but whatever it is encourages her to talk.

It's me who speaks up. "It's not that good, if you like spaghetti. The meat sauce is watered down and I'm pretty sure the meatballs are tofu."

Oliver scoffs. "They are not. How do you even know what that shit tastes like anyway?" He winces, side-eyeing River. "Sorry. I mean stuff. Don't swear. Mom and Dad don't like it."

Another nod.

I nudge him. "Trying to corrupt your sis already?" The joke makes River tense again, which makes me feel bad. Clearing my throat, I redirect the topic. "Their turkey sandwiches are pretty good. Nothing fancy, just deli meat, lettuce, tomato, and cheese. I wouldn't get their salad."

Oliver shudders in agreement. "Yeah, the salad bar is known for bugs."

River's eyes widen.

I nod. "One time Principal Ackerman was scooping out some lettuce and found a couple dead flies in it. It wasn't the first time."

She looks pale. "Gross."

Oliver and I both smile. "Yep."

Nervously, River lifts her eyes to meet mine. Her hair cascades around her face, blocking out everyone around us, kind of like blinders on a horse. "I ... like turkey sandwiches."

Drumming my fingers against the edge of the table, I push up. "I'll go grab—"

Oliver stands. "Nah, man. I've got it. They have fruit too, River. Want some of that?"

She swallows. "Um ..."

"I can go," I tell Oliver, assuming her hesitancy has to do with being alone with me. Can't blame the girl, so I'll do what I can to make her comfortable.

Oliver puts his hand on my shoulder. "It's my treat, dude." He looks at River. "Do you remember what I said earlier?"

Her eyes bounce between us. "Y-Yes."

His smile reappears. "Good. Now, I'm going to get us some halfway decent sandwiches and drinks. River, you good with water?"

She nods. He doesn't bother asking what I prefer because he already knows. Walking away, he weaves through the crowd, gaining attention from a few giggling preteens a few tables over. I chuckle and settle back down across from River.

Curiosity strikes me. "What did he tell you earlier?"

She shifts in her seat, yanking at the ends of her sweater sleeves. "That ... you're family." She takes a small breath, still not making eye contact with me. "And that family can be trusted."

My eyes dart to Oliver, who's schmoozing up one of

the older lunch ladies. His charm obviously works, because she laughs and shakes her head with a big smile on her face. Oliver's a people person, and definitely a ladies' man.

Emotion clogs the back of my throat. "Well then," I murmur, trailing my eyes back. "Not sure what to say to that."

We sit in silence for a short moment.

"Did you like the book?" She gives me a strange look which makes me clarify. "*The Scarlet Letter*, I mean."

She wets her lips. "Not really."

Her honesty makes me grin. "No? Did you finish it?"

She nods.

My eyes widen. "Seriously?"

Her shoulders rise.

"Impressive," I murmur, nodding in praise. Hawthorne isn't for everybody. Most classic literature isn't. "Do you like reading?"

There's a pregnant pause. "Sometimes."

"Have any hobbies?" I don't want to push her, but it seems like this is progress. Even if she doesn't answer.

Her eyes go to Oliver, who's still waiting to pay. The tray he holds is piled with food, probably more than he's supposed to have per meal. Perks of having charisma.

To my surprise, she says, "Drawing."

So, she's an artist. "That's cool. I can't draw worth a shi—uh, crap. I'm sure Bridgette and Robert can give you some materials if you're into that. They're supportive of hobbies."

She's back to silence, and I'm cool with it.

THE TRUTH ABOUT HEARTBREAK

Oliver is back in no time, passing out our lunch. He throws a small bag of baked potato chips at me along with my sandwich and diet Coke. He and River both have sandwiches, apples, and water.

"So," Oliver says smiling. "Let's talk."

FOUR

River / 13

Robert has a flat screen television installed in my bedroom when I'm at school. All because Oliver told him I should have one like he does. I've never seen one as big as the one in their media room, but this one isn't much smaller. Fifty-five inches, according to Robert.

Most of my time at their house is spent in the dining room doing homework. Bridgette tells me all the time I can go downstairs to the media room and watch TV or hangout in my room, but I feel like that'd be hiding. Oliver told me I don't have to hide here, so I don't. I'm trying to put in effort, so little by little I'll be more comfortable.

On Friday night, Robert and Bridgette ask if I want to go with them to some event in town. They're both dressed in fancy clothes, fancier than usual. Bridgette is even wearing diamonds around her neck that look expensive. I'm about to tell them yes, because I feel like I have to, when Oliver butts in and tells them we have plans.

Bridgette seems especially thrilled over our make-believe plans. She claps her hands and tells us to have fun and then ushers Robert out the front door. I'm about to go upstairs when Oliver stops me.

"You don't have to do that."

I turn slightly.

He tips his head in the opposite direction. "I didn't just tell them that to get you out of going. But trust me, you'll be glad I did. Charity galas are boring. Don't tell them I said that though."

My lips threaten to rise, so I force away the emotion threatening to leak through my protective shell. I like Oliver. Not because I feel like I have to as his new sister, but because he actually puts effort in. He sat with me every day at lunch so I'm not alone, and Everett joined us three times during the week.

Oliver told me to trust him and I ... well, I don't *not* trust him. That's a step in the right direction. I've always gotten along with people closer to my age. I've lived with a wide range of age groups—from toddlers to teens. The older kids were usually about to age out of the system. We got along because we understood each other, the fear of the unknown.

But Oliver's nothing like those kids. I worried about what it would be like to be around the son Bridgette and Robert always spoke so highly of. He's put together, with a lot of achievements. I'm lucky I haven't been to jail yet for robbery or assault. The victories aren't comparable.

He starts toward the kitchen. "I'm going to heat up some leftover Chinese from the other night. Want some?"

My stomach growls loud enough for him to hear. He laughs and waves me to follow, so I do. I sit at the stool by the counter and watch him dig through the plastic containers. I've had takeout before, but Darlene cooked us Chinese food from scratch. Except the cookies, she admitted she got them from the store because she didn't know how to get the little wrappers inside. Everything she made is way better than I've ever had before.

He remembers what I ate, pulling the sesame chicken out first and then starts dumping it onto a plate along with some sticky rice, dumplings, and veggie stir fry. By the time he's done, there's no room left. He pops it into the microwave to heat up and then fixes his own plate.

"Did you get a fortune cookie before?" He stops scooping out the rice and grabs something from the counter behind him. I flinch when a tiny object is tossed at me, barely catching it before it smacks me in the face.

"I ..." I fidget with the wrapper, staring at the little piece of paper peeking out from the folded cookie. "I don't really like them."

"Why not?"

Worrying my lip, I set it down. When I was eight, my foster mother smacked my hand away from a fortune cookie. I just wanted to know what it tasted like, I didn't know anything was inside. She told me some random person shoved the tiny piece of paper inside the cookie to mess with people like me, the naive child with hopes and dreams that would never come true. She said it was a pointless addition to the dessert, and I should just throw it away.

I settle on, "They're not real."

He shrugs, opening one up for himself. "So? They may be lame but they're kind of fun to read. You know, in a cheesy way." He cracks open the cookie and pops half of it into his mouth. His nose scrunches. "Except this one. This one sucks."

"W-What does it say?"

"It says 'it's raining outside.'" He makes another face and tosses the paper into the garbage. "First off, that's not a prediction. It's an observation. And it's not even right." Pointedly, he gestures toward the large window that, sure enough, shows the setting sun in the clear sky.

My fingers twitch to open mine. When the microwave goes off, he turns around to grab it, giving me time to open the cookie and crack it open. I don't eat it right away, just pull the fortune out.

Brighter days are ahead of you.

My lips twitch as I set the paper down on the counter. I mimic Oliver and crunch down on half of the cookie, my face twisting over the sweetened cardboard taste in my mouth.

Oliver laughs when he sees my face. "I take it you've never actually had one before?"

I shake my head.

He passes me a napkin. "You don't have to eat it. It's cool."

What does he want me to do, spit it out? I know

better than that. It's rude. I swallow and stick out my tongue in disgust. Replacing my plate in the microwave with his own, he turns around and sets my steamy dish in front of me.

"We don't have to sit in here to eat." He grabs two glasses, a couple napkins, and some silverware from the drawer by the sink. "Mom and Dad don't mind if we eat in the media room when they're not here, as long as we clean up."

He wants to go downstairs?

My body stiffens and I don't know why. Oliver won't hurt me, so being alone with him shouldn't bother me like it does. And the questioning look he shoots me when he sees my pale face makes me feel bad.

"What's wrong?"

I force myself to take a deep breath. "Isn't the media room ... yours?"

His brows pinch. "Nobody really has a claim on it, I just use it the most. Dad, uh, Robert goes down there a lot too. You just haven't seen him do it yet."

Oh.

When the microwave dings, he grabs his plate and sets it on the counter. Then he fills both our glasses with milk, because he says Chinese can't be eaten without it. It sounds kind of gross, but I go with it. As if his hands aren't full enough, he grabs a glass container of trail mix that someone bought from the store and gestures for me to follow him.

The media room is as big as I remember. I haven't

been down since last weekend, when I bumped into Everett. I just wanted to return the book I found when I explored the house after everyone went to bed. It's not mine and I know what happens when people get caught stealing.

Everett didn't seem to mind though. It surprised me, even if it shouldn't. Oliver told me Everett is practically my brother, just another family member I can count on. It's not that easy though. It never will be.

Trust isn't something that comes naturally. It's trial and error. But in the system, you can't afford the error part. Someone told me a long time ago that trust is like an eraser; it gets smaller and smaller until there's nothing left. I don't want it to disappear, so I don't use it much.

After settling on opposite ends of the couch with our food on the large glass table, Oliver turns the television on. He asks me if there's anything I want to watch, and I tell him anything is fine. Honestly, I don't want to watch sports. But I know he loves them, so I'll be fine if that's what he chooses.

Instead, he picks a cartoon I'm familiar with on Cartoon Network, making me smile before I can stop myself. Saturday morning cartoons used to be a must-watch whenever I lived somewhere that had cable. It used to be the only time I ever got to watch them. Even though it's a Friday, it's nice to see something from my past that isn't tainted.

We eat in silence while we watch a marathon of cartoons one right after the other. By eight o'clock,

Oliver is sprawled across one side of the sectional and I'm tucked into the other.

He offers me the trail mix he brought down, saying he's too full to eat anymore. I think he's lying, because I've seen him eat three times as much in one sitting before. But I don't turn his offer down, because I saw little M&M's mixed in with the assorted nuts and raisins.

"Mom does the same thing." Amusement lingers in his tone, making me glance up from my concentration on the food. I've picked out most of the candy-covered chocolate and a few almonds.

"She does?"

He nods. "It drives Dad mad, because he has a sweet tooth and usually doesn't eat anything else in it. I think it's why Mom does it."

My lips part in surprise. "To make him mad?"

He shakes his head. "More like to tease him. They're old high school sweethearts. I guess they've always been that way."

I ease back into my seat, focusing on the M&M's in my palm. One by one, I pop them into my mouth and refocus on the television. Oliver glances at me every so often but doesn't ask a lot of questions. I'm glad. Talking isn't my favorite thing to do, especially if it's about myself.

Sometimes I'll answer. Like when he asks me what my favorite color is. I tell him green. His is black, but I don't tell him that's not really a color. We sit in silence for a little while before he shoots off another one. What's my favorite movie? I don't have one. I don't watch movies. He seems shocked but doesn't press. He just tells me his is *The Hangover*. I don't bother telling him I have no clue what that movie is.

After a little while, we just watch the show without any other questions. He must have run out of things he thinks are safe to ask. I want to tell him nothing is safe, but I don't.

"Shit," Oliver mumbles, sitting up and nearly dropping the leftover trail mix onto the carpet. He catches it in time, another slur muttered under his breath, and then looks up at me. "I forgot I told a few buddies we'd hang tonight."

His dismissal isn't obvious, but I take it as one and gather up my dirty dishes.

"Where are you going?"

I stop. "To my room?" My tone is questionable, because I'm not sure what he wants me to do. Doesn't he want me to leave him alone to be with his friends?

He frowns. "It's cool. I'll just tell them to come over Sunday for game day. Everett is probably already almost here though. Mind if he sticks around?"

Why is he asking me? It's his house.

He gets up and takes the dishes from me, piling them on his. "Rhett's cool, River. But if you're still not comfortable with him, I'll tell him to come over another time. It's fine."

My cheeks redden over the thought of him turning down his own friend. He shouldn't have to because of me. And he's right, Everett *is* cool. Or cooler than most people I know.

"It's fine."

One of his brows quirk. "You sure?"

I nod.

He studies my face for a second before tipping his head once. Whatever my tight expression looks like must be believable. I guess it is. I don't want to be broken forever, never trusting. Oliver seems like someone worth risking being hurt over.

If he trusts Everett, maybe I can too.

Someday.

He picks up all our dishes. "Why don't you chill, and I'll go run these upstairs? Did you want anything else?"

When I shake my head he leaves me alone, nothing but the commercial in the background filling the room. I sit back down and curl my legs under myself, grabbing the throw pillow from the corner and hugging it to my chest. The material is rough, not really cuddle-friendly, but it works. I used to have a white stuffed elephant named Ellie that I'd carry around with me everywhere. Whenever I was left alone, I'd hold Ellie tight in my arms and tell myself it'd be all right.

It usually was. *Usually.*

Not even ten minutes later, footsteps come down the stairs. I expect them to belong to Oliver, not Everett. When Everett sees me curled up on the couch, he gives me a lazy smile and waves.

"Hey."

I swallow. "H-Hi."

He drops down in the spot Oliver had vacated and picks up the trail mix. When he sifts through the nuts and raisins, his nose scrunches. "Did Bridgette get in here again? Man, I really wanted chocolate tonight."

Something that hasn't happened in a long time occurs in the next moment. I laugh. Not loudly, of course. In fact, it's barely a giggle. More like a high-pitched squeak, short and abrupt.

Everett's eyes snap up at the noise before his lips spread into a wide smile. "Was that your laugh?"

I bury my head into the pillow.

"Don't be embarrassed," he says, a boyish, lopsided smile appearing on his face. "It's cute."

That makes my face burn hotter. *Cute?* I'm not even sure what my real laugh sounds like. It's certainly not like the one from the few shows I've seen; not like the women I see on the street or in school who look like the happiest people alive when they laugh with others. Their laughs are loud and warm and friendly.

"Anyway, it's good to hear." His voice is light, casual. It makes me glance at him through my lashes. His eyes are a striking shade of mint green, kind of like the girl's eyes in the York Peppermint Patty commercials. I've never seen anyone in person share the same shade. Unlike the girl, he's tan, lean, and his arms are wide with muscle like some of my old foster fathers used to look like. He's not scary like them though. "Oliver worries about you, you know. He wants you to be happy. Your whole family does."

My mouth dries up. He uses that word so easily, and it makes me wonder what it's like to have one. A family. I mean, I have one now. I've had plenty of them in retrospect. None of them were permanent though, and I want this time to be different. He's right, they want me to be happy. Nobody else has wanted me to be anything but quiet before.

I force myself to say, "I know."

He nods and doesn't say anything else until Oliver comes back down. He's holding two glasses of something green and fizzy, Mountain Dew I think. I don't like the taste of it, it's too sweet for me. Oliver loves the stuff though. I heard Darlene tell him there's soda running through his veins instead of blood.

"Thought you'd be chilling with your grandfather tonight," Oliver tells him, taking a seat in between the two of us.

My eyes go to Everett real quick. Why would he be with his grandfather?

Everett shrugs, sipping his drink. "He told me to stop suffocating him with my constant worry, so I figured I'd come over. The others doing game day?"

Oliver nods.

I feel a little left out, not that I mind. There's no reason I should be part of this conversation, but I don't want to offend them by trying to leave again.

Everett kicks his feet up on the edge of the table.

He's in his socks, which are off-white from wear. The bottoms have a brand stitched into them that I've never heard of, not that it means anything. Before Bridgette took me out, I only shopped at Walmart. Usually, my clothes came from there or other foster kids when they stopped fitting in them.

The hand-me-downs are still in my duffle bag tucked under the bed, even though I have a closet and dresser full of new clothes. All the new stuff is nice and not just fancy dresses like Bridgette wears. She took me to at least ten different stores and had me pick out things that are "my style." I don't know what my style is though, so she helped me choose casual things like jeans, sweaters, and a couple of plain dresses. She did pick out a few formal dresses for me when we go out to some fancier gatherings. Kind of like the gala Oliver saved me from tonight.

I'm not sure how I'll survive something that's supposed to have all those people if I can't even be around one of Oliver's friends. It makes me feel pathetic. More so than usual.

"What are we watching?" Everett asks, looking at the screen. It has moved onto some cartoon I don't know, and Oliver must not be a fan of. He takes the remote and channel surfs.

Everett doesn't want to talk about his grandfather, that much is clear. I don't ask why, even though I'm curious. I know my place, and it's not in his business.

The boys start talking about basketball, another topic

I'm clueless in. I tune them out and replay the conversation I had with Oliver. I haven't talked about myself to anyone for as long as I have with him. It's progress, really good progress that Jill will be happy with.

I wonder if I'll see Jill again. She's been my social worker my whole life. She doesn't look that old, but she's really in her late forties with no family of her own. She has a dog though. It's a tiny brown fluffball that she's let me play with whenever I'm around him. His name is Winston, which I still think is a weird name for a dog. But my name is River, so I can't judge.

When I hear my name, I startle back into reality. Both the boys are watching me expectantly, leaving my lips parting and cheeks pale.

"I-I'm sorry." Drawing in my inner cheek, I bite down on it. The temporary pain eases the tension that their focus gives me. I don't like when people stare.

"No big," Oliver dismisses. "Rhett just wanted to know if you made any friends yet. I should have probably asked that by now."

Are they asking because they want me to sit with someone my own age at lunch? Oliver told me he hopes I make friends fast and have someone to talk to. Maybe they don't want to come to and sit with me anymore.

Lie to them. "Yes." I nod for good measure.

There's a girl in my art class that tells me my paintings are pretty. Her name is Stephanie, but she prefers Steph for short. She and I are opposites in appearance. She looks healthy, not like my absent figure that needs more meat, something Darlene reminds me of daily. Her hair is so blonde it's almost white, which she says is natural and not bleached. And her eyes are a warm shade of blue, full of wonder and excitement unlike my dull and empty brown ones.

We don't talk outside of art, even though we share a few classes together. Sometimes she'll wave to me in the hallway, but I'm usually busy keeping my head down and watching my feet take me from point A to B.

Oliver shifts, pride lighting his face. "That's awesome, Riv."

Riv? I've never had a nickname before.

Everett doesn't say anything, just tilts his head and watches me. He does that a lot, watches people. It's like he's trying to figure everyone out, understand what isn't being said.

He looks like he sees through my lie and it sends a shiver racing down my spine.

My throat tightens. "I think ... I'm going to go to bed."

Oliver frowns. "It's not even nine thirty."

I'm usually in bed long before now. Not that I sleep right away. It always takes a while before I'm use to a new home. Except this one is different. I can explore at night, see rooms I'm too afraid to visit in the daytime. I wait until everyone is in their rooms to sneak out of mine. So far, my favorite place is Robert's office. It's lined with bookshelves on one wall and littered with paintings that look expensive. I've gone through two books so far, reading a few chapters a night. But mostly, I go and look at the artwork.

"I'm tired." Another lie.

Everett doesn't call me out on it, but I know he knows I'm just trying to get away. Maybe he doesn't want me around, he just pretends for Oliver's sake. He's a good friend in that way.

They both tell me goodnight and I leave before either can try convincing me to stay. When I'm changed in a pair of fluffy pajama pants with pizza slices on them and a comfy white shirt, I curl under the blankets and stare at the ceiling. It's made of fifty-eight white tiles, all pristine and clean without any flaws. Everything about this house is perfect.

How do I fit in?

FIVE

Everett / 17

I ace my Hawthorne paper and get out of taking the final, which eases anxiety I don't admit to anyone I have. Tests aren't easy for me, I need time. Perkins knows that even though I've never said anything to her. Unlike half of these teachers, she cares about her students.

When fourth period comes around, I skip out on study hall. Oliver is busy working on some last-minute assignment, so he doesn't pay attention when I tell him I need to be somewhere.

The cafeteria is still the same loud volume it always is during middle school lunch, but the difference is there's one less person. River isn't in her usual seat, and I start wondering if she was being honest on Friday when she said she made a friend. A few sweeps of the room reveal she's not in here at all.

Frowning, I consider going back and telling Oliver. But River lied for a reason. Whether she's embarrassed she hasn't made friends yet or because she doesn't want to be a bother, I don't know. My money is on the latter.

Thing is, I don't know where to look. She could be

B. CELESTE

hiding out any number of places to avoid this crowd. I've done it before, slipped away somewhere nobody would disturb me. For me, that place was the silent area in the library. None of my friends like being seen in there, so it gives me time to catch up on books without being messed with.

What's River's equivalent of that?

I check the library and gym for her with no luck and wander the halls for about twenty minutes before remembering something she told me shortly after we met. On instinct, my feet guide me to the art room in the east wing of school. Through the narrow window on the door, I see the back of her head, her red hair flowing down her back in a ponytail as she works on something in front of her.

Debating on disturbing her, I draw my hand away from the door before finally walking in. She doesn't turn but her body stiffens as I approach. Mrs. Cohen is helping another student in the lab positioned behind her desk, probably with some photography crap I don't comprehend. Art isn't really my thing, but I'm always impressed with what people can do.

Like River. Over her shoulder, I notice dark lines curved into what appears to be a woman. The charcoal she's using makes the drawing pop against the white stock paper, the open space visibly consuming the woman who looks to be in anguish. The medium coats the side of River's palm and pads of her fingertips from shading.

60

She stops moving completely, partially shielding the image with her arm. I step aside, pulling out the stool next to her and sit down.

"You're not at lunch." It's a stupid observation to make but it's out there.

She doesn't answer or move.

"Did you at least eat?"

Nothing.

My chin tips toward her drawing. "That looks good. What is it?"

It's pointless to ask because I know she won't answer, but it's worth a shot. When she doesn't say anything, I breathe in a heavy breath and exhale.

"Listen," I bargain, "Oliver doesn't care if you haven't made friends yet. It takes time for that to happen. I was here a few months before your brother started talking to me."

This time she looks at me, her brows furrowed in. From this distance, I realize her dark eyes are a shade of coffee, a little lighter than the espresso that I see Margaret drink sometimes. I've gained her interest at least, and that's a step in the right direction.

"So, did you eat?"

She blinks, the uncertain haze in her eyes slowly clearing. Then she shakes her head, her bottom lip drawing into her mouth. Her eyes lower back down to her project.

Glancing at the clock, I frown. There won't be enough time for her to get lunch and eat it at this point.

Tapping my fingers against the tabletop, I stand. "I'll be right back, okay?"

Walking out of the room, I head toward the nearest vending machine. It's not the healthiest, but at least it's sustenance. Oliver said Darlene offers to make River her lunch every morning, but she never accepts. I may not have known her for long, but I think River worries she's in the way—a burden. I see it every time Oliver asks if she wants to join us and she goes to her room instead. Even when Bridgette offers River something, she rarely accepts.

Slipping a few ones in the cash slot, I select a few items. I'm pretty sure River has a sweet tooth, so I choose regular M&M's along with pretzels and a brown sugar Pop Tart. When I make it back, she's right where I left her. Her project already has a few additional pieces to it, the curve of the figure's body reaching out to something; something she hasn't drawn yet or maybe won't draw at all. I pretend not to notice and drop the food next to her.

"You need to eat," I say plainly. "Oliver won't like it if he knows you're skipping lunch."

Her eyes widen as they meet mine.

I give her an assuring smile. "I won't tattle, but that doesn't mean he won't find out. I don't know if you've noticed, but he's kind of a know-it-all."

The curves of her lips waver like she wants to smile but refrains. They flatten back out, all hint of amusement gone in a nanosecond.

Brushing it off, I push the Pop Tart in her direction. "Personally, I think these are gross. I'm more of a strawberry Pop Tart guy. Or a s'mores. But the vending machine only had these, so it's what I got."

Her nose scrunches. "Strawberry?"

"Not a fan?"

Her head moves back and forth.

"Huh." I examine the other snacks. "I guess the only type of fruit I like are processed, artificial, and filled with sugar. Like these."

Another ghost of a smile.

"Anyway, you should eat one of those."

Before I can stand up, her lips part and eyes follow their way up to mine. In a quiet tone, she murmurs, "Thank you."

I nod. "No problem."

When I leave, I notice her hand moving to the M&M's instead of the Pop Tart or pretzels. I think back to the trail mix and smile to myself after remembering the missing chocolate candy.

She'll fit in just fine with the James'.

I WALK INTO OUR SMALL SUBURBAN HOUSE TO Granddad coughing up a lung. He says he feels better but he's lying. No wonder Grandma's heart gave out. He's too stubborn for his own good.

Margaret gives me a sympathetic smile and carries an empty bowl into the kitchen, probably Granddad's soup.

He's pickier about what he eats these days. It's because he can't stomach half the stuff he used to, which he chalks up to old age making his palate change.

I call bullshit.

He ignores me.

Dropping onto the couch and tossing my backpack onto the floor, I give him a once over. He's settled in his chair, the one Grandma bought him after he was diagnosed with pancreatic cancer. She wanted to get him something nice to rest in because chemo would wear him out. The footrest droops a little on the right side and the cushions are flattened from the amount of time he spends in it. He sits there every chance he can. It reminds him of Grandma, I think.

"Don't give me that look." He huffs out another raspy cough, making me frown. It sounds deeper than before, like it's settling in.

"What look?" I raise a brow, the picture of innocence.

He finally peels his eyes off the show he's watching. Every afternoon, I come home to see him consumed in *Judge Judy*. I used to sit and watch it with him, but I grew tired of the stupid court cases and drama. I witness plenty of that crap at school.

His eyes narrow, causing his wrinkles to crease worse than they already do without him scowling. Frankly, he's always been bitter. It's what makes him, him. But lately, his patience has worn thin, like he's tired. Tired of fighting. Tired of everything. One day after school I overheard him tell Margaret that he just wants to be with Mabel, my grandma, again.

"Don't be stupid," he scoffs. "You're looking at me like I'm on my death bed."

I hate when he says shit like that. "No, I'm not. Just wondering if I need to call Dr. Peters and get you a refill on those antibiotics."

He coughs again, this round wracking his whole body and making the chair creak. I keep my face neutral even though I'm wincing inside. A cough like that has to hurt his ribs but he acts as if it's nothing. Seeing him so sick causes the physical pain in my chest to spread in the deep crevices of my body.

"What's the point?" he hacks, his eyes hollowing. "They ain't working. What makes you think another round will? Doc told me it'd take a week's worth to kick in. It has been three, kid."

Which is why we should get you more.

I shrug like it's no big deal. "Well, I'm just saying it might be worth another shot. I'm sure Marge will agree with me."

She walks in the room, leaning against the couch. "I'm with Everett, Henry. You need to get some relief."

He grumbles under his breath, probably profanities. It makes both Marge and I laugh. At least he has her to keep him in line when I can't. They've been family friends for decades. Margaret was Grandma's friend long before she met Grandpa, and she took it upon herself to take care of him when Grandma passed away. She said she promised to look after both of us.

"Never break a promise," Grandma used to tell me when I was little. *"They're oaths to prove your trust to someone. Remember that, Rhett boy, okay?"*

When Granddad falls asleep, Marge and I head into the kitchen. She points me in the direction of the left-over soup she made for him, chicken noodle. I settle into a chair with a bowl and spoon in front of me, blowing on the steam to cool it down.

"He's strong," she states quietly.

"I know." He's always been the strongest person I know.

"He'll fight this."

When the salty broth hits my tongue, my stomach growls in anticipation for more. "I just wish he wouldn't complain so much. We're trying to help him."

Margaret pats my shoulder. "You know how he is. He doesn't like people doting on him or causing a fuss. We do both. It's his pride at stake."

I grumble about how stupid that is but know it's the truth.

"He's all I have, Marge." The truth comes out in hoarse, shattered pieces. If I lose him, I'll lose everything I have left.

She takes a deep breath and sinks into the seat across from me. Her small, wrinkled palm covers the back of my free hand. "You have me, Everett. I know I'm not your biological family, but we're family just the same. After all, I've changed your diapers. I've seen things."

Shaking my head, I fight off the heat that tries settling into my cheeks. She loves reminding me that she's seen my parts when I was a baby. And as a toddler, when I apparently would rip off my pants and underwear and streak across the front lawn naked.

There are pictures.

Margaret is family though. After I moved in with my grandparents, Marge practically stepped in when Granddad had to work, and Grandma couldn't bring me to run errands. They always told me family goes beyond blood. I'll always remember that, see it in every memory.

"I know," I repeat, because it's all I can think to say.

She stands up. "I best be going. Unless you're planning on going to the James'? I can stick around, make up the guest bed."

I shake my head. Oliver's parents have an event they're all going to. Some fundraiser for the local ASPCA. It'll be River's first experience at a charity function, so I figured it'd be best to sit this one out. Plus, I'm sure she's seen enough of me today.

"Nah, I've got homework to do." Lie. I finished all my homework for this week and already have half of next week's done. I'll probably find another book to read until I fall asleep once I get Granddad to bed.

Marge leans down and kisses my temple, the same thing she's done since I was little. She tells me I'm the warmest person she knows considering the circumstances, yet my heart feels frozen. Frosted. Calculated. I'd rather invest my time in making other people better than dealing with my own shit.

Some pasts aren't meant to be dwelled on. Too many bad memories that have no chance of mending. My heart was shattered past the white line on county route five, along with my jaw, eye socket, and arm. No amount of endearments can take away those memories.

"Have a good night, Rhett boy."

Rhett boy. Grandma's nickname stuck with Marge, and she's the only one I let call me that these days besides Granddad.

"Night, Marge. Thanks again."

She leaves like always, going home to get ready to repeat it all tomorrow. It's the same thing every day, seven days a week. She doesn't get a break because she wants me to.

He's my granddad, I'd tell her.

But not your responsibility, she'd reply.

But how can I turn my back on him after everything he's done for me? I promised him I'd do anything I could to make him comfortable, to make him better. And I'm a Tucker.

Tuckers don't break promises.

SIX

River / 13

A month has gone by since I moved in with the James family. Jill has stopped by twice, once every two weeks, to check in. She goes through a long list of questions about how I'm doing, asking about school and home and people I've met. It's protocol, I know, but I genuinely think Jill cares.

Some social workers see their fosters as a burden. One lady who resembled a bird with her large beak nose used to trash talk the kids assigned to her, saying they'll never get forever homes. I'm lucky to have Jill. Everyone says so. I'm one of the kids who spent most of my time with her, so a bond was bound to form.

Over the past month, I've started eating lunch with Steph, the girl from art class. Her last name is Malone, and she's one of *the* Bridgeport Malones, not that I know what that means. She says she likes me not knowing.

We used to talk about the art assignments, because it's common ground. But then she would ask me other questions, personal ones. Most of them I don't answer or skip. Like when she asks where my parents are. I don't know, so I can't tell her. In fact, I don't know anything about my father. Or when she asks if I liked the other homes I lived in. I didn't, but I don't say a word. I find that most people don't like the nitty-gritty of reality; they prefer seeing life through rose-colored glasses. I don't burst their bubble with the murky, gray truth.

Jill has always told me the past is the past. My mother left me to have a better life, and I finally have a chance at living mine.

"Don't dwell on what you can't change," Jill told me right before she left.

I try not to, I really do. But the picture of me being held by a stranger still lingers in my duffle bag under my bed. Sometimes I take it out at night and stare at it, trying to figure out if I really look like her or not. Jill says I do but I don't see it.

Bridgette saw me looking at it one day and told me my mother is beautiful. I thought she was just trying to be nice, but her face seemed genuine. I suppose the woman *is* beautiful. Her body is slender, her cheekbones are sharp, and her hair looks long and luscious. But all I see is the person who gave me away, the one who supposedly chose drugs over her own daughter.

That's not beautiful, that's tragic.

When Bridgette offered to get a small frame for it, I told her no. I tell her that a lot when she offers stuff; *it's okay* or *no, thank you.* The James' have already given me so much; a bed of my own and a closet full of stain-free clothing I don't have to share with anybody. They'll always ask if they can get me something, but never accept when I tell them they've given me enough.

During lunch on Thursday afternoon, Steph tells me about the time there was a food fight in the cafeteria. It started when the sixth graders declared war on the seventh graders during spirit week, some rally leading up to Christmas break. She said it was spaghetti day, so it was extra messy, and her blonde hair was stained orange for a week, which made her mom really mad.

Abruptly, she changes the topic. "Where's your brother these days? You know the tall one. I haven't seen him lurking in a couple weeks."

She's talking about Everett, not Oliver. I think she has a secret crush on him, because she asks about him all the time. The last time Everett came to the cafeteria, Steph smiled and invited him to eat with us. Her blue eyes got all big and cheeks grew pink, especially when he thanked her for the offer, but said he was just checking in.

I know he doesn't want me going to the art room instead of lunch, so I've only done it a few times over the last few weeks. Now that Steph and I are sort of friends, he seems happier.

"He's not my brother." I've told her that before, but she says he practically is. I guess she's right. Oliver says he's family too, so I might as well stop correcting her.

She shrugs, biting into her peanut butter and jelly sandwich. It's seafood day, but I finally agreed to let Darlene pack my lunch. She made me a ham and swiss sandwich with some chips, apple slices, and a cheese stick. She even added a tiny bottle of apple juice, Motts not any other brand because she must have noticed me sneaking a few glasses when I crept into the kitchen while she baked.

Steph doesn't give up on whatever pursuit she's on. I've noticed how determined she is in everything she does. Her persistence makes me like her, except for when she pushes me about Everett. I don't know why, but a funny feeling tightens my chest whenever she brings him up.

"Does he not like coming around anymore?" She twirls a strand of hair around her finger and looks around the room like she's hoping Everett will pop out from behind the trash cans.

I pick off a piece of the ham and mumble out an "I don't know" hoping that she'll drop it.

He's satisfied with me having someone to sit with, so he doesn't bother coming in. Sometimes he'll pass me in the hall when I'm walking to lunch, which I think he does on purpose to make sure I'm not sneaking off to Cohen's art room. Oliver says they have study hall somewhere in the high school wing, so it doesn't make sense why he's around here this time of day.

She stays quiet for a minute. Then, "He's popular, you know? I hear him and Oliver run the high school."

I've heard the same thing. Sports are a big part of Freemont, and it's basketball season. Oliver's navy jersey has the number one on it, which Robert says is the best he could have gotten. I wonder what that means for the seven on Everett's jersey. The gym teacher said he thinks they can win nationals, which sounds like a big deal. Oliver doesn't always come home the same time I do because he has practice after school, but everyone says he's going to take their team to the top, so I don't get why they need to practice so much.

Robert suggests I join a club to get more involved in the school. I think he got the idea from Jill when she was here last week. She told me getting involved in school activities would be a fun way to meet new people. We have different definitions of fun.

When I told Robert that I didn't want to join any clubs, he pushed the matter. He says the James family gives it one hundred and ten percent. He used to play football and Oliver plays basketball. Now that I'm a James, according to him, I need to participate too.

Bridgette thinks it's a good idea but told me not to rush into anything until I'm ready. Robert seems to think the exact opposite, like I should always ready to dive right in. I'm not like him at all and I wonder if he can accept that.

"I'm just saying," Steph continues, "they could probably make you popular by association. Brittney already noticed them sitting with you your first week here. I'm surprised she hasn't tried snatching you up for her own group of minions yet."

My mind tries recalling who Brittney is. There's a brown-haired girl that goes by Britt who wears tight clothes and lots of jewelry in my math class. She stares at me sometimes, but I usually ignore it because she'll whisper something to the blonde next to her. What's worse than talking about myself is knowing when other people are talking about me.

But I'm used to it.

Instead of skidding around the topic like usual, I'm honest. "I don't want to be popular. I just want ... to be invisible."

Her lips weigh down at the corners. "I get it, but I think that's impossible for someone like you. You're new, so everyone is going to want to claim you for their own clique. Plus, you're associated with the James family. They're a big deal in Bridgeport, if you haven't noticed. They even donated a bunch of money to Freemont to redo the football field and upgrade the gymnasium."

My lips part. It shouldn't surprise me that they did that, especially knowing how much sports means to Robert. Of course, he wants the gym to be in the best shape for games.

I just don't want people thinking I'm like them, the rich girl. I've got two pairs of jeans, three t-shirts, and a baggie hoodie to my name. Not money. Not fame. Nothing.

Steph must see the anxiety bubbling inside me, because she dismisses the whole thing. "But hey, you chose the right company on the invisible front. People say I'm annoying because I talk too much. I mean, sure, my dad is Bill Malone. But most people here don't care about that because he's nothing compared to Robert James."

My lips twitch again, and I nearly ask her what her father does. If he's like Robert, he's in some business trade. I've learned a little bit about what Robert does since coming here, but most of the stuff Bridgette tells me doesn't really stick. All I know for sure is that he's the founder of a large company called the JT Corporation that deals with investments in other big businesses.

"I doubt you're invisible," is all I can think to murmur.

She laughs, the sound smooth and carefree. "I am, but thanks for trying to make me feel better. You probably have it right. If we're invisible, people can't touch us. Right?"

I'm sure she doesn't mean literally, but it still makes me stiffen. Being the newest addition to a family like the James' means people watch me, waiting until they come up with an opinion. The teachers will smile and play nice, but their eyes flash with judgment they think they're hiding. I've seen it before at every foster home with nearly every person who took me in. They wait until I do something bad, something that will inevitably get me kicked out.

To them, I'm another body to feed on what little the government gives them in return. A burden, that's what I've been called the most.

"We should tattoo it on your head," my last foster mother

spit at me. *"That way nobody will be tricked by your innocent looks. A burden, that's all you'll ever be."*

I'm shaken by the loud ding of the bell that tells us lunch is over. Staring down at my half-eaten sandwich, I frown. Darlene won't like it if I bring all this leftover food home. So, I follow Steph up to the large gray garbage can lining either side of the wash station and toss the sandwich and fruit away. I keep the cheese stick and chips for later, knowing hunger will settle in the pit of my hollow stomach before last period.

"Ready?" Steph asks.

No, but I nod anyway. What else is there to do but grit my teeth and hold my head up high as I take things one day at a time?

I MISS THE BUS AND BRIDGETTE AND ROBERT ARE AWAY until later tonight, so I wander around the school while Oliver's at practice. He told me he'd take me home quick, but he'd miss the beginning of his drills. I should just suck it up and walk on my own, but I decide to stay behind and wait for him because I'm not comfortable going anywhere by myself yet.

Mrs. Cohen's brows go up in surprise when I walk into her room. She looks like she's ready to go home. It's almost three thirty, and most teachers high tail it out as soon as the last bell rings.

"Are you all right, River?"

"I missed the bus," I mumble, looking at the too-new

shiny finish on my shoes. Somehow, missing the bus feels like this big awful thing I've done, and I hate admitting it out loud.

"Do you have a ride?" There's a stack of papers clutched in her hands, ready to be put away.

I nod. I know I should use my words, but I can't make myself part my lips to get any out. Silence is safe.

She taps her chin and then a small smile forms on her face. Holding up one of her fingers as if to say, *wait here*, she disappears into the supply closet at the end of the room. Something shuffles and falls before she makes her way out with a large sketch pad in her hands.

"Take it." I hesitantly wrap my fingers around the yellow pad, looking at her skeptically. Her smile is as warm as ever. "You know where the supplies are. I was going to head out, but I don't mind sticking around. I enjoy seeing what you create, River."

She's giving me a sketch pad? It's huge, full of blank pages and endless possibilities. The two projects I've worked on have been the same figure, my mother. Or, someone like her. The charcoal drawing is Mrs. Cohen's favorite, because I left the woman's arms branching out into open space. I planned to draw a little baby, a toddler, a little girl that she yearned to touch.

I left it blank. Empty.

Every project needs to have a title, so I captioned it with *The Void*. It's not what I thought it'd be when I started. I'm not sure whether the woman is still my mother or me. Maybe it's both, reaching out for everything we can't have.

I settle into my usual seat and open up the pad to the first page. My fingers brush against the empty sheet as I wet my bottom lip. A month ago, I channeled my emotions into the image of the woman. Mrs. Cohen told the class our emotions are the best inspiration for true masterpieces. But I don't feel the same way I did when I first moved to Bridgeport. The hollow ache that echoed in silent desperation has closed a fraction. It's still there and probably always will be, but it's shaped differently.

I'm not sure how long I spend on my new picture before I hear someone call my name. I glance from the image in front of me to Oliver, who's walking through the door with damp hair and holding my backpack while his is slung over his shoulder.

"Sorry, Mrs. Cohen," he apologizes. "Coach had practice run a little later than planned."

He passes me my bag and looks at the colorful jumble of lines in front of me. They're woven together, in gray, black, and red, a mixture of lines that don't really have a start or finish.

"That's uh ..." His head tilts and eyes narrow like it gives him a better idea of what I've made.

I call this piece *Emotion*. It's a mixture of a weight I don't understand, a feeling foreign to me that sits on my chest. Eventually, it'll have other colors and hidden shapes. Right now, it's exactly what I feel, which is too much to pull apart.

"...interesting," Oliver finally settles on.

I can't help but smile to myself. He doesn't get it. I don't tell him that I don't either, because I'm probably supposed to. Instead, I let him help me clean up and gather my belongings.

Before we leave, Mrs. Cohen tells us to hold on and grabs a paper off her desk. She hands it to me with an expectant smile.

Art Club - every Tuesday at 3 PM.

"Consider it," is all she says before waving us off.

Oliver peeks over at the paper, nudging me with his elbow. "Are you going to join? Looks like it's right up your alley."

Nibbling my bottom lip, I read over the description. It doesn't say how many people are involved or what mediums we have to work with. It's probably open to anything but I can't be sure.

"I don't know. Maybe."

He gestures toward the paper with his open palm, so I deposit it into his waiting hand. His eyes scan over the information for a short moment as we make our way down the stairs and toward the front doors.

"Mom and Dad would be really happy if you did this," he points out, passing it back to me. "I know Dad seems kind of pushy about stuff, but he means well. Plus, it could be worse. He could be shoving you toward joining the cheer squad."

The thought alone makes me pale. Well, paler than normal. Being in front of people is not my forte, much less a stadium full of loud fans cheering on a sport I don't even understand.

He laughs when he sees my face. "Chill. He knows better than to suggest that. Even Mom told him to let it go, and she loved cheerleading."

Bridgette was a cheerleader? It shouldn't surprise me. She seems like the type that would be involved with that kind of stuff when she was younger.

"It's how they met, you know." He unlocks his car and stops outside the driver's side.

I tug on my backpack strap. It's mint green, kind of like Everett's eyes, with floral print. Bridgette picked it out for me. Its way better than the scrap of material I usually carried around. "Really?"

He nods. "I can tell you about it, but Mom really loves the story. Maybe she can share it when they get back later."

I've always loved love stories. Mostly because they give me hope. It's why I sneak books and devour the romance, waiting for my time to be swept off my feet and into the arms of a knight in shining armor. It's cheesy, really cheesy, but it's what keeps me going when I just want to stop. Stop feeling, stop hoping, stop wishing.

I say, "I'd like that," because I would.

I'd like that a lot.

SEVEN

Everett / 17

Granddad has finally been getting better after the second dose of meds kicked into his system a few weeks ago. His coughing fits are nowhere as bad as they used to be, so both of our anxiety levels have calmed down. He knows I won't be bothering him to drink fluids and rest despite wanting to tinker on some project in the add-on garage.

I'm walking around the kitchen of my home away from home making myself a quick snack before heading down to the media room with Oliver and the rest of the guys when quiet footsteps come in from the connecting dining room.

River still does her homework in there even though Bridgette tells her she can do it wherever she wants. Sometimes she'll escape to her room, especially if Oliver has the guys over. Unless it's an art project or some sort of free drawing, she stays put with her books and assignments stretched out across the long oak table top.

I tip my chin at her as she walks toward the fridge, pulling out the half-empty bottle of apple juice and then a clean glass from the cupboard. "Hey."

She changed when she got home from school. The jeans she's wearing are old, the knees ripped and not in a stylish way. The pink hoodie is two sizes too big and could be worn as a dress since it hits her body mid-thigh. Earlier, she had on black pants and a long sleeve shirt with a denim jacket. Nothing fancy but a three-sixty from her current attire.

Her greeting back is muffled as she pours her drink.

"Don't you have pajamas or something?"

Her shoulders straighten for a moment before she screws the top back onto the juice container and peers down at her attire. I didn't mean to offend her, but I don't get why she's wearing what I assume are her old clothes. Oliver told me Bridgette was in her glory when she went shopping with River, getting her enough clothing to fill two rooms. Knowing Bridgette, I don't doubt it for a second.

"I like these."

I go to ask why but stop myself. It's none of my business. Shrugging instead, I grab the sliced apple and put it onto a plate before taking the peanut butter out of the cupboard. After scooping out a good-sized portion and placing it next to the fruit, I notice River's pinched brows.

"What?" My eyes bounce between her and my plate. She looks like she's never seen anyone eat this combination of food before.

She shakes her head.

We talk on occasion. Sometimes she'll tell me about

her day before I prompt the question, which usually leads her to talk about her friend Stephanie Malone. I asked around about the chick and heard she's a good person to have as a friend. It's also obvious that River redirects the conversation to Stephanie, so she doesn't have to talk about herself.

"You really like those together?"

The doubt etched into her tone makes me halt everything I'm doing. "You don't? Apples and peanut butter are two essentials in life."

"I thought that was peanut butter and jelly?"

My lips split into an amused smile. "As far as I'm concerned, peanut butter should be its own food group."

Hesitantly, she walks over and examines the food closer. "I've heard of caramel apples but not peanut butter ones."

I gape. "You're kidding, right?"

She shakes her head, her hair falling from where it was tucked behind her ear. Fixing the rogue strand, she reaches out and takes a slice, her hand hovering above the peanut butter.

"Well?"

My voice startles her for some reason, and her eyes dart up to mine. "I-I should have asked. I'm sorry."

Why is she apologizing? "Don't worry about it. Just try it, you'll like it."

She studies me like she's trying to figure out if it's really all right. Nodding in encouragement, I lift the plate up, so the apple falls into the smooth, creamy butter.

Just as she's about to take a bite, Peter York comes strutting in opening his big fat mouth. "Is this the littlest James?" He makes a face at her baggy attire. "Did they not tell you how to dress? Man, where did you get those rags from?"

River drops the apple onto the plate and sinks into her hoodie. Her body steps back from Peter as he approaches, grabbing the apple chunk she was going to eat and popping it into his mouth in one bite.

Dickbag.

"That was hers," I growl.

His brow arches, always arrogant. "She wasn't going to eat it. Were you, Rachel?"

"It's River," I correct irritably.

He shrugs.

River is fisting the ends of her hoodie sleeves and staring between York and the door. Her tiny frame is tucked behind me, and it makes me feel protective. Something in her eyes darkens her previous curious features; fear.

It isn't until then I realize why she's wearing those clothes. She can hide in them. It's like how she uses her long hair to shield her face. Around strangers she reverts to the shy girl she was a month ago—quiet and non-existent.

"Go back downstairs, York."

"What the fuck? Why?"

My teeth grind as he glances over at River. I wonder if he sees what I do or if he even cares that he's scaring her. Knowing York, he doesn't give a shit. He's been bugging Oliver about meeting her since she started at Freemont High. Why would he care about a thirteen-year-old? Simple: she's part of the circle he's been trying to claw his way into since freshman year.

He's jealous, sizing up the competition for his way in. And if we don't keep an eye out for him, he will find a way to use River. Oliver's choice to keep him around makes sense now. Friends close and enemies closer and all that.

My gaze turns to River. "You can go."

She doesn't need me to repeat it. Her feet are darting toward the door long before I finish talking. Her apple juice is left forgotten on the counter, same with her homework on the table in the room over. The creak of the stairs as she practically bolts up them is all I hear.

"Nice going, York."

He throws his hands up. "What did I do? I was just messing with her. God, girls are so sensitive."

No, you're just an ass.

"You need to leave her alone."

His fists clench. "Or what?"

I step so close to him he flinches. "Why don't you test me and find out, York? Oliver and I won't let you use her for your own personal gain. She stays out of your agenda, got it?"

"I don't have—"

"Don't bullshit a bullshitter," I cut him off harshly. With my plate in hand, I shoulder past him, grabbing the glass of apple juice on the way through the archway into the hall. "Tell the others I'll be down in a minute."

"What?" he calls after me. "I have to stay away from her, but you can approach her whenever you want? Who's the pervert now?"

The comment makes me want to drop everything in my hands and punch him right in his smug ass face. He'd drop in an instant. But I don't give him the satisfaction of entertaining that disgusting remark. I just walk upstairs, set the apple juice in front of River's door, knock, and walk back downstairs before she can answer.

By the time I'm back in the media room, York is glowering at me from the seat in the corner and Oliver is arguing with Quinn over his cheating in the video game they're playing. York is smart enough not to say a word to me, so I eat my apples and peanut butter in peace.

OLIVER ASKS ME TO WAIT UP FOR HIM, SO I SETTLE against the row of lockers outside of the classroom. A few students I don't recognize stumble out, muttering about whatever the student counsel talked about. Something about the school semi-formal, but I don't care enough to know what their problem is.

The next person that walks out catches my eye, her long caramel legs are exposed by a skirt that definitely doesn't meet dress code standards. I'm not complaining.

When she notices me staring, she giggles and adjusts her brown hair, tucking it behind her ear.

"Hey, Everett."

Isabel Allen is a senior like Oliver and me. She's part of the student counsel with him, the co-captain of the cheer squad, and last I heard she volunteered at the homeless shelter in town. Frankly, she's a female version of Oliver. Only hot.

"Hey, Isabel."

"You can call me Issy."

I nod. "Rhett."

We stand there smiling at each other. Her lips are painted in a soft pink and glossed with something that make them look fuller and more inviting. Or it could be how she bats her painted lashes at me.

She steps closer to me, crossing her arms over her chest to make her boobs look bigger. They already fill out the white shirt she's wearing, but I don't mind a peep-show. "Are you waiting for Oliver? He'll probably be a few minutes. Trevor is giving him crap about not having a theme for the semi-formal."

So that's what the others were pissed about.

"I don't see why we need one," I admit.

She shrugs. "It's just easier to plan that way. Without a clear direction, the counsel won't be able to agree on decorations."

Seems like they aren't agreeing as it is now, but I don't tell her that. "Makes sense, I guess."

We're silent for a moment.

She clears her throat. "Are you going to Easton's party on Friday? I hear he invited the basketball team."

Easton Berkley is the quarterback for our football team. On his own, he's a cool dude. Laid back, drama free. But when he's around his teammates, especially during the season, he's annoying as hell. He'll laugh at their jokes even if they're demeaning and won't say shit. Not unless the captain, Joseph Anderson, says to quit it. But he's usually the one who starts shit, so everyone goes along with it.

"I'm not sure." Granddad may be doing better, but I don't know if I want to go out for long. Plus, parties around here are just excuses to raid houses, get drunk, and make stupid choices. I've been known to make a lot of those, and Oliver is the one who has to bail me out.

"You should," she says, brushing my arm with her fingertips. Her nails are long and blood red, one of them has some sort of design. Hell if I know what it is. "It'll be fun."

I tip my chin. "Are you going?"

Her lips spread into a sexy grin. "Of course. I wouldn't tell you to come just to let someone else try snatching you up."

A low chuckle shakes my shoulders. "Is that what you're trying to do, snatch me up?"

"Oh, I'm not *trying* anything." She backs up, shooting me a wink. "You're going to ask me out, Everett Tucker. Just give it time."

With that, she struts away.

Oliver walks out right after, noting the way Isabel adds a little swivel to her hips as she disappears down the hall.

He smacks my chest. "Did she finally make a move? 'Bout time, if you ask me."

My brows draw up as we start down the opposite end of the hall. "You knew she was going to do that?"

His laugh is loud. "Dude, Isabel has had a lady boner for you for like a year now. Probably longer. You're the only idiot who doesn't see the way she stares at you."

Huh. Guess I haven't really paid her much attention. Besides games, I don't see her around. We don't run in the same crowds, so there's no reason for me to know how she looks at me.

Oliver snickers and shakes his head, pushing open the side door that leads to student parking. "I swear, I don't get you. Girls fling themselves at you all the time and you either don't care or don't get it."

Girls don't *fling* themselves at me. That's ridiculous. Sometimes I'll hook up with someone at a party, but outside the occasional kegger, I don't have time to invest in anyone. Girls around here don't want a one-time thing, they want a commitment. Granddad's health keeps me busy outside of school and basketball, so there's not exactly time to entertain a girlfriend.

Oliver opens his car door. "You should go for it, bro. Issy's good people and she's hot. Can't go wrong with that, right?"

He's not wrong. "Maybe."

He rolls his eyes. "You'd be an idiot not to have some fun. We're going to East's party on Friday."

"You heard that?"

"I might have been eavesdropping." His grin says there's no *might have been* about it.

We climb in his car and buckle up. "I'm game for a party as long as Granddad is okay. Margaret likes having Friday nights off."

He nods. "No problem, man."

He pulls out of the parking lot. "My parents are taking River out that night, so it'll give us time to make some bad decisions. You especially."

"And what about you?"

The corner of his lips quirk up. "Don't worry about me. It's you who needs to get laid. Isabel is offering, so ..."

Sometimes I forget he's the son of Robert and Bridgette James. When he's like this, laid back, he's just a horny seventeen-year-old. It's like he's one of the guys. I doubt his parents know how much he drinks when we go to parties or the girls he's been with. I'm no saint, but Oliver is worse than I am when it comes to hookups.

I don't argue with him, so he takes it as a victory. Isabel Allen made her intentions clear, and Granddad does seem like he's recovering. What harm could a little fun bring?

The back of Oliver's hand connects with my chest. "I know that look. You're going for it, aren't you?"

I gruff out a reply as he pulls into my driveway.

Normally I'd go to his place, but his parents are having a family dinner. They don't care if I'm over most days, but they decided once a week it'd be just the four of them. I can respect that, I think it's good for them, for River especially.

Unlatching my buckle, I hoist my backpack from the floor. "See you tomorrow?"

"You know it."

"Eddy's at seven?"

He snorts. "See you there."

I slam the door and watch him drive away.

When I walk inside, Granddad is sleeping in his chair, and Margaret is knitting something with purple yarn. I'm not sure what it's supposed to be, it looks like a blob to me.

She glances up at me and smiles. "You're home early."

"Oliver dropped me off."

"Speaking of him—" She holds up what may be the start of a scarf. "I made his new sister something to keep her warm. Winter has been awfully mild, but I'm sure the cold is coming."

She's making River a scarf? "That's … nice of you, Marge. I'm sure she'll love it."

I don't think purple is one of River's favorite colors, but she's the type not to nitpick. Anything homemade will probably be really special to her. I see her face light up every time one of the James' gives her something money can't buy.

Marge watches me check over Granddad. "I think it's good we got him the extra meds."

Her lips press into a firm line, her eyes focusing on the project in front of her. Something flashes on her face, but she just nods in agreement without saying another word.

Margaret never stays quiet unless she has something upsetting to say. But I also know she won't tell me if she doesn't feel like it's necessary, so I don't push her.

Granddad's soft snores ease some of the worry that what she's holding back has something to do with him. His breaths aren't harsh or short but smooth and clear, which means his lungs are clearing up.

"Think he'll be okay on Friday?"

She studies me. "I'm sure he'll be okay. Do you have plans? I could—"

"It's just a party," I cut her off, waving my hand. "If he needs me, I can skip it. Freemont kids always have them, so if I have to—"

"Absolutely not!" She sets down her yarn and crosses her arms on her chest. "You're only young once, Rhett boy. You're going to go out and have fun. I don't have plans Friday anyway."

My eyes go to my grandfather. "Do you think he really needs someone?"

"No," Granddad cuts in, "he doesn't."

Go figure he's been pretending to sleep. He used to do that when I was younger and didn't want Grandma yelling at him over something stupid he'd done.

"Marge is right." He sits up, readjusting and searching for something. Margaret picks up his thick wire glasses and passes them over. "You can't keep using me as an excuse not to act your age, kid."

Sitting down on the couch, I grumble, "I don't."

They both look skeptical.

It's Marge who says, "We just want you doing more stuff on your own."

"I play basketball and hang with Oliver."

"But do you actually do anything?"

What do they want me to do? Get drunk, grope girls, and party until sunrise? I do that shit on occasion, once every month if not every couple of months. It's a good distraction but only a temporary fix from reality. The real world always comes crashing back into my mind like the goddamn Kool-Aid man.

"We play video games and watch ESPN." It should be enough to appease them, but it doesn't. Granddad especially looks disappointed. Then again, Grandma used to tell me all about his wild days before she reined him in and made him put a ring on her finger.

"Well, you're going to that party," Marge informs me. Granddad nods in agreement.

"Nice to know I have a choice."

They both snicker.

Before either of them can say anything, the phone rings in the kitchen. Margaret is up before I can go to answer it, leaving me alone with Granddad.

He asks how school is, so I give him the basic answer.

It's school. How exciting or different can it be from any other day? Nothing else is said between us before Marge comes in with a toothy smile on her face.

"It's for you," she tells me. "It's a girl."

"A girl?" Me.

"A girl?" Granddad.

Margaret nods enthusiastically. "She says her name is Isabel. Sounds real pretty, Everett. I hope she's at that party on Friday."

Granddad slaps the arm of the chair. "Well, I'll be damned. Miracles do happen."

Rolling my eyes, I grab the landline from Marge and walk up to my room to talk to Issy before she can hear any more.

By the end of the night, Easton's party will be the backdrop for my very first date with Isabel Allen.

EIGHT

River / 14

It may not feel like a long time to most, but three months later and I'm still shocked we've made it this far. After constantly moving, I finally start to settle into my new routine. The James' seem to understand what a huge milestone it is for me, for all of us really, because the four of us go out to dinner to celebrate the ninety-day mark.

That's something I'm still not used to. Well, one of the things. There's a lot on that list and it just keeps growing the longer I learn the habits of my new family. The James' love to celebrate. It seems like they have parties for everything. At least once a week they go out to some event where they dress up and mingle with other rich people and give away their money for different causes.

I mean, it could be worse. Most of the families I lived with in the past paid us no attention. If they went out, they made the foster kids stay in. On the off chance we were allowed to tag along, we weren't allowed to say a word. But here, I'm involved in everything. I'm the shiny new possession they want to parade around to their friends. Those people fawn over me and my circum-stances like I'm some sort of circus freak. I don't like the attention.

When my fourteenth birthday neared, I knew I would have to convince them not to make a big deal of it. Birthdays aren't special, they're just another day. Mine landed on a school day anyway, so everyone would be too busy with work and school to focus on me. I preferred it that way.

Two days before my birthday, Oliver mentions that Bridgette has been wanting to do a small get-together. *Intimate*, she calls it. No party, just a dinner of my choos-ing. But that isn't true, because I chose not to celebrate, and everyone is pushing me toward it anyway.

Oliver rarely ever comes to my room unless it's to tell me dinner is ready. Sometimes he'll yell goodnight on the way to his room, but he never steps foot into my space.

"Mom really wants to do this for you," he presses, examining a few books I checked out from the school library. One of them is by Jane Austen and the other by Charlotte Bronte. They're supposed to be good, but I can't get into either of them, so they just sit on the corner of my desk untouched, unloved. Kind of like me.

"I know she does, but ..." I fidget with the notebook placed in front of me on the bed, not really seeing my science notes as more than blurs of definitions and theo-ries. I consider everything Bridgette has done for me. I don't like parties, hate people paying attention to me, but it's the least I can do.

Oliver must see the moment my resolve crumbles, because he claps loudly. I flinch at the sound and draw back into myself. He's happy for his mom because he knows how much she wants this dinner. Maybe he wants one too. I'm not sure why though.

"It'll be small, I promise."

"What do you promise?" The deep voice behind Oliver belongs to Everett, I don't even need to look. Robert's voice is deeper, older, wiser. Everett still has youth in his, which makes sense since he's not even eighteen yet.

Oliver grins. "River decided to let Mom throw her a birthday dinner." Sometimes he'll correct himself when he calls Bridgette "mom" because he knows I can't call her that. Not yet.

Everett's eyes cut to me. "Wednesday, right?"

Heat spreads across my cheeks. He knows when my birthday is? I don't remember telling him. In fact, I know I never told him. But maybe Oliver did. I'm sure of it.

I just nod.

He nods once. "Cool. I know Bridgette won't disappoint. And Darlene makes some great chocolate cake."

"Maybe she wants vanilla," Oliver huffs.

Everett snorts. "No, *you* want vanilla." He glances back over at me. "Don't let your brother convince you to have vanilla cake. Unless you want that, but I'm pretty sure you don't."

How would you know?

Oliver sighs heavily. "I'm just saying, vanilla cake is good too."

"You also like that nasty ice cream shit."

Oliver gapes at him. "Ice cream cake is the best kind of cake. I don't know how we stay friends with your awful taste."

Biting back a smile, I shift on the bed. "Um, are you coming?" That's directed to Everett, but my voice is quiet and unsure, and I can't make eye contact with him.

Thankfully, he hears me just fine. "If you want me to, I'm there."

My heart does a summersault in my chest. I beat down the sappy smile that wants to stretch across my face. I don't want to think about why it keeps wanting to pop up whenever Everett is nice to me. He's nice to me a lot.

Everett tips his chin toward the door. "We still playing video games, or do you need to study for Hall's test?"

Oliver frowns. "Hall is giving us a test?"

The soft rumble of Everett's laughs echoes in my room, causing little goosebumps to pebble on my arms. "I guess we're studying. He mentioned it the other day. You know, when you were flirting with Viki."

Oliver side eyes me like I'm not supposed to know he flirts with girls. I hear things at school, mostly from Steph. She's into all the gossip, especially if it involves Oliver and Everett.

Instead of entertaining Everett with an answer,

Oliver says, "Like you're any better. I have it on good authority that you've been spending an awful lot of time texting Issy when you should be listening to lectures."

The sound of another girl's name tenses my shoulders. It shouldn't matter, but for some reason it does. "Who's Issy?"

Normally, I'd keep my mouth shut.

"Keeping quiet means less trouble," Jill always told me when she'd drop me off at a new home. Most people probably think it's awful that a social worker would tell a foster that, but Jill has always been realistic.

But I can't keep quiet now because I want to know who Issy is and why Everett is talking to her.

Everett sighs. "She's a friend."

"His *girl*friend," Oliver taunts.

Girlfriend? Steph never said anything about him dating anyone. Maybe it's because she likes Everett and doesn't want to admit it out loud. How many high school relationships last, anyway?

I don't hide the curve of my downward lips before Everett sees them. His eyes fill with sympathy. "Don't worry, River. You're still my number one."

The soft tone of his voice paired with those words make my whole body heat up. Oliver doesn't seem to notice my reaction, thank God. Instead, he pats Everett on the shoulder like he's being a good friend.

And he is. Everett is the best. I know better than to read into what he said. They're just words and words mean nothing. Actions on the other hand? Actions mean everything.

"Ready?" Everett presses, obviously over this conversation. I wonder why he doesn't want to talk about his girlfriend. Are they not really dating? Are they just friends?

I don't bother asking those questions and just watch them leave. His words ring loud and clear in my head.

You're still my number one.

But for how long?

STEPH COMES HOME AFTER SCHOOL WITH ME ON Wednesday to have dinner with the James'. It's all she talked about all day but promised not to let anyone at school know. Eddy O'Brien's birthday was two weeks ago and the whole art class sang him happy birthday.

No thanks.

Darlene suggested I give Steph a tour of the house. It's a bad tour, because I only know what a few of the rooms are used for, but Bridgette would be proud of me. It's what a good host would do.

Steph doesn't seem to mind that I don't know what some of the rooms are. When we get to my room, she jumps on the bed and exclaims how much bigger my room is compared to hers.

I haven't been to her house yet even though she's invited me over. Last month, her and some of her other friends were having a sleepover. I've slept in lots of people's houses, I just want to stay in mine.

Mine. The word feels funny to me. I've never used it when talking about homes I've lived in because they weren't mine.

"Are you okay?" Steph asks quietly.

Tears well in my eyes and I force them away. I don't want her to see me cry. They aren't sad tears, but I won't be able to explain that to someone who doesn't know what it's like to have my kind of upbringing. And I'm glad she doesn't. The scars I bare, both physically and emotionally, aren't worth anyone truly understanding the pain behind them. Or the relief that no one can hurt me again.

Silently, I nod.

She accepts my answer and climbs off the bed to examine my room. Not much has changed since I first moved in. The bookshelf in the corner has two shelves full of various books and knick-knacks that Bridgette saw me looking at the few times we've been shopping. On my desk there's a laptop I rarely use, and on the corner of my nightstand is a small frame holding the photo of my mother and me.

Oliver told me I should display it. When I asked him why, he told me that my mother will always be a piece of me.

"Plus," Oliver adds, "We wouldn't have adopted you if she didn't decide to be selfless enough to give you away."

I never thought of it like that. Over the years, I heard

my mother called lots of things. Selfless has never been one of them.

Steph rummages through my closet. "We need to look cute for the party."

I tell her for the second time it's not a party. Sometimes I wonder if she even listens, but I don't let it bother me. She's my only friend, and she's always so busy talking about herself that she doesn't ask personal questions about my past. I can't risk losing her.

I do talk to some other girls in art club. Mrs. Cohen spoke to my parents about me joining shortly after she gave me the paper with the information. I think Oliver mentioned it to them, because the paper disappeared from my backpack one night. I thought I just misplaced it, but the next day both Robert and Bridgette encouraged me to join.

"Why do we need to look cute?" I settle on the edge of my bed, crossing my legs under me.

Steph pulls a black dress out of my closet and holds it up to herself in front of the mirror attached to the back of the closet door. "Because it's your birthday, and the birthday girl always has to look cute."

I toy with the hem of my sleeve. "But it's not *your* birthday."

She rolls her eyes and flicks her blonde hair behind her shoulder. It's curly today. She said she spent a lot of time on it this morning, same with her makeup. The thick black eyeliner looks good against her blue eyes and she promised she'd teach me how to do the winged style. I said sure, but I don't really want to know.

Putting back the black dress, she takes out a different one. This one is burgundy and falls just above my knees, which means it'll be shorter on her because she's a few inches taller than I am. "*I'm* looking cute because Everett is going to be there. Plus, I'm your guest. We both need to be presentable. That's what my mom always says."

After thirty minutes of playing dress up, she tells me that I have to wear the cream dress hanging in the very back of the closet. It's lace and tighter than my other dresses. Bridgette picked it out because she said I have the type of figure I should enjoy while I'm young. Whatever that means.

It's a pretty dress, but there's a mesh cutout just under the bust that would show too much skin. It shouldn't be a big deal and to most it wouldn't be, but I don't like showing off that part of my body.

"I don't know ..."

She groans. "You're going to look beautiful, River. I'd totally wear this, but it would wash me out. Plus, I'm bigger than you."

I frown. She isn't that much bigger than me. Maybe when I first came here, but between Darlene and the James' making sure I'm fed, I've packed on over ten pounds. Twelve, to be exact. Darlene tells me I look healthier, and I guess she's right. It doesn't hurt to sit on hard surfaces anymore, and my collarbones aren't as prominent as before.

When Steph sticks out her bottom lip, my frown deepens. "Please, River? For me? I'm your best friend, so I'm obligated to dress you up and show you off. This dress begs to be worn tonight."

She doesn't know what's under my shirt. Very few people do, except Jill and the people who gave the marks to me. They're everywhere, clear as day. Some are little circles, and some are long thin lines. But they're all various shades of pink and white and jut out from my pale skin.

My mouth dries when she walks over and holds it out to me. Dropping my shoulders, I accept the dress. Steph claps and tells me how fun the night will be.

I don't agree.

When six o'clock comes around, Steph and I are both ready to go downstairs. Me in the cream dress and her in the burgundy one. Our makeup is vastly different. Unlike her winged eyeliner, mine is just around the edges of my eyes. She put some sort of pink shadow on my lids, a similar color on my cheeks, and finished off my lips with a clear gloss. She tells me it's neutral because she knows I don't like attention. When I look in the mirror, I don't recognize the girl staring back.

My auburn hair is pulled up on one side, clipped back by two black barrettes. The rest falls in waves down my other shoulder. The makeup I'm wearing isn't very noticeable except the eyeliner, because it makes my brown eyes look almost golden.

"I'm ... pretty."

Steph gives my shoulders a squeeze. "You've always been pretty, River. You're just extra gorgeous tonight. Ready to show yourself off?"

I flush over the thought. My arm wraps around the mesh part of the dress, covering the scars that peek out from the see-through material.

Steph must assume it's nerves. "It'll be okay. I'll be right there with you. Plus, you said it's a small dinner party, right?"

Lips twitching, I nod.

Her smile widens. "Good. Nothing to worry about then. It'll just be your family and Everett."

Repeating that as a chant in my head, I let her drag us downstairs. Bridgette sees us first, her friendly smile stretching into a happy greeting as her hand reaches out to me.

"Oh, River." She holds my hands and examines me at an arm's length. "I knew that dress would look amazing on you. Wasn't I right, Robert?"

Robert nods once. "You look beautiful, River."

My relationship with Robert is still limited, and guilt eats at me. He's been nothing but nice since I've gotten here. He gives me space and doesn't push because he knows about my past. Not the details, but enough.

"Thanks." My cheeks heat up.

Oliver walks over and gives me a funny look, his nose crinkling, then turns to Bridgette. "Don't you think that dress is a little short?"

My eyes widen. Is it too short? I quickly tug the hem down, but it just bounces back to where it sits mid-thigh.

Bridgette doesn't seem phased. "It's not too short, Ollie. Quit playing overprotective big brother and tell River how nice she looks."

He rolls his eyes but turns and smiles. "You do look beautiful, Riv."

Riv. He started calling me that more frequently. Sometimes I'll call him Ollie like Bridgette and Robert do, but usually he's just Oliver to me. I can't even get myself to call him the *b* word yet, but nobody seems to mind that I just call them by their names instead of the labels they deserve.

I'm just not ready.

Steph comes over and squeezes my hand when Everett comes into view. My grip tightens when I see a girl I don't know appear next to him. She's holding his hand.

"Happy birthday," Everett greets, smiling at me the way he always does. He looks different in the black silk button down and gray slacks. When he smiles, his face is brighter, friendlier. Without the smile, he looks unapproachable. I wonder if he does that on purpose.

"T-Thank you."

The girl tugs on his hand. "Babe, aren't you going to introduce us?"

Everett clears his throat. "Isabel, this is River. River, this is Isabel. My—"

"Girlfriend," she interjects. Her smile is too broad

and too bright. It doesn't reach her eyes as she scans my body from head to toe. "I admire your style, River. I haven't worn makeup that heavy since sophomore year."

My whole face heats up.

Everett shoots her a quick glare, his lips twitching at the edges. "Really?"

She bats her eyelashes. They're long. Way longer than mine. "Oh, I don't mean anything bad by it. She totally pulls it off! And that dress?" She gestures toward me. "Wow."

Steph squeezes my hand like she sees exactly what I do. I've been around plenty of fake people and this girl is one of the biggest offenders. What's worse is that she's pretty. Steph says that I am too, but this girl would be better qualified as stunning. Her skin is a natural olive tone that compliments her silky brown hair and she's tall; the tight dress she wears shows off her thin figure. She isn't sickly like I am, so I see why Everett likes her.

Bridgette saves me from engaging in anymore conversation. "Come to the kitchen. Darlene put out appetizers to start off the night."

I drag Steph along before she can make a comment to Isabel. She's not afraid to say what's on her mind unlike me. It doesn't matter if we see who Isabel really is, Everett obviously doesn't. If there's one thing I've learned, it's that people need to find out for themselves who's worth investing time in.

Dinner goes by quickly, even though some moments feel like they stretch forever. Like when Isabel asks me how being thirteen feels. It's Everett who tells her I'm fourteen. When she asks me how I like living in such a big house, I tell her it's nice. But that's not good enough for her, because she goes on a long rant about how lucky I am to have so much stuff considering where I come from.

When she says that, I stare at Everett like he betrayed me somehow. He doesn't know my background enough to tell her anything, but it seems like she knows enough to pass judgement.

Everett looks uncomfortable throughout most of dinner, like me. Maybe he feels bad that he told Isabel anything. Or maybe he regrets bringing her along. I like that idea more. I just wanted him here, not her. It's my birthday, after all. Shouldn't I get what I want?

You didn't even want this.

The entitled thought washes away my momentary anger. I have no right to be upset with Everett or who he decides to bring. This dinner is not just about me turning another year older. It's about my new family—Robert, Bridgette, and Oliver. And since day one, Oliver said family included Everett.

Steph asks Everett questions about school and basketball and college, but he doesn't really answer them. But I'm curious about what he's going to do, since he's graduating soon.

"Where *are* you going to college?"

The table gets really quiet from the little side conversations happening, and I squirm when all their eyes shift to me. At first, I'm not sure why they're staring at me in surprise. Bridgette and Robert the most. But then I realize it's probably because I never engage the conversation first. I'll answer somebody if they ask me something but that's it.

I guess I'm getting comfortable.

Everett's fork clinks against his plate. "Uh, the community college in town. At least for the first two years."

Robert perks up. "That's it?"

Bridgette puts her hand on his. "Rob."

Everett waves her off. "It's fine. I want to be close to home. Granddad seems to be doing better but I think there's something he's not telling me."

According to Steph, Everett has lived with his grandfather since he was little. When I ask what happened to his parents, she'd only tell me there was an accident a long time ago. I never pushed for more details because that's more than enough for me to understand him.

I can see why he wants to stay close to home. His relationship with his grandfather is all he has left. It's easy to comprehend someone who resembles yourself. I can empathize with him, even if our situations are completely different.

Robert doesn't stop. "I'm just saying, son, you could apply to better colleges and get an athletic scholarship."

Oliver cuts in. "He doesn't want to play ball in college, Dad."

Robert turns to Everett. "Why not?"

Bridgette clears her throat. "How about I get dessert?"

Oliver nods and offers to help.

Robert leans back in his seat. "You're a good player, Rhett. I've seen you grow since you joined the team with Oliver. I could make some calls and get you into the school Oliver is going to. Penn State, remember? It's a great school. A scholarship will ensure you're not in debt. What's the harm in that?"

"Family is more important than sports," I blurt from where I sit at the opposite end of the table.

I'm met by utter silence again.

Even Steph blinks at my outburst.

Bridgette reaches out and squeezes my hand, her hazel eyes are warm and glassy and look greener than normal. "You're so right, River." She turns to Robert. "That's enough of that talk, Robert. If Everett wants to go to community college, leave him be."

I notice Isabel looking at me with a funny expression on her face. Her eyes are slightly narrowed and her lips twitch downward, but when Everett glances at her, the tightness loosens.

The conversation is much lighter throughout the rest of dinner. Darlene made me a triple chocolate cake that has little pieces of chocolate chips in the mixture. The frosting is rich, and every bite explodes on my tongue. She knows about my sweet tooth and promised not to disappoint. I'm never disappointed in what she cooks, but especially not about this cake.

After dessert, I help Bridgette clear off the table even though she told me not to worry about it. I don't listen, just keep piling the dishes on top of one another. Following her toward the kitchen, I stop short when I hear my name being whispered by Isabel in the hall.

"I'm just saying, she's a little odd."

"Why would you say that?" Everett.

A loud sigh escapes her. "Come on, Rhett. She's a little girl playing dress up. Did you see her makeup? She looks ridiculous, obviously trying to impress *someone*. And don't pretend like you didn't see her stomach."

I nearly drop the plates I'm holding. Clenching them until my fingertips hurt, I wait until Everett replies.

"That's none of our business, Issy."

Issy. I hate when he calls her that.

"She's a cutter, Rhett. Shouldn't it be?"

A cutt—?

"River," Bridgette calls from the kitchen, "do you need help carrying the rest of the plates in?"

Quickly hurrying away from where I'm eavesdropping, I hand her the rest of the dishes without so much as looking her in the eye.

"May I be excused?"

Her hand brushes mine. "Are you all right?"

"Not feeling well."

"Oh, dear. Why don't you go lay down? It's probably all that sugar from the cake. I'll grab some medicine and make you some ginger tea."

I don't tell her that it's not the cake or that I don't

like tea. Somebody sneaks candy into my locker almost every day, so I'm used to the sugar. Sometimes it's M&M's and Skittles and sometimes it's Snickers and Reese's. Steph told me she wants a secret admirer to bring her candy, but then makes a comment about how she doesn't want to get fat.

The only reason I eat it is because I know Everett is the one who leaves them. I'm not sure how he gets into my locker, but I don't mind. When the first candy bar appeared, I asked him if he put it there and he told me no. But then he'd start asking me if I got my breakfast, and I realized the breakfast is the candy. So, when I started thanking him, he'd just smile and pretend he doesn't know what I'm talking about.

There's no way to avoid bumping into Everett and Isabel in the hall on the way to my room. When I come into their view, they both stop talking altogether. My arm goes to the mesh of my dress, and Everett instantly knows I heard. But before he can say anything, I run upstairs and get far away from them.

Bridgette comes up a few minutes later and passes me some pills and tea. She tells me I can open my presents tomorrow when I'm feeling better and leaves me alone for the night.

Before I finish pulling on my regular t-shirt for bed, my eyes scan across the scars. Shakily, my fingers graze the rough skin. I remember how I got each and every one of them.

My finger stops on the circular scar just above my

belly button. That one is from Mr. Davis's cigarette. He caught me sneaking into the kitchen for water after bedtime and told me I had to be punished.

I move my fingers upward to the curved pink line that stretches an inch long. It's from when I got in front of Mr. Marley when he was beating one of the younger foster kids for asking if he could go outside and play.

On the opposite side is a larger pink circle that's nearly white in color. It's one of my oldest scars. This one is curtesy of Mrs. Oakley. Another cigarette burn.

But the two deepest scars are just under my bust. They were given to me by the same man at my last home. Mr. Connors told us to follow the rules and he'd never have to reinforce them. But after a long day of school, all I wanted was to be left alone and I was stupid enough to tell him that. It was the last time I ever talked back. The two scars left behind are from a rusty butter knife.

I try not to think about it much.

Just like I try not thinking about the ones on my back, which double in number and size. There's little skin left untouched from the belt strikes.

Yanking on the shirt, I replay the words that spewed from Isabel's lips. I wish I would have been the one to permanently mark my skin. Then it would have been *my* choice.

Crawling into bed, I shove all the memories into the farthest part of my mind. They'll resurface whether I want them to or not.

They always do.

NINE

Everett / 17

Sometimes I don't know why I'm with Issy. She can be extremely cruel, something I never would have expected. Everyone at school loves her. She's got a large group of friends and a decent number of teachers who never have a bad thing to say about her. But when it comes to other people, like River, Issy doesn't know when to stop.

It's ridiculous that she has a problem with River in the first place. At first, I thought she just didn't like me hanging out with Oliver so much. After we officially started dating, I tried balancing who I spent time with. Oliver teased me for a while but understood. Issy, on the other hand, didn't seem to appreciate the effort.

Now I know Issy's real problem is that she thinks River likes me. Even if she does, so what? She's a teen with a crush. When I was fourteen, I had a thing for Macey Abrams. All the boys did because she was the first chick in our grade to get boobs. Point is, it's innocent.

The shit Issy said about River pissed me off, and I know River overheard. I'm not sure what, but she definitely got an earful. When she ran upstairs last night, she never came back down. Bridgette told everyone she wasn't feeling well, so the night ended early.

Isabel seemed fine after that. Satisfied, even. I told her when we left that she had to cut her shit, or we were through. Honestly, I've threatened it before. I'm not sure what that says about us, about me, but I never actually break up with her despite the way she talks to other people. But Granddad and Marge like Issy, and I like the distraction having her around brings me.

Today during fourth period, I skip study hall for the first time in months. River hasn't needed anyone to come sit with her in lunch room because she's gotten her own little circle of friends. But she never opened her presents last night and Oliver mentioned this morning she never even looked at the stack on the dining room table.

She has a thing about accepting stuff from people, I get it. But I want to apologize on behalf of Issy and hope that the gift I got her will make up for my poor choice of a dinner guest.

Her friend sees me first. Stephanie perks up and straightens her hair, giving me a wide smile. If anyone has a crush on me, it's her. But again, I don't care.

As I approach them, River stiffens like she knows I'm nearing. Her eyes go from the half-eaten food in front of her to me, widening.

"Hey."

Stephanie greets me first. "Hi, Everett!"

I just tip my head at her, my focus solely on River.

She doesn't acknowledge me at first. I sit down across

from them, which makes her shift and draw her hands onto her lap.

"Can I talk to you?"

Nothing.

My eyes go to her friend. "Alone?"

Stephanie frowns but nods, pushing up from the plastic chair. "I'll, uh, see you later?" River's eyes plead for her to stay, which makes my guilt become tenfold.

When it's just us at the table, she reluctantly glances over at me. Her brown eyes are dull and full of hurt that I'm responsible for. I know she didn't want anyone to do anything for her birthday, but she relented because it meant something to Bridgette and Robert. I'm the one who ruined it for her.

"River, I'm sorry about yesterday."

Her jaw ticks. "I'm not ... a cutter."

My body draws back over the abrupt statement. "I know you're not."

To my surprise, her head snaps up and angry eyes meet mine. Whoa. I've never seen angry River before. Not sure I want to again.

"How?" Her voice breaks. "How could you possibly know that, Everett? Y-You don't know anything about me."

My shoulders slump a little at her shaky tone. It means a lot that she's willing to show this much emotion, even if it's the negative kind. "I know I don't know you well, but I've been around people who've cut before.

Those marks Issy pointed out aren't from self-inflicted wounds."

Her body locks up as she draws back.

A few summers ago, I went to a junior sports camp for kids entering high school sports teams. I helped with the basketball kids, and one of them was troubled youth. He struggled with depression and anxiety and his arms and legs were covered in small cuts. I saw the ones Isabel pointed out last night, and they're not the same kind.

It pisses me off knowing the difference. Because somebody else put those on her body, someone else was responsible for doing that to her. But I've known from the beginning that she had a lot of bad shit happen in her life before her adoption.

I never knew it was physical.

Shutting off my brain from wondering what else she went through, I refocus. "I'm not going to judge you because of the scars, River. Okay? You can trust me. Always."

She doesn't say anything.

Shifting on the bench seat, I yank out the black jewelry box from my pocket. Her eyes follow my hand as I reach out and set it in front of her.

"You didn't open your present."

Her bottom lip draws into her mouth.

"It's not going bite," I tease. She doesn't seem amused, so I huff out a sigh. "Listen, I know what Isabel said isn't something you can just forget about. She doesn't get it. She doesn't get *you*. That's on her, though.

I told her if she ever said anything about you like that again, I wouldn't put up with it."

The box in front of her is the only thing she focuses on as she asks, "Why do you put up with it now?"

Good question.

I find myself shrugging. "I don't know. I guess I'm giving her the benefit of the doubt. She's never been around people like you before."

That gets me another offended look.

"Shit." I wince. "I mean shoot."

"You can swear. I don't care."

"You should."

Her small shoulders rise. "I've heard people say worse."

I nod once. "I'm sure," I agree, with a slight nod, "which is all I meant before. Issy hangs out with a certain type of crowd. People around here come from money and families that have one way of living. Your past isn't something she's experienced, so she doesn't know how to deal with it."

I'm met with silence.

"Do you trust me?" I ask quietly.

I need her to say yes. It might physically hurt if she answers any other way. This girl has been through hell and back and I want to know every moment someday. She needs to trust me to reveal that sort of thing, to find someone to confide in.

"I don't know." I deserve her hesitation, but it still stings.

"Well, you can," I prompt, nudging the gift closer to her. "If not now, then in the future. I'm here for you just like Oliver. Okay?"

Hesitantly, she takes the box. "I'm not even sure what that means," she admits softly, peeling off the red ribbon that's around it.

"It means I have your back."

Her eyes are distant when they peer up through her lashes at me. They're not angry or sad anymore, but glassy with an emotion I've never seen before when I've caught her looking at me.

Hope.

"O-Okay."

I just nod toward the present.

She takes a deep breath before opening it, her lips parting when she sees what's resting in the velvet holder. I picked it out from a jeweler in town. When I saw the little charm, I knew I had to get it for her.

"It's ..." Her fingertips brush against the silver paint brush and palette that hangs from a matching silver chain. She doesn't seem like a gold girl, so hopefully this is okay.

"Do you like it?"

Silently, she nods.

A relieved smile forms on my lips. "Good. I know how much you like art, so I thought it would be a good birthday gift. The place I got it from has other charms, if you want to add more to the necklace. The guy tried getting me to buy the bracelet, but I thought this would be different."

"It's perfect." Her voice cracks a little as she pulls it from the box. I'm about to offer some help getting it on when she unclasps it and puts it around her neck with no difficulty. Pulling her long hair out from under the chain, she positions it so it rests over her shirt.

It suits her.

"Thank you, Everett."

"You know, most people call me Rhett."

Her fingers wrap around the charm. "I'm not really like most people."

My chest eases from the guilt. "No, you're certainly not. That's why I like you, River. You don't feel entitled just because you know the right people. But that doesn't mean you can't let them in. Whatever happened to you in the past doesn't have to dictate your future. You're safe now."

She blinks back what I think are tears.

Just as I'm about to ask if she's all right, my phone goes off in my pocket. Brows pinched, I pull it out and glance at Margaret's name across the screen. My stomach bottoms out. She never calls me while I'm at school.

"Marge ..."

"I'm sorry, Rhett boy," she sobs.

My fist clenches the cell until I hear it crack and I think it may break.

"I'm so damn sorry," she whispers.

TEN

Everett / 20

Almost three years later.

The party is in full swing by the time I navigate my way through the throng of vehicles on the front lawn of the cabin. I should have been the first one here, it's my property after all. But I knew the high school kids would get word of the small get together and swarm the place. I didn't feel like surrounding myself with idiots too early.

Plus, Isabel and I got into it right before I left. Not even in person, because she's too busy shopping with her friends two hours away. She loves telling me what I should or shouldn't do, like agreeing to throw parties.

"We're twenty. Adults now."

"So?"

"You shouldn't be entertaining children."

When I remind her that we were teenagers not that long ago, it only fuels her to snap back. It's tiring, this shit we go through. Our relationship is a roller coaster I don't want to be on. So instead of waiting for her at my apartment like she wanted me to, I left.

As I weave through the haphazardly parked cars, people greet me and slap my back. I make conversation with some of them, but most just get a tip of the chin or nothing at all.

Alcohol. That's what I need.

After fights with Issy, I prefer being alone. Which, let's face it, is ninety percent of the time. I'm used to my introversion, and nobody questions it because they are too. It's not hard to be alone, even in a party with drunk assholes surrounding me. They're all too busy making fools of themselves to care about what the host does.

Can't say I blame them. I *was* them.

It's why I don't care if they have parties here. Sure, Granddad's old cabin is a sacred place. When my childhood house sold, I wanted to keep this. Between the money he left me and the money from my parents' death, I have no financial problem keeping this and a place for myself in town. Either way, it's a great location for a party. Far enough away that towners won't care about the noise, and isolated so people aren't stupid enough to get into mindless trouble like drinking and driving.

I rarely have parties anymore—maybe once or twice a year, especially since graduating high school and starting college out of state. When Granddad died from an advance relapse of undetected cancer, I took Robert up on his offer to get me into Penn State with Oliver. I got a full ride and we both played basketball like nothing changed.

Except everything did. Issy and me became more

serious and she would come see me every other weekend or vice versa. We talked about moving into a place together after I finished my associate degree in business, because Robert offered both Oliver and I positions at his company. It's not what I expected, but I had no other plans. The only thing I knew for sure was that I couldn't stay away from Bridgeport forever. Regardless of Granddad's death, it's still home.

On the off chance that I do decide to let the partiers come, like tonight, I use it as an escape from my own problems. After all, I have plenty of them to choose from.

Isabel being the biggest.

By the time I make it out back by the lake behind the cabin, half of my beer is already gone. I settle on the log facing the clear blue water with the moon's reflection on the surface and a cigarette in my hand. It's a nice place to relax because most people stay inside or on the front lawn chugging cheap beer or hooking up. The few people that are by the water are talking and joking and it's just enough noise to keep me from thinking too much.

The thoughts don't even last long when they do start to resurface, because the silence is cut into by a familiar soft voice. "Since when do you smoke?"

I glance up just as River takes the empty spot next to me on the log. It's cool tonight and she's just wearing a pair of jean shorts and a tank top. My gaze settles on her chest for a brief moment, and I can't help but notice her nipples pebbled against the cotton of her thin top. I look away hastily. If there's anyone in the world I can't look at like *this,* it's River.

I look back down at the unlit cigarette in my hand before my eyes bounce back to her. Her gaze is curious, narrowed, like she's trying to figure something out. "I guess for a while now."

Her lips do that thing where they twitch in silent judgement. She doesn't want to say anything but worry floods those annoyingly bright brown eyes. "They're bad for you."

A lot of things I partake in these days are bad for me, but she doesn't need to know that. Smoking takes off the edge. Life has been hell since Granddad's death. College sucks, my social life sucks, my dating life ... hell. It's not even worth mentioning at this rate.

So, I settle on assuring her. "I don't do it often. Just when I'm bored."

This time, her lower lip draws into her mouth by her two front teeth. Now I know something is on her mind.

"What's going on, River? Oliver said you weren't coming tonight."

Sometimes I keep tabs on her, but usually stay out of her business. Half of the time Oliver fills me in on her life since we're not around as much to see her. I know she's involved in the art club after school still and that Bridgette and Robert celebrated her getting on the Principal's List with her 4.0 grade average. She's smart. Other than what Oliver freely tells me, I don't pry. Much.

What I know for sure is that River doesn't like

parties. It makes me wonder if Stephanie Malone or one of the many artsy kids she's friends with are hanging around here somewhere.

One of her hands flatten against her bare thigh, right below where the hem of her shorts rides up. If she's not careful, she'll flash the people in front of us her ass. Her other hand wraps around a familiar silver chain. Although the charm isn't showing, I know it's there, tucked under her shirt. She does a quick sweep around us, her fingertips digging into her thigh until little crescent indentations from her nails appear on her milky skin. The other partiers are too busy drinking, laughing, or making out to pay us any attention.

"I, um ..."

I wait.

Her hand reaches for my beer, her long fingers wrapping around the lukewarm bottle as she draws it up to her lips. There's something on them, I realize. Lipstick, I think. Since when does River wear makeup? I haven't seen her do that since her fourteenth birthday party, not too many months before Oliver and I moved way.

She takes a small sip and makes a face. I'd normally chuckle over her obvious distaste for alcohol if I wasn't worried. I know she doesn't drink, never had an interest in it from what she told me during one of my visits to the James estate. I teased her about staying out and partying and she replied with blatant annoyance over the topic. This isn't like her.

She clears her throat nervously, shifting on the log

and looking anywhere but me. The ground. The lake. The trees. "I want to ask you something."

I itch to grab the bottle back from her but don't. Alcohol asks for trouble, but it seems she's already searching for it.

"You can ask me anything," I reason, toying with the cancer stick in one hand and squeezing her knee with the other. "Anything, River. Really."

Her dark eyes lock on my palm where it rests on her leg. The skin just above her knee is warm, too warm. And the problem is, I like it. But I push that sick thought away, far away.

For a few short moments, she's quiet. Then she says, "Yeah?"

She's making me nervous now. "Of course."

There's another pregnant pause. It's torturous to have her so quiet knowing that she's found her voice after the past two years. "Iwantyoutotakemyvirginity."

The cigarette in my hand drops into the dirt. What the fuck did she just say? Her beet red face makes me think I didn't mishear her, which makes it that much more shocking.

River wouldn't say that ... wouldn't ask something like that of me. Right? I mean, I'm still with Issy. Our on again-off again relationship is rocky at best, but I'm pretty sure our current status is *on*. Maybe River doesn't know that. I doubt my dating status is something she and Oliver talk about.

My mouth dries up. "River," I rasp.

Jesus, it's a million degrees suddenly. The fire crackles in front of us like it's taunting me, and the wind does nothing to cool down my overheated skin. Pin prickles spread up the back of my neck. And worse, it spreads into my groin.

River's hand clenches the bottle tighter.

I blow out a breath. "I can't ... uh ..."

She downs the rest of the warm liquid in one long chug. "You always tell me I can trust you, right? With anything?"

My heart goes haywire.

Thumpthump.

Thumpthump.

Thumpthump.

"Yeah." It comes out a croak.

"I trust you with this," she whispers.

This. Her virginity.

Fuck.

My hand rakes through my disheveled hair, making the moppy blond mess probably look worse. I mean, I'm honestly glad she's a virgin. I've been wondering what kind of shit she's dealt with in the past, and the things I hear about what some men do to the young girls in the system... The thought alone makes me want to fucking strangle somebody.

Blowing out a heavy breath, I try turning her down gently. "I will always mean that, okay? But you're sixteen for Christ's sakes. I can't do that. You're ... River. You're young. Oliver would—"

B. CELESTE

Her eyes pop out of her head. "He wouldn't know."

People would talk. Sure, they're used to seeing us together. But not at a party. If we disappear somewhere, gossip will spread. It's happened before and I won't subject her to that. She's not the lanky thirteen-year-old I knew. She's grown up. Her figure is fuller, her curves are more noticeable, and she's ... yeah, she's pretty. Gorgeous, even. People would definitely start talking if they saw us disappear into a room.

I blow out a heavy breath. "I'm not sleeping with you, River. I won't."

I shouldn't.

I can't.

Jesus, I never thought I'd have this conversation with her. I'm twenty, for crying out loud. She's jailbait in every sense of the word. As happy I am knowing she fully trusts me, this isn't the moment I want her cashing that in.

Regret instantly washes over her face. I try squashing it and tell her it's fine, but she hops up and nearly loses her balance before I can grab her. Quickly correcting herself, she jerks away from my extended hand.

"O-Okay." She backs up.

"Riv—"

She runs off into the crowd of people.

I know she won't want to be found, so I sit there like a goddamn idiot soaking in what just happened. The cigarette on the ground begs to be smoked, so I pick it up and brush off the dirt.

River, the girl I've known for three years, just asked me to take her virginity. My heart still pounds loudly in my chest, so much that it hurts. I worry Oliver, wherever he is, will hear it.

But that's not the only thing that stirs ...

"Fuck."

I drop my head into my hands.

ELEVEN

River / 16

I lose my virginity to Asher Wilks that night.

TWELVE

Everett / 20

Bridgeport is different after you grow up. The same people who treated you like another idiotic teen show you respect as soon as you come home with a paper in your hand that says you're trained for employment through a university. Thing is, I've still got another two years before I can do half of what the other people at JT Corporation does.

The city seemed a lot smaller before, like there wasn't anywhere we could have gone without someone knowing about it. I guess we just needed to know the right places, because seeing it in this new perspective just proves there's a lot I haven't experienced.

The apartment I have on the outer edge of the city gives me just enough isolation from the buzzing traffic while still letting me in on the soft noises of car horns, yelling, and construction. I need the noise, it drowns out the demons in my head I don't want to think about.

"Mr. Tucker," a man with gray hair greets. He's got one of the local newspapers tucked under his arm and a large Styrofoam coffee cup in his hand with Landmark's logo inked into the side.

"Mr. Calloway." He used to be one of my father's friends. I vaguely remember him with dark hair and a youthful smile, usually at a get-together my family would host for the holidays. After all, the *T* in JT Corporations stands for Tucker.

By right, I've always had a place in the company whether Robert James pulled strings or not. I just never wanted it. Not until Granddad died, and I had to grow up and figure out what to do with my life.

Mr. Calloway takes the empty seat across from me, setting the paper down in front of himself. I haven't seen him in years. Once my parents died, most of their friends paid me no attention. Why would they? They thought they could get the job my father was no longer alive to keep, and I was just some boy who had no purpose to them anymore. They were nice to me because of my parents, and without them I became nothing.

I didn't care until now.

"Can I help you with something?" My voice is void of enthusiasm, hopefully getting my point across that his company isn't welcome. I like drinking my morning coffee in peace.

"I was just checking in."

Bullshit. We both know that's not what this is. What he really wants to know is if I'm taking a spot in the company shadowing Robert. Once I get a grasp on things, I'm sure to move my way up the corporate ladder and get promotion after promotion like my father had done. Once Robert feels comfortable enough, he may give me my father's portion of the company, putting it back into the Tucker name like it belongs.

Calloway must be one of the people who filled his spot all these years. He's threatened by me. He wants to know my motive.

I play his little game. We're coworkers, after all. Civility is something I know too well. "I'm doing well. Robert has been showing me the ropes at JT and I think I'll do my parents proud."

One of his large eyebrows raises. "And is that what you want, son? To work at the company?"

I set my coffee down and inch forward. "Let me tell you exactly what I want, Norm." His eyes widen at the sound of his first name. "I want this interrogation to be over, because we both know you don't give a shit about me or how I'm adapting. You care about your position at the company because you want everything my father had. So, yes. I want to work at the company, because I want to make my parents proud. Is there anything else you'd like to waste my time with?"

Yeah. Civility can kiss my ass.

He stands abruptly and grabs his belongings. Offense takes over his face but it's a rouse. I know when people are pretending, and this guy is a world-class act.

Through gritted teeth, he says, "Well, I hope you have a good day, Mr. Tucker."

"Mmhm. You too, Norm."

His eyes narrow before he turns and leaves me to my brooding. A satisfied smile tips my lips when I see him yank his phone out and dial somebody as he disappears down the sidewalk. Probably one of his bitch boys at work that he complains to. Even Robert knows he has them.

The satisfaction wears off after a group of the local kids come strolling through the door of the café. It's a college hangout that serves fancy drinks for too much money, so of course teens and college youth would swarm the place.

Normally, I ignore them. But one of the cocky assholes is someone I'm too familiar with. About two weeks ago, the blond-haired cowboy Casanova came strutting in like he was king of the world. I paid him little attention until I heard him bragging to his friends that he bagged the James girl at my party.

River.

Yeah, my fist got real acquainted with his face after that little remark. Some of the satisfaction his presence stole comes back when his faded black shiner comes into my view. It's almost healed, but still evident that he got his ass handed to him.

When he sees me sitting in my normal seat, he pales. I just grin and give him a small wave, which makes him grumble something to his friends before sulking out of the café.

I may have told him I never wanted to see him here again, much less talking shit about River. Truth is, I didn't know if he was even telling the truth. River doesn't let just anybody into her life and losing her virginity to a Wilks is nothing like her norm. Then again, it's been two years since I've known what her norm is.

She's changed. Grown up.

Not long after I threatened Asher Wilks, I decided to get the details. Not all of them, just enough to figure out if he's trying to be cool by lying through his ass. Unfortunately for me, he wasn't. More than four people saw River and Asher walk out of the party and to his car. All their stories were the same; the two had their hands all over each other. One of the people I spoke to even told me they were pretty sure they hooked up right there in his fucking Civic.

It still pisses me off that River let him touch her. She deserves more than just some hookup in the backseat of a car. If I had just told her yes, she would have been treated with the kind of respect she deserves.

Subconsciously, I know my anger is because of more than River deciding to give it up to Asher Wilks. It's deeper than that, but I won't admit it. I've always had a soft spot for River because she's a kindred spirit.

That's all it's allowed to be.

Isabel shows up while I'm working, so Robert's secretary directs her to the small office that's right outside of Robert's master suite. She comes in wearing a tight blue dress with her cleavage hanging out and a pair of fuck-me heels that make her long legs look ten miles longer.

My girlfriend is sexy, I'll give her that.

"I thought we planned to see each other for dinner later." The greeting obviously isn't what she expects, because she frowns at my less than amused statement as she approaches my desk.

She rarely stops by. Sometimes she'll bring me lunch if she knows I forgot to grab the sandwich I make for myself, or sometimes she'll stop by for other, more salacious, reasons. Most of those involve her getting on her knees underneath my desk and sucking my cock. She never cares when I tell her no, and I don't stop her whenever she takes me out of my dress pants and wraps those painted ruby lips around me.

The look in her eyes tells me she's not here for that, and frankly, I'm glad. Issy gives some of the best head I've ever had, but I'm not in the mood.

"I just thought it'd be nice to say hi."

I know her better than that. "Issy," I drawl.

Her shoulders slump. "Fine. You've been acting really weird lately, so I thought maybe I'd come by and help you out of your funk."

She *is* here for office sex.

"I'm really not in the mood."

A sultry smile curves her red lips. "You always say that."

When she steps closer, I hold my hand up. "I mean it,

Is. I've had a shit day and I don't want to do this right now."

Her arms cross on her chest, pushing her breasts up. The neckline of her dress does nothing to hide what she's packing under it. "You've been giving me excuse after excuse as to why you're not in the mood. We haven't had sex in two weeks, Everett."

My jaw locks. "Keep your voice down. Nobody needs to hear about our relationship, especially not our sex life."

"Or lack thereof," she grumbles.

Leaning back, I blow out an exasperated breath. "What do you want me to say, Issy? Settling back in Bridgeport has been difficult. I'm trying to get a routine down and it hasn't been the easiest transition. I've told you about the people who don't want me back. I need to prove to them I can handle this."

A sympathetic smile eases her tense expression. "You're right, I'm sorry. I just miss you, Rhett. I thought having you back here would be better for our relationship, but it still feels like you're hundreds of miles away."

Rubbing the back of my neck, I try figuring a way out of this. I feel bad for her, I do. I've been as distant as she's claimed, and I didn't really lie to her. I am trying to get a routine down here while taking classes at the community college to finish the rest of my gen eds. It's a lot of work to balance.

"Tell you what," I bargain, "I'll grab some dinner on the way home tonight and we'll stay in. Sound good?"

She perks up. "You don't want to go out?"

"No, baby. I think we'll be very busy inside."

Her eyes flash knowingly, and she kisses me goodbye in satisfaction. Truthfully, sometimes it's easier to let sex talk for us. We don't have the best conversations otherwise, most of them lead to arguments. If sex is what keeps us together, then so be it.

Robert steps into my office not long after Isabel leaves. "You going to finally put a ring on that finger, Everett?"

My eyes widen. "Uh ..."

He chuckles. "They don't make girls like that anymore, son. You might want to claim her before it's too late. But no matter. I came to tell you we have a meeting with the district board in ten minutes over in the west wing conference room."

"Okay," I rasp.

His amused smile is what he leaves with, walking in the direction of the conference room he mentioned.

He thinks I should propose to Isabel? Shit. That means she's probably thought about marriage too. It's a logical next step for us, since we've been together for three years. But it's a step I can't force myself in to taking.

Not yet.

Probably not ever.

THIRTEEN

River / 16

Bridgette tells me that Oliver is coming home for the long weekend. I'm excited to see him and ask how college has been. He calls sometimes and tells me about his classes and his games, which we all go to once a month. I never thought I would have missed him this much when he moved to Pennsylvania, but I do.

The excitement wears off quickly when I overhear Robert tell Darlene to make sure there's enough for an extra person. He doesn't need to say who it is, because I already know in my gut.

After I figure out Everett Tucker is joining us, I quickly make plans with Steph. She asked me during the week if I wanted to come stay at her place tonight, because her and some other girls are doing a movie-slash-sleepover. I told her no because of Oliver, but now I feel like it's my only way out.

Everett used to be someone I looked forward to seeing walk through the front door. Another first for me. Men ... we still don't get along. But he gave me no reason not to trust him and proved time and time again that he's always going to be there for me. Except for the night of the party.

Facing him after what I asked is too much. I've avoided all conversation that leads to him, because seeing his disgusted face that night replays on a loop in my head. It hurts.

Not just because he rejected me, that stung. But the chances of us ever being the same are low, and knowing I ruined our friendship, if that's what you call it, makes my heart feel like it's being stabbed. Only I'm the one holding the knife.

Robert tries to get me to stay home, but Bridgette assures me it's fine if I go to Steph's. I've only slept over at her house once before and made Bridgette come get me when I started having a breakdown in the middle of the night. Thankfully, it was just me and Steph. I lied and told her I didn't feel well, which is why I was crying. She bought it, I think.

Anyway, Oliver will be home all weekend, so it isn't like I'm skipping out on spending time with him. I can see him when I'm back tomorrow. He'll probably be proud of me for facing my fears and sleeping at Steph's house. I just hope I'm stronger than a year ago.

Pulling out a new overnight bag that Bridgette bought me a while ago, I stuff some clothes inside. Pajamas, jeans, and a blouse for tomorrow, and some cotton panties that Steph made me buy when we went shopping with her mother a few weeks ago. She tried getting me to buy lacey underwear, especially after she found out about

Asher Wilks. But I refused, because nobody else is going to see what I'm wearing underneath my clothes.

My chest stings thinking about Asher. He's a senior who takes classes at the community college part-time. Everyone loves him. He's smart, witty, and on the football team. When I saw him at the party after the whole Everett thing happened, I let his flirtations get to me. I used him.

A few days after the party, people at school started whispering when I passed them in the halls. I tried convincing myself I was being paranoid, but Steph pulled me into the women's bathroom, demanded everyone inside get out, and then made me spill. Turns out, the whole school knew I slept with Asher.

But that isn't what got the most buzz. The morning Steph made me tell her what happened, Asher Wilks came to school with a black eye and split lip. Supposedly, he got the injuries during football practice. Steph said that's impossible, because his helmet would have protected him.

People kept connecting the dots and figured someone who knew me must have found out about us hooking up. The term still makes my spine crawl. I know I shouldn't have slept with him, shouldn't have handed him my virginity, but Everett didn't want it and Asher did.

Pulling myself from the thought, I grab a new outfit to change into before heading over to Steph's. Bridgette took me to get my learners permit for my driver license, but I still need more hours before the six-month hold lets up so I can take the actual test. Honestly, I'm not sure I want to drive. It's Steph who keeps telling me I need my own car, so Bridgette and Robert don't have to drop me off whenever I want to go somewhere.

Just as I throw my shirt onto the floor, my bedroom door opens. Yelping loudly, I spin to see who it is only to gape in disbelief when I see a tall, broad form filling my doorway.

"Oh my God." My voice is high-pitched and squeaky as I dart into my closet and out of Everett's eyesight. I'm in my bra and jeans, and the top of my pink polka-dot panties are peeking over the waistband of my pants.

"River," he calls, his voice rough and unsure.

Everett just saw me in my bra.

Grabbing the first shirt I see, I yank it on and force myself to take a few deep breaths. He won't go away until I face him, I know that. It doesn't make my heavy steps ease the panic building in my chest as I peek at him over the edge of the closet door.

His eyes are dark as he stares at me.

He's mad.

"E-Everett, what are you doing here?"

He isn't supposed to be here until five, same with Oliver. It's only three-thirty.

"Your back," he whispers.

"I ... I never left," I answer in confusion.

He swallows, his throat bobbing. "No. What happened to your back? Were those ... are those?"

My whole body freezes.

My back.

The front of me only contains the scars left by cigarettes and dull knives. But my back ... those are worse. They stretch from my shoulder blades to just above my butt, with very little skin left untouched. I forget about those marks most of the time. Out of sight out of mind. But the memories of the belt slashing my skin always remind me when I'm at my weakest.

"River." His voice is firmer. "What the hell happened to your back?"

Forcing myself to step out of my closet, I cross my arms over my chest. "That's n-none of your business, Everett."

"None of my business," he muses dryly. He shakes his head, looking anywhere but me. "It would have been, River. If I agreed to sleep with you, it would have *become* my business."

Nausea sweeps over me. "H-How? You wouldn't have seen them. Y-You would have only seen ..."

He waits for me to finish the sentence, but I can't. He's looking at me with so much intensity it drowns out my words.

He takes one step closer, but I'm too frozen to back away. "Believe me, River, if I had you, I'd have *all* of you. There's not one piece of skin that I wouldn't see, touch, or kiss."

Oh my God.

A funny tingling sensation settles into the pit of my stomach the same moment my body heats up. My cheeks feel like they're on fire as images of what *could* have happened flood my mind. But those images are shattered when I realize he's being serious—he would have seen everything. All the scars, deformities, and flaws that are reminders of everything I've gone through.

"I guess that means Asher Wilks didn't see everything?"

His words slice me worse than the belt did.

"What?" My voice is barely a whisper.

His eyes narrow. "Asher. Wilks."

Everett knows about Asher. How could he not? We had sex at *his* party.

Now my face is full-blown on fire, and Everett knows why. "Yeah," he gruffs, "how'd that turn out for you, River?"

He's definitely angry with me.

What does he want me to say? Asher Wilks *didn't* see everything. He stuck his hand up my shirt, pulled off my shorts, and didn't even completely take off his jeans before we were doing the deed. I didn't want him seeing everything, and he didn't seem to want to either.

Everett doesn't want to know that, even if he asks. He's upset, lashing out. I deserve it. I always mess up, always do the wrong thing.

So, I remain silent.

His fingers rake through his dirty blond hair. It's longer than I remember, floppier and unkempt compared to the party three weeks ago. The messy look works for him and the light stubble lining his jaw makes him look older, like an adult instead of a twenty-year-old college kid.

"Why?" he finally asks, breaking the silence.

"Why what?"

He throws his hands up. "Why did you do it? Why *him*, River? Is it because I wouldn't? I was doing you a favor, okay?"

A *favor?*

Anger bubbles up. "I don't need any favors from you, Everett."

He laughs coldly. "No? Because you sure were asking a big one at the party."

His words hit me at full force. I stumble back a little, flinching when they sink in.

"Shit." He grips the back of his neck. "River, I didn't mean that. I'm just … processing this. I want to understand why you did that."

Does he really? It seems like he doesn't want to know anything. Not about this. He's just trying to figure out how to deal with it.

The truth is, I lost my virginity because I was afraid of somebody else taking it. It's a stupid term, if you ask me. Your virginity isn't something you can misplace, you give it to someone. Preferably, someone you trust. Maybe even someone you love.

That's why I wanted Everett to have it.

I'm not sure when I realized I loved him. I think I kind of always have. When I was thirteen, he was the only one I looked forward to seeing outside the James'.

He made me feel special, like I wasn't some foster kid in a place I didn't belong. He made me feel like I fit in.

So, yeah. My virginity should have been his. If it goes to the person you love, he should have said yes. But he didn't, because he doesn't love me. Oliver mentioned not long after the party that Everett and Isabel are still together, though he doesn't know why. It was like ice water being dumped on my head.

Everett doesn't belong to me, but to her. Issy.

It makes what I did with Asher feel less like a huge mistake and more like moving on. But I haven't moved on at all. I'm deeper into the pit of despair than I was, only now I have one less thing that belongs to me.

Because I gave it to Asher.

A boy I don't even like.

After spending time with strange men in the past, I realize that virginity is a sacred thing. People tried taking it, tried doing things nobody as young as I was should have experienced. The thing is, I'm one of the lucky ones. A lot of girls don't make it out with their innocence.

Giving my virginity to Everett was meant to be a ginormous deal.

It also means giving it to Asher Wilks was probably the stupidest thing I've ever done.

"River." Everett's voice snaps me from my train of thought.

Bolting toward the overnight bag on my bed, I zip it

up and throw it over my shoulder. "I have to go," I whisper brokenly.

"That's it?"

"What else is there to say?"

He stares at me for a long, uncomfortable minute. Then he shakes his head, something dark flashing in his eyes.

When I walk past him toward the door, he calls out my name. I stiffen, afraid of what he's going to say. My grip on the bag tightens as I face the stairs, tasting freedom in any form that doesn't have Everett in it.

All he says is, "Your shirt is on backwards."

FOURTEEN

Everett / 20

Dinner at the James' last night is no different than it was before Oliver and I left. Except the obvious void where River usually sits.

Robert asked Oliver how school was going and tried encouraging him to move home early to work for him like I am. Oliver declined his father's offer like I knew he would. He's not interested in working at JT Corp. Then again, I said I'd never end up there either. Look at me now, the epitome of a lost boy looking for the right path.

My apartment is a three-bedroom, two-bath in the isolated side of town. It's bigger than one man needs, but I like my space. Plus, Issy finds herself here more than not. She doesn't think I notice her clothes slowly taking up half of my closet or the unnecessary lotions and conditioners littering my master bathroom.

I know what Issy thinks. If she moves her things in, I'll have no choice but to let her stay permanently. She still lives in the guest house at her parents' place. In her mind, we're ready to move in together for good.

What Issy can't grasp is that I don't want to share my

space. When I lived with Granddad, I didn't mind. Having someone to care for made it easier. But I'm older, Granddad is dead, and Isabel isn't the type of person who wants to be cared for. We're too alike in that way, not wanting anyone to be responsible for our wellbeing.

I didn't stop her from coming over late last night. We've been spending more time together since she swung by the office, which appeases her enough not to complain. It's best that way, giving her what she wants within reason.

Her sleeping form is stretched out next to me, my black blanket covering her naked curves. She likes waking up to me pressing kisses down her neck or combing my fingers through her dark hair. But that always leads to sex and I just want to move on with my day without entertaining her.

Quietly, I slip out of bed and leave her to sleep. The coffee pot is set up, probably by Issy. She knows I like going to the café for coffee, but she doesn't like my habit. Especially not when she's still in my bed.

Sighing, I flick on the machine and pull out a mug from the shelf. Issy probably won't be up for another hour, not to mention in the bathroom for at least an hour and a half getting ready for classes.

She travels to a college forty minutes away, some fancy private school her dad pays for. It's funny that she still lives at home, considering he's paid for everything else. I guess it's harder to control people if they're not close to you.

Somehow, my mind conjures the image of an auburn-haired, pale-skinned teenager at the thought. River can't be controlled. Not by the James's money, not by her past. She's a wildcard, uncontrollable compared to the rest.

Maybe that's another reason Issy doesn't like her. She realizes River has a freedom that she doesn't. It isn't about some stupid crush or the fact that she's part of a rich and well-known family.

I underestimated Isabel Allen.

When the coffee is done, I down my cup, dress in my running gear, and write Issy a note. I won't be going my normal route, so she can't "accidently" bump into me like she's done hundreds of times before.

My feet take me down Third and Fifth Avenue and hook onto Chestnut Street. The wind whipping my face as my sneakers propel me forward does nothing to erase the thoughts from yesterday's conversation with River. It heightens the anger, the hurt, everything I told myself not to feel.

I stop in front of the white house with a single blue door and a large bay window to the left. Two cars are parked in the driveway. A flower garden is planted in the front yard by a small cherry tree.

Catching my breath, I walk up to the front door and ring the bell. A blonde-haired, middle-aged woman answers with a friendly smile.

"I'm here to pick up River James."

FIFTEEN

River / 16

I wake up in the guest bedroom at Steph's house feeling the success of my first real sleepover. Lena Donovan and Vanessa Kingsley are staying in Steph's room with her, but Steph told me I could have my own so it's easier for me.

One day, I'll be brave enough to tell Steph everything. I'll show her the scars because I *want* her to see them. I'll tell her the story and maybe find some closure in having her know the truth about me.

Shortly after Oliver and Everett moved away for college, I closed myself off from everyone. Steph would come over and we would do homework and talk, but I never felt like I could open up to her. She loves talking about college and the future. I've never thought about mine before, never thought I'd have one.

Bridgette and Robert decided I should see a therapist once a week. I didn't talk to her either. Or the shrink after that. Or the one after him. None of those strangers understood me like they said they did. They just kept pushing and pushing until I nearly lost it at my last session.

I did something I never thought I would have to do again. I begged Bridgette not to make me go back. There were tears, lots of them, and she promised she'd never put me through that again. The only thing she asked was that I talk to someone, to let them in.

The first year following my adoption, I finally told Bridgette about my last home. I told her about the dirty dishes, the moldy food, the alcohol and drugs. I told her about the way the man of the house hit us and yelled at us and threatened us if we stepped out of line. I wouldn't tell her anymore because the way she looked at me changed. She saw me with something deeper than sympathy. She looked at me with pity.

I hate pity. Pity makes people weaker, like it's the only thing they're willing to see when someone's past becomes too much. Just telling her about my scars nearly broke her.

But Everett ... they didn't destroy him. He looked sad, angry, an array of mixed emotions, but not once did he let pity slither into those minty eyes. It makes me believe he's the only one I can truly bare my soul to. All those deep-seated burns and bruises could spill from my lips and end the haunting memories that control my everyday life.

The painful reminders etched into my skin are like a painting I never want revealed to the world. But for

Everett, I'd display them with a spotlight on every inch of marred flesh.

I'm halfway to Steph's room to see if the girls are awake when I hear my name being called from downstairs. Curious, I change direction and grip the railing as I descend the carpet steps to see Steph's mom, Aubrey, smiling at me.

Everett is standing beside her.

He looks different. Instead of jeans and a tee or a suit, he's wearing black running pants and a loose tank. Sweat dots the front of the neckline, shifting the light gray color of his shirt to granite. I've seen Oliver in similar clothing when he goes to the gym, but he doesn't fill them out quite like Everett.

Everett is taller than Oliver, always has been. He's also bulkier in all ways possible. His shoulders are wide, his upper arms are huge, and his waist is toned. Probably more so now than I remember. A little over a year ago, I saw Oliver, Everett, and a few of their friends playing basketball outside our house. They were all shirtless, but Everett caught my eye because unlike the others, he had abs.

He's leaner now, so I can only imagine what's underneath his shirt.

Snap out of it.

"What are you doing here?" I don't mean to sound rude but based on the twitch of Everett's lips that's exactly what happens.

Aubrey answers for him. "Everett is here to take you

home, darling. I'm sure the girls are still sleeping, so I'll let them know you left."

Steph mentioned having a big breakfast before going swimming in their pool out back. I've been trying to figure out how to talk them out of making me join them, so seeing Everett should be a relief. It's not.

"Bridgette said she'd pick me up," is what comes out of my mouth instead.

Everett's fist clenches before loosening up at his side. "She's busy, so I volunteered. Figured we could walk since it's a nice day."

Walk? With Everett? *Alone?*

"Um..." Do I really have a choice? "I have to get my bag."

It takes me less than three minutes to gather my stuff before I'm back downstairs. I could have stalled, but what's the point? Everett would still be waiting for me ten minutes from now, just maybe a little angrier.

Waving Steph's mother goodbye and thanking her for letting me stay over, I follow Everett out of their house. He takes my bag and throws it over his shoulder despite my protests, ignoring me when I tell him I'm capable of carrying my own stuff.

He greets me with, "We need to talk."

"No, we don't." There's nothing we need to say that hasn't already been said. He rejected me. That's that. I moved on with Asher, even if it left a sour taste in my mouth, and now it's time for me to put Everett firmly in my past where he belongs. I know he'll never be mine, maybe even counted on that, because it's the only way I can protect myself. He can't hurt me anymore if I don't give him the chance to.

He sighs heavily. "You went out of your way to avoid me last night, River. I don't like that. We're friends, right?"

Are we?

"I don't know," I murmur hesitantly.

He stops walking. "Really?" His tone is dubious, like he can't fathom why I wouldn't know what our relationship is. "That's bullshit."

He spits out the words so harshly that I wince. His eyes close for a split second before they reopen, looking much softer than before.

"I didn't mean to scare you."

"You didn't." It's a lie.

He knows as much. "You don't have to pretend with me, you know. We're too much alike in that way."

Curiosity takes over. "What way?"

Everett and I are polar opposites. He's social and popular and not afraid to speak his mind. I'm nothing like that, like *him*. Sure, I talk more than I used to, and I ask questions without feeling like I need to throw up, but I'm a far cry from being as sociable as he is.

"We both pretend because it's easier," he states, finally walking along the sidewalk again. He exhales a weighted sigh, glancing up to the sky like maybe it can give him an answer to a question he desperately needs. "We put on an act, but we can't really fool everyone."

"Why not?" My voice cracks.

He eyes me. "Because there's always going to be somebody out there who knows us better than that."

I don't answer.

"I don't like when you avoid me."

We're back to that? "I wasn't—"

"What did I say? Don't lie to me."

My teeth grind. "What do you want from me, Everett? I don't want to talk about the stupid party or what I asked of you and Asher Wilks."

"Well, I do." The words are gritted out between his teeth, his tone raised, and it instantly puts me on the defense.

"Too bad!"

I never argue, but this feels like the perfect time to start. Everett can't just swoop into my life and demand answers. He's never done that before, which is why I've always liked him. Maybe he *should* ruin that for me. It'll make the crush I've been harboring go away.

"I can't believe you." I try walking ahead of him, but his long legs eat up the distance between us easily.

"Well, believe it."

"This is practically kidnapping!" I sound like a ridiculous petulant child, but right now I can't bring myself to care. It was scary asking Everett to take my virginity, showing my vulnerability and how much he means to me, and it was tossed back in my face as if it meant nothing. Very few times have I ever allowed myself to feel angry or entitled or judgmental, but right now I'm feeling all three. He doesn't get the right to act like *I* owe *him* something.

His deep chuckle unnerves me. "You walked out of the house willingly, River. That's hardly kidnapping."

What? Did he change his major to pre-law?

Grumbling under my breath makes him chuckle louder. His amusement makes me angry, but I don't feed him with more disgruntlement.

"Why do you care about what I do anyway?" I ask, my voice now soft and devoid of any fight left. I focus on my feet instead of him.

"That's a stupid question."

You're stupid.

"We're friends," he points out. "Friends look out for each other. They're also supposed to stop each other from doing stupid things."

"Like kidnapping?" I mutter.

"Like sleeping with douchebags."

My heart stops.

"Wilks was talking about it to a group of people at the Landmark Café. It's like you were a prize to him."

Tears well in my eyes that I battle to fight off before they fall. "S-Stop talking."

"Do you know how hard it was for me to stop hitting him before I took it too far?"

I come to a staggering halt. "What?"

He doesn't say anything.

Shock creeps into my chest. "*You* were the one who rearranged his face?"

He just shrugs.

"But why?"

"Because I care, River. Why else?"

Why else? There are plenty of reasons somebody punches a person after talking shit. I'm used to people doing that—talking smack, not punching people. At least not for me.

"You say you care, but when I asked you to ... you didn't do it. You wouldn't—"

"No," he cuts me off through clenched teeth, "I wouldn't. I didn't for a lot of reasons. I already told you I was doing you a favor by rejecting you."

I flinch at the word *rejecting*. It's painful to know the only guy I've ever liked, felt comfortable with, did me a *favor* by rejecting me.

"It's because of Oliver, right?"

They're best friends. Brothers, practically. Their relationship is better than mine and Oliver's, so I get the risks. It doesn't mean I have to like them.

His fingers thread through his hair. "It's not just about Oliver. You're young, River. There are guys worth your time that are your age. And, yeah. Oliver is my best friend and your brother. Not to mention you and I are friends. That kind of thing, what you asked of me, could have ruined the friendship."

Seems like it's already crumbling.

"So that's why, okay?" His voice is softer now, less wound up. There's one important piece of his life that should have been number one on his list of *Reasons Why I Can't Have Sex with River*.

"And Isabel?" I prompt.

He goes still. "What about her?"

"You didn't mention her."

"What's there to mention?"

That you're together. "Lots."

He's silent.

I stop and turn to him. My chest hurts over thinking about them, much less asking the question that needs to be said aloud. "Do you love her, Everett? *Really* love her."

"Of course, I do." His answer is too defensive to be believable, like it's not me he's trying to convince.

"Then you should have told me that you couldn't sleep with me because you love her," I whisper, wishing I could punctuate the word with a jab of my finger to his chest. But I don't dare touch him. Every time I do, I feel something work its way inside of me. Something I need to let go of. "Oliver, me, my *age,* shouldn't have mattered if you truly believe that."

Shifting on my heel, I walk farther down the street. His footsteps fall behind me, soft but evident. He trails a few feet away, not lining up with my short strides like before. He doesn't want to talk now that the topic is on him.

"She's the type of girl worth marrying," he finally says, making my heart pinch, because he's implying *I'm* not the kind of girl who's worth forever. "And I will, because that's what people want and expect."

But what do you *want, Everett?*

I take a deep breath and force myself to push through the ache. Physical pain is easier to handle, I'm used to it. Emotional pain ... that's a new type of warfare I'm defenseless against.

"I guess it's good you love her then."

STEPH ALWAYS DRAGS ME ON SHOPPING TRIPS I DON'T want to go on. Sometimes she bribes me with promises of a ginormous pretzel from the food court. Based on the tight fit of my jeans, it's really showing.

What I don't expect is to be peer pressured into trying anything on. But Steph pulls me into the swimsuit section, aka my worst nightmare. Everything they have would reveal pieces of me I don't want anyone to see. Bikinis, one pieces, tankinis, they would all show my scars.

I try telling Steph no, but she's insistent. I even tell her I can't swim, which is true. Everett told me he would teach me on my fifteenth birthday, but it never happened. Why should someone who doesn't know how to swim buy a bathing suit? Steph says she'll teach me, but if I managed to talk Everett out of it, Steph should be easy. She's not though. She's a mastermind.

It's how I end up in a dressing room with an armful of suits that will not make it into my wardrobe. Steph chose every color in the rainbow, and if I hadn't been permanently scarred, I'd consider entertaining the idea of wearing one somewhere. The royal blue one is especially pretty, the bottoms have cut out sides and the top has a crisscross back.

"Just try on one," Steph calls from her dressing room. She's trying on every swimsuit in her size. No exaggeration.

To appease her, I slip off my clothes and slide on the blue suit. It's a little tighter than I expect, I'd need a size up. Then again, I'm not buying it, so who cares if it hugs my hips wrong?

"Well?" she prompts.

"I don't like it."

I'm completely shocked when the curtain whips open, and Steph says, "I'll be the judge—"

I cry out and quickly close the curtain again. It's too late though. She's seen the ugly marks painted across my back. Tears well in my eyes as an anxiety attack forms. My lungs tighten and my chest hurts, but I manage to change back into my clothes before I completely shut down.

It's two minutes and thirty-seven seconds before I force myself to walk out of the dressing room. Steph is still in her swimsuit and if I wasn't so embarrassed, so horrified, so *angry*, I would tell her the hot pink number looks amazing on her tiny frame.

Her voice is quiet. "Why didn't you tell me?"

It's the same reason I didn't tell Bridgette or Robert or Oliver or Everett. I don't *want* to. I don't want to relive those moments of pain and terror. Telling those stories would be setting myself back from all the progress I've made.

The whole thing makes me glower. "When could I have told you? Even if I wanted to talk about them, you're too busy talking about your plan to be popular and all the fancy clothes you want to buy to fit some stupid stereotype that I don't get a chance to say a word. Your problems aren't like mine, Steph. All you've ever had to worry about is whether to buy Prada or some knock off. Pink or blue? Stilettos or flats? I need to worry about people seeing these disgusting marks that I have to live with for the rest of my life, right along with the memories of how I got them! Don't you think that if I wanted to admit I've been beaten because I was hungry, or some other god-awful reason, I would have?"

I suck in a deep breath, clenching and unclenching my fists. I've never blown up before and never thought I would at Stephanie, my only true friend.

Hurt spreads as her lips weigh further down at the ends. "You know," she whispers after a long moment of playing with the bikini top string in her hands, "I think those scars make you pretty badass."

And that's all she says about it before we pretend it never happened.

That's when I realize Steph gets me way more than I give her credit for. She's a great friend.

But I'm not.

That's the day I make a vow to not only be a better friend, but a better person as well.

SIXTEEN

River / 18

Two Years Later

The volunteers tell us to line up outside the double doors in the order we practiced. Alphabetical, of course. I think they should have been creative and made a pattern, because the boys are in blue caps and gowns and the girls are in white. Girls dominate the boys in numbers, so there's way more white than blue and it looks dumb.

But what do I know?

Someone snickers behind me. I peer over my shoulder to find Gavin Wilks, Asher's little brother, murmuring into his friend's ear while staring directly at me. They all start laughing loudly until a teacher steps in to shush them.

The music starts playing inside. I can hear the soft hum of the middle school band getting ready for our entrance. Gavin keeps snickering and I know it's at my expense. He kept saying that the girls should have worn blood red, not white while we were getting ready in the back. Most people thought it was a period joke, but I know it's a purity one. Or lack thereof, I guess.

Gavin has been harassing me ever since he found out I had sex with his brother. I usually ignore him, but it's hard to right now. Another teacher hushes them, but their stares burn holes into my back.

Anxiety creeps up my stomach and settles into my throat. I think I may vomit. There will be hundreds of parents in the Opera House, the same fancy setting of every Freemont graduation. It's hot, stuffy. The gym would have been better.

Suddenly, someone grabs my hand. My heart jumps in my chest and settles when I see Steph. Someone tells her to get back in line, but she ignores them.

"Together?" she asks.

A smile spreads on my lips. "Together."

We get yelled at by the volunteers for being out of order, but we don't listen. When the doors open, we walk hand in hand down the aisle. There are supposed to be two columns of people. Steph stands in the middle with a huge grin on her face and not one care over the weird glances we get.

Then I see my family.

Yeah, *family*. Bridgette and Robert are standing, and Robert has a camera up as we near him. Steph makes a face which makes me laugh. The camera goes off. When the little white light from the flash clears my eyes, I see Oliver. He's hooting and clapping, and it makes me smile.

Steph tugs on my hand, squeezes it, like she's saying *we made it.* And we did.

Next to Oliver is Everett in his tall, muscular glory. My heart lurches a little in happiness despite how weird we've been toward each other for the past year. But the excessive beating does a nosedive when I see the small body tucked behind him.

Isabel Allen.

Oliver never said Everett was bringing her. He thought they broke up again. Well, he didn't tell me that exactly— just that he didn't know what their current status is. I guess their status is like it always is when it matters most; on.

Steph doesn't let me drown in the deep pit my emotions take me to. She squeezes my hand again to bring me back. Not before I glance over my shoulder to see something flash in Everett's green eyes. Pride.

The dress under my gown matches his mint hues that have always fascinated me. I didn't buy the dress because it reminds me of him. Bridgette made me try it on because it makes my hair look redder. Plus, I fill it out in a way that makes me look like an adult.

Steph and I walk up the three narrow steps to the stage, where the principal and superintendent frown at our mixed-up arrival. The principal seems to care less than the superintendent. I guess his reputation is on the line, the school board may get on him about how disoriented the progression was.

Too bad.

Steph finds the right seat in the row behind me, which makes the few people in her way stumble and glare. But Steph doesn't care because that's just who she is.

When everyone is on stage, the principal announces the class of 2013 and tells us all to sit. My eyes drift to the crowd to see Robert snapping more pictures until Bridgette pulls him down. It makes me laugh that it isn't the other way around.

Robert and I bonded after I accidently broke the picture frame holding the image of me and my biological mother. It was an accident, and the picture itself is fine. But seeing us under shattered shards of glass made an ache settle in my chest and tears streaming from my eyes before I could stop them.

Jill reminded me during the last visit we had that I shouldn't think about the past. It was shortly after I snapped at Steph when she saw my naked back. But how can I forget my past? I'm painted in memories. Carved by pain.

Robert saw me crying and asked what was wrong. He told me he'd get me another picture frame, that I didn't need to worry. I told him I wanted to find my birth mother. Just like that. Something that random should have been more surprising, but he just nodded, cleaned up the mess, and told me he'd hire a private investigator to look into it.

A year later and we're no closer to answers. Robert

says we won't give up and I believe him. We've been close ever since.

My eyes trail over to Everett, who's saying something to Isabel. Her body is angled toward him, leaning close as she whispers in his ear. He isn't smiling, in fact he looks angry. I want to know why but force myself to listen to the speech that the salutatorian makes.

Blah blah future ahead of us. Blah blah making great memories. Blah blah we'll rule the world. We won't. Well, most of us won't. There are a few people who will probably do really well in life. I'm not one of them and neither is Scotty Berge, the current speaker.

Refusing to watch Isabel whisper sweet nothings into Everett's ear, I glance at Steph. She grins and gestures toward something in her lap. Her phone.

I'm in the second row, hidden by broad bodies, so I pull my cell out.

Steph: We did it, bitch.

I normally hate being called that, but I know Steph doesn't say it in a demeaning way. It's just what she does.

I answer, **we haven't done it yet.**

She rolls her eyes at me. **Close enough.**

Tucking my phone away when the first row is announced to stand, I try calming my speeding heart. It's just a quick walk to the podium, a few handshakes, and then an even quicker walk back to my seat. It shouldn't be a big deal, but my anxiety is making it.

Steph must sense that because she puts her hand on my shoulder in comfort.

She mouths, *you can do this* when my row is told to stand. I'm the third person in. I didn't wear heels because I'd fall. I could fall in flats, I'm talented like that.

The first person walks.

I move.

Oh my God.

The next person is called.

My heart is all I can hear.

I slide to the end.

"River Jean James."

Somehow, I make my feet move forward. The thundering sound of my heart drowns out the clapping from Steph, but I see her do it. It isn't until I'm shaking my clammy hands with the superintendent and school board that I break out of the spell when I hear my name being shouted.

It isn't Robert or Bridgette or Oliver who yells the loudest. It's Everett. He's standing, hollering, and clapping those big hands of his until the sound overpowers my heartbeat.

I stop half way to my seat and stare at them. My family. Robert takes more pictures and my eyes well with tears. I'm sure Bridgette is crying too. But me, I don't like to cry.

I let the tears fall anyway.

Emotion clogs the back of my throat. I'm overcome with pride and happiness and fulfillment. I raise my hand and wave to the people who have given me this chance, this piece of paper displayed in the navy blue holder in my hand.

When I get back to my seat, Steph hugs me from behind. For once, I squeeze her back. My cheeks are still damp when she walks, my voice the loudest in her little group of friends. I clap like she did for me and laugh when someone in her family section whistles and screams.

She doesn't make it back to her seat right away. Instead, she poses in the middle of the stage. Her family takes pictures, she does a little dance which makes the crowd laugh, and she finds her seat.

I turn to her. "*Now* we did it."

She giggles. "Love you, River."

I sniff back more tears. "Love you, too."

SEVENTEEN

Everett / 22

River is stopped by a few kids on her way out of the dressing room in the back where she smiles and waves and entertains them with answers to pointless questions. I know her better though. The smile doesn't reach her eyes and her stiff posture screams discomfort.

When she finally breaks free, she beelines right for us. Oliver steps out and picks her up, spinning her around until she squeals. He laughs and sets her down. Her face is red, and her eyes are a bright shade of brown, glazed over from tears. Happy ones, I think.

"I'm so damn proud of you, Riv," Ollie exclaims, squeezing her hand.

Robert clears his throat. "Language."

Oliver rolls his eyes. "She just graduated, Dad. I think she can take a few swear words, especially if they're in praise."

River giggles, and the sound warms the pit of my chest that's long been iced over.

Bridgette sidesteps Oliver and wraps River in a tight hug. They embrace for at least a minute, Bridgette whispering in River's ear and both looking on the verge of tears. Again.

I wait my turn until Robert is done before I unlatch my palm from Issy's and wrap River in my arms. My cheek rests against the top of her head and the sweet scent of green apple from her shampoo takes over my senses. She settles into my hold, melting into my chest, her arms mimicking mine around my waist.

"Proud of you, River," I tell her under my breath.

A little shutter wracks down her spine when my breath caresses her scalp. "Thank you, Everett."

She never calls me Rhett. It's always Everett, and I like it. With her, she could call me anything. Just like she's River to me. Always has been and always will be.

A throat clears, drawing me away. It's Isabel, who's shooting me a dark look. Her glare shifts to a broad smile as she turns from me to River.

"You must be so glad to be done with this boring place," she notes, squeezing River's hand. River winces and I wonder if Issy squeezed too hard.

"I-It wasn't so bad."

Isabel laughs. It's dry. "You don't have to lie. High school sucked. Think about all the things you have to look forward to now. I mean, you're free to do whatever you want. Not that you're *not* used to that by now."

What's that supposed to mean?

River frowns.

Issy shrugs. "You know, being a foster and whatnot. I hear they do what they please anyway. But now you can do that, and it won't be frowned upon. Know what I mean?" She gives River a conspiratorial smile—as if Issy knows *anything* about what being a foster kid is like. She lives in a delusional world that I want nothing more than to drag her out of.

It's Robert who steps forward. "She hasn't been a foster in five years, Isabel. She's our daughter. And while I'm sure some foster children do what they please, it's not good to stereotype." His eyes on Isabel are completely full of disapproval, and even though his gaze isn't directed at me, I feel I'm the one being reprimanded.

River's wide eyes are grateful at his defense, but she doesn't say anything.

Issy blushes, flattening out a nonexistent wrinkle in her black dress. "I didn't mean anything bad by it, Mr. James. Honest."

I call bullshit.

Isabel's default setting is catty. She isn't as bad as she used to be, but she has her moments, especially if those moments involve River. Over a year ago, we experienced some rough shit that put us both on edge. Most people would have called it quits, but somehow it made us stronger. We understood each other's pain.

But I still have moments when I look at her and wonder why she can't cut the crap. I compare her to everyone else, put her on a pedestal. I know it's not fair, she's Isabel; incomparable. It doesn't stop my brain from picturing other people's reactions to the arguments we get into. Like when she leaves a wet towel on the bathroom floor of my apartment we live in together. Or when she bitches at me to take the garbage out or clean the dishes or cook dinner with more greens and I don't want to because work drained the piss out of me.

We get on each other's nerves all the time. Robert says that's what happens when you live with a significant other. The honeymoon period wears off when you realize you have to share your time and responsibilities. I'm not sure we ever had a honeymoon period to begin with.

River dismisses Issy's nonsense and turns to Bridgette. They talk about the get-together they're having at their house. It's a barbecue, according to Oliver. I asked Robert at work yesterday if they needed us to bring anything.

"Just your beautiful bride-to-be."

He's still trying to get me to propose; has been for two years now. Isabel mentions our future at least once a week. I appeased her when I agreed to her moving in, but I can't agree to anything else.

The crowd starts dispersing, so we all head toward the parking lot. There are crossing guards directing traffic on the busy street, making sure there are no accidents. Despite Isabel trying to keep me next to her, I fall back and meet River's strides step for step.

"Are you excited to be done?"

She likes school, even though it took her a solid year before she started getting involved with things outside of art club. I'm pretty sure she only joined that because it made Robert and Bridgette happy, even though she loves the subject matter. During her sophomore year, Oliver mentioned her volunteering after school at a local art studio, cleaning up after one of the local youth groups comes in and paints before their parents pick them up. She tried joining the book club that the library hosts but didn't like it. The kind of books they discussed weren't her thing.

"A little," she admits. She glances from the ground to me. "I'm sad. Is that weird?"

Shaking my head, I brush her arm with mine. Her cheeks color. "I don't think that's weird at all. You grew a lot at Freemont. Issy's right, though. You can grow a lot in college, too."

Most people find themselves during their higher education experiences. Me? I think I just realized who I'm not. I guess that works too. Someone like River, who has so much to offer the world, would flourish in college if she lets herself.

At the beginning of her senior year, the guidance counselor told her to apply to at least two colleges. She told him she wasn't going, which prompted him to call the James'. Someone like River, with a 4.0 grade point average, who's well-behaved, and involved in clubs, is exactly the type of person colleges want to accept. Not to mention she'd get a full ride.

Truthfully, we were shocked she wasn't valedictorian, but two of her class grades dropped right before they processed who would give speeches at commencement, and I don't think it's a coincidence; especially because one of the classes was English.

She fumbles with the diploma holder in her grasp. "Did Oliver tell you I decided to go to Bridgeport Community College?"

He did. "Why didn't you go to one of the bigger universities that accepted you? Ollie mentioned that you had at least three options."

She's quiet for a moment. "I like it here. Bridgeport ... it's become my home."

Something warms in my chest. An easy smile forms on my face as I take her hand and squeeze it. It's an innocent gesture, but her whole face heats up as she glances at our joined hands. And when Isabel glares back at us, River's face gets redder as she unlatches herself from me.

My palm feels cold. Too cold. Not even Isabel's fiery gaze could warm me.

Clearing my throat to clear the frog lodged inside it, I nod once. "I'm real glad to hear that, River. You deserve a home; a family."

You deserve everything.

Her eyes are focused on something in front of us, narrowed in on Issy. I follow her gaze to Isabel's left hand. What is she looking for?

When she realizes I'm staring, she blushes. "Robert said you were, uh, taking things to the next level with Isabel."

Shit.

Dropping my voice so Issy can't eavesdrop, I murmur, "Did he now?"

She just nods.

"I'm not."

Her head snaps over to me, her hand brushing fallen strands of auburn hair behind her ear. "Oh. That's …"

I wait.

She doesn't finish the sentence.

Isabel's eyes keep darting back to us. I give her a tight smile and nod of my head. She's too busy looking at River. More like glaring, actually.

We make it to our cars, which are parked next to each other. Isabel doesn't climb in right away. She watches me and River as Bridgette and Robert advance to their vehicle.

Issy says, "Why don't you ride with us, River? It'll give you and Rhett more time to catch up."

Her offer surprises me. "You can, if you want to," I agree, shifting to face River.

Her eyes bounce from Bridgette and Robert to me. "Um …"

Bridgette nods and smiles. "Go ahead, sweetie. We'll be right behind you guys."

Oliver waves and climbs into the back of their vehicle, not fazed by the offer made by his best friend's girlfriend. He doesn't find our dynamic weird. He thinks it's cool that River and I get along so well.

Like siblings, he always says.

The term makes me feel sick as fuck.

Isabel's smile seems genuine, which makes me wonder if she's really trying to make things right with River for my sake. It chips away some of my resentment that I tell myself isn't there, but always is, lingering, taunting, haunting me.

"O-Okay," River finally answers.

I hold the back door open for her and she climbs in. The green dress she wears flows in the slight burst of wind, lifting the edge enough for me to see a glimpse of white lace panties underneath. My cock stirs.

Jesus.

This is going to be a long night.

THE BARBECUE LASTS UNTIL THE SUN GOES DOWN, AND most of the friends River invited over left to go to parties being held around town. She's invited to tag along but declines.

I watch her while I nurse a beer at the picnic table in the backyard. The patio where she's standing talking to Oliver is lit up by small solar lights. It gives her milky skin a yellow glow. Ethereal.

Something Oliver says makes her laugh, and her laugh is low but feminine and makes my eyes narrow in on the curves of her full lips. She replies to the joke, making Oliver double over before shaking his head and clinking their glasses together. He's got beer, she's got water.

Bridgette told her she can have some wine since she was staying in, but she declined. I've only seen her drink once, at my party two years ago, and not a day since. It makes me wonder if she blames the alcohol for her lack of filter. Though I think we both know she wasn't drunk; the alcohol was liquid courage to ask me what she did.

Isabel is mingling with some old friend from childhood. Taylor or Tyler or Travis. I'm not sure. Honestly, I don't care. As soon as she started talking about how much money he made, I tuned her out. Money doesn't mean anything to me, she knows that.

"Of course, it doesn't," she always says in response. *"You're loaded because of your parents. It's not like you need to worry. That's why we're alike."*

But we're not alike in that way. She's materialistic, a firm believer that money can buy happiness. The money I have is blood money, only in my account because my parents are dead and buried six feet under. Money doesn't make me happy, it pisses me off.

When Oliver goes off to who knows where, I find myself wandering toward River. She's still standing in the same spot, sipping her drink until it's empty.

"Want more?" I ask.

She gives me a small smile. "No, thanks. If I keep drinking, I'll be running to the bathroom all night." She winces and blushes. "I guess you didn't really need to know that."

I just chuckle.

She clears her throat. "Isabel looks like she's having a nice chat with Peyton."

Peyton? Fuck, I was way off.

"Uh, yeah. They go way back."

She nods.

"Want to go inside for a bit?" It's getting cooler and her skin is pebbled with goosebumps. Most people are chatting about business or politics with Robert and Bridgette, so nobody would really miss us if we go inside to warm up.

I guide her in, my palm pressed into the small of her back. We go to the kitchen where she deposits her glass into the sink. I head toward the cupboard and pull out some peanut butter and then beeline toward the apples.

She knows what I'm doing instantly. "I blame you for my addiction to those." There's teasing in her tone, which makes me smile as I slice up the fruit into wedges.

A few weeks after I tried getting her to try apples and peanut butter, I left a plate of them outside her bedroom door. Peter York scared her off the first time, so she never got to have any. I didn't leave a note or an explanation. Just knocked on her closed door and left. I see her nibbling on the snack every time I visit.

When I'm done, I put enough peanut butter on the plate for the both of us and head over to where she's sitting at the island.

She takes a slice and dips it in the peanut butter before taking a large bite. Her moan makes the front of my pants tighten, but I try forcing the yearning away and grab an apple too.

"These are so good," she says with her mouth full. She used to care about having proper manners. I think she was afraid of being scolded if she was caught being unladylike. But she knows she can be herself around me.

"Told you so," I muse.

She finishes the first slice and grabs another, taking a large portion of the peanut butter with her.

"Hey now, save some for me."

She scoffs. "There's plenty."

"Not before you're done with it."

Her eyes narrow. "Are you implying something, Everett? I like food, what can I say?"

If she's asking if I think she's fat, she's way off. She's curvy in a dangerous way, her hips and thighs filled out in all the right places. There was a time she was self-conscious of her new figure, especially when guys took notice. I'm definitely one of those guys, but I told her not to worry about any of them. As long as she's happy and healthy that's all that matters.

"I like that you like food," I admit. Issy lives on rabbit food; lettuce, carrots, or some other insanely healthy option. It's not like I don't enjoy a hearty salad occasionally, but the look Issy gives me if I order a damn cheeseburger annoys me.

"Steph says real men appreciate the type of women who can eat them under the table."

Her words make me choke on my apple slice. Well, maybe not her words. It's the image of her on her knees under the table in front of me that my mind conjures up out of fucking nowhere. It nearly kills me.

She pats my back, worry carved into her features. "Are you okay?"

I wave her off. "Fine."

She rolls her eyes and grabs her glass from the sink, filling it with water. Passing it to me, she raises her eyebrows and waits for me to take a sip. Once she's satisfied, she takes her seat again.

"Went down the wrong pipe," I murmur.

She doesn't comment on it.

After we're done with the snack, she sets the plate down on the counter. I itch to do something I keep telling myself not to.

I touch her.

The pad of my thumb grazes the corner of her mouth. Her breath hitches, then blows out slowly against my finger. The thick lashes around her chocolate eyes flutter closed for a moment, absorbing the moment. I do too.

"Peanut butter," I whisper.

My finger trails over her bottom lip, feeling it tremble beneath my touch. She's affected by me, always has been. I'm not sure when I started realizing it. Maybe after the party. Maybe after Isabel accused her of having a crush on me. Who the fuck knows?

What I do know is that I like the way she shakes for me. I love how her eyes close and her breath changes and her cheeks color into the prettiest shade of pink I've seen on a woman. I want to tell her it's not just her, that I feel it too.

But I don't. I never do.

"What the hell?" a shrill voice shrieks from the corner. My hand quickly falls to my side when I turn to find Issy staring daggers at us. I realize I'm nearly standing between River's legs, and I'm not sure when I got there.

Taking a step back, I clear my throat. "I got River and I some snacks."

Isabel glances between the two of us, skeptically. I get it, her doubt. Her disbelief. There are trays of food still outside, some hors d'oeuvres that Robert and his business friends like, some plain sliders and deli meats. We shouldn't have needed to come in here, alone, for a snack.

Isabel straightens. "I think it's time we go home, Everett." Her tone is deadly, allowing no room for argument.

When she calls me Everett, it means I fucked up. I suppose I deserve it this time. Glancing at River, I give her an apologetic smile. She's flushed, her chocolate eyes darker than normal, and she's speechless.

Not in the same way she was before. She's processing. I touched her—I've never done that before, never told myself I had the right to.

I *don't* have the right.

But she didn't stop me.

"Goodnight, River," I tell her.

She blinks, her teeth biting into her lower lip—the same one I caressed. I still feel its silky texture on my thumb.

"Goodnight," she whispers.

We haven't been the same since she asked me to take her virginity, since I punched Asher Wilks for taking it, or since I saw her marred body. We'll never be the same. After all, there was no peanut butter on her lip.

AFTER

EIGHTEEN

Everett / 27

Present Day

Everett. We made a mistake.

That tiny sentence still haunts me every time I let my mind drift to the way her husky, broken tone said those four fucking words.

We didn't make a mistake.

The mistake, if that's what you want to call it, was waiting all these years to finally experience what it's like to feel her tight pussy squeeze my cock—to know what her salty skin tastes like, her lips, her neck. I've wasted years not knowing what the weight of her supple breasts feels like in my palms or the way her nipples pebble when my mouth wraps around them or the soft, breathless noises she makes when she comes.

The mistake is me not realizing what I could have had all along. The mistake is me. Always me.

Jesus. I've made a lot of bad choices in my life. Like never telling my parents how much I love them or not being there to say goodbye to Granddad. Hell, leaving town to pursue something I've never been interested in, leaving someone I care about behind, is just another stupid decision I need to deal with. The only thing I've done because I actually wanted to is kiss River James; to make a move. *Finally*.

But she thinks it's a mistake.

She regrets it.

It's a sucker punch to the gut every time my memory takes me back to her hips grinding against mine or her riding my palm when I fucked her with my fingers. The way her eyes rolled, her lips parted, her world stopped, was because of *me*. She can regret it all she wants, but I don't. Not one second of it.

The only thing I regret is how she feels now that we crossed the line.

I'll cross it again if she'll let me.

NINETEEN

River / 23

The brushstrokes leave behind a blur of emerald green across the stark white board, the gritty material blemishing the flawless curves of the form. Another layer and the imperfections will be covered completely; smooth and beautiful. That's what you need to do, add layer after layer until nobody can see what's underneath.

A soft melody lulls from the speakers in the back storage room. Melanie says it helps the kids concentrate, so I keep it on even after the youth group leaves. It's instrumental, wordless, which I usually despise. It isn't distracting enough like the words of someone else's struggles serenading my guilt. But it does the job, fills the silence now that I'm the only one left in the Painter's Choice studio.

The new groups of kids I've started teaching are part of a special program sponsored by the Bridgeport Community Center, who also happens to own the art studio. Usually, the youth groups are just children whose parents can't pick them up after school, so they send them to afterschool activates the church puts on in town. But after reaching out to Jill, my old social worker, I set up a program to offer classes to foster kids in the area. After it was approved by the church board, of course.

Mrs. Cohen used to teach me how to channel my emotions into my projects, so my hope is that these kids can too. It's been a success so far, and it makes me feel fulfilled knowing I can be part of their lives somehow. Even if it's just by bringing them somewhere to go besides back home to who knows what. I can tell these kids have stories, we all do. Once you're a foster kid, you never really stop being one. Robert doesn't like when I say that, but he doesn't understand.

I never try to make him.

Examining my canvas, my eyes travel the long stroke of the green circle. Grabbing a new brush, I wet it and dip the bristles into the white paint of my wooden palette, mixing it into the emerald tone and swirling them together. There's a hollow inner circle, still empty from the board. It'll be black, maybe navy blue. I'm not sure the mood yet.

The outline of the light green hue I've created is a dark shade of blue, not quite royal or navy but somewhere in between. It's a unique color, one that's hard to capture.

Before I can fill in anything else, I'm startled by the bell ringing on the front door. Melanie walks in with a smile on her face when she sees me positioned in the front of the empty classroom, hovering over a new painting.

"I thought you'd still be here."

She goes in the back and flicks off the music. The studio is drowned in a deafening silence. Setting the paint brush down, I push off the stool and wipe my stained hands on a damp paper towel.

"The kids were good today," I note, leaning my shoulder against the doorjamb to our office. I got a part time job here teaching art classes to the local youth, mostly the fosters since I pitched the program. Sometimes I'll fill in for Melanie, like today, and teach all the classes that come in.

Her smile widens as she organizes some paperwork on her desk. "I'm glad. How'd your class go? It's only the third one, right?"

The Church board had to weigh in on the decision of allowing me to bring fosters to the studio. Their extensive knowledge of local foster homes makes them extremely beneficial in swaying the vote.

I was too determined to start this program to to let a room full of stuffy old people stereotype these children, most of whom just wanted a safe place to hang out. The head of the clergy listened to my speech and watched my presentation, but ultimately stretched their final vote over a month-long period. When I finally got the okay, I had to figure out how to contain my emotions because it seemed like they flooded me at once.

"They're adapting, I think." Shuffling into the office, I sit on the torn upholstered chair. It's blue and uncomfortable but it was a donation from a local business, so we keep it around.

She leans back in her seat. "And everything else? How's life. I know you don't like talking about yourself, but you seem like you need to talk about something."

Melanie is over ten years older than me, twelve if memory serves, and she's perceptive. She knows I'm a foster kid, which is why I wanted to implement the new program into our schedule, and that I was adopted by the James'. Over the past few years of working for her, she's seen me interact with Oliver when he stops in to see me "do my thing" and Bridgette if she's in town running errands. A few times, she even saw me with Robert if there's a meeting in the building we share with other businesses.

But the one person she's only seen twice with me is Everett, and there's good reason. She just doesn't know it. If I keep pushing those reasons away, I won't have to think about them either.

I do though. Every day for the past three weeks, I've been taunted by the memories of callused caresses and husky moans. My brain has nothing better to do than to replay that guilt ridden, ecstasy-inducing night repeatedly.

Swallowing past the lump in my throat, I force a smile. It hurts my face, like I'm cracking in half at the seams. "I've just got a lot going on. You know, with school and whatnot."

I finished my bachelor's in Art History and moved onto a master's in Education. Both degrees will come from Bridgeport Community College despite Robert trying to get me to go to a bigger university for my master's program. I thought about it but opted not to keep walking away from my problems. From *him*.

No. Not him. *Them*.

I see them everywhere and it suffocates me. They're on my morning walk to Landmark Café where I get my lavender tea, or the short commute to BCC for evening classes.

My mistake haunts me.

"If working is too much—"

"No!" I exclaim quickly. "It's the only thing that keeps my mind off ... school. You know, stressful things."

Her eyes narrow in skepticism, but clear of doubt before she nods. "Art has a way of being the very thing we need to cope with life."

That's why I stayed. I could have left, could have avoided my problems. But I've never done it before, and now that I'm stronger, I won't throw in the towel. Art is the only way to run without actually leaving. So, I paint. I draw. I sketch. I mold. I let my brain, my heart, and my soul do the talking, the running.

Clearing my throat, I stand. "I'll clean up and be done for the day before I head up. Do you need anything else?"

Her head tilts. "If you want to finish your project, feel free. Something tells me you're nowhere near done with that painting in there. I see it on your face. You have a lot to say, and if painting it helps, I won't stop you."

She starts gathering some papers, which gives me a chance to slip out. Facing my painting, I realize she's right. If I don't finish this tonight, I may not have the inspiration tomorrow. It's weird how my feelings fuel me these days, eat at me in ways I wouldn't allow them to before.

I wish I could turn them off.

I send a text to Bridgette since I'm supposed to come for dinner.

Be there late.

NOTHING BUT THE GLOW OF THE DIM STREETLIGHTS cascade through the front windows of Painter's Choice. There are planes of glass stretching from floor to ceiling in the front of the building, revealing a quiet night beyond the glass.

The white earbuds plastered in my ears sing to me as I finish the last part of my painting. Sinking into my stool, I absorb my newest creation. My heart hums in satisfaction as my eyes roam across the minty green and black and white that form the iris; tortured with guilt as it looks out into the world. The black pupil within tells a story, a hand reaching out and grasping a ball of orange and yellow flames. Smoke lines the edges of the canvas, leaving no open space. Everything is consumed by fire, by feeling, by torment.

I shriek when the earbuds are yanked from my ears and nearly fall off my stool as I bat my arm at the person behind me when a familiar musky scent overwhelms my senses.

"You shouldn't have your earbuds in when you're alone in an unlocked building," Everett scolds in a deadly tone, his eyes hollow and as dark as the bags resting beneath them.

My heart is still racing from the unexpected intrusion.

"Why do you care?" My words are biting. He's the last person I want to see right now.

"Don't ask stupid questions."

My teeth grind. "Why are you here?"

His eyes narrow. "What did I *just* say?"

The harshness of his cool tone snaps me out of my surprised haze. "You have no right to talk to me like that."

He cants his head to the side. "Don't I?" His eyes shift from me to my painting. Something flickers in them. Realization. "Is this your way of saying you want me to catch on fire?"

"What? No."

The tension he holds in his shoulders doesn't ease. In fact, his corded muscles tighten. He's suddenly too tall, too overwhelming. I stand back.

He notes the movement, his nostrils flaring, but doesn't say anything. Maybe he knows whatever will come out won't be pretty. I don't do well when people yell, and he looks like he wants to scream.

What does he want me to say? To do? He can't deny that what we did was a huge mistake. If anyone should be eaten alive by guilt, it's him. *He's* the one who has a girlfriend.

I'm just the one with a crush.

The other woman.

He finally huffs. "What? No, hello?"

My hands tighten into balls. "Hello."

"Don't do that."

"What?"

He doesn't respect my personal space like he used to. Instead, he takes a massive step forward until all I see, feel, and smell is him. "I woke up *in your bed* and you were *fucking gone*, River. I think that warrants a conversation. Now, I've given you time. Nineteen days, to be exact. No more bullshit."

That's what he thinks this is? *Bullshit?*

He doesn't stop there because he knows I'm too stunned to speak. "I've had a lot of time to think, to *really* fucking think about what we did. And you know what I've come up with?"

My lungs sting when I force a deep breath. "W-What do you think?"

"That I miss you."

I miss you, too.

It's such a quick internal response that I nearly choke on

the words. They're not a lie. I miss Everett. I miss his friendship and his wisdom and his wittiness. He makes me laugh
and smile and sometimes angry, but only because he pushes
me in ways nobody else has; without force or ill will. He does
it because he wants to see me flourish even if it's annoying.

Like when he helped me study for math classes in
undergrad because statistics kicked my ass. Or when he
helped me dissect a Dickens novel when I had to write a
twenty-page paper on thematic ideologies on Victorian
literature. He made sure I passed even when I set myself
up for failure. He never let it happen.

"I miss your warmth," he adds, taking an impossibly
close step to me. "I miss your voice." His polished Cole
Hann black dress shoes brush the tips of my Walmart
five-dollar ballet flats. "I miss the feeling of your skin
against my palm."

Can't. Breathe.

His fingertips graze my arm, up, up, up, until they're
somehow tangled in my hair. *How did they get there?* I tell
myself to push him away. I don't. *God*, I don't want to.

His fingers tighten around a fistful of hair, but it
doesn't hurt. One more step and my chest is flush against
his and I'm afraid he can feel the way my nipples pebble
under my thin dress. I'm affected by him, even when I
shouldn't be.

Always when I shouldn't be.

"We didn't make a mistake," he whispers, his lips
brushing my ear. His breath causes goosebumps to form
on my arms and a shiver to rake down my spine.

"You heard that?"

"Every fucking word."

My eyes close. "We did, though."

"You'll never be my mistake, River."

There's a strong pull to let him inside the deepest parts of me, to let him soak into every crack and crevice, to rip my heart wide open.

But I can't.

Stepping away from his touch, I blink past his blurry figure. "But you'll always be mine, Everett."

Because you love her.

His throat bobs and brows pinch in as he takes me in. My heart hurts on a whole different level right now and I worry it might shatter me completely. Art can't fix what we've broken.

"I see." He stuffs his hands in the pockets of his navy slacks and it's a bad time to notice how good he looks, but he does. He looks amazing. All business. Sexy and sinful, with his muscular body filling out his work attire. I think he works out more than he ever has before, and I wonder if it's his way of coping like painting is mine.

It makes this hurt more.

"You should go." My traitorous voice cracks, revealing how much this hurts me. If he thinks I'm doing this because I *want* to, he knows the difference now.

I'm doing this because I *have* to.

For the both of us.

He doesn't say one word as he turns on his heel and walks out. He doesn't slam open the door or bang it closed. Externally, he's poised, together, calm. Internally, I know him better than that. He's facing as much turmoil as me; burning, breaking, pleading.

When he's finally gone, I allow myself to speak the words he didn't need to hear. "I miss you, too."

TWENTY

Everett / 27

I've learned how to absorb a lot of blows in life, but River may just be delivering the hits that take me down for good. I was too young to remember my parents' death, and only have Granddad's passing to compare it to. Because that's what losing River will feel like; death.

She may not know it, but she's been the one consistent thing in my life for years. The only other person who comes close to that is Oliver, but he doesn't even surpass his little sister's place in my life. And that's the fucking problem.

I can respect River's choice to push me away. A long time ago she asked me if I rejected her because of my friendship with Oliver, and while I told her that wasn't completely the reason, it *was* a big portion. We're all friends, and anything between us could risk that dynamic. But something already happened, and there's no fucking way I can forget it. Even if she wishes I would.

Nineteen days without a single word spoken between us felt like three weeks without everything that's essential to me—sun, water, oxygen. It's cheesy as hell acknowledging that the only decent thing in my life is her, but it's true. Issy can give me her body, her opinion, and her attitude, but not even she can give me her heart. I think she's stopped trying. Deep down, she knows I don't want it.

We've been together nearly ten years, and neither of us can move forward. Three years ago, I almost bought her a ring. Two years ago, I almost let Margaret give me her old wedding band to give to her. One year ago, I wondered what the hell I'm doing with my life for the millionth time.

I haven't thought anything like that so whole-heartedly again until nineteen days ago when I met River James at the Landmark Café. Her usual lavender tea sat in front of her with a chocolate scone on a plate left untouched. She got it for us to split. It was supposed to be an innocent meeting—two people catching up.

River left with Stephanie Malone over the Christmas holidays, leaving me without air for over two months. It left me worried, despite her being tagged in photos of the grown women smiling and playing tourist at the usual landmarks; the Hollywood stars, the Hollywood sign, Warner Bros. Studio. Realistically, I knew she was fine. But no amount of reassuring texts or photos could make me believe it until she was back.

Subconsciously, I was more worried she wouldn't return after getting a taste of freedom. But she did. Because, like she always says, Bridgeport is her home.

We sat at the café for three hours while she told me all about her trip. Where she stayed, what she ate, the places Stephanie dragged her to. She said it was fun, but she missed us. Missed *me*.

Despite how that night ended, in a tangle of tongues and limbs, I know she still feels the same way. She didn't have to say it back when I told her how much I missed her, I saw it in her glassy eyes as she fought with herself. *Do I or don't I.* She chose not to feed the growing tension, but I heard her heart, felt it beat wildly when her chest was pressed against mine.

That day at the café, I'd given her a present. A welcome home gift, I told her. But really, I just wanted to buy her something special. I've given her things during the holidays and birthdays, I still sneak candy to her when she least expects it because I know she's still obsessed with M&M's, but I couldn't resist buying her a new charm for her necklace when I saw it in the jewelry store's window in town.

The charm is silver like her other one and the chain, but this one signifies more than she can ever know. Next to the paint brush and painter's pallet I know rest between her breasts is a broken heart, split right down the middle with a jagged line.

My heart. Because this is as close as I can ever get to giving it to her.

I took it off her that night.

Nothing but skin. That's what I needed between us. Not the necklace, not the memory of our youth, just bare warmth. And I saw the silver chain still hanging around her neck yesterday at the studio, which only cements what I already know.

River James will always be mine, even if she doesn't want to be. Even if she can't be.

So, no. I don't blame her for what she said. I don't blame her for one goddamn thing. The night we shared was one of the most consuming experiences in my life, like two halves of a whole finally forming for the first time. She can live in her make-believe world where she pretends it never happened, where I was never inside of her. But in the real world, the memory of her calling out my name and tightening around me is burned into my brain for all of eternity.

I'll have River James.

Even if it completely ends me.

OVER A WEEK AFTER THE ENCOUNTER WITH RIVER AT Painter's Choice, I walk into my apartment a little before ten o'clock to see Issy waiting for me. She's sitting in her usual skimpy pale pink pajama set at the small table offset by the kitchen, a cup of hot water with lemon steaming in front of her. It helps her sleep.

Dropping my keys onto the counter and peeling off my itchy blazer, I walk over to the sink and fill a glass of water. She hasn't greeted me, I haven't greeted her. I know something's wrong.

When I take a seat beside her, she finally looks at me.

I'm surprised to meet hollow eyes that are usually full of sass and attitude. Isabel's face is bare like it usually is before bed, but she looks ghostly.

My throat tightens when I swallow, and I wonder if she can hear my heart.

"You okay?" I ask, forcing my voice to stay steady.

Say yes.

Isabel has gone through just as much hell as me over the years, probably more. After she got a degree in fashion design, she interned for a local artist specializing in custom attire made for Broadway shows. The business was shut down for some embezzlement scheme and she lost her credentials. After working for her father as a secretary for a year, she found a job similar to the one she interned for in the town over. But that's not what makes me respect her.

She can face the deepest pit and still come out alive, climbing, fighting, and doing what it takes to survive. That's the way Issy's always been. It's why we always find our way back to each other when we separated. It's why I made the promise to her after what we lost.

I'll always be here for you, Issy.

I never go back on my promises.

But sometimes ... fuck, sometimes I wish I could. Because the tension that rises whenever we're in the same room with our clothes on transpires into something darker and painful when those clothes are off. We connect physically, sometimes mentally in our endeavors, but never emotionally.

"You've been working late," she comments quietly, her fingers lifting the teacup to her lips. Their natural rosy pink color looks lighter, paler.

"Robert's deal with Steinburg, Inc. went through a few days ago, so we're swamped sorting through the paperwork and making sure the proper forms are signed." It's a big deal for JT Corporations to have one of the largest pharmaceutical companies linked to us. It means triple the funding, and more chances for raises and promotions.

She nods once, setting the cup down on a coaster. I think it's stupid we have them. Who cares if the furniture gets marked? It's mine anyway, not hers. But she likes them, so I don't verbalize my distaste. I have no right.

Clearing my throat, I stare at my untouched water. I'm parched for reasons I can't think about now. Not when I'm looking at the woman I broke in more ways than one.

"Where do you go?" she finally asks.

"When?"

Her shoulders rise. "When you're here but not here. You're just ... gone. I don't even remember how long it's been like that."

I don't answer her.

Her eyes lock on mine. "Aren't you going to say something? Anything?"

My dry lips part, then close.

She grips her cup a little too tightly. "I always do the

talking for us and I know you hate it. You hate a lot of things, Everett. But I've tried over and over again and why? What's the point?"

"I don't know what—"

She holds up her hand. "All I want is to see you put effort into our relationship like you used to. Remember when you'd take me out on dates? When you'd pick me up flowers or chocolates or presents? That stuff is nice. It's what boyfriends do for their girlfriends."

Swiping my palm down my clean-shaven jaw, I let out a soft exhale. "I've been so busy with work and the fire department that I haven't been giving you enough attention. I'm sorry."

Her jaw ticks. "Believe it or not, I don't always expect attention. Just something to make me believe that you're here for a reason. Hell, that you're here *at all*."

Anger bubbles in my veins. "I *am*."

She glances away, lips pressed in a firm line as she contemplates something. "You were at the fire station the past few weeks, right? Like last week? You were helping Steve train the newbies."

"For a while, yeah." I only spent about forty minutes there last week before leaving for the studio because Steve had it handled and two of the trainees didn't even show up. We weren't both needed there for what little was left to be done.

The fire department became my home away from home shortly after Granddad's cabin caught fire from faulty wiring a few years back. Thankfully, not much damage was done. But the more I spoke to the chief, the more interested I was in volunteering. Now I'm there at least once a week, sometimes more, depending on what's going on at work ... and home.

Her head tips once. "Good."

I don't say anything.

She closes her eyes and grabs the cup, finishing off her drink. "Sometimes I wish you would just explode whenever I tell you off. Get angry, Rhett. When you just sit there and take it ... it makes me feel ..."

"It makes you feel what, Isabel?"

She just shrugs.

"Why do you want me to get pissed?" I doubt quietly. "What the hell will that do for us? Nothing will change if all we do is argue."

Her lips twitch, then flatten. "Nothing is changing *now* when we're not. We're stuck in the stupid cycle like we have been since—"

"Don't," I crack.

Her eyes narrow. "Is that what it'll take? Reminding you that we screwed up? That we're never going to be whole? You know why I want you pissed, Everett? Because then I'll know you *care*. That you *feel* something."

Once again, I'm silent. Not to piss her off, but because I'm afraid of what will leave my mouth if I open my lips. The truth lingers in the pit of my chest, straining to break free from the cage it's locked in. I'm in a deeper part of hell than Lucifer, but I can hear his satanic laugh.

She pushes off the table. "Why doesn't anything I say make you react anymore?"

Finally, I say, "They're just words."

She shakes her head, moving away from me and toward the bedroom. "Well you should really think about that, Everett. Because they shouldn't *just* be anything."

Raking my fingers through my hair, I rest my elbows on the edge of the table.

"I'll pick up dinner tomorrow," I offer weakly, knowing damn well it's too late to make amends for everything. For us. For years worth of bullshit. For not being able to feel anything for her despite what I've put her through.

"Don't bother."

Our bedroom door clicks closed and the soft sound of the lock turning crushes any ounce of hope I had left for some form of relationship with the woman behind the oak wood.

I set up the couch with a pillow and blanket and fall asleep to the utter silence of the apartment.

TWENTY-ONE

River / 23

Oliver is always a welcome face to see. When he went off to Penn State for college, I missed him like crazy around the house. When he'd come home for breaks, I would run into his arms at full speed. Now he visits once or twice a month since he lives a few cities over with a girl none of us have met. It makes his visits that much more exciting. He catches me when I throw myself at him, grunting but still spinning me around in circles.

"You're not as light as you were, Riv."

Frowning and brushing my frizzy red hair behind my ear, I peer down at myself. "Are you calling me fat?"

When I was thirteen, I barely weighed one hundred pounds. All my bones stuck out because I'd been starved at my last home. Hell, at most of my foster homes. It wasn't until my first physical that Bridgette took me to shortly after my fourteenth birthday that the doctors discovered just how brutally I'd been treated. I made Bridgette stay in the room with me, where she held my hand and held back tears when she saw the truth hiding beneath my clothes.

Not just my malnutrition, not just my scars, but the misshapen formation of my bones where they'd been struck, broken, and apparently healed wrong—the dips of my ribcage that belts and fists and other objects hit and cracked and broke. Bridgette learned the truth that day, saw it for her own eyes. And she didn't see me as some broken, hideous monster like I was afraid she would. She cried for me, for not being able to stop it from happening. The tears she shed were for the present and the future, where I would never have to worry about another mark again.

And for the first time ever, I cried in front of not only her, but the doctor. She promised I wouldn't have to talk about it to anyone unless I wanted to, which is another reason therapy didn't work. I never spoke a word to the professionals.

My body will always hold the marks, although some are faded, but I don't look the same despite them.

Oliver rolls his dark eyes playfully. "You're the farthest thing from fat, River."

I give him a tiny smile.

Bridgette and Robert come into the room next and greet him with big hugs and bigger smiles. It gives me time to really look him over. His dark hair is chopped short and professional looking, but his style hasn't changed. He's sporting jeans and a black long sleeve shirt and a pair of gray Converse I think he's had for at least four years now. Maybe he wears business attire at his job, some tech company, but I doubt it. Oliver isn't anything like Robert.

He tried working for his father, but it only lasted a month before he accepted a job that led him to where he is now.

To my surprise, he's got dark scruff lining his jaw that matches the color of his dark brown hair. It looks weirdly good on him, especially when he smiles, and his right dimple pops out. He's happy, which makes me happy.

Bridgette keeps hounding me for answers on his girlfriend because she thinks he's told me about her. I don't even know her name, just that she's pretty and works at the company with him. Over the years if he was catching up with Tommy and Quinn, his old high school buddies, they would brag about all the girls they've hooked up with. He was no different, but he would always give them a scathing glare if I was within hearing distance. I would always ask him for the most details, which riled his friends up and earned me a narrowed eye from him. For someone who constantly brags about the notches in his bedpost, he sure doesn't like talking about the details.

Darlene still cooks for the James' part time, so she prepared a big dinner for Oliver. He says he has big news to share with us, so I thought he was bringing his girlfriend home to introduce her to the family. I guess I'm sort of still a hopeless romantic despite my poor taste in men.

Internally, I cringe.

Everett isn't a bad person, but what transpired between us is horrible. It grates on me that I still have feelings for him that tingle and flutter if he's around or if

THE TRUTH ABOUT HEARTBREAK

someone says his name. I tell myself it's my body's way of remembering what transpired between us, a natural reaction.

But it's not.

I want to tell someone. Steph would die if she heard what I did. Not just because she used to have a crush on Everett, one that lasted until he graduated and it was "out of sight, out of mind" for her, but because I'm not this person. Well, I guess I am. But I'm the last person she would expect to do something so drastic.

I can picture it now, the twenty questions. After Asher, she asked me things that made my face set on fire. Not from the memories of our time together like how I feel thinking about Everett and me, but because I was embarrassed and ashamed.

"How big was he?"

"What did he do to prep you?"

"Who was on top?"

Those were G rated questions compared to what she would ask now. Over the summer, I experienced grown up Stephanie in full force. Like when an L.A. native asked me out to coffee and offered to show me around the city and Steph practically shoved me at him and told me to tell her what kind of package he carried. I'm so inexperienced that I legitimately thought she was talking about an actual package.

Snapping out of it when Oliver mentions going back home tonight, I frown. Usually he stays for at least a day.

But he's not single anymore—he has someone to go home to.

My heart hurts a little more.

"Want to go into town for some pastries before I leave?" Ollie asks me, nudging my arm with his elbow. He wiggles his eyebrows. "I'll even get you an extra triple chocolate brownie for later."

Apparently, my stomach likes the sound of that because it roars to life and makes him laugh. I want to say no, because I'm afraid of who I'll see. But Oliver can't know I'm avoiding his best friend because then he'll ask questions that he *definitely* can never learn the answers to.

My guilt runs deep for multiple reasons, not just because of Isabel. He's my brother's best friend and my family treats him like another child. I'm afraid I'll ruin the relationships he's made between the members of my adopted family.

Ollie knows I trust Everett, but he doesn't need to know the boundaries that are now splayed open between us.

I tell Oliver I'd love to go with a forced smile he doesn't seem to see through. Out of the two of them, Ollie and Everett, he isn't the one who knows when I'm pretending. It's eerie how well Everett can see through my lies.

It's going on four o'clock, and if Oliver wants to leave before dark, that means we only have a few hours together. It also means he's probably going to drop some big news and then leave. Well, not before getting me chocolate. I guess I'm getting more perks than our parents.

After we're digging into the pot roast dinner, Oliver's favorite, and Robert makes small talk about Oliver's work, which he doesn't understand any more than Bridgette and I do, he reveals the big reason he came.

I know it's serious because he sets down his fork and everything. Oliver is always eating something, so it makes me nervous. "The company I'm working for is opening a new branch that they've asked me to run."

Bridgette claps. "Oh, that's wonderful!"

A big, proud smile stretches across Robert's face as he reaches over and squeezes Oliver's shoulder. I just smile when he looks at me, but he sees how happy I am for him. It's the one thing I let stay written on my face.

Oliver clears his throat. "It's in Chicago."

Bridgette makes a tiny noise that I think only I hear. Robert's hand stills on Oliver's shoulder, and then drops.

"Chicago?" I ask. "As in ... Illinois?"

"The very one."

Bridgette dabs her napkin across her lips. "Wow, Ollie. That's ... it's amazing news. Really."

He gives her an unsure smile. "Really?"

Robert composes himself. "Chicago has a lot of great opportunities, and it sounds like this one would be silly to pass up, son."

Relief is evident on Oliver's face, and his whole body eases into his chair. "I'm glad you guys think so. I was a bit worried, to be honest."

"It's a long way away from New York," Bridgette admonishes, "but I've always wanted to visit the windy city. Perhaps during its *less* windy season."

Seeing the support from Robert and Bridgette makes me even happier for Ollie. I mean, I'm sad that he's leaving. Really sad. But I don't want him to see that. He's grown up in ways I don't think he's even acknowledged yet, but I do. It's easier to see how people have changed when you're a fly on the wall, experiencing everyone in their natural state. He's got a girlfriend, a job, and now he's moving away.

His family is proud of him like they always are, like he works so hard for them to be.

It makes me wonder if I can ever find the type of strength to do what he's done. Visiting California for a few months is nothing like moving there permanently. The idea of separating myself from the one place I've learned I can depend on sounds terrifying. When you grow up not belonging, and finally find that forever kind of place, it feels like the destination you've been searching for all along.

"River?"

I blink. "Huh?"

Oliver chuckles. "I asked what you thought about it."

I reach over and grab his hand, which makes his lips curl up. "I'm really, really happy for you. But the free desserts you buy me will be missed."

Everyone laughs.

"And I'll miss you," I add, smiling.

He flips his hand over, so he can squeeze mine once. "You're the little sister I never knew I wanted, River. But I'm glad I got you. And I'm really proud of you and everything you've accomplished."

Emotion threatens to leak from me in any way possible; tears, word vomit, sobbing. I take a few deep breaths and try avoiding the tear-filled gaze Bridgette watches us with.

"And you're the ... brother ... I've always wanted," I whisper.

I think even Ollie wants to cry.

I THINK I'M MADE OF MORE CHOCOLATE THAN WATER and blood. If a doctor tried drawing anything from my veins, I think it'd be in some form of yummy melted sugar. It's really no shock I'm bordering the "average" weight category now.

Oliver has a cup of coffee, bitter black with no cream or sugar, and a corn muffin in front of him. He's picking it apart, like there's something on his mind.

Biting into the brownie, I take my time savoring the sweet flavor. "So ... how's your girlfriend?"

A knowing smirk lifts the corners of his lips. "She's no longer holding that title since the promotion was offered to me."

"Oh. I'm sorry, Ollie."

His shoulders lift. "Honestly, I'm not surprised. She's a good girl who loves being near her family."

"But if it's love, she should want to be with you," I find myself whispering. That's what true love is—making sacrifices and changes for the other person.

His eyes are dull and sad, but he doesn't let it drag down his lips. "Oh, River. I like that you think that. But love isn't so black and white, okay? It's a complicated thing."

I lean back, frowning. "But it shouldn't be. Love is ... *love*." My voice is weak, my belief nothing but shattered expectations that I know first-hand.

Maybe he's right. Everett and I aren't black and white. We're technicolor, too blinding to sort through.

A thought crosses my mind. "Is that why you never introduced us to her?"

"Yeah. I want to make sure the girl I introduce to my family is *the one*, you know? It's ... yeah, shit, it's cheesy." He doesn't wince when he swears or tries correcting himself. "I want to show her off because I know we're it for each other, that she's the only one."

All I can do is stare at my half-eaten brownie. My appetite is nonexistent, even for chocolate, because now I'm wondering about Everett. He doesn't have family to introduce Isabel to, but has she introduced him to hers? They've been together for ten years—a whole decade. There's no way he hasn't been around her parents before.

"Hey." He taps my hand. "What's up?"

My throat tightens. "Just thinking."

He waits.

"Um ..." I force myself to break off another piece of

my brownie. The frosting on top gets on my fingers, so I lick it off. "I guess I was just wondering when you think you'll meet the one?"

I'm not thinking that at all. Though Oliver is twenty-six, he's bound to find someone eventually. And Chicago is a big city, he'll probably meet the love of his life there. My mind just doesn't want to wander to depths I can't resurface from, depths that involve my brother's best friend.

"I don't know." He takes a big bite of his muffin again, nearly finishing it. "But if you're worried that I'll somehow forget about you if I do, you're wrong. You're my sister, River. You're a big part of my life. Nobody can get in the way of that."

Wetting my bottom lip, I nod.

While the conversation is still hot, I redirect the subject. "Do you think Everett found the one? You know, with Isabel?"

His tongue clicks, like he's wondered that himself. "You know how I said love isn't black and white?" I nod. "Well, I think that applies to Everett and Isabel the most," he tells me. When he sees my confusion, he enlightens me. "Not everything is what it seems, Riv. Everett is a man of his word, and even if it kills him, he keeps it."

I'm still not sure what he means, but I don't ask. If I do, I risk him suspecting my intentions with the answers. What I do know is that Everett Tucker promised Isabel something and now he'll take that to his grave.

He deserves to be happy, but I don't think he feels the same way. And if I were him, maybe I'd think it too. Even if he decided to be happy, that doesn't mean he'd choose me.

He already did, hope whispers in my ear.

But I know better than to believe a silly thing like that.

TWENTY-TWO

Everett / 27

Painter's Choice is barely lit when I pass by after five on Friday night. Work dragged significantly since our last deal closed, which means there's a lot of sitting around and doing nothing. I texted Oliver to see if he wanted to grab some drinks, but he said he wouldn't be back in town until Sunday.

Knowing Isabel would be out with her friends like she has been every night this week, I don't feel like going back to an empty apartment. Not when I feel like the walls are caving in around me.

I turn into the studio, listening to the little bell chime. It closes in twenty-five minutes, so it doesn't surprise me to see the main room cleaned up and chairs resting upside down on the tables.

Making my way toward the back office, I'm surprised to see a blonde-haired woman sitting at the desk. When she hears me at the door, she glances up from the computer screen.

Clearing my throat, I stuff my hands in my black

slack's pockets. "Sorry, I thought someone else would be here."

She smiles, leaning back. "You're here for River, right? I've seen you around before."

"Uh, yeah."

"I'm Melanie. I work with River."

Ah, her boss. I've heard about her from River over the years. She used to tell me how much she looked up to her. I expected someone much older, but I doubt she's even forty.

"Anywho," she dismisses, "I sent River upstairs about half an hour ago. Our last class canceled on us and we haven't had any walk ins, so it's been a slow evening."

I know how that feels.

"Well, thank you."

Located on the second floor of this building, right above the art studio, is River's two-bedroom apartment. It's small, and the second bedroom doesn't have anything specific in it, like she can't decide what to do with the space. I keep offering to build her bookshelves, so she doesn't have to have her little collection of novels stacked on her desk in the bedroom, but she never lets me.

She moved in almost two years ago, though sometimes still spends the night at the James's house. I think it's nights when she's feeling off, when she needs familiarity. I wonder if she left her bed the morning after we had sex to go back to her childhood bedroom.

When she announced that the space was offered to

her, Robert and Bridgette told her she'd always have her bedroom at their house. I helped them move her stuff in, since Oliver was away. The full bed, dresser, and desk are all new courtesy of her parents. So are the small appliances like her microwave, coffee pot, and crockpot. Those Oliver and I bought her. She insisted on buying everything else—a used couch from a thrift shop down the road, a coffee table that looks like a dog gnawed on three of the four legs, and a TV stand with a miniscule television that I'm not sure even gets used.

Bridgette always makes a face when she sees the hand-me-downs littering River's apartment, but I think it suits River better than any new furniture could. She worked hard and saved money for every item she bought and fought tooth and nail on the things we got her. It took Oliver convincing her that it makes their parents feel better knowing they can provide for her. It's not a lie, not some trick to get her to submit. Naturally, River is the daughter of two of the most caring people I'll ever know. They want to make sure she's taken care of.

When my feet hit the narrow wooden steps that lead up to her apartment, I loosen my gray tie and roll my shoulders back. She won't like me showing up unexpectedly, but I won't give her another option. I'm not asking for much, just her company.

The landing just before the roughed-up door creaks under my weight as I raise my knuckles to the wood. Knocking lightly, I take a step back and listen to muffled shuffling before the deadbolt turns and the door opens.

Her lips part when she sees me, her eyes swarming with confusion and surprise, but I don't let her get a word in. "Do you want to grab a burger with me?"

She stands there staring at me with wide eyes. It gives me a second to note the black sweatpants and loose white tee she's wearing, which she must have changed into after work. Her hair is tossed into a messy bun, with a few auburn strands fallen and framing her face.

Shifting on her feet, she studies me warily. "Burgers? Is that, um, a good idea?"

"Have you eaten?"

She pauses, then shakes her head.

"Then, yes," I conclude, "I think it's a great idea. I'm hungry and your brother isn't around, so I need a dinner companion."

Once the words are out, I internally cringe. I set myself up for the skepticism crossing River's face, because we both know there's one person who *should* be my dinner companion on any given day.

Wetting my bottom lip, I jut my thumb behind me. "Listen, all I'm suggesting is a quick dinner. Neither of us have eaten, and we're friends. Friends eat together."

They also have unbelievably hot sex sometimes.

I don't add that part.

She hesitates, worrying her lips and glancing between me and the floor. Her shoulders drop, showing her resolve. That and the small sound of her rumbling stomach.

"Let me change," she finally answers, stepping aside

to let me in. I take one big step into her familiar territory before she closes the door behind me. "Um ... just, uh, make yourself comfortable. There may be some bottled water in the fridge or something if you want a drink. Which you probably don't, since we're going out and all. Not *out*, out!"

Pressing my lips together to mash down my wavering amusement, I study her reddened cheeks. She's cute when she's mumbling, and even cuter when she's embarrassed. The faint color of her blush makes her cheekbones pop in a way that highlights her natural beauty.

She closes her eyes, takes a deep breath, and then points toward her bedroom. "I'm going to stop talking now and go put on real clothes."

With that, she disappears into her room, clicking the door shut behind her. Thoughts of her beautiful body surface in my mind. Her luscious skin and full curves are unforgettable.

I settle on the couch, throwing my arm across the back and crossing my ankle over my opposite knee. Her apartment has a few photos lingering on the walls, and if memory serves, the one of her and her biological mother is in her bedroom. The ones displayed in the living room area are of Bridgette and Robert, and another of them with Oliver. On the corner of the TV stand is an image of the five of us at her graduation party, all dressed up and smiling at the camera.

I'm sure she has more, probably some of her and Stephanie or the other friends she's still in contact with.

But it seems like the people that mean the most to her are on display for everyone to see in the main room.

I smile knowing I'm still one of those people.

When her door reopens, my eyes go to the tight skinny jeans hugging her long legs. Her hips flare in a way I don't remember them doing before, and the denim is clad against her pert ass. That I *do* remember. Well. My gaze flicks to the black sweater that hangs off one of her shoulders as if it's too large for her, yet it seems to narrow into the curve of her hourglass figure unapologetically. I guess that's the style, and I have no complaints. River looks beautiful.

Her hair is still in a messy bun, which makes me smile. She usually has it down unless she's working on some art project, but I prefer it up, so she can't hide from me. I don't want her to hide around me. Not tonight, not ever.

"Ready?" I ask casually, pushing up off the couch.

"I feel underdressed," she murmurs, scoping out my typical workwear. I could have gone and changed out of my slacks, button-down, and tie, but I didn't want to. There's a chance I wouldn't have come here if I went home first.

"You look fine, River." *More than fine.* But fine seems like a safer word than beautiful, no matter how badly I want to see those cheeks pinken again.

She slides on a pair of ballet flats by the door and grabs her jacket from the iron hook on the wall. It's not cold out, but I know she freezes easily.

I open the door for her and make sure it's locked before we make our way downstairs. Melanie is just walking out of her office and waves when we head toward the front door. River has keys to the front and back doors as well as two sets to her apartment. I think she comes downstairs and paints whenever she feels the touch of her muse.

When the night air cascades around us, River is glancing at anything but me; the storefronts, the street-lights, other bystanders walking down the opposite side of the street.

"Where did you want to go?" I prompt, keeping my hands stuffed safely in my pockets. Hers are wrapped around her jacket and hugged close to her chest. She's already cold, but she doesn't want to show her discomfort.

Her response makes me chuckle. "I thought you had a plan since *you* asked *me* to dinner."

Grinning, I nudge our shoulders. "I have an idea, but I wasn't sure what you were in the mood for. Obviously, the diner has great burgers and kickass milkshakes. But Undercover East has specialty burgers."

I have a feeling I'll know which she'll pick, so I slow my pace since one of them is closer than the other.

She exhales softly. "I have been craving a chocolate milkshake for a while now."

"Diner it is."

I direct us across the street, putting my arm in front of her when a car speeds past us going well over the limit.

She rolls her eyes at my basic instinct but doesn't push my arm away. When we're inside Pop's Diner, we're greeted by Patty, one of my personal favorite waitresses, and take a seat at one of the side booths.

Neither of us look at the menus Patty sets down before we shoot off an order. Two milkshakes, one vanilla, one chocolate, and two cheeseburgers with everything on it, and fries. Patty smirks knowingly and swipes up the menus, putting in our usual. We used to come here a lot, but it has been a few months.

My eyes take in the modern diner. It's not like the fifties-style you always see on television. The walls are light yellow, the wood paneling is dark brown like the tables and chairs, and the upholstery of the booths are red. Soft music plays from the speakers at the corners of the dining room, some eighties song I don't know well.

I glance at River, who's fiddling with her thumbs on the table. "You know what would make this place even better?"

Her lips quirk. "Patty already told you that they won't cut up apples and give us peanut butter."

A grin tilts my lips at our shared love of the snack. Maybe it's stupid, possibly pathetic, but I love that we have something that's ours and *only* ours. It makes me chuckle. "I don't know, I feel like I can wear her down."

Patty shows up and sets down our milkshakes and two straws. "No, you can't. But nice try, kid."

She reminds me of Margaret, who I need to see soon. Her daughter gives me updates on her health since she's slowly slipping, which I guess is expected at eighty-two. I think she'll be gone by Christmas, and the thought tears me apart. She's the only thing I have left that's a reminder of Granddad. Of *family*.

River's voice breaks me out of the heartbreaking thought. "Are you okay?"

"Fine."

She knows I'm lying but chooses not to comment. "Thanks for suggesting this. I was just going to pour myself some cereal."

"Let me guess," I muse, "Frosted Flakes?"

She ducks her head. "Maybe."

I poke her with her unopened straw. "Thought so. I'm surprised you haven't had a cavity with all the sweets you eat."

Now she makes eye contact with me, her lips twitching in amusement. "And who's to blame for that? Those candy bars didn't just magically appear in my locker."

"It's plausible."

"Mmhm."

"And," I add, "you're welcome. I truthfully didn't want to go home and heat up leftovers. I've needed a burger for a solid week now."

"Why haven't you gotten one then?"

I shrug. "Been busy."

Plus, I cooked for Issy and me. Three times out of the week, she would leave right after getting home from work, leaving me alone to eat chicken salad or garlic roasted pork chops. Hell, if I knew she was going to give me the cold shoulder, I would have made burgers sooner or grilled up some steak.

Changing the subject seems necessary right now, before the tension grows in the silence. "How's everything been with work and school? Oliver mentioned you've been swamped."

After Oliver announced the big move to his family, he called me up and we made plans to grab lunch. I can't say I'm surprised that he wants to get out of the state. He loves his family, but he loves traveling more. It's all he ever talked about growing up.

"Bridgeport just doesn't have what I need, you know?"

I don't know, because Bridgeport has the very thing I need and it's sitting across from me right now.

"I've been using the classes I teach with the foster kids as experience toward my field hours and student teaching for school," she explains. She proceeds to tell me about doubling her credits to try graduating a semester early, but she doesn't think she can. I tell her she can do anything. She blushes again.

Knowing River's determination means she'll succeed. She's driven to prove herself to the world, to the people in her past who told her she'll never make it. Now she has not only a high school diploma and bachelor's degree, she's about to have a master's degree, too. As far as I'm concerned, they can kiss her ass.

We're quiet after our food arrives, concentrating on the steaming plates in front of us. I want to tease her when she dips her fry into her milkshake. She used to call me disgusting when I would do that very same thing.

"So ... how are things with you?" she inquires after nibbling on her pile of fries. Patty knows how much she loves them, so she always gets more than the usual helping, which means I can steal some.

Swallowing my burger and wiping off my mouth and fingers with a napkin, I give her a small nod. "Good."

"Good. That's ... yeah, good."

More silence.

I sigh. "Things shouldn't be weird between us, River."

She meets my eyes. "I disagree."

"Fine. Let's talk about it."

"Talk about why I disagree?"

I nod once.

She stares at me like I'm crazy.

"Okay," I press, "I'll start. We've been friends for, what? Ten years. We've eaten lunch together too many times to count. I know what it's like to see you closed up, and what it's like to see you pissed off. Frankly, I've seen everything in between. This—" I gesture between us with my pointer finger. "—is bullshit. We're *friends*. Nothing has changed."

"*Everything* has changed, Everett."

"Why?"

Her eyes narrow. "You know why." She says it under her breath, side-eying an older couple sitting near us at the counter as if they care what we're talking about.

"What we did is natural. It's—"

"*Cheating*," she hisses under her breath, voice cracking and pained.

I cringe at the word, at the reality and truth of it. It makes my chest ache in ways I can't describe. Not for me, for Issy.

"What?" she doubts, breaking a fry in half and staring at the soft interior. "I'm sorry if you don't like that word, but it's what we did. We both know it."

"I'm not denying that."

"Then don't deny that it was a mistake."

"It—" I shut my mouth when she shoots daggers at me for trying to do exactly what she said not to. But I want to drill it in her head that it's a lot of things—perfect, heart stopping, memory inducing, but *not* a mistake.

Leaning over my half-eaten burger, I lock eyes with her. "I have done a lot of shit things in my life, and I won't deny that hurting Isabel is one of them. But things between us are complicated beyond understanding, River."

"So uncomplicate them."

"It's not that simple."

"Why?"

I don't answer, instead, I lean back and pick up my burger to take another bite.

River wraps her hand around her glass and shakes her head. "I want to understand why you're with a woman that you don't love. You've told me over and over that you do, but I don't buy it. Nobody does, Everett, except Robert."

Telling River about the promise I made to Isabel is going to ruin the perfect night we're having. In fact, this entire conversation could take a turn for the worse. It could sever our friendship completely. I would ruin her if she ever found out the truth.

"I do love her," is what I come up with.

"Bull."

"I do," I grind out, jaw ticking. Sighing, I set my burger back down and rub my jaw. "I will always have a special place in my heart for Isabel, okay? We've been through a lot together. Ten years of being in a relationship means a lot to people, to us. It means we have a lot of history."

River plays with the lettuce on her burger, which only has a few tiny bites taken out of it. "I can see that," she admits. "But I also know that's your default answer when the real one is too much for you to admit."

Drawing back like I've been struck, I stare blankly at her. "What are you talking about?"

Her dinner is now long forgotten as she meets my confused gaze. "When I was fourteen, you told me I'd always be your number one. Do you remember that?" I nod. "When I was fifteen, you told me I'd always have you. In fact, you say that to me at least five times a year. Not that I'm counting or anything. Then, when I was sixteen, you told me you rejected me because I deserved someone better, someone my age who was worth my time. But my favorite is just shy of my high school graduation, when you came up to my bedroom after I walked in on you and Isabel kissing by the pool while Ollie and that chick he was with at the time swam. You knew I was upset, said I had every right to be, but do you remember what you said right after that?"

My mouth seems impossibly dry right now, and my throat feels like something is jammed in it. Emotion. That's what it is.

"You'll always have a special place in my heart, River." That's what I told her that night after seeing her distraught face. That single sentence eased some of her pain like I hoped it would. It wasn't a lie. River James will always have a special place in my heart. Just like Issy.

She dunks another fry in her milkshake. "So, you see, that's what you tell people when you can't face the truth. It's a cop-out."

My fists automatically clench at the accusation. "That isn't a cop-out, River. It's far from it."

Her brow raises, as if to say, *is that so?*

I shove my plate away from me, and it clinks into my untouched milkshake that's more like cold soup at this point. "I can't explain to you how ridiculous it is that you don't see how much you mean to me. I don't tell just anyone that they have a place in my heart. I'm not an asshole."

Her silence is like a slap to the face.

Finally, she replies, "It seems like you're just as lost as me. Sometimes I wonder if we're too much alike, trying to find our ways in this heinous world. But then I think how stupid I'm being, because we're nothing alike. You have friends. You have a girlfriend. You have a nice apartment, a great job, money, and a future. What do I have? A crush on somebody who I can't be with. Who isn't mine to have feelings for, but the very person I can never get enough of."

Her words halt my breathing. "I've always been yours, River."

She shakes her head, tucking strands of hair behind her ear. "You were never mine."

I watch her sip on her milkshake and eat her fries and nibble on her burger, all while she avoids looking at me.

"Tell you what," I bargain, "I'll tell you about Isabel and me when you tell me about the scars I know you're hiding under your clothes."

She sucks in a breath.

"Yeah," I murmur more harshly than I intended, "didn't think so."

I ask for the check.

TWENTY-THREE

River / 23

Walking out of the Leavenworth Liberal Arts building on campus, I note the dark clouds rolling across the gray sky. I'm not even half way to the bus stop when a raindrop hits my cheek, then all hell breaks loose, leaving me bolting to the nearest building.

Drenched and cursing at myself when I see my ruined notes from class, I glance out the double doors I'm hiding behind and watch the rain shower the earth. Sighing, I set my stuff down on a plastic chair against the wall and ring out my thick hair, tying it up in a bun so the wet strands don't cling to my neck and cheeks.

My cell phone died an hour ago. I can practically hear Bridgette chastising me in my head about how I should always carry a charger in my bag. Half the time, I don't even use my phone, much less remember where my charger is.

A black clock on the wall tells me it's almost eight pm. I'm not sure when the rain will let up, but it doesn't look like any time soon. Clearly, I chose the wrong day to walk to school.

Robert always tells me to check the weather before I leave my apartment. I didn't do that either. *Go me.*

Before I figure out my next move, the other set of double doors across the tiny entry open behind me.

There's a grumbled murmur before a familiar voice says, "River?"

My body stiffens as I turn to face Isabel. She's in a raincoat, because *she* must have watched the weather channel. Her dark hair is highlighted with caramel strands and pulled off to one side. She's got on shiny black rain boots that reach her mid-shin, protecting her tight jeans from the oncoming rain.

Clearing my throat, I give her a lame little wave. "H-Hi, Isabel. Um, what are you doing here?"

It's none of my business, and I don't expect her to answer. Everett isn't here for her to put up a front. She can be as mean and miserable as she wants.

Shifting her large, expensive-looking purse over her shoulder, she glances between me and the outside doors. "I've got an old college friend that works here. She's a biology professor."

I nod, unsure of what to say. Cool? I hope you had a nice visit? I stick with silence.

She sighs, and I can only imagine it's in irritation. "Do you need a ride or something?"

My eyes widen over her kind offer. "Oh, um, n-no. I'm good. I'm sure the rain will let up soon."

Studying me for a moment, she finally blows out a sharp breath and then shakes her head. "It's supposed to storm the rest of the night. Come on, I'm parked in the visitor parking just over there."

My stomach bottoms out. Being alone in a car with Isabel Allen sounds terrifying, and not just because she obviously hates me. She seems like the kind of person who can smell fear and guilt, and I'm sweating it from every pore at this point. I mean, I slept with her boyfriend of ten years, the guy she's supposed to marry one day. What kind of person does that make me?

"I really don't think—"

"Everett would kill me if I left you here. Just because we're not on great terms doesn't mean I want him to hate me any more than he already does." Once the words are out, she winces and swears. "Forget I said that. Grab your stuff and let's go."

But I can't forget. She's more open about whatever is going on between them than Everett, and it doesn't sit well with me. For some crazy reason, I begin gathering my things and follow her to the doors. She hits the unlock button as we speed walk toward the black sports car and we both quickly climb in.

The sound of the rain splattering against the car is the only thing I focus on as I buckle the seatbelt. She's quiet too as she starts the vehicle and blasts the heat, then turns on the lights and wipers.

I clench my soiled notebooks in my lap and look out the window as she pulls out of the spot and toward the road leading off campus. Most people are out of classes by this time of night, though some grad students have classes until almost ten. Been there, done that. I switched to earlier classes and made it work around my studio schedule. Thankfully, I have no social life to ruin.

Isabel reaches out for the radio, but then pulls her hand away. "Do you like music?"

My brows arch. "Y-Yeah?"

She gives me a funny look. "Can I ask you a question?"

Everything inside me stops. My heart lurches to my throat and chokes me, but somehow, I nod, despite the fear clenching my stomach.

Her hands wrap tightly around the steering wheel. "Did you see Everett last week for dinner?"

Relief filters through my body. I thought her suspicion of our escapades was about to be announced in the form of screaming. "We went to the diner for burgers," I answer quietly.

"At least *you're* telling the truth."

Did Everett lie to her about our innocent dinner?

"He told me he was at the fire station," she informs me quietly, as if reading my mind. Her voice is nothing more than a murmur, and I detect humility in her, emotions I haven't seen her wear before.

I'm an awful person.

Feeling bad for her, I try relinquishing some of her doubt. "He might have gone after we ate. He left before he finished eating and I don't know if he went home or not. I mean ... I guess he didn't, or you'd know. So, yeah. He probably went to the station."

Heat creeps into my cheeks over my rambling. I'm pretty sure she doesn't care, she normally wouldn't. But her eyes do seem to lighten over the idea.

He purposefully held back telling her we had dinner together. Isabel already hates me for some unknown reason. I'll never be her favorite person and he probably didn't want to start another fight between the two of them.

There's a burning question that I tell myself not to ask, but my heart outweighs my brain's sense of logic. "Do you love him?"

For the first time since we got into the car, she turns her focus fully on me. "Of course I do, River. That's a stupid question."

I wet my chapped bottom lip. It stings but I ignore it. "I just ..."

"What?" she snaps, and I feel slightly better knowing she sounds like herself again. It quickly goes away when those narrowed eyes burn mine like oil to a fire.

Fiddling with my hands on my lap, I take a deep breath. "I just know that you two aren't, uh, engaged or anything and you mentioned that you haven't been on great terms. Sometimes people ... fall out of love, I guess. It happened with my brother."

Using Oliver as a cover is weak, and I acknowledge that. But telling Isabel what she's suspected for years now —that I'm in love with her boyfriend—is not an option, especially not in a moving vehicle she's currently operating.

"Oliver and Everett aren't alike when it comes to relationships." Her tone isn't as bitter as I expected. It's level and oddly calm. "Everett and I have gone through ... some stuff. We've broken up and gotten back together and have a lot of baggage."

"What makes you come back?"

Her laugh is cold, chilling away any humanity she showed before. "*He* comes back to *me*. I admit, I only got together with him in the first place because he was a mystery. Girls like mysteries, right?" She doesn't wait for me to answer. "But then I got him, and then his grandpa died and he got ... I don't know, dark? Lonely? The excitement of it all kind of faded."

She shrugs. "I think that's when we started having problems. His version of fun and mine are different. I thought he should go out and do stuff to get his mind off his family, but he wanted to sit around and mope. Then when I went out, he would get all pissed that I wasn't with him. But I ... guess I sort of get it. I remember what you said at your birthday party I went to, about how family is important. I'm not an idiot like a lot of people believe. Everett loved his grandpa more than anything in the world, more than me. Nothing I could do would make him feel better.

"You know, when he left Bridgeport for college, I thought for sure we'd break up, but he didn't want to. He said he needed something that connected him to home. It made me feel loved for once in my life. That's when I really knew how I felt, that I knew we were meant to be together forever."

He wanted something that connected him to home. The words sucker punch me in the gut. I was fourteen when he left. What did I expect? I couldn't be that person for him.

I know he and Isabel visited each other a lot and would hang out with Oliver and the other friends they made at Penn. Ollie would tell me how annoying she was whenever we chatted over the phone and mention how he's surprised Everett can stand her clingy personality.

"But yeah," she concludes as she slows down to pull onto the street I live on, "I love him. I probably shouldn't, because he doesn't show it, but I never exactly had the role models to show me what real love is anyway. Despite how weird he's been with me lately, I think he loves me too. Just in his own unique way."

He says he does.

But do I believe it?

She puts the car in park outside Painter's Choice and turns to me. "I know you don't owe me anything. I haven't been very nice to you over the years. Or, you know, at all. But can you try convincing Everett to just tell me how he feels. *Really* tell me. I don't want to guess anymore."

My heart thumps so loudly in my chest I wonder if she hears it. It hurts, and I'm half-tempted to peer down to see if I can watch it propel right out of me.

She stares at me.

Thumpthump.

Her brows raise.

Thumpthump.

My lips part. "I-I'll see what I can do."

Her smile is weirdly genuine.

"T-Thanks for the ride."

When I'm safely inside my pitch-black apartment, I sit on the couch. There's a weight on my chest that has been lingering since the night Everett stayed over. Since we …

Closing my eyes, I brush my fingers where I feel like a red A should be.

It's ironic that I stole Everett's copy of *The Scarlet Letter* when I was thirteen. I lied about finishing it. I wonder if Hester ever gets her happily ever after?

OLIVER'S TWENTY-SEVENTH BIRTHDAY GET-TOGETHER doubles as his going-away party. On May third, the day before his actual birthday, everyone gathers in the back-yard of the James estate and barbecues, swims, drinks, and celebrates Oliver's achievements.

Everett is late. Not that I'm looking for him. It's just hard *not* to notice someone so prominent missing. Plus, I've been avoiding him. Or, trying to. Ever since Isabel asked me to talk to him for her, I haven't given myself a chance to be alone with him. Deep down, I know I owe it to her to fix whatever they do have between them.

After all, Everett makes choices every day to stay

with her. The glaring truth is that he'll always pick her, whether he believes I'm his or not.

He called me the day after Isabel dropped me off and asked how I was. I told him I had to go, that class was starting. It wasn't. Then he texted me the same night and asked if I was at the studio. I told him I was meeting up with friends. Afraid he would come by, I forced myself out with a few people I go to school with. I had water, they had shots, and I went home an hour later so it wasn't a lie.

Two days ago, Melanie mentioned that Everett stopped by to see me. I actually was out with a study group preparing for a final exam. I never called him back or answered his text when I got home. I ate, changed, and went to bed.

I don't like not talking to Everett. But keeping quiet seems like the logical option. If I do what Isabel asks, I risk losing him forever. If I don't ... well, the fantasy lasts.

But so does the guilt.

One of the girls I hung out with the other night during our study group, Emma, asked if I'd be willing to go out with one of her guy friends. She wants to do a double date, and go bowling, but I told her I'd have to think about it.

I should say yes. I haven't been bowling before, as embarrassing as that is to admit. I should text her and say that I would love to go, because how else am I going to move on from the man I can't have?

But you did have him.

And therein lies the problem. For one night, for less than twelve hours, I had Everett Tucker. I felt his smooth skin and his hard edges and his gentle touches and demanding kisses. One night would never be enough.

But it will have to be.

Pulling out my phone, I click on Emma's name and take a deep breath. **If you still want to do that double date, I'm in.**

I don't wait for her response before turning off my phone and setting it on the plastic table by the lounge chair. Walking over to the pool, I sit on the edge and sink my legs into the heated water.

It's unusually warm for May. The winter was rough, nothing like the nonexistent one I had when I first arrived here. It stayed below zero the better half of December and January, and stormed and flurried most of February and March. Thankfully, California saved me from most of the horrid temperatures. April couldn't decide what it wanted to do, but as soon as May hit, it was sunny skies and eighty-degree weather.

Someone splashes me and laughs. Looking over, I see Oliver swimming over to me with a wicked smile splicing his face in two. When I see the mischief flash in his brown eyes, I try pushing away but I'm too late.

He yanks on my leg until I'm pulled into the water with him. Thankfully, I'm wearing a dark t-shirt and cut off shorts. Nothing would show, not my scars or something inappropriate.

Steph kept her promise to teach me how to swim. We

used her pool and she showed me how to float and then doggy paddle. She never made me wear swimsuits, though I have occasionally. Only around her, since she knows what I hide on my skin anyway. I keep a few suits at her house for when I want to cool off when she visits her parents, but that's not often these days. She got a job as a personal assistant to some rising Hollywood actor in Cali.

Oliver laughs when I try brushing my hair out of my face, but its heavy and sticking to my cheeks. "You look like a drowned dog."

Frowning, I wring it out. "I wonder why."

He feigns innocence.

"I can't believe you're leaving tomorrow," I murmur, swimming back over to the edge and leaning against the side.

Leave it to Ollie to move on his birthday. I guess he'll be starting his new job first thing Monday morning, so he wants to give himself time to settle into the apartment and get a lay of the land. That means in twenty-four hours, I'll have to say goodbye to the very first person who I considered a friend.

He swims up next to me, mimicking my casual stance and throwing his arms up to rest against the warm pavement. His hair is wet, making the brown shade look almost black. Little droplets of water cascading off his body hit the patio behind him and dissolve instantly.

"It does seem pretty crazy." His eyes rake the yard, like he's memorizing every nook and cranny.

I nudge his side with my elbow. "I'm going to miss you, Ollie."

His eyes turn to me and a soft smile tips his lips, making his little dimple pop out. I wish I had one like it. Robert has one too, on the opposite side.

"I'll miss you too." He splashes me with water, making me laugh and splash him back. "I know it'll be pretty weird here for a while, but you can always call me. Okay? We can Facetime if you want, too."

My nose scrunches. He knows how much I hate technology. But I will take him up on the offer to call. We may not talk often as it is now because I don't like being a bother, but not speaking to him at all may kill me.

Before I say anything, his attention shifts behind us. "Well, it's about time."

Brows pinched, I turn to see what he's talking about. Everett is shaking hands with one of Robert's friends. His dark wash jeans fit his long legs well and the plain white tee hugs his muscular arms in a way that has my heart doing little flips in my chest. Pressing my lips together, I wait for Isabel to walk out behind him from the house.

She doesn't.

Oliver hops out of the pool, leaving me alone with my thoughts. Like noticing how Everett's hair looks brown today, and I wonder if it's wet like he just got out of the shower or if he has some sort of gel in it. The top kinda flops everywhere like it's styled, so my guess is the hair products.

Ollie and Everett clap hands and say something to each other. I force my gaze away and stare at the rippling water as I move my palm back and forth. It distracts me, which is what I need.

Suddenly, a wet strand of hair is flicked off my shoulder. My gaze snaps up to Everett, who's kneeling next to me. One of his tan elbows is resting on his bent knee; the other is hanging loose beside him. His smile is white and broad and friendly.

He looks ... different.

"Hey, River."

"Hi." My eyes go around him. "So, um, where is Isabel?"

His lips twitch microscopically. "She couldn't make it."

I can only think to nod. Not letting my mind take me to the reason for her absence, I note someone waving in our direction. Reid something-or-other. Another friend of Robert.

When Oliver notices him, he waves back and tells us he'll catch up with us later. Leaving Everett and me alone is not a good idea. Who knows what will leave my mouth?

As Ollie gets farther away, I feel my heart pick up speed. Every surface of my body becomes hyperaware of how close Everett is. Even if my brain tells me to stay away from him, my body ... I've never been able to control my reaction to him.

He doesn't give me a chance to speak. "I was hoping we could talk. Do you mind?"

I swallow. "Um, now?"

"Preferably."

"Here?"

He rubs his jaw. "I was actually thinking somewhere quieter. Want to go inside? It looks like you could dry off."

Déjà vu hits me, taking me back to the night of my graduation party. It was the first time Everett touched me in a less-than-innocent way. I felt my mouth burn where he touched me for months after that.

The tiny voice in my head tells me not to do it; to turn him down instead. What could he possibly have to say to me? But I shut that voice away, and let Everett help me out of the pool and into the house.

To my surprise, Everett follows me upstairs. When I get to my room, I glance over my shoulder at him. His hands are stuffed in the pockets of his jeans and his expression is light, eased compared to normal.

"I can wait ..."

Shaking my head, I blow out a tiny breath as I open my door. "I'll, uh, change in the bathroom. You can come in."

Bad idea, my inner voice tells me.

I ignore it.

He follows me in and sits on my old bed. I still have clothes hanging in the closet for when I stay here, so I grab a white sundress with yellow sunflowers on it and head into the bathroom.

It doesn't take me long to peel out of my wet clothes and dry off. I'm in my sundress with my wet hair in a bun and heading back toward the door in less than five minutes. Everett is still sitting on the edge of my mattress, his long legs bent over the side and arms resting beside him as he leans back. When I walk out, he straightens and smiles.

"You look ..." His eyes take in the basic cotton dress. It stops mid-thigh, probably too short to wear, but it'll keep me cool. "Beautiful," he finishes in a quiet tone.

Rubbing my wrist, I take a seat next to him. Our legs accidently brush and my heart bursts, forcing me to take a sharp breath.

Walk away, the voice commands.

I sit still.

Everett turns, his leg lifting slightly on the bed, so his knee is pressed against my upper thigh. Swallowing seems hard when all of my emotions are crammed into my throat.

His large hand rests on his knee. "Isabel went back to her parents' house last night. We, uh, got into a pretty bad argument."

I stop breathing.

His eyes sweep the room. "She hasn't called or texted and I think ..." Finally, we lock eyes. "No, I *know* that we're through. She never leaves. And she has every right."

Tell him you don't care, the voice pleads.

But I do.

"You broke up?" My voice is nothing more than a raspy whisper. The words taste funny in my mouth and my heart doesn't drum as hard as I thought it would.

His head bobs once.

Oh my God.

Isabel and Everett broke up.

Everett is *in my old room.*

His hand moves to mine, which rests on the comforter between us. He links our fingers, and the sensations tingling down my arm make my heart start beating faster in my chest with anticipation.

"W-What does that mean?"

He shifts closer, his nose nuzzling my ear until I think I die a little. "It means that I can do this without you pushing me away."

I don't get a chance to ask him what he means before his lips are crushing mine in a heated, rough, all-consuming kiss. My lips part almost immediately and his tongue slips in and tangles with mine. I moan when he threads his fingers in my hair and bites down on my lower lip. He tastes like peppermint and smells like pine, which means he spent time at his Granddad's old cabin.

He grips my hips and lifts me until I'm straddling his lap. One of his arms hooks around my waist as the other dives back into my hair for a bruising kiss. My body takes over and shuts out the voice that's begging me to stop this madness, grinding into his hardness that's pressing against the softest part of me.

A low, hungry growl is what I'm rewarded with. I rock my hips over him again until his fists tighten in my hair and he tips my head back and nips my neck.

"Fuck, you feel amazing on top of me," he groans, meeting my movements until we're both panting.

I'm burning with need between my legs, trying to get the friction I so desperately desire to ease the pressure.

"Everett," I plea, threading my fingers through his hair and keeping the rhythm I've set against his erection. The rough material of his jeans has my eyes rolling back as my movements become jerky.

Before the night with Everett, I only fooled around a little with one guy. Before that was Asher Wilks when I was sixteen. My experience is limited, and it makes this need so much stronger.

"I've got you, baby," he whispers, his kisses becoming sweeter, gentler, as he slips a hand between us. My hips push into his palm as he reaches under my dress and moans when he realizes I never put on panties.

"So fucking wet," he notes as he runs his fingers over my slick heat and circles my clit in slow, circular motions. I'm so turned on it isn't funny. In fact, it actually hurts, this need for him. It's nothing like I've ever felt before, and when he finally slides his fingers into my arousal, I buck my hips into him and ride out the sensations.

He slides one finger in and out of me until I'm whimpering his name and digging my fingertips into his scalp. When he slides in a second finger and hooks them, I gasp loudly and writhe on his lap.

"Beautiful," he repeats in a strangled voice, kissing me and claiming me and picking up the pace with his fingers.

I ride his hand, meeting him thrust for thrust until my legs start to quake. "Oh God, Everett. That feels so good. Don't stop. Please don't stop. I-I'm going to—"

I don't finish the sentence before he circles my clit with his thumb and presses down, making me come harder than I ever have before. I'm about to cry out loudly when he captures my mouth with his, drowning out the orgasm with a searing kiss.

He keeps his fingers inside me as I ride out the wave and my hips settle again, and then pulls them out ever so slowly, kisses me gently, and puts both of his fingers in his mouth. His eyes flash as I watch him taste me. It's the most erotic thing I've ever seen, and mixed with my pounding heart, I think it might just end me.

Before we can say anything, Bridgette calls my name. Her voice sounds close, like she's nearing my room. Jumping off Everett's lap, I panic and look around.

"The bathroom!" I whisper, yanking on his arm to get him to move with no luck.

Amusement flickers across his face as he watches me have a heart attack. "I'm not hiding, River. We didn't do anything wrong."

Bridgette's heels click right outside my bedroom and the knob turns with a soft knock before cracking open.

Everett quickly adjusts himself in his jeans and leans back, looking innocent like we didn't just fool around in my childhood bedroom.

B. CELESTE

Bridgette peeks in and smiles when she sees us. "Oh. Hi, Everett. Sorry, I was just checking in. Someone said you were up here changing." She turns to me, seemingly not suspicious of anything. "If you give me your soaked clothes, I'll throw them in the wash for you to take home before the night is over."

Nodding, I turn on my heel to collect my clothes that are heaped in a pile on the bathroom floor. Before I head back in, I stop short when I hear Bridgette talking to Everett.

"Isabel is downstairs," she tells him softly, causing me to hold my breath. "She says she's been trying to reach you. You better go see her, she looks worried."

I told you so, the voice murmurs.

Tears well in my eyes. Everett sees me standing in the cracked doorway, his eyes hollow and wide. Did they really break up or did he just tell me that?

Jaw quivering, I fight off the tears. Taking a deep breath, I walk out and pass Bridgette my clothes.

She pulls my cell out of her pocket. "I saved this from getting wet. Your brother is showing the young Calloway twins how to do cannon balls in the pool."

Accepting it, I just nod. Forcing out a *thank you* is too hard and I'm afraid it'll say too much. My voice will crack and show how much I hurt, how much I'm shattering and splintering internally.

When it's just Everett left sitting in my room, he bolts up with an unreadable expression on his face. "River, I—"

"*Leave.*"

"I can—"

"Please leave," I whimper, barely able to hold it together for another second longer. My hands shake as they clutch my phone and he reaches out but I quickly move away.

His touch would burn me, and not in a good way.

He realizes I won't relent and rakes a hand through his hair before walking out of my room. Sitting on my bed, I wipe away a few stray tears and power on my phone again.

There's a message from Emma about the double date waiting for me when it loads.

David can't wait to meet you!

My chest aches. **I can't wait either.**

TWENTY-FOUR

Everett / 27

The walls of my apartment are closing in around me. They have been since I got back from Oliver's going-away party with Isabel hot on my tail. What's worse than that was stepping into the building only to see her father glaring daggers at me and telling Issy to go inside while we chat.

Nobody wants to be on the bad side of Blake Allen, which is why I've done everything in my power to stay on good terms with him. To say Isabel's appearance at the party after she packed a bag and left to her parents was surprise enough, but Blake?

Fuck.

It's plenty bad having to relive the moment of River's absolute dissolve. I didn't lie to her—would never lie to her—but for the first time in ten years, I don't think she believed me. In fact, her clear rejection makes me wonder if the trust we've always shared is gone for good.

All because of Blake Allen.

I knew there was a reason Issy put up with my shit. Hell, I put up with hers over the years too. After meeting

Blake and Gianna, I knew where Isabel's tenacity came from. She was raised to get the best in life and never settle for anything less, which made me wonder why the hell she wanted me. But then circumstances changed and Issy and I were tied together in ways neither of us expected. Her parents found out and encouraged me to propose, to cement our future.

Then everything went to shit.

Blake showing up sent me into a downward spiral to rock bottom. Between hurting River and then getting sucked back into the world of the Allens, I had no idea what to do. And when Mr. Allen gave me the black velvet box that contained a cherished Allen heirloom, I knew what he expected. No, what he *demanded*.

"It's time, Everett. You've had ample opportunity to live your life, but it's time for you and my daughter to live one together."

Honestly, the words didn't sink in until he slapped the box in my hand and walked away. The ring I have yet to look at weighs on me just thinking about sliding it onto Isabel's finger, and I know I've cornered myself for good.

I'll always be here for you.

And I have been.

There's a soft knock on the door before Issy pops her head in. We haven't spoken much since the party or her father's visit. I think she's giving me space. She must know what he gave me, but she doesn't say anything.

Until now. "It was inevitable, wasn't it?"

Our marriage. "Why now?"

"Why *not* now?" she argues, sitting down next to me

on the mattress. "When you said you wanted to wait until you graduated college, I waited. Then you said you wanted to settle into your new position at the company, so I waited longer. You barely showed any enthusiasm when I finally moved in, and I chalked it up to the death of your bachelor pad. But what's the excuse now?"

The truth is on the tip of my tongue, and I'm two seconds away from saying River's name when she says it instead.

"I asked River to talk to you, you know." Her statement shocks me, grabbing my full attention. "The night I drove her home from campus, I asked her for a favor. But she never spoke to you and then I found out you kept lying to me about where you were, and I lost it. Can't you see we're perfect for each other?"

A dry laugh bubbles from my pressed lips. "How are we perfect for each other? We do nothing but fight."

"We both know what it's like to lose someone important to us," she whispers, her palm moving absentmindedly to her stomach.

Closing my eyes, I feel her move my hand on top of where hers rests. There's nothing there but a memory of what our future almost held. And, sure, I would have given her a ring if fate hadn't intervened ... but it did.

"We've lost so much." Her voice cracks. "I don't want to keep losing you, Rhett. You promised I wouldn't lose you."

My heart pounds in my chest as emotions threaten to pour from my tear ducts. I did promise her that. She needed me the most the day she found out she was pregnant, and we needed each other even more the day she miscarried.

It took months before either of us were ready to go back to normal. Normal being stupid fights about equally stupid things. We were stronger because of the loss of our unborn baby but spiraled out of control since. I tell myself not to break my promise, to stay because I know she needs me, but it gets harder the further we seem to drift apart.

Isabel Allen doesn't need me at all.

She needs *love*. A love I can't, and won't, be capable of ever giving her.

"You deserve the world, Issy."

Her shoulders tense. "I deserve a man who's as dedicated as you. That's why my father gave you the ring. Don't you get it? They approve, even after everything."

But they shouldn't.

It eats at me that Blake Allen is adamant about me marrying Isabel. I haven't proved shit to him, and I admit as much. I work hard, almost too hard, so I can support myself and prove to the disloyal assholes at the company I'm just as good as they are.

"Don't you think it's strange your family supports our less than stable relationship? How many times have you gone to them when I was treating you like an asshole?"

Her lips twist downward. "They know that nobody is perfect. Look at them, Rhett. You see how they are as a couple. Plus, Daddy loves how invested you are in our future. He knows I'll be well taken care of when you get the company."

And there it is.

Blake Allen wants to be tied to me because I'll be the CEO when Robert retires, since Oliver wants nothing to do with it. Between the money I got from my parents' and Granddad's death, along with the trust fund left in my name from my father's share in JT Corporation, I'm set for life. With a shiny title like CEO next to my name, someone as greedy as Blake Allen can associate with me and get the type of clients his business is sorely lacking.

He doesn't give a fuck about his daughter's happiness.

Removing my hand from her hold, I shift to face her better. "Can I be frank with you?"

"Of course."

"Your father is a dickhead."

Her lips part.

"And, yeah, I'm not much better," I add, giving a terse shrug. I won't bullshit her right now, because her dad and I aren't as different as I'd like to admit. "But at least I want you to be happy. He just wants my money, to be related to me when I have a better title. Can't you see that he's using you?"

Her jaw clenches and teeth grind as she stands. When she flattens out her white blouse and flips her hair over her shoulder, I know I'm in for fight number one million and two.

"You're right," she snaps, "you're no better. Obviously,

you think I'm stupid. But I can tell that you're using me, too."

She walks over to the dresser and pulls something out of the wooden jewelry box I bought her that rests on top. Storming back over to me, she shoves a white piece of paper into my chest.

"I know damn well you didn't buy anything for me," she hisses, causing me to glance down at the receipt from the jeweler in town. It's from when I bought the broken heart charm for River. "But for a microsecond, I had hope that maybe you were buying a ring. So, yeah. Maybe I am as stupid as you think I am."

"Isabel—"

"Screw you, Everett."

She walks out of the room.

But it isn't the end—not like it should be. Blake Allen has warped his daughter's mind to believe that love shouldn't factor into marriage, and the thought pains me. Just not as much as breaking my promise will.

Crumpling the receipt up and throwing it behind me onto the bed, I rest my face in my open palms. "Give me some fucking guidance," I groan into the empty air.

Nothing happens.

TWENTY-FIVE

River / 23

David Chen is a twenty-six-year-old post grad student who's working on his PhD in Education. He's of Asian descent, his hair and eyes are the same shade of brown-black, and his skin is the kind of natural tan that makes me look albino standing next to him. Not that it's hard to do with my milky complexion, I guess. At least he's not much taller than my five-five stature. I'd guess five-nine or five-ten, so he's taller than me without making me feel like an albino *and* a midget.

I almost backed out until I called Steph and she gave me her version of tough love. Her put-on-your-big-girl-panties pep talk made me laugh in a way only she could accomplish. Our conversation should have lasted ten minutes tops, but my freak out led to her pressing me for the real reason I called. Steph knows me better than to believe I'm nervous about meeting a guy. New people will always terrify me, but Emma and her boyfriend Luke would be with us. I know Emma wouldn't put me in any type of danger.

I spilled my guts about Everett. And, of course, there

were a lot of questions regarding his anatomy. Questions that I'm glad she couldn't see me blush over. But as soon as I mentioned what happened between us at Ollie's party, her Mama Bear mode turned on and she cussed Everett's name.

To my surprise, she didn't tell me what a huge mistake I made. She never judged or told me I was going hell. Then again, I didn't expect her to. When she congratulated me and said I had to compare penis sizes with David, I knew she didn't think differently of me.

"You've loved him forever, River. The important thing is that you acknowledge when to cut your losses."

But I didn't. I mean, not really. I could have, *should have*, cut my losses when Everett offered to walk me home that night from the café. I *should have* waved him goodbye instead of inviting him upstairs. I *should have* stopped him from brushing his fingers against the broken heart charm on my chest.

I let my heart do the talking that night when I threaded our fingers together on my chest, when I stepped into his warmth, and when I let him lift my hair up to unclasp the necklace from my neck.

Nothing but skin.

So, no. I took too long to cut the losses I should have snipped that night, and maybe even long before then. Isabel Allen has been Everett's since they were teenagers. I was naïve to think I could love him from afar, like it wouldn't matter to me that he stayed with her.

David Chen is nothing like Everett, even though he's

only a year younger than him. He's lively and fun and dorky. Hearing the story of how Emma met him in undergrad at some small college downstate makes me laugh as we eat cheese pizza at the bowling alley. When Emma and her boyfriend find out I don't know how to bowl, they tease me mercilessly.

Emma and Luke are not originally from Bridgeport, both having traveled from other states to attend school here. Maybe if we were in business classes, they would recognize my last name as being one of the founding families. But to my small group of academia friends, I'm just River—an awkward, introverted loner who's been sheltered her entire life.

If they only knew.

Emma and Luke laugh as I try holding the mint green bowling ball. It was the only one they had left, which seems kind of cruel.

David comes up behind me. "Want me to show you?"

He takes the ball and demonstrates how to hold it properly. I'm glad he doesn't put his arms behind me or guide my arm back. He's giving me personal space, not pushing. When I do as he says, I let it go too early and it rolls the wrong way.

Emma squeaks and pulls her legs up before the ball strikes her feet. My face burns in apology when I quickly fetch the ball and try brushing off their loud cackling. It *is* kind of funny, but mostly embarrassing.

David gives me one more pointer before gesturing for me to try again. This time I get a split, which seems perfectly named because there's no way I can knock out the pins still standing on the opposite ends. I try. Gutter ball.

By the end of the second game, Emma and Luke dominate. Turns out, neither David nor I are good at bowling. Although, he's better than me by a long shot.

We go back to our table and finish the greasy pizza. David tells me he's hoping to continue teaching history somewhere local because he loves the area. David in Bridgeport? I can tell Emma likes the thought of it. For me, not her. It's easy to see how much she loves Luke.

"River is an art teacher in town," Emma raves, shooting me a wink. "You should see her work at the studio. What's it called again, River?"

Gnawing on my inner cheek, I sheepishly look in David's direction. "It's Painter's Choice on the corner of Main and West Ave."

The same white, friendly smile he's worn all night appears again. His two front teeth are a little crooked, I notice. I like it. They aren't straight or too white like Everett's.

Stop thinking about Everett, my inner voice chastises.

Unlike last time, I listen to it.

Ripping the napkin up in little pieces in front of me, I try keeping the conversation going rather than shutting down. "Um, you should check it out. You know, if you want. They have some of the kids' artwork hanging up. It's nice."

David's eyes lighten. "I'd like that."

Emma beams. I blush.

"What do you like about—"

"What part of history do you want to—"

We stop when the other starts talking, making Emma and Luke laugh.

"Why don't you two talk?" Luke suggests, nudging Emma's arm. "How about we go across the street for some froyo?"

Her eyes widen. Emma's been talking about frozen yogurt for weeks now but keeps saying she's too busy to get some. I guess she hasn't just been telling me that but bothering Luke too.

Emma turns to me. "Is that okay?"

I admitted before the boys showed up that I was nervous. She probably thought it was first-date jitters. That's what Steph called it. And it partially is, but it's so much deeper than that and I can't tell her without admitting what I've done to get here.

"Of course." I cringe when my voice comes out a little higher than normal, which makes Luke snicker behind his closed fist. Waving them off, I stare at the pile of torn napkin bits in front of me.

"Here," David offers, sliding out of the booth and rounding the table so he's on the opposite side of me. He pushes the empty plates away and crosses his arms on the edge of the scratched-up wood. "Better?"

My lips part and I blink. "You didn't have to do that."

He leans back, moving his crossed arms to his chest.

"So, what's it like to teach art? That has to be fun, right? I loved art class when I was younger."

Art is an easy subject to talk about. "It's great. The kids I teach need the kind of release that art can offer them. They can paint their feelings. The stuff they put on the canvas or paper isn't an object, it's their anger or sadness or happiness or joy. You know?"

Surprise flickers across his face, then washes away into something like awe. Dipping my head down so my hair shields my face, I clear my throat. "Sorry, I just get extremely passionate."

"Don't apologize. I think that was the coolest description of the job I've ever heard. I'm pretty sure my art teacher just told us to draw whatever was in her lesson plan."

My lips turn upward. "My teacher was a big inspiration to me. She made me realize that I could use paint or clay or charcoal to express myself when words were too hard."

When I dare peek at him, he's watching me with interest. I force myself to keep eye contact and stop fidgeting. Drawing my hands onto my lap and locking them together, I say, "I bet it'll be fun to teach history. What is your focus?"

He grabs his glass of unsweetened tea from where he was sitting and pulls it in front of him. "Right now, it's Global Studies at Freemont. I'm just filling in for the previous teacher's maternity leave."

"And after that?"

His shoulders raise. "I'm hoping to become a professor and teach college kids about significant wars in U.S. history."

"Oh. Wow."

His cheeks redden. "It's no big deal. History to me sounds like art to you, only lamer." That gets a giggle from me, which makes him look victorious. "My parents own a Chinese restaurant and wanted me to go into the business. You know, take over after them. But I've never really been interested in the industry. It's always been history for me—teaching."

An easy smile stretches on my face, because I get it. As soon as Mrs. Cohen invested time in me, I realized it has always been art for me.

"Are you close with them?" I find myself asking, drawing the plastic straw from my water into my mouth and taking a sip.

David heaves a heavy sigh. "Yeah, I suppose. My dad more than my mom. Neither of them expected me to be in school for as long as I have, much less go the teaching route. But Dad has been supportive through the whole thing and Mom ... well, she just worries. You know how mothers are."

My mind drifts to Bridgette and all the times she calls and checks in on me or texts asking how things are or randomly brings pre-made meals by my apartment to make sure I'm eating. "Yeah, I do."

"What about you and your family?"

Wetting my bottom lip, I nudge the sweating glass

away from me. A ring of water rests where it sat, so I run my fingers through the liquid. "Uh, Oliver, my brother and I are pretty close. He just moved to Chicago for work. Bridg—um, my parents and I are pretty close." Dropping my shoulders, I worry my bottom lip. "I'm adopted, actually. My relationship with the people who adopted me is hard to explain. I love them. They saved me, to be honest. I'm not sure what would have happened to me if I stayed in the foster system."

His shocked face is unsurprising. His eyes widen, lips part, and no words escape his mouth for a few awkward seconds. Pity is the only thing missing from those dark chocolate eyes, which surprises me in return. "That's ... wow. They sound like amazing people, River. How long have you been with them?"

"Ten years."

He smiles warmly, then the corners of his lips twitch. "Can I ask ... do you know who your biological parents are? Have you ever thought to ask?"

The question makes me squirm.

"You don't have to answer," he dismisses quickly. "I sort of suck at the whole first-date thing. I, uh, may have done some stupid online dating crap I'm not proud of. You know, pretending to be someone I'm not to get dates. But I don't do that now!" He adds that last part when my eyes bolt to his. He rakes a hand through his buzz cut. "Geez, sorry. Maybe you should talk now?"

The plea makes me laugh, which causes him to join in. "For the record, I don't really know anything about my biological parents. I asked Robert, my adopted dad, to help find my mother but we never had any luck tracking her down. So ..."

He nods thoughtfully. "So, what's your favorite color?"

Pressing my lips together to hide the amused smile over the abrupt subject change, I let my tense shoulders ease. David Chen is a nice person; someone I can picture hanging out with again. Maybe even date long term.

The thought crushes me a little.

I whisper, "Mint green."

TWENTY-SIX

Everett / 27

When I was fourteen, I woke up in the middle of the night from the first bad dream I had in almost two years. Hair stuck to my sweaty forehead and my heart raced from the memory, because that was what it was. I wanted nothing more than to believe being in that car again was just a nightmare, but I remember it too well.

The crushing metal.

My mother screaming for me.

The final flip that left us upside down in a ravine that dropped twenty feet off the road.

I was little, only five, but I remember the way the car smelled metallic and something moldy as the water seeped in from the flooding rain we'd had leading up to the accident. The roads were slippery, and the other driver took the curve too fast, slamming into the front end of my parents' car and sending us over the edge of the shoulder.

Everything hurt, and just thinking about it makes the same bones I broke ache in a new way. It's the same memory I bolted awake at two this morning from, only my grandparents aren't here to soothe away the past.

Grandma had sat at the edge of the bed and combed her fingers through my hair, humming the same song I could never figure out the title to, to calm me down. It worked.

"You won't have them forever," she promises, brushing my damp cheeks with the pad of her thumb. "Sometimes the conscious mind lets the bad break through when we're most vulnerable. Be strong, Rhett boy. Like I know you are."

The day before, I had been told I didn't make the basketball team because I was failing two of my classes. Coach knew I was a good player and an even better shot, but not even he was above letting my grades slide. Making the team would be my chance at a scholarship and a future somewhere far away from Bridgeport and I messed it up.

It's no surprise I relived the worst day of my life after the shit show that's become of it now. The ring Blake Allen gave me to give to his daughter is gone, and part of me is relieved; like it vanished when the pressure got to be too much. Realistically, Issy moved it somewhere until she was ready to push the idea on me until I broke, but I can't make myself do it.

I'm sick of living by Blake Allen's rules, old promises, and outdated lies. Isabel Allen may think she's not worthy of love, but she is. And there are plenty of other people in Bridgeport with connections like mine, just maybe not with the same bank account.

And, frankly, I'd fucking give her the money if I knew that's what she really wants. But Issy, while materialistic, is more than a number on a check. She can pretend money can buy her happiness, but the older we get and the more she settles, the more I see the change in her. What she wants, I can't offer. She just stays because of her father. I'd have better luck paying that asshole off if it means setting Isabel and me free.

It's two thirty-eight when I leave Isabel sleeping in our bed. She's dead to the world and doesn't move an inch when I brush a strand of dark hair out of her face.

"We're both going to be happy one day." It's a new promise, one I can keep without it poisoning me like the one tattooed under my skin.

I'm not sure what to expect when I get to Painter's Choice. I know the doors will be locked and that the chance of River being up is slim to none, but I can't help feeling like there's a pull to try anyway.

When I arrive, there's a single light illuminating from the back of the room. The soft glow of red hair pulled back into a long ponytail flowing down her back has me taking a deep breath. Every time I look at her, it's like I'm seeing her for the first time. She's effortlessly beautiful, and everything about her screams that she's mine. My knuckles wrap on the glass door.

She jerks up and looks over, and it's too far away to know for sure, but I imagine she's scared. Nobody should be knocking on the front door at two in the morning, least of all me.

When she sees who it is, she doesn't move right away, just stares. I take a step back and shove my hands in the pockets of the jeans I slid on before leaving. Paired with the gray Henley, I'm a little cool from the late-night air, but I had to leave and didn't care what I threw onto my body as long as it got me out the door quicker.

After a moment, she sets down whatever she's working on and walks in my direction. My hungry gaze slides down her body, which isn't covered by more than a short pair of pink pajama shorts and a white tee. When she unlocks the door and pushes it open, her nipples pebble.

She's not wearing a bra.

Fuck.

"You can't be here," she whispers, not moving away from the door.

I step forward, closing in the distance between us. The slight breeze drifts her familiar green apple scent toward me, easing some of the pressure in my chest. "I know you probably don't want to see me, but I just ... *I* really wanted to see *you*."

She glances behind her, drawing in her bottom lip with her front teeth in contemplation. I want her to let me in, to show me she still trusts me, but I can't ask that of her—to expect that anymore.

When she steps aside, I let my shoulders drop into a neutral position as I walk into the warm studio. My arm unintentionally brushes her hardened nipples, and she sucks in a sharp breath before forcing herself away, closing and locking the door again.

She crosses her arms on her chest, much to my dismay, covering herself. "How did you know I was up?"

I wet my lips. "I didn't," I admit sheepishly. "I just needed to see you and hoped you were."

"And if I wasn't?"

"I would have waited." It comes out a whisper, a quiet vow, and I'm not sure she believes me. Drawing her attention to the sketch pad resting on one of the tables, I head toward where she was working. "New project?"

She walks beside me. "Everett, I really think you should go. It's late and you shouldn't be here."

"Why not?"

"Because your girlfriend is at home." The words are spit bitterly at me and I take the hit as I deserve.

It's my only time to try explaining to her what really happened the day of Oliver's party. "She told me she was done when she went to her parents. I really thought she was going to stay there. That—"

Her eyes narrow into skeptical slits. "So, she didn't actually say she was breaking up with you?"

Raking my hands through my hair, I try reasoning with her. "Usually 'I'm done' means the same thing, River. I don't ... shit, I don't expect you to understand. Hell, hate me all you want. I know I deserve it."

Her eyes close and I want to know what's going through her mind. The white scar on her bottom lip disappears when she presses them into a flat line, and then scrubs her palms down her tired face.

"I don't hate you, Everett." She shakes her head, brushing back what little pieces of hair escape her ponytail. "It would be so much easier if I did, but I can't. I can't ... stop holding onto whatever there is here, and I know it's wrong."

When I reach out to brush her hand, she moves away and sits back down on the stool in front of her drawing. Charcoal pencils scatter the work station around the paper.

"You should leave," she says, not looking at me once. Her hands pick up one of the charcoal sticks, and that's when I notice her skin is blackened from them.

I should really listen to her.

...but I don't.

TWENTY-SEVEN

River / 23

His hard muscles press against my back, causing my breath to catch in my throat. "I like this." I have a feeling he isn't talking about the drawing. "It's serene but also ... sexy. Dark."

Gulping, I find my voice. "It's not really anything yet. I haven't made up my mind."

"About what?"

Everything.

"The picture."

"Hmm."

He stays like that—his stomach to my back. I feel every breath and heartbeat as it syncs with mine. The room seems hotter, like the heat kicked on. It does that sometimes, kicks on for no reason. My skin gets all flushed and hot, but I don't dare move.

He does.

Reaching forward, his fingers brush the side of my arm. Down, down, down until he wraps those long, tan fingers around one of the charcoal pencils.

"If you're not careful, you'll make a mess," I warn,

knowing how easy it is to stain clothing with art supplies. Everett wears expensive stuff. Even the jeans and gray shirt he's wearing look like they cost more than my rent. He won't want them dirty.

"Is that so?"

"Y-Yes."

"Don't do that." His mouth is right by my ear now, his breath caressing me. My breasts tingle from our closeness, aching for him to palm them like I remember him doing during our only night together.

I swallow. "What?"

He shifts so his arm is right against mine, trapping me between him and the wall on the other side. I can't escape. "When your emotions get the better of you, you stutter. If you're angry, sad ... other things."

"O-Other things?"

His husky chuckle is all I hear in reply.

Suddenly, he lifts one of the pencils and marks my arm. It's just one little black dot on my right wrist. It'll easily come off.

"I held you there," he tells me, the tip of the pencil moving upward and making another dot at the crook of my arm. "And there. Remember? You were lying in bed, I was hovering over you, but you kept squirming. Your body wanted more, and you wouldn't sit still. So, I took your wrist in my hand and squeezed, not hard—just a warning, so you'd know that I'd let you touch me when I wanted you to."

Now my heart is pounding so hard I feel it drumming

in my ears. The heater is definitely on. I'm on fire. Over-heating.

"Then when you tried wrapping your arms around my neck to kiss me, I grabbed your arm here—" He makes a line at the crook of my elbow. "—and flipped you onto your stomach. Remember, River? Do you remember what I did then?"

Oh, God did I ever.

His callused palms ran down the sides of my still-clothed body. He'd taken off my necklace first, then my earrings. His hands worked magic along the curves of my body, gripping the flare of my hips in the jeans I wore.

After flipping me over, he lifted me up, so I was on my hands and knees. The wrap shirt I wore tied around my middle, so he slowly undid it and massaged my bare skin after it fell open. His fingers teased the sliver of skin just above the waistband of my jeans, which left me swallowing back my moans. I squirmed with need, already feeling wetness dampen between my legs.

I think I said his name—no, whimpered it, because he kept touching me without *really* touching me. And the need I had for him was so foreign to me because I was practically a virgin. My body caved to desire as he tortured me by stripping me slowly until I was completely bare to him.

"I think you remember well." The charcoal pencil slides up my bare arm, leaving a solid black line in its wake. "If the wall out front wasn't glass, I would mark every single place I touched and kissed. You'd be a new kind of artwork. A fucking masterpiece, River."

He rolls his hips into me and a low groan escapes my lips when I feel how hard he is. Reason escapes me, the fight over his appearance here long gone. All I can think, smell, and feel is him, just like that night.

"Do you trust me, River?" Everett grabs something out of his back pocket. A square foil packet.

"Always."

He kisses me with fervor and sits up on his knees, flicking the button of his jeans open and slowly sliding down the zipper. Anxiety and desire and lust all course through my veins when he gets off the bed and strips down completely.

Naked Everett is like a statue of a Greek God, all carved with muscle upon glorious muscle.

After rolling on the condom, he climbs back over me, lowering himself down. He touches me, my breasts, palming and massaging them until I writhe and whimper and moan. His mouth covers one nipple, then the other, then trails down to my belly button.

"N-No." It comes out choked when his lips land on my lower stomach and I realize what he wants to do. "I'm not r-ready for that."

He draws back up, kissing me gently once, twice, a third time. "We can wait."

"I want you. Just not ... that."

When he starts massaging my inner thighs, spreading them ever so slightly, I feel the burn between my legs increase. But not as much as when he finally enters my slick heat inch by agonizing inch. He groans my name and buries his face into the crook of my neck and kisses, licks, and sucks the salty flesh there.

And I come alive.

As he moves in and out of me, whispering how beautiful I am, all I can think is how we got here. How I invited him upstairs and how I told him that I loved my new charm. The broken heart is unconventional, but beautiful all the same because, in a way, I know what it represents. Or, what I want it to. That he's mine, even the deepest, most shattered part of him.

When he reached out to touch the charm, I threaded our fingers together and let his touch linger. The warmth felt good. He didn't stop me when I wrapped his arm around my back, hugging his body to mine. He only stepped closer, his other hand threading into my hair, as he leaned his forehead against mine.

We'd never been that close, and neither of us could stop with just one touch. Not when there wasn't anyone to stop us, to pry us apart.

"I've wanted this for too long, too fucking long," he whispers into my skin, biting down on the area just above my collarbone.

What he's doing hurts at first, but the pain turns into pleasure as he pumps faster and plays with my clit. I try meeting his thrusts, lifting my hips up, which earns me a loud moan as he goes deeper and deeper.

"Fuck, River." He takes my arms and keeps them above my head, threading our fingers together as he drives into me over and over. His lips crash on mine as one of his hands palms my breasts one at a time. I writhe, feeling my legs quake, as they bend and capture either side of his hips, latching on for dear life.

His mouth lowers and bites down around my nipple, sucking

and gliding his tongue over the pebbled tip until I'm crying out his name, free falling from the sensations. His release comes right after mine, his body lowering down as he kisses me in every direction possible.

"That's how your first time should have been, baby," he tells me, nuzzling his nose into my neck.

I'm startled when my hair is released from the ponytail it's in and Everett's hands comb through the thick strands. I'm turned on from the memory of our first time, of how full I felt with his thick length inside of me, which causes me to squeeze my thighs together and squirm on the stool.

"I should have told you yes all of those years ago," he whispers, his fingers skimming my neck. "I should have showed you what it's like to be loved the right way."

Those words snap me out of what he's doing, and I quickly stand up and back away from him and the fantasy I'm sinking back into.

His brows pinch. "River?"

"How can you possibly show me what it's like to be loved the *right way*? Jesus, Everett! You can't even love your girlfriend the way she deserves!"

His eyes widen and he stumbles as if he's been shot. I'm not ashamed to be holding the smoking gun.

What is he doing here with me when there's a woman in his bed? A woman he's told me time and time again that he loves, that he'll marry because people expect him to. It's been ten years and she's still not wearing a ring.

He says he's not a liar, but he is.

He hates saying he's a cheater, but he is.

And us? We're toxic.

Even if he won't admit it.

"I'm done." I keep backing away, pinning him with a look of despair and anger. "I can't keep putting myself through this, Everett. You say you'll never hurt me, but you are. Every day that you love *her*, you stay with *her*, you're killing me. And I deserve so much fucking better than that. Than *you*," my voice cracks, just like the heart charm dangling from my necklace.

Everett Tucker doesn't have to break my heart, because I broke it myself by loving him.

It's funny how the heart can still hurt over something it has expected all along. But I guess that's not entirely true.

The truth about heartbreak is that there is no such thing. It's your soul that shatters, along with every fiber of your being that screams for another person.

Gripping the wall leading to the hallway, I make eye contact one final time with the man I've held on to since I was thirteen. The man I've depended on and trusted and crushed on and loved—loved achingly, desperately, and completely. Our love has brought nothing but pain, to a place where I'm considered the *other woman*. I'll never be the one he puts a ring on, who he shares his bed with, we won't have children and grow old together, because ten years ago he made the choice to do all those things with her.

I'm not a doormat, and I won't be second best. I deserve so much more than what he wants to give me.

"Don't talk to me again unless you figure out what you really want from life, Everett. I can't keep living like this. We're not good for each other."

His green eyes glaze over. "Don't say that, baby."

"I'm *not* your baby."

Sniffing back tears, I blow out a shaky breath. My chest hurts. It's as though my ribs have caved in from all the pressure and misery and hurt.

Before spinning around and locking myself away, I whisper, "But I could have been."

TWENTY-EIGHT

River / 23

The rest of May passes in a blur and June starts with torrential rain storms and dreary weather that makes my mood worse. I'm supposed to start an Education Law class at the end of the month, but the idea of going to campus every week for the next two months makes me feel like I'm suffocating.

Oliver calls and checks in on me once a week, and I've called him a few times asking how things have been in Chicago. He doesn't need to tell me he loves it; I hear as much in his voice when he tells me about all the sites he's gone to. To my surprise, his favorite is The Art Institute, where he wants to take me when we visit him toward the end of summer. He says it reminds him of me, of home.

It made me smile.

The small break from college leaves me with more time to help Melanie at Painter's Choice. I work fulltime hours helping co-teach her classes to get a wider variety of experience. The foster kids will always be my favorite, and most of them seem to enjoy the atmosphere.

There's one twelve-year-old who never wants to participate. She sits in the corner at every class with an iPod she said she found at her old foster home. Someone accused her of stealing it, not finding it, and she doesn't deny it. Whatever she listens to puts her in a trance, because she closes her eyes and absorbs the music like I do with art.

I don't expect everyone to be as invested in painting as I am. I just want them to find some sort of relief. When I approach her, I'm slow and calculated because I know sneaking up on anyone in her position is a dangerous game. But I also know if she's comfortable enough to lose herself here, she feels safe.

"Charlotte?" Kneeling next to her, I give a small smile when she pops her eyes open.

The chair she's tipping back settles onto the hardwood floor, and she swallows nervously.

"Not in the mood to paint today?"

Her blonde hair is matted with knots and I wonder how long it has been since it was properly combed or cut. It's pulled back, so I can't see how long it is, but I bet it goes halfway down her back.

"I never want to," she tells me, glancing at the chipped-blue device in her hand. The screen has a tiny crack in the corner, but it looks like it's still in decent shape.

"Do you like music?"

She doesn't answer right away, just plays with the

iPod. Her thumb brushes over the arrows that skip through the playlist. Oliver gave me his old iPod when he started using his phone's music app. I accidently broke it a few months later when I got paint into one of the plug-in slots. He told me he could get me a new one, but I opted to use my phone like him.

Eventually, she nods and sets the iPod on her thigh.

Standing and pulling over a chair next to her, I settle into the hard plastic. "Have you considered doing something with music, like playing an instrument? Maybe art isn't your medium, but music can be."

Her lips part, and then close, promptly. Before the first class I held, I told them that I understood them a little better than some. I never went into the details of my stay in the system, but I wanted them to know they could talk to me if they needed to. It doesn't seem like too long ago I was in their shoes, unsure of what to say and do and who to trust.

I'll always have those problems, but the James' have given me a safe haven. These kids need one from me, and Melanie and I are willing to get them to that place.

"Charlie," she finally whispers.

My brows arch.

Her cheeks color. "I like being called Charlie, not Charlotte."

"Well, it's nice to meet you, Charlie." I hold my hand out toward her, not expecting her to take it. She stares for a moment before her palm slides into mine. I notice a few pink scars on the back of her hand, hurt seizing my heart. One of them looks like a cigarette burn.

Dropping our hands, I set mine into my lap. "It's okay if you don't like painting or drawing. What if there were programs at the school you're attending for music? Do you go to Freemont?"

She stays silent, and something about the way she evades my eyes makes a little red warning alarm ring inside me. "Remember what I said on the first day of class, Charlie? This is a safe space."

Picking up the iPod, she squeezes it tight in her grasp. "I don't think I believe you. Not all of us are lucky like you."

Inhaling slowly, I give her a tiny nod. "I know I'm very fortunate to have had the opportunities I did in life. But that just makes me want to make a difference in other people's lives. If you want to do a music program, I'd love to help. Expression is the best way to deal with things beyond us."

I startle when she bolts up, the chair flying backward and smashing into the linoleum floor. "What if I don't want your help? Just because you want to make a difference doesn't mean any of us wants to be your charity case!"

When she runs out of the studio, I quickly run after her outside. But she disappeared in the crowd of late-afternoon people on break grabbing coffee from the Landmark Café down the street.

Rushing back inside, the other kids stare at me with wide eyes.

"Do any of you know where she'd go?" I try keeping my tone even, but I'm afraid. If she doesn't turn up, she'll be considered a run-away. I'm trusted to keep these kids safe while they're here, not run them off.

One of the boys raises his hand. "Charlie likes hanging out at the old baseball factory. You know the one by the train station?"

Melanie comes out of her office. "I'll watch them, River. Go on."

She knows the repercussions Charlie would receive if the van showed up and she wasn't here. I wonder if Charlie knows those consequences, or if she has long ago given up. When I was her age, I understood it all too well. That was right before Bridgette and Robert started to take interest in me, and my expectations of them sticking around were low.

I'm grabbing my keys and running out the back door to where my car is parked, and head to the only spot I know to look. If she's not there, I don't know what I'll do. Calling Child Protective Services can't be an option. If I promised these kids safety, I don't want to risk ruining it by doing something drastic.

But Bridgeport, while a semi-safe city, is no place for a twelve-year-old girl to roam alone.

It takes me nearly ten minutes to get to the factory because of traffic, which is more than enough time for Charlie to arrive by foot. If she's come here before, she knows shortcuts. I scoured the streets on the way over with no luck, so I'm crossing my fingers that she's somewhere on this abandoned property.

Getting out of my car, I take a look at the beat-up brick building. The lot smells off, like mold and mildew, and the walls are covered in various colored graffiti. My nerves pick up and course through my veins as I step toward the broken front door.

"Charlie?" I cringe when a flock of birds flutter over me from the sound of my echoing voice in the empty building.

Gripping my keys tightly in my hands, I walk around further, glancing into any nook and cranny she may be.

"Charlie, are you in here?"

I squeak when a mouse scurries past me, jumping backward and making my spine shudder. Why can't mice be cute and friendly like the ones in *Cinderella* that Steph made me watch with her when we were younger?

Swallowing past my nerves, I stop at one of the many doors leading out of the main lobby. There's no noise or voices that I can hear, so I push the doors open one by one.

No Charlie.

Brushing hair out of my face, I turn around and stand on my tip-toes to peer out one of the broken windows. The glass is missing from the corner of the windows, as if someone threw rocks at them. Considering the stones littering the dirty floor, I believe that's what happened.

When I catch familiar blonde hair peeking out from

the corner of my eye, I shift to see Charlie poking her head around the corner of the hallway I had yet to check.

Relief floods me. "There you are!"

Her lips waver. "Are CPS coming to get me now? I bet Connor ratted me out, right? He's such a tattletale."

I don't want to talk about Connor. "I didn't call Child Protective Services, Charlie."

Those big green eyes I know she has widen. "Why not?"

Walking over to her, I stop a few feet away. She wants space, so I'll give her space. "I told you before, I want to make a difference. If I called them, what good would it have done? You'd be in trouble."

"But ..."

I wait, crossing my arms on my chest.

"But I yelled at you," she murmurs.

I shrug it off, because there's a lot worse she could have done. Some of the kids in class have files ten times thicker than mine, and while I didn't read through them, I was warned of "violent tendencies" which made Melanie a little nervous to sign off on to the idea.

But even she says everyone deserves a chance, and we seem to be the people willing to hand them out to the kids who need them most.

Gesturing toward the door, I give her a reassuring smile. "Are you ready to head back? We'll make it back in time before you're picked up, so no need to worry." I notice the dark dirt staining her jeans. "We'll just say we played outside today."

When she smiles, I welcome the idea of having a new friend.

A COUPLE WEEKS FOLLOWING THE DOUBLE DATE WITH David, Emma, and Luke, I decided to reach out to David using the number he gave me. Emma told me after our last final that David couldn't stop talking about me, and Luke even admitted that he hasn't seen him like that before.

So, I ask if he wants to see the studio.

Melanie was teaching a class when he stopped by, so I gave him the tour. There's not a lot to see because it's a small building, but he seems to genuinely enjoy the art hanging on the walls from the kids. Although, I'm pretty sure he didn't get what most of it was supposed to be.

After the tour, we went out to the diner for an early dinner. Patty almost put in my usual when I opted to get a chicken parmesan sandwich instead. David teased me for coming here so often, and I blushed.

That day at the diner, I learned a lot about him. He grew up as the youngest of two, with an older sister, and has very strict parents. While they don't get his choice in careers, they support him and his endeavors to become a teacher. He doesn't have a middle name or a favorite color, though he wears a lot of red, so I tell him that must be it. He goes with it, because he's a nice guy.

He found out that, outside of art, I enjoy reading. Mostly romance, but sometimes I'll read non-fiction biographies about infamous criminals. He didn't seem surprised when I told him I binge-watched all the Ted Bundy Confession Tapes on Netflix, or the original series the company has of true crimes.

I bet Everett would be shocked over my obsession in television shows. Sure, violence terrifies me, but there's something about the psyche that makes me want to know why people do bad things. I suppose getting in Ted Bundy's mind isn't a healthy choice, nor are the other criminals featured in the documentaries I watch, but it's an interest I never had before—never thought I would. And change is good, it's important.

It's why I keep hanging out with David. After the date at the studio and diner, it was a movie and ice cream a few days later. Turns out, we both love mint chocolate chip flavored anything.

After the movie and ice cream was a walk in Fuller Park, where David didn't once reach for my hand like I thought he would. I kept asking myself if I wanted him to and could never come up with a response before my emotions knotted and made it hard to think.

Now we're sitting in Underground East, one of Bridgeport's fancier dining establishments. I've been here once or twice with the James' for special occasions; Bridgette's birthday and celebrating a deal at Robert's company. Everett has asked me to eat here with him and Oliver before, but I never did.

Part of me feels bad I agreed to come here, not because I don't enjoy David's company. It's expensive, and I know he's not making much more than I am right now, especially because his contract is up for the maternity leave he's covering. I ordered the cheapest chef salad I could find, and it was still over ten dollars.

Then again, it didn't stop me from ordering dessert when he asked if I wanted anything else. I was still hungry after the sorry excuse of servings they offered me of lettuce and toppings, so I said yes.

David leans over his carrot cake toward me, his eyes drifting off to the side. "Do you know that woman, River? I think she's staring at you."

His gaze is pointed toward someone across the restaurant. Trying not to give myself away, I brush some hair behind my ear and glance in the same direction. There's a woman who *is* looking this way, but she doesn't look familiar. From this distance, it looks like she has dark brown hair, almost black. But she's sitting in the shadows off to the side of the room, so besides her straight hair, I can't tell much about her.

Shaking my head, I focus back on my chocolate parfait. "I don't think so. She must be looking at somebody else."

His brows pinch skeptically, because we're the only ones in this section of the dining room. Piecing off another forkful of his cake, he tries redirecting the conversation. "So, would you be interested in attending an event with me next weekend? It's sort of a family thing ..."

A family thing? Choking on my spoonful of sugary

goodness, I pat my chest and take a sip of water. Is he asking me to meet his family, because that seems like a big deal?

He must sense my anxiety. "It's really not a huge thing. I mean, it'll mostly be my cousins. My niece is having a party for her fifth birthday and they're doing a potluck. Nothing fancy and there's no pressure."

Except there is, because I remember what Oliver said about people meeting the family of someone they're dating. And I don't think I *am* dating David. I mean, he's nice and we've hung out quite a bit in the past few weeks, but he hasn't even really made a move besides a kiss on the cheek the night we strolled through the park. I didn't mind that he never made a move, because I wasn't ready. I figured that out just now from the pounding rhythm of my heart.

Before I can answer him, the woman who was sitting across the room, steps up beside our table. Her hands fidget in front of her loose, stained black dress as her brown eyes focus on me. This close, I realize her hair is a dark shade of red, almost like mine but tinted with brown like it has been dyed a few times. Her skin is pale, maybe paler than my milky white, and she looks nervous.

"River? A-Are you River?" Her voice is a low, shaky tone, like she's not sure she should be here.

David's eyes bounce between us in uncertainty, gauging my reaction to the stranger.

Shifting back, I draw my hands to my lap, unsure of

what to say. Obviously I'm River, but a stranger shouldn't be coming up to me and asking.

"River Jean Scott?"

My body goes on high alert as the woman locks eyes with mine. The sharp breath I inhale burns, because I haven't heard that name in ten years. When I was officially adopted, Jill told me I could take the James's name if I wanted. It seemed like a perfect way to start over.

"It's me," the woman moves closer. "It's your mom. You're *real* mom."

David's eyes widen as he reaches over and places his hand on mine. I must be pale. No, ashen. Because standing in front of me is a ghost. Not a memory. Not a salvation. A person who has haunted me since I was old enough to understand what being a foster kid meant.

David's hand squeezing mine pulls me back to reality. "I-I don't know who you're talking about. I'm sorry, but we have to go."

David doesn't argue as he pulls out his wallet and drops money onto the table. Going the long way around the chairs, I tuck myself behind him, so there's no contact between me and this woman.

My birth *mother*.

She doesn't have to tell me anything more, I know the truth. I see it in her straight, pointed nose and heart-shaped lips. The bottom one is fuller than the top, like mine. Her eyes are the same round shape and color; only her lashes look much darker and frame her eyes better. This woman is undoubtedly who she says she is.

But that doesn't mean I have to face her this way.

"Can we go?" I whisper to David, wrapping my arm around his.

He draws me in closer to his side, keeping me away from the woman as he walks us around her defeated form. "Of course."

Neither of us looks back.

TWENTY-NINE

Everett / 27

June is a whirlwind of business proposals made by half-ass companies that waste more of our time than it's worth, but Robert wants to expand the business past its usual routes. We've already tripled our profit, and all the employees have gotten raises, even the interns. More money means more power, and I'm not sure I'm on the same page as him about it since I'll be the one running everything when Robert decides to retire.

It's not the business I'm worried about right now. Thankfully, Robert has never spoken of retirement, though I'm sure Bridgette would like him to consider it. He's still got time, plenty of it, but that doesn't mean it won't pass by quickly. Then where does that leave me? In charge of a corporation I don't think I can run on my own.

That I don't want *to run on my own.*

There's a lot of shit I don't want to do that I settle with. I'll accept the company and responsibility, because I don't hate it. I've shadowed Robert for the past seven years and grown quite close with some of the people who work with him. Especially those who worked with my father when the two first opened the doors here. I bring baked goods to Betty, the receptionist downstairs, and in return she gives me advice. Mostly unsolicited.

The morning after Isabel closed the bedroom door on me, I came to work on three hours of sleep. Issy left before I ever woke, and I was worried until her father informed me she was at the guest house. He was eerily calm considering he'd just demanded I propose to her, which made it all the more unnerving to me.

As soon as Betty saw the bags under my eyes she started *tsking*. *"You are simply too young to be this lost, boy. Your father wouldn't want you looking like the walking dead, now would he?"*

But how am I supposed to know what my father would want? My memories are limited to him rubbing my hair after coming home from work and showing me how to hold a pair of scissors. He died before I could really learn anything about him.

That morning, Betty went into the little kitchenette area and poured me a cup of coffee. I already drank one cup on the way to the office but needed more to wake up.

"You're just like him, you know," she tells me, taking her seat at her desk again. *"I know how much being there for people means to you, because it meant the world to him. But you know what meant more? Happiness."*

Betty seems to know a lot, more than I give her credit for. Ever since she told me that, I've kept it with me. My father was said to be a lot like his parents, and my grandparents always reminded me of the importance of keeping my word when I promise something, of helping the people who need it most. Betty is right, my parents would both want me to be happy more, and I'd like to think some promises are worth amending if it means getting there.

That night, I asked Isabel to dinner. The pressed black dress she wore was tight, short, and paired with the kind of jewelry that I imagine a ring would look great with. But I had to crush those expectations between the appetizer and entrée. Telling her that I wasn't going to marry her went about as well as expected.

There was yelling, lots of yelling, in the middle of Undercover East. People stared and whispered and the waitstaff had to ask us to leave. But not before I told her I'd stay at the cabin while she collected her things from the apartment. She needed her space, and I was more than willing to give that to her.

"You said you'd be there for me!"

"This is *me being there for you, Issy."*

"Don't fucking call me that, Everett!"

She always preferred it when I called her Issy. It makes sense that she refuses that type of familiarity with me now.

"You deserve to be happy, Isabel."

"What if I am?"

But we both knew she wasn't. *Isn't.*

When the staff asked us to leave, Isabel followed me out of the restaurant and shoved my shoulders back as soon as we hit the sidewalk. Names were called, names I damn well deserved, and tears were shed. That shit killed me, *still* kills me. Issy only ever cried the day at the hospital when the doctor told her she miscarried.

I promised her I'd be there, that she'd never lose me like she lost our child, and I plan on keeping my word. She'll always have me, as a friend, as a memory, as someone to count on, she just needs to get past this—to move on.

True to my word, I've been staying at the cabin for the past two weeks. I don't call or check up on Isabel, because I know she won't reply if I do reach out. I know her after all these years, which means I also know the fight she'll put up until the final nail is in the coffin.

A knock on my office door has me snapping out of la-la-land and glancing up at the two men standing with firm faces. Robert's isn't as tight as Blake Allen's, but neither of them look particularly happy. Though I'm sure Robert's displeasure has to do with Mr. Allen's appearance here, since the two don't get along. They're practically rivals, which is why the break from Isabel is almost therapeutic for me. I know Blake's end game of getting me as a son-in-law includes clawing his way into JT Corporation, and he doesn't deserve it.

It seems fitting that we're both losing shit we spent years building. I'm sure Issy thinks I don't care about her at all, but that's the farthest thing from the truth. I do love her, just not the way I should have. Once she finally detaches her claws, then she'll be able to experience the soul-burning kind of love that will surely consume her.

"Gentlemen," I greet, staying seated behind my desk. Dropping my interlocked fingers into my lap, I lean back in my office chair. It creaks under my weight. "What can I do you for?"

Robert clears his throat, nudging past Blake's tense form. "Betty tried getting Mr. Allen to understand that he had no business coming here, but he insisted it was important that he see you. If you'd like, I can call security."

Blake's eyes narrow, wrinkling at the corners. "I bet you'd like that, wouldn't you, Robert? This matter doesn't concern you, though."

Robert simply shrugs. "I imagine not, but I can't see why it's so vital you have to storm into my company."

Clearing my throat, I wave my hand in dismissal. "It's fine, Robert. Mr. Allen and I can talk. I'm in between meetings at the moment. Apologize to Betty for me."

Robert shoots one last suspicious glance at Blake before closing my office door behind him. Truthfully, I'm surprised it has taken this long before we encountered each other.

"I gave you a ring for a reason, Mr. Tucker," Blake begins, sauntering to the front of my desk and bending over it, so he's in my personal space. "You can't expect me to keep my mouth closed after wasting ten years of my life on you."

His angry tone and spat words make me laugh, but he

obviously doesn't see the humor in them. "Don't you mean your daughter, sir? She's the one who's stayed by my side for ten years, not you."

He slams his palm against the edge of my desk, nearly knocking off a snow globe with the Golden Gate Bridge in it. Rescuing the keepsake River brought me back from her trip to California, I carefully place it out of his reach.

"There's no need for violence here," I inform him plainly.

"Then don't *bullshit* me, boy," he growls back, fingers clenching the edge of the wood desktop. His knuckles are turning white and his face is red. I momentarily consider taking up Robert's offer on calling security.

But I deserve this, in a way.

"You never loved my daughter."

"That isn't true at all." Unlike him, I keep my voice level. There's no point poking the fire and making everyone in hearing distance know my current situation. "I love Isabel very much, which is why I hope she finds someone who will make her happy. And, to be honest, you have no right to defend her. You only care about the benefits you'll get from the person you tie her to."

His dark eyes narrow in on me, and they remind me of Issy's when I say something stupid. "So what? Do you honestly think my parents cared about finding true love for me? This is a business world where you fight to survive. You can't make it if you don't connect with the right people."

Scoffing, I stand to his level. "It's a new world, Mr.

Blake. Isabel shouldn't have to be *tied* to anybody unless she wants to be. We both know that we were never good for each other."

"Funny," he growls, "you didn't seem to think of that when you knocked up the little slut."

I'm in front of him before he can even blink, but he doesn't flinch from our sudden closeness. The tips of my Nordstrom brown leather shoes are pressed against his cheap knockoffs. I'm usually not one to throw around my money, but for someone who talks big about what money can buy, he isn't spending it.

"Tell me, Mr. Blake," I bargain, "how does it make you feel that somebody half your age is more powerful than you? You must be hellbent on building yourself up by any means necessary to use your daughter's darkest days against me in an argument that doesn't truly have anything to do with her. Or are you just heartless? Do you not care that you lost a grandchild? Maybe a little boy who you could have taught the business to or a little girl to fucking *protect* against assholes like you and me."

Scoffing, I straighten up to full height, which gives me a few inches on him. "You may think that the pregnancy was some big mistake, and maybe you're sadistic enough to be happy it didn't work out, but I will never let you fucking talk about your daughter or unborn grandchild like that again without at least one of your front teeth missing. Is that understood?"

He's seething now, nostrils flaring and eyes darker than they've ever been. The devil is in this man. Driven by greed and all six other deadly sins. "You'll always just be trash with money who never deserved her."

Flattening my white dress shirt, I give him an indifferent shrug. He's using words, tactics to piss me off. It won't work. "Neither one of us deserves to have Isabel in our lives. Unlike you, I'm man enough to admit it. Just like I can admit that I may be garbage, but you'll always be a superficial, heartless jackass who can't see past a goddamn dollar sign. Now, you best be leaving before I *do* call security. I'm sure your reputation would take a hit if pictures of you being forcefully removed from the premises were published."

His jaw ticks. "Isabel used to tell me that you were different than the other men," he drawls, stepping back. "Turns out, she doesn't know you at all. My, how money changes people."

"You don't know me at all, Mr. Blake."

An evil grin slices his face. "I know your father would be disappointed."

With that, he walks toward the door and steps out before I can even think of a reply.

Dropping into my seat, I scrub my palm across my face. Picking up the snow globe, I shake it and watch the glitter freefall in the fluid. I'm lost in thought, of wondering if the dickhead could be right, when another knock sounds from my door.

"Your father would be proud," Robert says, walking in with his hands in his beige pants pockets. He notes the snow globe I'm holding and then sits down. "Let me ask you something, son. What's the real reason you're letting go of Isabel?"

My lips part and hands withdraw from the globe. "What do you mean?"

His shoulders raise. "It could be as simple as what you say; that you want her to be happy. I don't doubt that for a second. But anyone who dedicates ten years to a person must have a bigger reason than that."

I'm in love with your daughter.

Wetting my lips, I heave out a heavy sigh and palm my tired eyes. It feels like I haven't gotten a decent night's sleep in months because of everything that's gone on.

"Blake Allen has taught her to believe that true love isn't real," I answer carefully. "I want her to see that isn't true. Just because her parents are stuck in a loveless marriage doesn't mean she has to be."

"And that's what it'd be for you two? A loveless marriage?" He rests easily in the chair, one leg crossed over the other with his hands resting on his stomach.

"Yes," I breathe audibly.

He clicks his tongue. "I've seen how you look at her, but I've also seen how you act around her. One is vastly different than the other, driven by two very different things. I may be old, but I know the difference between lust and love. Can't say I'm surprised by the inevitable, but also not sure I understand it."

Breathing is suddenly difficult, and I know it's because my guilt is sitting on my chest like an anchor.

The truth is between us, lingering in the air until I silently suffocate. My lungs burn as I force even breaths, because Robert can't find out this way that I love River or how far I've crossed the line in my relationship.

"Is there somebody else?"

His question stops my breathing altogether. I can't correct the shock of it before he notices my widened eyes, and I can only hope he can't read the rest of my emotions; the shame, the desperation, the torture.

He tips his head once. "Thought so. I know you didn't ask for any advice, but you're like a son to me, so I'm going to give it to you anyway. Whoever you truly love needs to wait until you can give her every piece of you. It won't be fair to you, her, *or* Isabel if you offer what you have now, because that isn't much. Love ... it's a precious thing. If you feel like you've found the real deal, then I'll stand behind you in any way possible. Just do me a favor."

Emotion crackles my words. "What?"

"Treat her well."

He walks away, leaving me staring at the empty chair he occupied.

THIRTY

River / 23

David picks me up at ten o'clock to take a two-hour drive to his niece's birthday party. The normal date it was scheduled for was cancelled because his niece came down with a cold, so they're throwing it today instead. I considered making an excuse, any excuse, as to why I couldn't go. But the idea of leaving Bridgeport for a little while seemed like a good idea.

Now we're halfway to a small town I've never heard of with some 80's rock band filling the silence between us but doing nothing to ease my nerves. I try focusing on the lyrics, but they don't keep me from biting down on all my nails until they're just gross, ragged shards.

David told me the party is princess-themed, because his five-year-old niece is into Disney royalty. When I asked if I should get her a present, he told me not to bother. But showing up empty handed with no food or a gift seemed like a bad first impression, so I opted to get her a little charm bracelet that I found at a thrift shop. It has pink, white, and silver charms on it, all girly things like crowns, makeup, and shoes. Honestly, I don't know if she'll like it, but from what David told me, she won't hate it.

He brought an Asian dish that's his mother's favorite recipe, spicy chicken with vegetables, I think. Thankfully, neither of his parents will be there. It doesn't ease my anxiety over meeting the rest of his family though.

When he pulls over for gas and something to drink, I slide out and meet him inside. My sweet tooth is ten times worse when I'm nervous. Bridgette says she's the same way and that I fit in with our family of stress eaters.

Walking down the candy aisle, my fingers graze over a packet of plain M&M's in the cardboard holder. Biting down on my bottom lip, I remember the first time Everett bought me a pack of them, then all the candy bars after. Suddenly, I don't want candy anymore.

By the time I pick out a bottle of water and bag of pretzels from the next aisle over, David is inside snatching up his own snacks for the road. He doesn't have a sweet tooth like me from what I've noticed. Sometimes he'll order cake or pie if we're eating somewhere, but he mostly chooses healthier alternatives or just steals pieces of my sugar stash.

After we're buckled in and ready to finish our journey to his sister's house, I shift in my seat with my hand buried in my pretzel bag. "What does your sister think I am to you?"

He glances at me for a moment, a shy little smile

curving his lips. "I told her we're friends, but ..." I wait for him to finish. "But, uh, I think she suspects it's more."

My hand stills around a pretzel. "Is it?"

His eyes snap to mine in surprise before returning to the road. We're surrounded by highway and trees and off to the side in the distance are buildings. Maybe houses. Maybe businesses. "Uh, I don't know. I mean, I wouldn't mind if it were more, but I won't pressure you into anything that you don't want."

Inhaling slowly, I sink into the seat cushion a little deeper. "We haven't really done couple things."

He chuckles softly. "I think we go out more than Emma and Luke do."

"But we never hold hands," I blurt. My cheeks heat up at my outburst. Why would I point that out? I'm not sad that he doesn't hold my hand or make moves on me. Besides a few cheek kisses or lingering hugs, there's nothing more between us.

I'm okay with that, I think. We're not dating, so there aren't expectations. Deep down, I guess my subconscious is demanding certainty. Like if David is going to be someone I invest my time in, I should know what it means.

But it shouldn't be considered an investment, like it can be lost.

"River?"

I startle. "Y-Yeah?"

He rubs his jaw. "I, uh, asked if you wanted us to be official. You know, like boyfriend and girlfriend?"

The car becomes too quiet. The radio is turned down, so not even music can fill the gap between us right now.

He blows out a breath. "It's fine, really. I wasn't really sure if you were inter—"

My eyes widen at his reading of my silence. "No! I mean, yes, I'm interested. But it's complicated, David. I like you and think you're fun to hang out with."

"And if I held your hand?" he asks, his lips curving up in a teasing smile.

"I ... I wouldn't pull away."

Something flashes in his eyes. "Slow."

My head jerks back. "What?"

"We'll go slow," he assures me. "I think slow is good, you know? If you're not in a place to have a label, then this could be perfect for us."

Does he really want that? It seems like he wants more, but I can't read him. Emma keeps asking if we're together or not and says that David likes me. *Likes me,* likes me. But when we're together, I don't see it in his eyes. Then again, do I even know what I'm looking for?

No, you don't, that pestering voice comments silently to me.

Shoving it away, I find my own voice amidst the sound of wind hitting the car as it flies down the highway. "Slow. I ... I like slow."

David's smile broadens.

. . .

SPENDING THE DAY WITH THE CHENS WAS surprisingly fun. Jossy, David's niece, asked us to play tea party with her. Seeing David sit on the ground around a table half his size and try picking up miniscule plastic teacups with his big fingers was one of the sweetest things I've ever witnessed. It never stopped him from telling her how good the tea was (it was dirty water) or how delicious the food was (it was plastic).

His sister Asa talked with me about art and school and her little brother. Never once did she ask what we were, if we were dating or planned to, and I knew David was to thank for that. Slow. I could do slow. Right?

When she went to tend her daughter, I asked David why her name seemed more traditional to Asian culture, and he told me that she was born in China, but his parents didn't want to live by the one-child rule, so they moved to America for a fresh start. A year after they settled into the States, they had him and opted for an American name in hopes he would fit in better than Asa, who struggled with the culture difference.

After a late lunch and presents, David and I left to travel back to Bridgeport. Jossy loved the bracelet and asked me to help put it on. My nerves were extinguished and replaced with contentedness, because a few years ago, I wouldn't have even given this type of thing a thought—dating, meeting somebody else's family. That version of me was scared of the world. I think I'll always be in some ways, but not like I was.

I'm stronger.

And when David dropped me off and walked me to the door in front of Painter's Choice, I knew what he was going to do. He would lean in and press his soft lips to my cheek and tell me goodnight. The old me would stiffen until he retracted, tell him goodnight, and walk inside.

I didn't want to be the old me anymore.

When he leaned in to peck my cheek, I turned and captured his lips with mine. He startled but didn't pull away, instead, pressing a little deeper against me. I waited for something to happen; the tingles in the pit of my stomach, the fire in my chest, the desire building until I couldn't take it. None of that happened, leaving me empty and thinking about the way I felt when Everett kissed me and touched me and talked to me in a low, raspy voice. I thought about all the things I shouldn't while another man kissed me.

When David drew back, his eyes were brimming with hope. Mine didn't look the same. He could tell, because he cleared his throat, squeezed my hand, and left.

I spent all night remembering the distraught expression on his face. Maybe it resembled mine, because I thought kissing David would make me forget about kissing Everett; forget everything I did with him that was off limits to me.

It doesn't really work that way, I guess. After a restless night of tossing and turning, I slip on a pair of black yoga pants and loose tee with an unknown logo across the front that I bought from a thrift store and head toward Landmark Café for much needed coffee. I could have made some with the machine Oliver bought me, but I can't make specialty ones like the café does. Right now, caffeine and sugar are two must haves to get me through the day.

It could be the lack of sleep, or the way I tried—and failed—sorting through my feelings for David, but my gut told me today would be a bad day. When I got to the counter to order a caramel iced coffee and chocolate scone, they told me there were no scones left. Then I spilled my coffee on my shirt when I bumped into some guy in a suit, splattering coffee on his expensive looking shoes and got a dark glare as I offered him napkins.

They say bad things happen in threes.

Walking outside into the warm summer air with my coffee in hand, I stop when I see a familiar face shoving at the door of Painter's Choice. It's locked because it doesn't open for another hour and a half, and Melanie won't be there for at least another thirty minutes to set up.

But Isabel Allen is on a mission. She must sense me watching her, because her head turns and her dark hair swings around her from the abrupt movement. When she captures my eyes, it only takes one look for me to know that something very bad is about to happen. She struts over to where I'm frozen in front of Landmark Café and faces me with such venom in her eyes that I can feel the poison seep into my veins.

Her eyes drift downward at something, and I wonder if it's at the coffee stain dousing my shirt, before a sudden pinching sensation tingles at the back of my neck. She lifts her hand, now clenching my charm necklace, and flares her nostrils when she sees the heart dangling next to the one that has sat lonely for over nine years.

Flinching back when she shoves the necklace in my face, my heart doubles in speed because her face tells me that she knows everything. The coffee I'm holding nearly slips again, so I clench onto it a little too tight until cool liquid slides down my hand. It's sticky and gross but I don't dare move right now.

"You know what, River?" She growls my name so loudly that people down the street turn to see what the ruckus is about. "I used to think that you were a threat when we were younger because you had the poor fucking orphan girl routine and Everett wrapped around your finger because of it. But he told me I had nothing to worry about, and you know what? I believed him. I believed him because you were fourteen and he was almost eighteen and getting ready to leave the state for bigger and better things. My hatred for you went away when he picked *me* and stayed with *me*."

She throws the necklace on the ground with all the force she has, and I half expect her to take her pointy heel and smash it into pieces. "I should have known that the feelings he had for you, the need to protect little innocent, naive River, would change over the years. But you know what? I never, *never* would have thought that *you* of all people would be willing to ruin a fucking family when you never had one for so long. I guess I really am as stupid as you must think, huh? I let my guard down, asked you for *help* with my relationship, and you were fucking him all along, weren't you?"

"I-I-Isabel, I—"

Her palm strikes me faster than I can blink, and I stumble back from the stinging blow. Dizziness sweeps my vision as I cradle my cheek with my free hand, blinking past the blurry tears forming in my eyes.

Someone gasps from the crowd surrounding us, but I don't move or try to defend myself. I've taken harder blows, and this is the only one I've ever deserved.

"Don't you dare lie to me!" she hisses, pointing toward the necklace still laying discarded between us on the sidewalk. "My uncle is the jeweler at the shop Everett buys those charms from. He custom makes them. And when he saw Everett shopping, Everett told him it was for someone special. The joke is on me though, isn't it? I waited and waited for him to show me what he bought, even thought it was a stupid engagement ring. When I found the receipt for less than a ring would cost, I knew I would have nothing to show for it. Uncle Donny told me it was a charm he got, not a ring, and that was all I needed to know."

Tears stream down my cheeks, not from the pain of her hit, but from the audience around us hearing our argument, witnessing the worst mistake I've ever made come to light.

Even her voice is getting shaky, and I realize there are tears in her eyes for a totally different reason than my guilt. She's mourning. Angry. Destroyed. "He's never at the firehouse when he says he is and lies about who he's out to eat with like I'm not supposed to know. What the hell gives you the right, River? Huh?"

Shaking my head vehemently, I try telling her the truth, how sorry I am, how there's no reason that could make this better. But the words are stuck in my throat and that only makes her angrier.

When she waves her hand in the air, I see something flash on one of her fingers. A ring. A ring with a large diamond in the center that looks like it costs more than the entire art studio and apartment above it.

She sees what I'm looking at when a slow, sadistic smile spreads across her lips. "Oh, this little thing? I'm sure you're surprised to see it, but maybe it'll finally get the point across. You may have had my *fiancé's* body, but you will never have anything more than that. He will always choose me. Do you know why, River?"

Speechless. The ring on her finger makes me speechless. I'm not sure why, because everyone expected this to be where their relationship would lead. But Everett's waited so long that I honestly thought he would end it once and for all before he ever proposed.

"Because of the baby," she whispers.

The ...?

Nausea sweeps through me.

Everett is going to be a dad?

She steps up so close to me that I choke on her expensive perfume. "He didn't tell you that either? I guess you never were much to him after all, were you? Guess he tricked us both."

She laughs but it's a dry, dull sound. "I don't know why you think you're the only one who deserves a free pass in life. We all have pasts that we want to change, pieces of our lives we want to escape from. You won the fucking lottery getting the James'. Some of us aren't so lucky on the family we're given, but at least this little scandal will put you in your place. Far away from the James family when they find out."

Oh my God.

Isabel bends and picks up the necklace from the ground and shoves it into my aching chest. "Everett Tucker is my way out, don't you get it? Without him and his money, I'm stuck under my father's thumb. This necklace, the memories of you two, will be the *only* thing you have of him. Do you understand?"

Breathless, I nod. There are so many emotions waging through my body that I can't quite figure out.

Her hand pushes off me, causing me to stumble backward into the brick wall and catch the silver chain in my hand.

With a flick of her wrist, she turns and glances over her shoulder. "Get ready, River. Your life in Bridgeport is never going to be the same."

The crowd that's gathered around our show parts for Isabel as she walks away from me. When she disappears, I'm left with gawking eyes, a sore cheek, and a necklace with a broken clasp ... and a family that's going to hate me forever.

THIRTY-ONE

Everett / 27

The news is everywhere by lunch, and I'm ready to go find River when Robert shows up at my office with his hands in his pockets and disappointment dulling his graying features.

Tensing where I stand behind my desk, I hold my breath and wait for his reaction. There's no possibility of letting myself explain the situation, he's probably heard the rumors by now. Many friends witnessed the confrontation first hand while they were grabbing breakfast on the way here. The moment they arrived back in the office, the hasty, judgmental comments and stares began.

It's as though I've transported back in time to witness catty high school girls tearing everything to pieces.

He blows out a heavy breath. "I told you to treat her well, Everett. But I guess my advice the other day was too late, wasn't it?"

My lips part to answer, but he shakes his head and walks away, the door to my office closing slowly behind him.

I sit back down and put my face in my palms.

THIRTY-TWO

River / 23

There's a knock at the front door of my apartment, echoing in the dead silence surrounding me. I've been avoiding all contact with the outside world since Isabel confronted me yesterday morning. Shutting myself inside, taking time off work, closing myself in my guilt and sin and shame, is the only thing I can do.

"Sweetheart," a soft, familiar voice calls from the other side of the door. A silent sob wracks my body at the sound of Bridgette's voice. Tears fall harder down my face as I squeeze a pillow tighter to my chest.

Maybe if I squeeze hard enough, it'll burst from the seams. It's what I want to happen to me, because the emotions bloating and tugging on my insides makes me feel like I'm two seconds away from combusting.

Everything hurts. My eyes. My body. My heart. It hurts for Isabel and for my family. It doesn't hurt for me, because I'm the maker of my own destruction.

I deserve this pain.

I accept this pain.

Another knock. "Baby, can you please open up for me? I need to make sure you're okay."

She wants to know I'm okay?

Knowing she doesn't hate me, at least not completely, makes my bare feet glide toward the front door. Shakily, I unlatch the chain and undo the deadbolt before flicking the lock and finally revealing the woman behind it.

She normally looks put together, like the world can't touch her. Today, her eyes are muddled with worry and something else, something bad, and her makeup-less face makes her look older than she really is. The corners of her eyes are wrinkled with exhaustion, and her lips are curved down in the type of frown that makes me realize just how heavy the consequences of my actions are.

A sob breaks loose inside of me; a sob for Bridgette, the woman who's always happy and positive. It's a sob for Robert, who is probably trying to rein in the havoc I've caused at the company.

Dropping the pillow that I helplessly held onto, I take one blurry look at Bridgette and completely shatter into millions of tiny pieces.

"*Mom*," I rasp in a choked plea, falling into her open arms. "I made a mistake."

Her arms instantly engulf me in a tight, warm embrace. Her own damp cheek rests on the top of my messy hair and she guides us inside and out of the cold draft created by the hallway air vent.

Her lips brush the crown of my skull, caressing my

knotted hair as she says, "Oh, baby girl. You're not the only one."

Soaking her shoulder with my tears, I squeeze her tighter to ground myself. I need her, my mom, now more than ever.

She strokes her fingers through my hair and hushes me in comfort. "It'll be okay, sweetie. I know it doesn't seem like it, but you'll get through this. You're strong."

Another wrack of sobs escapes me. "I'm n-not though. I did something bad and I don't know how to f-fix it."

Drawing back, she uses the pads of her thumbs to swipe at my cheeks. Sympathy lingers in her glassy eyes. "River, you can't fix something like this. I know you want to, I know you feel awful, but it happened."

Lifting my arm and wiping the sleeve of my shirt at my cheeks, I try blinking away the remaining tears. "Do you hate me?"

Her eyes widen before she hugs me quickly again. "I could never hate you! And I know you probably think the worst right now, but Robert doesn't either. He—your father—is just a bit ... startled at the moment."

Startled? That isn't the word I was expecting her to say —disappointed, angry, and a slew of other adjectives, sure.

"He *should* hate me though."

She guides us over to the couch, picking up the pillow I dropped and setting it in the corner of the cushions. "Sweetheart, we both love you so much. You are our miracle. Do you understand that? We tried to have more kids with no luck after Oliver, and as soon as Jill told us about you, it was like something clicked. You were the missing piece we needed to feel complete and nothing, *nothing* you do will ever ruin that for us."

But how? How can I hate myself so much and get only love from people who I can ruin with this scandal? Isabel is right. What I've done doesn't just impact her relationship with Everett. It risks everything Robert has built, his morals, his loyalties.

"I think you're punishing yourself enough, don't you?" she asks gently, holding my hand in between hers. She reaches into the purse I didn't see hanging from her other shoulder, producing a tissue from inside. Dabbing my eyes, she gives me a warm smile, a familiar one that I've seen thousands of times grace her elegant face. "I'm going to give you some motherly advice that I want you to truly think about, okay?"

Sniffing back tears, I give her a tiny nod as my only reply.

Once my face is dry, she sets the tissue down on her lap. "Bridgeport will always be your home. Robert and I will always greet you with open, loving arms. But maybe it wouldn't be a bad thing if you got away for a little while." Seeing the stricken expression of my face, she quickly adds, "Not because we don't want you around. We talked about it last night, and I truly think escaping for a little while will help you *and* Everett. You both need space, time to let the gossip cool down, before you face each other again."

Staring at my lap, I absorb her suggestion. I always thought leaving Bridgeport would be running away from my problems, no matter how big or small. Bridgette could be right. Leaving for a little while could be exactly what I need to clear my conscience and free my soul. It would also give me time to figure out what I want, because every time I've tried before, I was suffocated with my decision.

"Do you love him, sweetie?" Her voice is quiet, curious, and maybe a little knowing. She's watched me grow up, watched me blossom and change, so surely she's watched me pine for Everett Tucker all these years.

Pining isn't the same as loving though.

"Yes."

Her hand squeezes mine again. "Then let him go until he can figure things out with Isabel. Distance makes the heart grow fonder. It did for your father and me, you know. We went to separate colleges on different sides of the country, and our love never dwindled. If it's truly love, and I believe it is knowing that boy, then you will find your way back to each other."

Swallowing back my rising emotions, I press my lips together. "I ... I could ask Steph if I can stay with her and her boyfriend. She's been trying to get me back to California ever since I left."

Bridgette pats my leg. "I think that's a good idea. Get

a tan, have some fun, do something for yourself. Everything will be waiting for you when you're ready."

But how will I know when that is?

That annoying voice in my head answers, *when it stops hurting.*

Closing my eyes, I wonder if that's even possible. Just seeing Everett's face, remembering the fury on Isabel's, leaves a gaping hole in my chest, especially when my brain replays the image of Isabel's ring and what she said about ... *the baby.*

I make a choking sound and brush hair out of my face. "California will be good," I whisper brokenly.

Maybe if I tell myself that over and over, I'll actually start believing it.

THIRTY-THREE

Everett / 27

Robert asked that I take some time away from work to stay at home and "deal with things". It really just keeps the assholes at the office from coming by and cracking jokes or giving me shit about throwing away a perfectly good relationship. Half of them talk about Isabel like they know her well, and shit, maybe they do. But they don't know what our relationship was like.

At first, I ignored them. What else could I do? Then I blew up at Cody Anderson from accounting in front of the entire fifth floor when I had enough of him running his mouth.

Half the office on the eighth floor has bets placed on how long I'll last in my position with the new information they've gotten from town gossipers. From what I hear, the pot is high, and I'd be lying if I said I'm not nervous about the repercussions I'll face when Robert really wraps his head around what I've done with his daughter.

It doesn't matter that he sees me as a son or known me longer than her. River is his daughter in every way but blood. She's his first priority. I just hope he can forgive me eventually.

My apartment has been vacated for over a week now, and I've only been there long enough to see if Isabel really left. The furniture and dishes she bought are right where I remember them always being and a handful of clothes still hang in our closet. It looks like it did before she moved in, not quite settled but slightly lived-in.

The apartment never felt like home, and Isabel might have filled the emptiness, but it never changed how I felt about my indifference to the place. She, on the other hand, loved it. It used to be bland with neutral walls and empty shelves and cupboards until she decorated the space. In my haste to move on, I never thought about her just staying there permanently, but maybe that's exactly what she needs.

The cabin is where I feel the memories the most. This sense of security, of belonging, wraps itself around me just like I imagine it did for my father growing up. Pictures of my family litter the walls, fireplace mantel, and shelves. Trophies and game heads from hunting competitions my father used to compete in with Granddad hang around the living room, and it still smells like I always remember—pine, cinnamon, and the great outdoors. Isabel used to hate coming there for parties because the wood is worn, the floors creak, and the décor is dark and monotone. But I like simple. Simple suits me.

After getting internet installed, I set up the old guest bedroom as my home office. Robert thinks I should speak to Isabel, but I know Issy. She needs time away from me, and the few short weeks it has been since I asked her to move out of the apartment isn't enough considering the years I'm saying goodbye to. It isn't like they meant nothing; we had our good days along with the bad. The bad just won out.

When I do see Issy, it'll be during working hours, so her father can't trap me at their house. Plus, we're less likely to argue in a public setting. I'm just as guilty of losing it at bad times as she is, she's just louder. But if there's one thing Blake Allen taught her, it's to save face.

The apartment won't be enough of an apology to her, but hopefully it helps. I don't expect her to forgive me by any means, just to understand why it has to be like this.

Closing my laptop and pushing off the desk, I wander into the kitchen where my cell is plugged into the wall. The farther away it is from me, the less chance I have at reaching out to River. The calls I made right after hearing about the confrontation were left unanswered, so I knew texts would find the same fate.

Plus, I promised Robert not to bother her until she was ready. It's the only thing he asked of me before telling me to go home. But home isn't as simple as four walls and a roof.

Home isn't a place. It's a person. And mine is somewhere suffering as a wrecking ball threatens to tear down her walls.

I'm the instigator.

I'm the person who pulls the lever.

All because of one night.

No.

All because of *ten years.*

I just hope there will be a hell of a lot more to come.

THERE'S A WOMAN YELLING MY NAME. SHE SOUNDS worried, kind of like Mom did the one time I wandered off in the store alone. I wanted the blue rubber ball in the cage. But this woman is shrieking and older and familiar.

"Where is he? Where's Everett?"

I try moving but shooting pain makes me cry out until soft hands and lulling voices tell me to stay still.

The woman yells again. Sobs. "Everett! Where is my grandbaby?"

A man is telling her to take a deep breath, his voice is raspy kind of like Dad's but deeper. Another voice is closer, younger, warmer. She tells me that I'm okay. That they're going to fix me.

Everything gets fuzzy but the pain goes away. My veins feel cold when something trickles through them, then warms, until my body goes still. More voices. More yelling.

I can't open my eyes, but I think someone enters the room. There's a lot of crying and whispering and I hear my name.

"Rhett boy," a voice says, "it's okay now, we're here for you. You're going to get through this because you're strong. Understand?"

Somebody agrees, the raspy man. "I promise we're going to take care of you. Your grandmother and I will make you better. Do you know why, son?"

Grandpa calls me son.

"Because we're Tuckers," he whispers close to my ear. Sleepiness washes over me suddenly. "And Tuckers always keep their promises."

I jolt awake with the sweaty, scratchy sheets clinging to my body. Forcing my legs over the side of the bed, I rest my elbows on my knees and thread my fingers through my damp hair.

Sometimes I think the cabin has *too* many memories. It's why I chose to sleep in a different room than the one I spent my childhood in. My grandparents' room was across the house, my father's old room next to that, and my childhood room a few doors away from there. This one is clear across the house, but not far enough to ward off unwanted memoires.

Waking up in the hospital was a terrifying experience. I was in and out of it for days because of the medicine they pumped into me, but my grandparents were always there like they promised. They took me to their house after a month of corrective surgeries and recuperation, wearing a bright blue cast on my arm, bruises on my face, and a large cut down the side of my neck that the doctors said would scar from the seventeen stitches it needed. One of the nurses called it a battle scar, which I thought was cool at the time. It wasn't until much later I acknowledged most battles ended in death, and I was the only survivor.

Running my hand down the curve of the old wound, I close my eyes. Taking a few harbored breaths, I push myself up and toward the kitchen for some water. It's three in the morning, almost four. Too early to run. Too early to start the day.

Just ... too early.

Funny, considering I'm usually too late.

When I check my phone, I don't know what I expect. There aren't any missed calls or texts waiting for me from anyone important. Not even Oliver, and I wonder if he knows. I doubt he'll be in the dark for long, even a thousand miles away. People talk.

In fact, I disabled my social media accounts, the few that I had, because everyone talked too much. I got nasty messages on Facebook and even worse comments. But when I went to River's page ... she got the brunt of the hate. Last I knew, she still had it. In fact, I may have checked up on her last night before bed. It's pointless because she never posts.

Probably a good thing right now.

The night I asked her to the café, I never intended to end up in her bed. Have I fantasized about it? Fuck yes. My right arm has more muscle mass from the workout it always gets thinking about her naked. River has meant something more to me for longer than I like to admit. It has been years of quick glances, longing looks, and secret wishes that I've kept bottled up.

I fucked up and can't go back. I don't want to. Everything about the past has been done wrong. Moving forward means redoing what I should have done to begin with.

Tell River how beautiful she is.

Tell River how much I care.

Tell Isabel I'm sorry.

Picking up my phone, my finger hovers over River's name in my contacts list. My promise to Robert is what makes me close out of the app, down a glass of water, and go to the living room.

Phone in hand, I sit down on the cool material of the cloth couch and heave out a long, heavy sigh. Closing my eyes will bring new nightmares, old memories. Sleeping will trap me in with my conscience.

Clicking on Issy's name, I shoot her a quick text to ensure that I fix at least one thing in my power.

Can we talk tomorrow?

I'm laying on my back staring up at the dark ceiling that dances with shadows of tree limbs outside the front window when my phone buzzes on my stomach.

10. Don't be late.

Huffing out a quiet laugh, I shake my head and shut my eyes. At least Isabel hasn't lost her charm. Maybe that's a good sign. Or a very, very bad one.

That's the last thought I have before falling back into the darkness.

THIRTY-FOUR

River / 23

L.A.X is swamped with busybodies swarming baggage claim trying to locate their things. I learned last time I visited that you have to use your elbows to get through or you'll just stand there forever. The only reason I found that out was when Steph came searching for me after waiting nearly an hour outside. She didn't hesitate to shove her way through the crowd and demand to know where my bag was when we couldn't find it.

I'm not like Steph though. I barely tap people as I make my way through the heavy crowd grabbing their bags from the conveyer. I do manage to pull my black rolling suitcase off and yank the handle up as soon as it's on the ground next to me and search the huge room.

When I called Steph and asked her if I could still stay with her like she offered hundreds of times before, she squealed so loud in my ear, I think it started bleeding. Her boyfriend, Mason, and her made up the spare room and told me it's mine whenever I need it.

I've never met Mason, but I did talk to him during one of my many phone calls with Steph. She always has it on speaker phone, so sometimes he'll crack a joke or intervene when she gets riled up about something to do with work. That's how they met, on set of the indie film they're part of. Mason has a small roll as a side character in it and Steph got promoted to helping with costumes. They seem like they're in love, but I don't exactly have the best judgment on what love really is.

As soon as I get through a bulk of the crowd, Steph starts jumping up and down and waving her arms around. She looks the same as last time except tanner, if that's possible. I wonder if she spends more time outside now that she isn't the assistant to some stuck-up movie star anymore.

She's wearing a long sheer white maxi dress with a slit that goes up mid-thigh. Like usual, she's in Gladiator sandals with a huge purse hanging from her shoulder. Her long sandy blonde hair falls in waves past her shoulder, and she's got a pair of sunglasses folded in her hands as she yells my name.

I miss Steph's energy. Sometimes it made me feel like a failure for not being more like her, because I was her exact opposite. But it worked better that way. Her mom said we balanced each other out, which I think she liked because Steph sometimes got a little *too* crazy before we became close friends.

"You're here!" she shrieks, bouncing over and wrapping me in a tight hug. She smells like suntan lotion and coffee, and when she pulls back there are tears watering her baby blues. "I can't believe you're really here, River!

Mason is probably sick of me saying that you're staying with us, but I'm just so excited! I mean, the circumstances could probably be better, but who cares?"

Steph catches me when a guy with a buzzcut shoves past me on his way out.

Once I'm stable, she turns around and shoots daggers at the guy. "Hey, watch where you're going, asshole! Yeah, I'm talking to you, buddy!"

The guy is long gone, not caring that somebody is yelling at him. But that's Steph, calling out people without a worry in the world.

Turning on her heels, her big smile greets my tired eyes. "I'm really sorry about everything going on at home, babe. But we're going to have so much fun here!"

I never told her the details about the Isabel thing. She doesn't know about the ring or baby, just that Isabel gave me a much-deserved bitch slap and told the whole east-end of Bridgeport that I had an affair with her boyfriend.

Her fiancé, the pesky voice in my head reminds me.

She takes my suitcase despite my protests and we start heading toward the front doors side by side. "How did you even find out about all that stuff anyway?"

Making an unattractive snorting sound, she gives me a *duh* look and rolls her made-up eyes. "I have this thing called social media. You do too, if memory serves. And let's just say the haters are out to get you on Facebook."

My eyes lock on the sidewalk as we step onto it. Tiny ants walk in a haphazard line, some toward the cracks and others toward the mayhem. I wonder if they know they don't stand a chance or if they just don't care.

Steph reaches out and takes my hand, keeping it wrapped in hers. "The haters are just jealous, River. Honestly, most of the people talking about it are chicks from school that Everett never paid attention to. Even *before* that evil hoe."

Shoulders sagging, I let out a tiny, defeated sigh. "Don't call her that. If anybody deserves name calling, it's me."

It's why I haven't been on Facebook. I normally go on a few times a week to see what everyone is up to, mostly Steph and Oliver since they're both active online.

The thought of Ollie seeing the comments everyone's warned me about makes my stomach bottom out. I've come to terms with my family seeing me differently. Bridgette ... *Mom* ... reminded me right before I got on the plane that they love me. But I wonder if that extends to Oliver?

My hand gets squeezed. "I mean it, River. Those girls are just jealous they didn't get to see Everett's cock, too. He didn't hook up with many girls at parties, so there's a lot of people who missed the mystery that is Everett Tucker."

Those words make my chest hurt. Isabel called him a mystery the night she gave me a ride home; she said that's what drew her to him. But he was never a mystery. Not to me.

"Can we not talk about it anymore?" I plea quietly,

letting her pull me across the busy street toward one of the parking lots.

Jumping up onto the curb and easily wheeling my bag behind us, she wiggles her eyebrows at me. "Sure thing. Let's talk about everything we're going to do while you're at Casa de la Stephanie. First, your hair."

"My hair?"

An evil grin spreads across her face. "I seem to remember you telling me once that you'd only let me dye your hair if you did something stupid. You know, because then you'd deserve the punishment that is girly fun. Which, by the way, is ridiculous. No worries, I still love you anyway. But some might define your actions with Everett as stupid. Not me though, because I'd jump on that dick—"

"Steph!" I scold, feeling my face heat. "I thought we weren't talking about it anymore?"

Tipping her head back and groaning loudly, she stops beside her car. "Ugh, fine. You're no fun. All I'm saying is that you came here to let loose and live a little, so I'm going to help you do that."

Blinking back doubt, I ask, "By dyeing my hair?"

She nods enthusiastically, her red lips stretched into a huge grin. "Damn straight. But don't think I'm letting you off that easy. I remember lots of things you said you wanted to do that one time at Kenzie's house when we were talking about life dreams."

My eyes widen as she unlocks her car and opens the backdoor, slipping my suitcase onto the leather seat. "But we were all drunk from the wine she snuck out of her mother's cabinet!"

Steph doesn't care. "So? Now is your chance to finally be somebody you never let yourself be in New York. California is literally the perfect place to reinvent yourself."

Swallowing past the lump in my throat, I shake my head. "What if I don't want to reinvent myself? Maybe becoming somebody else isn't the answer. I mean, I'm not here to make more stupid choices."

"And I won't let you."

I eye her.

"Okay, I won't let you make *many*."

That sounds more like her.

"Just trust me. You trust me, right?"

"Of course."

More than anyone.

She takes my hands again. "I just want you to be happy, River. So does your family. It may not seem like it now, but you *can* find happiness without you-know-who. Give it time, okay?"

After years of wanting the same person, I wonder if I really can. Thinking about every encounter, every heartache of Everett and Isabel, the answer seems so clear.

I whisper, "Okay."

MY LONG AUBURN HAIR IS NOW "LUSCIOUS LAVENDER" according to the box, and I wonder why I let Steph win this battle. It's too different, and I've never done well with change.

"It's only temporary. Stop fussing."

She's been telling me that for two days now, after catching me play with the locks of purple or seeing my reflection in the mirror. It's not bad, just ... different. I don't look like me anymore. Steph makes me her plaything every morning, putting makeup on me—more than my usual foundation. Unlike the first time she made me up, I sport the famous winged liner she loves so much.

Mason Combs is definitely the perfect match for Steph. He mellows out her crazy, especially when she tries dragging me out to clubs every night. Well, the past two anyway. Something tells me he won't be able to stop her if she keeps insisting I "let loose" by dancing my heart out. Steph doesn't give up, which is unfortunate because she knows I can't dance to save my life. I have two left feet.

But Steph likes to get her way, and I think Mason knows that. It's why she chooses what to eat every night and picks what movie to torture him with. He never argues, unless Indian food or *Dirty Dancing* are the selections.

Like tonight.

"Babe, you know I can't eat that." He's sitting on their suede couch with an arm draped across the top while Steph goes through her takeout menus. "What if we cooked?"

That doesn't seem to suit Steph. "Are you kidding?

We can't cook to save our lives. Do you remember when you tried making me dinner for our one month anniversary?"

My eyes bounce to Mason. "What happened?"

He starts laughing. "I set the toaster on fire trying to make her toast. She loves breakfast, so I thought breakfast for dinner would be romantic. Eggs, toast, pancakes, the works. Instead, I almost burnt down our place."

A giggle escapes my lips. "That is kind of romantic. You know, the thought. I wish someone would burn toast for me."

Steph throws a menu at me. "Edible toast is better, but I digress." She tosses the Indian takeout brochure to the side. "Okay, what about pizza? We can't hate on pizza."

Pizza does sound good right now, but Mason tells Steph that he has a shirtless scene to shoot tomorrow.

Steph picks up her cell and hops onto the counter. "Well River and I don't, so I guess you'll be eating a salad while we indulge in greasy, cheesy goodness. Won't we, River?"

Mason frowns at his girlfriend. "You're an evil, evil woman."

Steph blows him an air kiss. "But you can't get enough of me. If you're a good boy when the pizza arrives, I'll breathe near you so you can get a good whiff of all those yummy carbs." She turns to me. "Aren't you glad we're not actresses? All those body restrictions and diets would kill us."

Me without sugar is a bad idea. It's like Bridgette without tea or Robert without coffee—nobody needs to see that. The thought of them makes me frown.

Steph misinterprets my sullen expression. "Don't worry, Riv. We don't need all the drama that comes with acting anyway. Working on set around B-listers makes me realize what kind of bullets I've missed. Remember when I wanted to be one? Or a model? I mean … I'd have to stop eating cake. It just wasn't meant to be."

Her outburst makes me laugh. She wanted to be a model when we were sixteen when one of the girls in our grade got some catalog gig at the mall, where she was featured in local ads and magazines for a homegrown clothing company. She tried dieting to lose weight that, in my opinion, she didn't need to lose, but her mom wouldn't let her keep starving herself for some ridiculous dream. It hurt Steph's feelings until she started eating her much beloved desserts again. All was forgiven and she moved on with the next dream. I think she wanted to be a pastry chef.

After the pizza arrives, Steph puts on *Sixteen Candles* and tells Mason that Michael Schoeffling is on her free pass list, which Mason explains means that Steph can sleep with him without repercussions of Mason breaking up with her if she ever meets the celebrity. Steph tells me his is Anna Kendrick, who apparently, is also on her list.

It doesn't surprise me.

My nose scrunches. "Isn't Michael Schoeffling old now?"

"He's not even sixty," she argues quickly, smacking Mason when he chuckles. "Dolly Parton is on Mason's list! I mean, *come on!*"

Mason gives me a *well, duh* expression, his lips pressed flat together. "Can you blame me? Her tits are huge."

Steph shakes her head. "They're also fake. At least hold out for someone with natural boobs the size of your face. I imagine they're more fun to play with."

Heat creeps up the back of my neck over their conversation. "Can we maybe change the subject?"

"Fine," Mason relents. "Who's on your list, River? Tell us about all your freaky fantasies."

Steph laughs. "Do you still have a crush on James Marsters? I totally wouldn't judge you because that man is a silver fox now."

Mason's eyes narrow inquisitively. "Is that the dude from *Buffy?*"

"Spike!" Steph chirps with a nod.

He scoffs, stabbing the last piece of lettuce in his chef salad. "At least it's not Robert Pattinson. I mean, real vampires don't sparkle. That's fucking boring."

Steph pokes Mason's knee from where she sits next to him on the floor. "I bet if Dolly played a sparkling vampire you'd love it."

He grumbles something under his breath that I can't understand.

Steph turns to me. "He's just bitter because I made him watch *Remember Me* without giving him any warning."

THE TRUTH ABOUT HEARTBREAK

That makes him speak up. "I'm just saying, a little warning would be nice! I swear you watch the most depressing movies, woman. Like the time you made me watch *Marley and Me.* You're a sadist."

Steph and I both laugh while he shakes his head and collects our empty plates. My stomach is full, and the movie is nearly over, so I grab my phone and text my parents to let them know I'm all right and that I'll probably head to bed soon. It makes them feel better when I update them every night.

Just as I'm setting my phone down, Steph snatches it up and opens the camera app. Shuffling closer to me she flips the camera screen to selfie mode and fluffs her hair.

Nudging my shoulder, she smiles into the camera. "Say cheese, River. We need to show off your hair and prove to the haters that they can't stop us from having fun."

Frowning, I glance at her. "I'm not sure that's a good idea. I don't want to feed their hate. Let's face it, Steph. They're not wrong to call me out on anything."

Her playful expression turns grim and serious, eyes narrowing to slits like I'm about to be scolded by my mother. "Nobody deserves to be treated the way they're treating you. Do you understand me? They're petty bitches who have nothing better to do than spew hate."

I don't say anything.

"*But*," she relents, "I'll only post this to my Instagram account. We don't have many friends in common, and nobody appreciates drama on there. So, smile already."

Rolling my eyes, I wrap a strand of hair around my finger and nervously turn to the phone. Forcing a smile on my face, Steph smushes her cheek against mine and makes a silly face, sticking her tongue out. It makes me laugh, which is when she takes the picture.

I admit, it's cute. We look carefree like we did when we were younger, and our only worry was what we'd have to eat at the school cafeteria. She sends herself the picture and then plays around with filters on her Instagram page. Whatever she chooses makes my hair look more lilac than lavender.

She shows me the final product, only captioning it with *What's happenin' hot stuff?* before posting it to her ten thousand followers.

Not even a minute later, she squeaks and shows me her phone. "Look! It's already got thirty likes and people are saying how much they like your hair! And, wait—" Her eyes squint as she reads a comment. "Why does that name sound familiar?"

"What name?"

"Peter York." She clicks on his username, which brings it to his profile. "Hey, isn't this one of your brother's friends? They played basketball together, right?"

Inspecting the image, I shudder. I remember him all right. Whenever Oliver would have game days, he would wander around the house. If I was doing homework at the dining room table he would bother me and ask a million questions until one of the others told him to leave me alone. Usually, that was Everett. But sometimes

Tommy and Quinn would step in when I was too nervous to speak up for myself.

"What did he say?" Part of me doesn't really want to know, but someone who used to hang out with Oliver and Everett would probably have something to say about the little scandal in Bridgeport.

Grinning, she wiggles her eyebrows at me, which always freaks me out. "He said you look hot with purple hair. Oh! He commented again." Her smile instantly disappears, but she tries hiding it before I notice.

"What?" I whisper.

She waves her hand in the air. "It's nothing important. You know how guys are—"

I take her phone and read his new comment, sucking in a sharp breath when my eyes scroll over the lewd statement.

Send her my way when Tucker is done with her. You know, unless she's only into unavailable men.

Steph quickly takes her phone and deletes the comment. Giving me a sympathetic look, she squeezes my arm. "Hey, don't listen to that asshole. I sort of remember people saying what a douche he was in school. I guess he never changed. I mean, it's no wonder he's single!"

It doesn't help me feel any better, but I force a sad smile anyway. "I'm getting kind of tired. I think I ate too much. Mind if I go to bed?"

Her shoulders drop. "Sure. See you tomorrow, River.

We'll grab some pastries before I have to go to work. Okay?"

I nod before telling Mason goodnight and slipping into the darkness of my room.

What did I expect to happen? Until something bigger comes along, I'll be the topic everybody talks about no matter how far away I am from home.

Curling up onto my side, I think about Bridgette and Robert—Mom and Dad. I fall asleep with tears rolling down my cheeks.

THIRTY-FIVE

Everett / 27

Isabel's office is littered with blueprints of clothing designs, colorful fabrics, and bags of feathers and buttons I imagine will wind up on some sort of outfit. The bright pink and white walls match her perfectly, just like the lime green armchairs in the corner of the room. I'm not sure who designed the office, but it seems like it was made for her.

The secretary right outside the elevator doors must know who I am because she perks up instantly and tells me Isabel's finishing up a meeting down the hall. The young black-haired woman directs me to Isabel's office, which I've been to a few times when she first started, and find myself looking at her personal items.

There's a picture of her and her mother from high school graduation, both wearing big smiles and black dresses. Next to that is her parents, their smiles neither big nor reaching their eyes. Hanging above those in a silver frame is a picture of us. My arm is wrapped around Issy's waist and she's tucked into my side. One of her hands is resting on my pec and her pink painted lips are stretched into a big smile as I look to my right. Almost as if I'm staring at her but ...

"That was my favorite picture of us."

Her voice startles me from going back to the day it was taken. Turning with my hands in my pockets, I watch her walk into her office with folders tucked in her arms.

The heels of her stilettos click against the floor as she walks around her white desk, setting the folders down in front of where her chair is positioned in the middle.

"Was?" I question, strolling to the chair across from her. I don't sit. Not yet.

She laughs coolly. "Like it's a surprise that it's not?" She shakes her head, pulling out her seat and sitting. Her eyes go to the one behind me, so I take it as an invitation and settle into the firm cushion.

"I suppose you're right, given the circumstances," I agree quietly.

She huffs, rolling her eyes at me. I shouldn't be surprised that she doesn't look different. Her makeup is done in full and her white dress is tight and pristine. She's professional, not showing one ounce of emotion.

"It's not for reasons that you think," she murmurs, typing something on her phone. She taps it a few times before turning it to me. It's the same picture that's framed. "Do you see what I see? A happy couple? Two people in love? I remember that day so well, Rhett. We were at a fourth of July party at the James's house. Robert was grilling and you offered to help but he wouldn't let you. People were swimming, Oliver was off flirting with who knows what girl. I asked Bridgette to take a picture of us before lunch was ready. When I saw the picture, my heart felt so full because you were looking at me with such ... love."

Her eyes trail to her phone screen for a moment, her smile disappearing when she clicks a few more things until a different image pops up. "Stephanie Malone posted this picture the day before I confronted River. It was some lame throwback Thursday post I nearly skipped over. Recognize it? It's the same moment Bridgette was taking the picture of us at the barbecue. I didn't pay it much attention until I realized that your eyes weren't focused on me in this picture. They're looking at River. Funny how perspective can really change things, huh? She was, what—seventeen here? Eighteen? Stephanie didn't even realize what bag of worms she was opening when she posted this picture of little miss perfect River James. But it made me open my eyes for the first time."

"Issy ..."

She holds up her hand. "You came here to talk, so let's talk. Let's talk about how long you've been in love with your best friend's little sister. Let's chat about all the feelings you've had for her when you were *inside me*. Were you picturing her every time you made me come? Every time you fucked me?"

Cringing over her words, I shake my head. "It wasn't like that."

"I bet not," she retorts, lips twitching before

returning to their flat position. "I'm sure that's why you had to find out what it was really like to be inside her, right? Because I couldn't do it for you. Maybe I never really had."

"Jesus, Isabel. That's not—"

"No," she growls. "*I'm* talking."

I shut up.

She sets her phone down. "You know, I think I've always known. I was fucking jealous of a fourteen-year-old and you made me feel stupid for it. Maybe you didn't love her then, but it wasn't long after when you realized that what you felt was more than just protectiveness for Oliver's helpless sister."

I'm not sure what to say, if she even wants me to say anything. Her eyes go to the picture on the wall and she sighs. "Your eyes were so bright, so warm in that picture. When I look in them, my heart used to feel all fuzzy knowing *I* made you look lost in the stars."

My tongue weighs heavy in my mouth, forcing me to keep quiet.

"After I saw that other photo, everything started making sense. You have a snow globe that River gave you in your office, and pictures of you two together in your apartment. In *our* apartment. There are so many memories of you two that you display for the world to see, Everett. Why not me? Huh? There's nothing in your office to remind you of me. Your apartment barely has anything of us besides the furniture I brought in. But everywhere I turned when I was packing my things was

River. Between the receipt I found for the charm and the picture ... I just ... I lost it. I have always wanted you to look at me the way you look at her.

"And you know the saddest part? When I confronted River that day, I didn't realize just how far you two had gone. Sure, I accused her of it, but I never would have thought either of you would cross that line. I knew there were emotions, *feelings*, but it wasn't until you told me how sorry you were that I realized you legitimately cheated on me."

Scrubbing a palm over my rough stubble, I try finding the words. There are so many ways to apologize, but none of them would fix this. Nothing can. They're just words. Even though I mean them, actions are the only way to make this right.

"You're right, Issy. I took things too far and nothing I can say will make it okay."

She crosses her arms on her chest. "It looks like we finally agree on something."

My eyes capture something on her finger. "Why are you wearing your grandmother's engagement ring?"

She holds out her hand and snickers at the piece of expensive jewelry hugging her slim, tan finger. "Honestly? I wore it to freak out your little side-piece and just liked having it on. It reminded me of everything I've ever wanted."

I'm on high alert, scooting forward in the seat. "What did you tell River, Isabel?"

Her brows lift. "She didn't tell you?"

"We haven't spoken."

Interest washes over her face. "My, my. That makes me feel good. It was probably the news about our baby that did it."

I choke on air. "What the hell are you talking about? Our ..." My eyes trail to her stomach, which is hidden under her desk. "Are you telling me you're—"

She eyes me hard. "If I were pregnant, I would have told you sooner. I'm a bitch, not a monster. Think about it, Everett. I would have used that as a reason to get you to put this ring on me for real."

So why the hell would she say anything about the baby we lost? Does she not care anymore? Does that not fucking destroy her like it does me?

Not a monster, my ass. "How could you bring up our unborn child to her? That's seriously screwed up."

"You don't get to judge me," she snaps.

"Don't I?"

She leans forward, fierceness flaming in her dark eyes. "You messed up first, buddy. I acted out of anger and I'm justified. Why should I care what she thinks? All I wanted was for her to feel as humiliated and destroyed as me."

I lose it then. "But you're not destroyed for the same reason! Face it, Issy. We don't love each other. You didn't want me to marry you because I was the one."

"Don't you dare—"

I gesture between us. "*This* is why we never were going to work out. Our relationship was so fucked up.

We hurt each other. We fight. We use each other. It's not healthy. It's not what either of us needs."

"And River James is what you need?"

Yes. "The apartment is yours," I tell her instead, ignoring that conversation. She already knows the answer.

"I don't want your fucking pity!"

"I'm not giving you *pity*, Isabel." I take a deep breath and lean forward. In my softest voice, I say, "I'm giving you *freedom.* That's what you really want, isn't it? The ring on your finger was supposed to be your way out, but it doesn't have to be the only one."

She blinks. "You're ... serious?"

"The rent is paid for the next year," I answer, locking eyes with her unsure gaze. "I know it's more complicated than that with your father, but it's a step in the right direction. You make good money doing what you love. There's no reason he has to control you, much less who you marry. Just because he made bad business choices doesn't mean you have to save him. Parents aren't supposed to rely on their children, it's the other way around."

This time, she's speechless.

I reach into my pocket and pull out the single key resting in it. It's the last one to the apartment, since she still has the other.

Leaning forward, I rest it by her phone in front of her. "I'm not asking you to forgive me, Isabel. The shit I've put you through will be something I regret for the rest of my life. All I'm asking is that you find happiness. Do what you want. Live in the apartment you've told me all these years you love. Redecorate. Fall in love. Prove to your father that true love exists. Just be happy, Issy. Not for me. Don't do shit for me. For *you*."

I'm shocked to see her eyes glaze over as she peers down at the key. Her fingertips graze the ridges before she blows out a steady breath. "We really are horrible for each other, aren't we?"

"Afraid so," I murmur.

She nods once. We sit there for a few moments in silence, but it's not uncomfortable. It's what we need right now.

Pulling open her desk drawer, she pulls a folded piece of paper out. At first, I don't recognize it. But when she passes me the yellow, crinkled, paper, I know exactly what it is and what's written inside.

"For the record," she whispers, eyeing the paper between us, "I don't hate you, Everett. I don't particularly like you right now, but hate is the furthest thing I feel. When I found this letter as I packed, I couldn't make myself read past her name. What we had may not have been real love, but I *do* love you. If I read this letter, all of that would go away. We'd have nothing good left between us."

Accepting the letter I wrote nearly six years ago, I blow out a quiet breath, like I'm dispelling my anxiety and worry. "I love you, Issy. We'll always be friends."

Isabel laughs, brushing tears from under her eyes and

sniffing back more from falling. Even tears can't break her. Not really. "Let's not get carried away. I still think you're an asshole."

That makes me smile. "Let me know what furniture you want to keep, and I'll get people in there to remove the rest of my things. Make a home out of that place, Issy."

She doesn't ask me where I'll live, because she probably already knows. The cabin is my home. River is my home.

Hopefully, she'll find hers.

THIRTY-SIX

River / 23

July boils me alive in the California heat, and I'm not sure I'll ever complain about New York summers again. My hair is a frizzy mess that Steph has to teach me how to tame, and I'd say she's mastered it based on her silky-smooth strands.

In the few weeks I've been here, Steph has kept her promise to make me live. When I want to stay in and watch movies, she takes me out on the town. We've seen new stars on the Hollywood walk of fame that have been added since I was here last, and she's shown me some of her new favorite places; restaurants that cost a kidney to eat at, hidden diners that remind me of Pop's in Bridgeport, and food trucks that offer any type of food we could want.

Sometimes I'll go to set with Mason and Steph to pass the time, though Steph claims she's the one who keeps convincing me to go. I just like looking at the setup they have, so when she's assisting in costume, I wander around the lot. It's not large, because of the low budget, but it's still impressive.

When I hear Steph yelling my name and running over to me with wide eyes, worry ceases me. "What's wrong? Is Mason okay?"

She grabs my arms and tries catching her breath, holding her chest as she sucks in as much oxygen as her lungs allow. "I need to ask you a huge favor. One of the set crew members showed up super high and got fired, and they need someone to step in to touch up a few things today. Maybe tomorrow, too."

My mouth goes dry. "Steph, I can't—"

Her blue eyes turn pleading as she yanks on my arm. "Pretty please? It's just painting, Riv. They won't expect you to build anything. Plus, I told them you majored in art, so you're practically qualified!"

"I majored in Art *History*," I correct her, glancing at a group of people who seem to be watching us in wait. Panic courses through my frozen limbs.

"Hey, look at me."

I obey, trying to force myself to calm down before I have a full-blown panic attack. I started getting them my senior year of college when I thought for sure I'd flunk my math class. Evidently, Everett saved me like he always does. No ... *did*. Past tense.

"It's just painting, River. I promise," she begins, voice softer than the panicky tone she gave me before. "You know how to hold a paintbrush, and I haven't seen you do anything art-related since you've been here. Don't think I haven't noticed the sketch pad that's been in the same place all lonely and sad in your room."

B. CELESTE

Glancing down at my sandaled feet, I count to ten backwards and finally relax. "I'm not inspired, is all."

"You're not letting yourself be," she counters with a sad frown dulling her face. "I know you promised Bridgette and Robert that you'd try. But are you?"

I don't answer.

She doesn't let up. "You've always wanted to make them proud, so do that. Help out on set, do what you love, paint or draw or whatever when we get home. The best friend I knew back in Bridgeport hasn't been living with us over the past month. The ghost of her has been. And don't think I won't sage the house or call Father Thomas from the Catholic Church down the street to perform an exorcism until my bestie returns."

There's no stopping the ridiculous laugh that bubbles out of me. She claps and jumps, wrapping me in a quick, tight hug.

"There she is." She squeezes my hands and gestures toward the people staring. "They're going to give you what you need and tell you what to do. It's so simple even I can't mess it up, so don't start overthinking like I know you want to."

She pulls me over to the set crew and introduces us all. The person in charge, Briggs, is in his late fifties with salt and pepper hair and a gray beard that covers his less than amused expression.

Before Steph leaves she whispers, "Don't worry. Briggs always looks like this. It's his version of resting

358

bitch face, except 'bitch' is more like 'bored'. Go show them what you've got, babe!"

Then she runs back to whichever trailer she's working in today.

Briggs assesses me and sighs heavily, like I'm not who he's looking for. "Well, you're not high, so that's a good start. Come on, kid. We've got a lot to do today."

I remember what I said I'd do while I was here—live, be happy, and not let anything get in the way of doing something great. This could be the first step at keeping that promise.

Mom and Dad will be proud.

STEPH COMES HOME AFTER A LONG DAY ON SET WITH A huge smile on her face and an envelope in her hands. Dropping it onto my lap, she stares at me until I hesitantly pick it up. She's giddy and bouncing where she stands, her hands waving for me to hurry up.

Tearing it open and pulling out the contents, I inhale a sharp, surprised breath. "Uh, why am I holding a check from your employer?"

She squeaks. "They paid you for your help this week doing the sets! And Briggs asked if you could be put on for the duration of the film, because there's always work to be done like you did this week. You got that man to like you, River. I didn't think that was possible."

It's probably because I don't talk unless someone prompts me. The others chit chat and joke around while they work, but I never know what to say. Briggs will sometimes come and ask me how I'm doing and inspect whatever project he gave me, just nodding before moving on to the next person.

"I'm being hired to work there?"

She bolts toward me, dropping on the couch and tackling me in a hug. "Yes! How exciting is this? We'll see each other on set! You get to paint and be creative and I get to help dress people and make them look pretty. I mean, how awesome is this?"

"Uh..." My shoulders rising is my only response. I never thought I'd work on a film set. The week has gone by fast and it's been a nice distraction, but it makes me remember the youth group I said goodbye to last month. Those kids are where I want to be, and Melanie and I spoke to them about me needing this time to heal, so I can be the best person for them when I'm back. Working another job feels wrong.

"We need to celebrate," she informs me, quickly standing and pulling out her phone. "I know how you feel about clubs, but there's this really laid-back place I know—"

"No!" I groan loudly, dropping the check onto the coffee table.

She winks. "Sorry, I'm not familiar with that word. We're going to get dressed up, put smiles on our face, and wait for Mase to get home. He'll be our escort tonight."

There's no point arguing with her. When she pulls me off the couch, it's to her room and not mine. She helped me unpack, so she knows what I have in my closet isn't club material. The huge walk-in closet in her room is definitely sporting options for the occasion though.

She rifles through a few things, the scraping of hangers against the bar making me wince, before squealing and yanking out a black scrap of fabric.

"What is that?"

She laughs and tosses it at me. I don't catch it before it hits me in the face, sliding into my hands. The material is soft and stretchy, and it looks like there's a design in the middle.

"It's a bandage dress. It'll look hot."

I don't want to look hot. In fact, frumpy seems to be the perfect style for me. Nobody pays attention to frumpy.

"Don't look like I just told you that your puppy died," she pouts, sitting down next to me.

"But—"

"I'm going to level with you because we're friends." She faces me with a stern expression. "You've been pining for the same guy your entire life. Don't think I never noticed when we were younger. Just because I liked Everett didn't mean I had claim. He always paid attention to you, so I get why you fed into that. And I'm not saying that's why you fell for him or whatever. He might have been the first nice guy you encountered who didn't make you feel scared, but I do think he always had some feelings for you. But after what happened, I think you deserve to try new things. Date new people. You already went out with David, right? And it didn't work out. Who knows, maybe you'll find someone tonight or on set or somewhere that will make you forget about Everett Tucker."

Her version of forgetting means using other men, but I don't want to be like Everett. He used Isabel to fight his feelings for me. He used me to distract himself from Isabel. Using people gets you nowhere but in a tangled mess of what-ifs and unrequited feelings.

Steph must sense my ill feelings toward the idea, so she sighs lightly. "You're River Jean James, a fighter and a survivor. Let Everett drown in you, River. Let him see that you can't be controlled or manipulated or beat down by old choices. Stop crossing oceans for people who won't even jump over puddles for you."

And that's all it takes before I'm secured in a black bandage dress with my purple hair in loose waves down my shoulders.

I don't want Everett to drown in me.

I just want him to float away.

THIRTY-SEVEN

Everett / 27

I'm back at the office after two weeks of working from home. Shit in town has died down, especially after Isabel started resurfacing around Bridgeport buying things for her apartment. It hasn't been forgotten, but it's better than listening to people whisper about me every waking second.

Robert won't admit it, but I think he may have warned people not to say anything about the topic— maybe even threatened termination. He's a well-respected man, so people listen to him. But there are a few who test him until he makes sure they know he isn't playing. Whether he did it for me or River, I don't know.

Not wanting to push my limits with his patience, I haven't said more than I've had to since I started back at the office Monday morning. Robert went over a few deals he wants me to look into and that's all. No updates on River. No talk of his thirtieth anniversary plans with Bridgette.

He hasn't called me out or gotten angry over the situation, and I wonder if it's building until he can't contain it or he's choosing his battles carefully.

The *beep* of the intercom stationed on my desk tells me Leigh, the new secretary on our floor, is trying to get in touch with me.

"M-Mr. Tucker?" Her voice is shaky and nervous. "There's a man who insisted on talking to you and he seemed awfully—"

She's cut off by Oliver slamming the door against the wall as he storms in.

"I see that, Leigh. Thank you."

I lean back in my chair and try speaking before he can, but he's next to me yanking me up before I can say a word.

"What the *fuck*, Everett?" he growls, slamming me against the white cement wall behind us. I let him, despite standing a few inches taller and having more muscle mass than him. He needs to work this out on his own.

From the corner of my eye, I see Robert standing outside my office. He doesn't intervene, just watches silently along with Leigh and a few others.

Oliver's fists twist my white dress shirt as he shoves me against the wall again. "You told me nothing bad would happen to her, Everett. I *asked* you if something was going on with my little sister and you *lied* to me."

Pointing out that he asked me when we just started at Penn would be pointless. I *did* tell him nothing was going on between River and me because there wasn't at the time. He suspected she had a crush on me and I assured him he had nothing to worry about. He may not have liked Isabel but having her in my life seemed to ease his worry over my feelings for River.

His hands are shaking as he pushes off me, leaving me against the wall. He doesn't raise his fist or try to punch me. That isn't Oliver James. He's not violent unless he has to be and apparently, I'm not worth the hassle of a swollen hand.

"I won't hit you," he murmurs, stepping away and raking his hand through his abnormally long hair. He's wearing a pair of jeans and a plain gray t-shirt. Bags are under his angry brown eyes, making his anger dim compared to the exhaustion.

Robert nods once at the back of his son's head, like he's proud. That's all he does before he turns back into his office, waving in dismissal for people to do the same.

When I'm sure Oliver is calm enough to hear me out, I push off the wall and flatten out my wrinkled shirt. "I'm not going to justify what's been done. Just know that I never lied to you when I said you had nothing to worry about back then. It wasn't until a little while later that I even started looking at her that way."

"*That way*," he scoffs, dropping into a seat across from my desk. He drops his face into his hands, his elbows propped against his knees.

After tucking my shirt back into my navy slacks, I take my own seat again. The door can stay open for all I care. Let people listen and pretend they're not.

He straightens up and eyes me. "I get that shit with you and Issy was never good. But why River, Everett? Why my sister?"

With a loose shrug, I return, "Why *not* her, Oliver? She's gone through hell and back, experienced the type of pain I can relate to. But unlike my sad excuse of a life, she channels hers into her passion and lets it make her stronger. I admire her strength and ability to trust and love and fight. I'm not sure I know another woman like her."

I'm not sure I want to, I add silently.

He blows out an exasperated breath. "I wouldn't have cared so much if you weren't so set on staying with Issy. River didn't deserve the kind of treatment she got from you. I'm not saying she's innocent in all of this, but she might not be as strong as you think."

That makes my jaw tick. "Why not?"

He eyes me skeptically, like I'm not supposed to be irritated he would question his sister's strength. "My dad asked me if I knew that her birth mother found her. I think he was asking the wrong guy about it."

Leaning forward with wide eyes, I stare at him in surprise. "Her birth mother?"

He grumbles something under his breath. "I guess that answers that. Yeah, her birth mother found her not long before she left. It must have shaken her up not to tell our parents about it."

I remember River mentioning that she wanted to

know about her mom, but never thought anything came of it.

Then something clicks in my head.

"What do you mean she left?"

He rolls his eyes in disbelief. "Come on, man. Like you didn't know." When I don't bother trying to speak, his brows raise. "Wow, you don't know? She's been in Cali for the past month. A little over a month at this point. She's with Stephanie."

Swiping a hand across my jaw, I shake my head. "I promised Robert I wouldn't reach out to her until she had some time to think. I didn't ..."

His shoulders seem to ease from the squared position they held. "Well, she didn't seem to tell anyone then. A tweaked woman came up to my mother one day when she was running errands claiming to be Savannah Scott, River's biological mother. And, I got to say man, Mom showed me a picture and they look too much alike for it to be a lie."

Why wouldn't River mention it to anyone? Meeting her birth mother had to be hard, she shouldn't have had to go through it alone. If it happened after our fallout, then I wasn't going to be the person to be there, but she had Bridgette, Robert, and Oliver.

"She must have had her reasons, Oliver. What if this Savannah person came up to River in the same state she did Bridgette? It could have freaked her out, maybe embarrassed her. You don't know what went through her mind, so I wouldn't question her strength."

He's quiet for a moment, his jaw ticking like I hit a nerve. "You're right."

Nodding once, I sit back in my chair.

He studies me like he's trying to figure something out, eyes roaming over my blank expression, until he shifts where he's sitting.

"You know," he murmurs, "if the circumstances were different, I would have congratulated you two. River deserves someone with a head on his shoulders. And you deserve someone who acts like they care about more than what money can buy. But I swear to God, man, if this does become something more then you need to cut ties with Isabel. For *good*."

"I've already cut ties," I assure him. "In fact, the last time I saw River I was going to tell her that I was ending it for good. We just never got to that point before—"

"Stop," he groans, holding up his hand. "I really don't need the details of you and my little sis. That's just ... weird."

Now I roll my eyes, chuckling softly. "I wasn't going to say anything bad, but fine. Point is, it's just River. It always has been."

Seriousness takes over his face. "If you really mean that, then fine. But I won't hesitate to punch you if you screw up, Rhett. I mean it."

Tipping my head once, I say, "I promise not to hurt her any more than I have."

He knows what promises mean to me, so he tips his head once and moves on. "Speaking of punching, there's somewhere else I need to be. I came right here after getting off the plane."

Pushing himself off the chair by the wooden arms, I stand and watch him walk toward the door. "Is that all I get? You don't hit people, I do."

Asher Wilks wasn't the first person I lost my shit with, just the one I got the most satisfaction from.

He glances over his shoulder. "You really aren't keeping tabs on River, are you?" When I shake my head, he sighs and pulls his cell out of his pocket. "Stephanie has been posting pictures of them doing stuff in Cali, and Peter York likes to run his mouth and comment on some of them. I took a few screenshots before they got deleted and told Steph to block him, so he couldn't keep doing it."

Passing me the phone, I suck in a sharp breath when I see River. Her hair is purple, pin-straight and falling longer than I remember past her shoulders. She's wearing makeup that makes her look older. Her eyes appear golden brown and her lips seem fuller from the pink color on them.

"She looks ..."

"Different, I know," Oliver says.

"I was going to say beautiful."

He scoffs. "Jesus." Ignoring the comment, he gestures toward the bottom of the image where a *peter_york_ny* commented using less than respectful words about River's appearance.

My fists clench.

Oliver deposits his phone back into his pocket. "You're more than welcome to come. I know where he is right now. But let me do the punching. I've been waiting a long time for a chance to knock him on his ass."

Laughing, I tell Leigh that I'll be away for the next two hours and to take messages if anyone calls for me.

"I always thought you liked the asshole."

He snorts as we leave my office, my door locking behind me. "I wanted to make sure I kept an eye on him. He was after me and the position for captain. Couldn't let him have it, so I needed to make sure he wouldn't sabotage me."

Considering he finished the season as Captain of the Freemont Patriot basketball team, I'd say it worked. York threw a temper tantrum and dented a few lockers in the main hall as he stormed out of Coach's office after the news.

"Nobody messes with my little sister," he tells me as we step into the elevator. "That means you, too, just so we're clear."

Oliver James, always the protective older brother. I'm glad River has him. I just hope she'll have me.

THIRTY-EIGHT

River / 23

The indie film *Through with Heartbreak* has only one more month of filming left, which means four more weeks of working. I don't mind, even though Bridgette and Robert told me I should be having fun instead. Working is fun, even if it's slapping red paint on a wall or touching up something in one of the set designs.

Briggs isn't a fan favorite among the rest of the set crew. I heard Olivia, one of the few girls who also works set, tell one of the guys that she thinks Briggs was part of some scheme at a different location, which is why he was shipped to work on a B-list movie.

I'm not sure why everyone hates him. He doesn't say much, but he isn't afraid to hold back criticism either. Last week, he told me that I'm not painting a mural, so I should have been done long before he came over. It didn't bother me, maybe embarrassed me a little. A few people near me snickered, which made me blush, but Briggs told them to keep working.

I spend a lot of time watching the actors and tend to

get lost in the scenes. Everyone says it won't get any buzz because of the budget, but the story is captivating. Half the time, it's why it takes me twice as long to finish painting something. I'm too enamored with what's going on in front of the cameras.

During lunch break, Steph meets me outside the makeup trailer with salads she bought down the street. When Emily, one of the makeup artists, sees my hair, she gasps.

"Who did that to your precious locks?"

My roots have grown out so much that my natural auburn tone is shining through, and the purple has faded to a lackluster gray. Steph tried getting me to redo it, maybe pink this time, but I told her I wanted my old hair back. She got to play around, but changing my hair won't actually change me.

"Steph did," I answer, pointing my plastic fork at my best friend.

Steph sucks in a sharp breath. "Traitor!"

Emily turns her narrowed eyes on Steph. She can't be much older than us, maybe thirty. The other makeup artist is almost forty and very sensitive about it, as we learned two weeks ago when one of the personal assistants asked her what cake she wanted. She broke down crying and locked herself in her trailer.

"Do you like it?" Emily asks me, sitting down next to Steph at the picnic table.

Taking a strand of hair and examining the bland tone it has faded into, I shrug. "It's okay, I guess."

Emily snorts. "Loyalty." She eyes Steph. "I should wallop you for ruining such beautiful hair! Do you know how rare it is for people to have that color naturally?"

"Ruining?" I squeak.

Steph waves at me. "Your hair is fine. Emily is just a drama queen. I think this is her way of asking if you want your old hair back—which, by the way, I was going to ask her to do anyway when the color faded."

I know Steph has been busy. She's been working longer hours because costumes have needed to be tweaked for reshoots and final scenes. Sometimes she gets home later than Mason, so he and I will watch television and either order dinner or I'll cook something for all of us. I'm no chef, but I don't burn toast like they do. Mason has deemed me safe to use the kitchen.

Emily claps. "I have time after four-thirty. Do you want me to do it then?"

I'm done at four, so I give her a tiny nod.

When Emily is satisfied, she pops up from the table and saunters away.

Steph laughs. "She's been wanting to mess with your hair since you started. I can't say I blame her, even I have hair envy."

Frowning, I touch my wavy tresses. "It isn't that big of a deal. In fact, having this much hair has been awful in this heat. I don't know how you do it."

I've always had long hair. It's nearly halfway down my back now, and even longer when Steph straightens it. The problem is, it's also thick and heavy, which is *not* a good combination in the high-ninety heat we've been experiencing.

Steph fluffs her golden locks. "It takes dedication, babe. Plus, my hair isn't as thick as yours. Emily could totally cut it for you if you want. It doesn't have to be super short, like to your shoulders or something."

The idea causes me to freeze for a moment. My hair has always been a safety net for me, and even though shoulder-length is still long, it would be a huge step. I don't really need a safety net anymore—I haven't for years.

Going back to my half-eaten salad, I blow out a small breath. "You're right, maybe I'll have her cut it."

We finish eating in silence.

BY THE END OF THE WEEKEND, I FEEL LIKE A NEW person. Emily said that happens when you reinvent yourself in the simplest ways; like chopping almost seven inches of hair off. The wavy tresses of auburn now rest just below my shoulders in a new layered style that makes tolerating heat easier.

I decided that having my old hair back meant having my old face back too. Steph complained all morning when I wouldn't put makeup on. The faded scar on my bottom lip is noticeable, and my pale skin isn't as smooth or hidden by pink blush.

Mason notices me first the first day I'm back to old

River. "I think this is the first time I've seen you really smile, River."

The comment makes my cheeks heat, because that's sad. It isn't like I'm unhappy here. But playing dress-up and trying to let loose by being someone else didn't feel right. Steph dragged me to three different clubs, where I wore a different tight dress and styled hair each time. I wouldn't dance with anybody but her, and that became hard when guys would come up behind us and grind like their lives depended on it. Mason threatened to punch one of the jerks who came onto me and wouldn't take no for an answer, so we left.

"I feel like me again, whoever that is."

He watches me fill a bowl with Froot Loops that I bought yesterday at the store. "So, does this mean no more clubs?"

Shuddering, I shake my head and pour some milk over the sugary cereal. "No more clubs."

Steph walks in the room. "You two are so boring. Why do I love you?"

"Sex," Mason replies.

His reply makes me laugh, though my face is probably red. I don't really care about PDA or sex jokes. I'm no prude, obviously. But sex is still a weird topic, especially because the last time I had it was with a man in a relationship. Mind-blowing or not, it was wrong. It's never something I talked about with him before, it just sort of happened. And before him was my lackluster experience with Asher Wilks, and I prefer not remembering that giant mistake.

"Anyway," Steph directs, looking at me devouring my breakfast, "I should have an early day today since they're finishing up final scenes before the reshoots. Since Briggs will probably do the same with you, I was thinking we could hit some local stores. I have an extra paycheck I want to spend."

Mason groans. "Babe, last time you said that you brought home enough clothes to fill another closet."

She pats his clean-shaven tan cheek. "At least I didn't buy the goat that old man on the corner was trying to sell me. It was super cute."

He grumbles out something sounding like an agreement. Steph pecks his cheek and turns to me expectantly.

"So?"

My shoulders rise. "Sounds fun to me. I think Briggs mentioned to the crew yesterday that we were stopping at one because we'd be busier next week when they start re-filming."

She jumps and claps, her bouncy white blouse exposing her trimmed stomach. I remember when she first moved to Los Angeles to attend UCLA. She was approached by an agent who told her she had the perfect figure to model, which fed into her teenage dreams. But after one photoshoot for some fancy clothes designer, she decided she hated it and kept studying design at college.

Work goes by quickly, and while I wait for Steph to finish up some last-minute adjustments on an outfit, I hang out outside her trailer.

Briggs is sitting at a picnic table eating, so I wander over and sit down. I know him well enough not to be scared. In fact, I like Briggs and his no-bullshit demeanor. If there's one thing I've learned, it's that I appreciate people who don't hide behind masks and lies.

"What do you want, kid?" He says it with a mouthful of food, but it doesn't bother me. Oliver used to do the same thing when it was just us.

My stomach grumbles when I smell the peanut butter coming from the potato bread he's holding. It makes me want apples, but I tell myself to let it go. At least for now.

He gives me a funny look then reaches into his lunch pail and pulls out another half. Passing it to me, he tips his chin at it. "Anyone tell you that you're too skinny?"

"Yep."

"Huh." He bites into his PB&J. "Not sure if you like peanut butter and jelly, but I noticed you didn't eat earlier with the others."

My mouth waters. "I don't want to eat your lunch. Plus, one of my friends and I are going out. I thought maybe we'd get something to eat then."

He studies me for a second with an expressionless face. There's no confusion, interest, or anger. Just ... indifference. "You should probably eat to tide yourself over. I heard the lead had a meltdown over her outfit for the last scene, so your friend is going to be in there for a while."

To make his point, he pushes the sandwich bag closer to me. "Why are you being nice to me? I mean, thanks, but why?"

"You don't annoy me ... much."

His response makes me crack a smile, and it's all I need to pull the sandwich out and take a bite. The creamy peanut butter hits my tongue and makes my stomach sing in praise.

I heard about Jasmine Phillip's breakdown, but didn't realize Briggs paid any attention to cast drama, much less that Steph is my friend. We're kind of alike, both wallflowers noticing the little things most others don't.

"So, what's your story?" he asks, balling up his empty sandwich bag and stuffing it back into his lunch pail. He opens a bag of potato chips and dumps it onto an unused napkin between us.

"What do you mean?" I reach for a chip and bite down onto it.

He leans back, folding his arms onto the edge of the table. "Everyone comes to L.A. for a reason, but you're not like half the wannabes that show up here. You have a story."

Staring at the sandwich, I think about my little story and how much I don't want to talk about it. "Um ... I came here to get away for a little while. Steph— Stephanie is my best friend. We grew up together in New York. She offered me a space to escape, and here I am."

He accepts the answer and continues eating, not bothering to ask questions. Instead, he says, "I came here when I was twenty-three for a girl. That was, what? Over thirty years ago now. Shit, I'm old."

He's over fifty, hardly old. But I guess in this world it is. I'm glad I don't live in it fulltime, because there's no way I'd fit in or survive.

"Did it work out with the girl?"

He laughs, but it's dry. "Nah. She entertained me for about a year before she met someone bigger and better. You know how it is, kid. People around here want success, not love."

That's so sad. "You really loved her?"

"Sure did." He brushes off crumbs from his hands and sits back. "But it wasn't real love or she would have stuck around."

I frown, suddenly worried over what Everett must think. I'm no expert on love, but I don't want him to think that I'm not in it with him. "What if she didn't stick around because she needed space?"

He eyes me, head tilting. "Ah. I see."

He sees what?

He nods, crossing his arms over his chest like I've seen Robert do when he gets all serious. "The escape you came here for is from a guy, huh? Well, let me tell you something, kid. Laura, that's the girl I followed here, has always wanted to be famous. When she met a rising star one day in town, it didn't matter that I came hundreds of miles to be with her. I thought she'd come back because that's what people in love do. But love isn't that simple, there are all different kinds. I suppose we were in lust, or some lower level of love that made it easy for her to leave when the moment suited her."

My chest feels heavy.

He nods toward my food as if to say, eat up, so I take another bite. "Was it easy coming here and leaving him?"

"No, of course not."

"That's a good sign then."

"Do you believe in that? Signs, I mean."

His lips press together in contemplation. I'm surprised he hasn't told me to go away yet or to stop talking. Briggs is a cool guy. He reminds me of Robert, and it makes me homesick.

"Signs are what people bank on when there's too much doubt in something they want to believe," he tells me slowly. "I looked for signs that would tell me Laura was coming back and dumping the tool she left me for." He shrugs loosely, like he doesn't care. "You can ask the universe for a sign or guidance, but it won't do you a lick of good, kid. We see what we want to when we're good and ready."

Playing with the crust on the bread, I contemplate his answer. He's not wrong, I guess. I used to rely on signs all the time when I was younger and waiting to be saved. Nothing ever happened and the hope fizzled out.

"Did you see what you wanted?" My voice is quiet, unsure. It's none of my business what happened to him, but he's still here after moving for somebody that didn't love him back. It seems like there's a reason he stayed behind and maybe it's a good one.

"I found love in other things. Work."

My brows raise in skepticism.

He chuckles. "I know people think I'm an asshole, kid. Truth is, I just want to see things done right. I enjoy what I do. Film directors hire me for smaller side jobs during the summers, and I have my own contracting business that takes up most of my other time."

"So, you're like … successful?"

He grins. "Something like that."

Picking off my crust, I set it on the table and glance up at him again. He's watching me with an amused smile on my face. "What?" I ask, brows pinching.

"My daughter does the same thing."

I gape. "You have a daughter?"

He nods once. "Probably a few years younger than you. She never liked crust, so she'd sneak it to the dog when she thought nobody was watching."

When I was little, I used to sneak my crust to the dogs my foster parents had. After moving in with the James', Oliver would eat them for me.

"There are many kinds of loves out there, but it's the real thing that's hard to find, because it's extremely rare," he tells me in an uncharacteristically soft tone. "Sometimes you meet that one person in your life who holds all of that love for you and then some."

But how could that be Everett to me?

"Could those people hurt you?"

He taps the edge of the table. "They're the only ones who have the power to hurt us. But it's only us who has the power to forgive."

THIRTY-NINE

Everett / 27

When five o'clock rolls around I notice Robert's office light is still on. Usually, he's gone by four thirty to have dinner with Bridgette. After locking up my office door, I make my way toward his. Stuffing one of my hands into the pockets of my black slacks, I rap my knuckles against the glass.

Absentmindedly, he glances up at me, then down at the small clock sitting on the edge of his desk. His brows draw up as if he's surprised it's so late already.

Walking in, I lean my shoulder against the doorjamb. "I thought you'd be home by now. I know Bridgette makes pot roast for you on Wednesdays."

A ghost smile appears on his face. "I suppose I lost track of time. I'm sure she's wondering where I am."

Nodding, I press my lips together. I should probably go too, not that I have anyone waiting up for me. The cabin will be empty and quiet, two things I've grown accustomed to but still don't like. Isabel brought noise in to my life, a distraction. I'm glad we've parted ways, but it makes the demons taunt me in louder voices.

He leans far enough back in his chair that it squeaks under his weight. His arms rest crossed on his chest as he studies me. "Is there something on your mind, Everett?"

There's been something on my mind for nearly two months now. Shit, for years. But I've kept my distance from Robert because I thought that's what he wanted. He hasn't reached out to me, scolded me, or told me off about sleeping with his daughter. We're strictly business like he is with the rest of his employees.

Not having Robert around is like losing my father again.

Clearing my throat, I push myself off the doorjamb and walk further into his office. "I, uh, thought maybe we could talk? I owe you an apology."

One of his gray brows arches, but he remains silent. Dropping onto the leather chair across from him, I tap my fingers against the smooth material coating the arm.

"I love River, sir." It might not be the best way to start the conversation, but it's straight to the point. I know how much Robert likes that. "I won't apologize for that, but I will apologize for what I've put her through. As well as you and Bridgette."

His palm scrapes against his jaw. "I've known about your feelings for quite some time, son. If you expect surprise from me, you won't get it."

I blink. "You knew?"

He chuckles, straightening up and linking his fingers together to rest them on the desk. "I suppose you wouldn't remember the night you told me you loved my daughter. You were about three sheets to the wind when you dialed me to come get you."

What? I haven't drank since ...

He fills in the gaps. "It was about, oh, six years ago or so when I got a call from you. It was nearing midnight, if I remember, because the wife asked where I was going so late. I just told her you needed me and went to the bar you said you were at. The bartender was pouring you another drink, but I took it from you because the last thing you needed was more alcohol. You looked rough, Everett. I thought it was because it was almost the anniversary of your grandfather's death, but you've never let yourself go even after he first died.

"When I paid the tab and got you out of there, you were rambling on about things that made no sense to me —something about Isabel. I managed to get you back to my place, down a few glasses of water, before you told me what had happened to the two of you. Now, I've never told you how sorry I am for your loss. Figured you wouldn't remember telling me anyway, and you never spoke of it since. But, for the record, I am sorry. Losing a child in any form is ... it's a tough thing to cope with. I don't think you know this, but Bridgette and I had many of the same experiences trying to have children before we decided to adopt."

I didn't know that. When Gianna Allen fell asleep next to Isabel at our apartment after I brought her home from the hospital, I snuck out to go to the bar. I let them be and left to get out of my head. I don't remember calling Robert or telling him anything. In fact, the last thing I remember is waking up on the couch at my apartment. Issy and her mother were both still sleeping in our bed, curled up next to each other in an embrace only two mothers would understand.

"I was getting you some aspirin when you told me you loved River. You said, 'I'm sad, Robert. Not just for the Issy and the baby, but for River.' And I asked why you'd be sad for her, you told me it was because you loved her, but you couldn't be with her."

My throat tightens and heart drums rapidly in my chest. I told River's father that I loved her. Jesus.

He lets out a heavy sigh, glancing toward the wall at nothing in particular. "You told me that you made a promise to Isabel you wouldn't break, which meant loving River was impossible."

Leaning my elbows on my knees, I bend forward and place my face in my open palms. Why the hell would I admit that to him? And why wouldn't he tell me about this sooner? He's been holding this back for six years, for Christ's sake.

Robert's calm tone breaks me out of my thoughts. "Jack used to tell me that promises are the foundation of any good relationship—it could have been anything from romance to business."

Jack. My father.

"You never talk about him," I murmur quietly, peering up at him.

He shrugs. "Honestly, son, I didn't think you'd be

ready to hear the stories. Jack Tucker was a good man. He never let anybody down because he lived off fulfilling those promises. But you know what, Everett? I never believed the same things he did. Promises aren't what make the foundations of good relationships, commitment is. We can promise people anything, stretch ourselves thin to maintain them, and then waste away from guilt when they can't be achieved. You can't promise people anything, son. You're setting yourself up for disappointment, for failure. Sometimes it takes more than that to prove what you're willing to do for a person."

His words strike me silent, as I lean back in the chair until I'm staring at him in wonder. If anyone knows my dad, it's Robert James. And if Robert can admit that my father's methods of life were less than realistic, then maybe I can too. At this point, I have to. I've lived my whole life believing Tuckers have to keep every promise they make.

I promised my grandma I wouldn't steal cookies from the jar at night. I promised my grandfather I wouldn't sneak out to meet up with girls after I turned fifteen. I promised my parents that I would make them proud.

Even before breaking my promise to Isabel, I knew that some were impossible to keep.

"As for River," he adds, voice firmer than it was before, "She made her own choices. I know my daughter, Everett. The things she chooses to do are thought out and based on emotion. I wish I could say logic played a hand in what you two conspired in, but she tends to think with her heart. That makes her vulnerable, in many ways, but it also makes her strong. I'm not saying that I disapprove of you two being together, I think I've always expected it to turn out that way, but I'd like to see you two be there for one another in better pretenses."

"What do you mean?"

He grabs a stack of papers and slips them into his bag. "She's in California to figure out exactly what she wants from a clear perspective. Sometimes, distance is a blessing in disguise. It makes us realize who we need in our lives and who we don't. I have no doubt in my mind she'll be back here soon enough for more reasons than just seeing us again. I just hope when she comes back, she's ready to face the consequences. Bridgeport isn't a forgiving town, son. People will talk about this for a long time. If you two really want to be together, if this type of love is the real thing, you need to be prepared. She's been through enough as it is, so I worry how she'll cope."

River is stronger than anybody here gives her credit for. I don't promise him I'll protect her through the chaos. I don't even promise him that everything will be okay.

Promises mean nothing.

"River will prove to us all how strong she really is," I finally settle on, nodding once to my own statement. "And I will be there every step of the way, because we're in this together."

He stands, grabbing his black messenger bag and slipping the strap over his shoulder. "To us, you've always been family, Everett. We'd be glad to have you as part of it permanently. Frankly, I can't think of one person who'd be better for her."

He holds out his hand to me and I take it. I guess the James and Tucker families were always meant to be together in one form or another. When River is ready to come back, I just need to prove it to her.

FORTY

River / 23

After the crew celebrates the final official filming day on set with cake, pizza, and beer that Steph says tastes like watered down piss, everyone starts saying their goodbyes. There aren't many people I feel emotional over never seeing again, but I can tell that isn't the same for everyone else. They've become a family during the past year of filming.

I've only known the set crew for about two months, and Briggs is the only one I talk to for more than two minutes. Occasionally, we eat lunch together and chat about random things. He tells me about his daughter, Maci, and I tell him about the kids I teach back in Bridgeport. He tells me more about how he met his wife, and I tell him about how painting became my first real love.

Briggs doesn't ask about Everett, so I don't really offer him any information. What can I say? If he knew the truth, that Everett is engaged and having a baby with the woman I cheated with him on, he'll probably see me differently. I don't want to risk him thinking of me in a bad light, especially because he's become like family to me. He doesn't judge me about being adopted or the scars that sometimes peek out of the thin shirts I wear to keep cool.

He always says, "We all have pasts, kid," and then keeps doing whatever we're doing at the time. Usually eating. We both love peanut butter, even though he refuses to dip apples into it.

Briggs is in the corner of the air-conditioned room all by himself when I approach him. He looks like his broody self, but I can tell that he's going to miss it here.

"You should be over with the youth celebrating," is how he greets me. I don't listen to him and lean against the wall, watching everyone else like him.

Shrugging, I glance back at him. "I don't really know anybody, and I don't drink. The cake wasn't bad though. Did you get a piece? It's marble, but I mostly ate the chocolate chunks."

That makes him chuckle. "Yeah, I got some. More of a vanilla man, myself."

My nose scrunches. Everett is too.

I'm not sure why I think of him all of a sudden, but his image sticks with me. Everett eats chocolate if I'm the one who requests it, like when Darlene makes cupcakes or cookies for my birthday, but he's like Oliver and prefers vanilla otherwise.

"What's the look for?" Briggs gestures to my nose, which I realize is still scrunched up.

"Vanilla is so boring. Everett, uh, my friend likes it."

He cracks a grin. "Your friend, huh?"

Blushing, I brush my hair behind my ear.

"I like your hair that way better," he states, changing the subject. He doesn't need to ask who Everett is, he obviously knows. "It doesn't look like you're trying to be someone else. Honestly thought about bringing baby wipes to clean off all that makeup when I first saw you."

My lips part in hurt. I didn't think the makeup was awful, just overdone. "Did I look *that* bad?"

He shakes his head. "Not bad, just not you. And before you go and tell me that I don't know who you even are, I know you well enough to see you're more comfortable like this. If you were my daughter, I would tell you that you don't need all that other stuff. It just hides all the shit that doesn't need to be hidden."

Instinct has me touching my bottom lip.

He notices. "I don't mean your scar, kid. People around here play dress up to become somebody they're not so people like them. You've got that natural essence about you where you don't need all of that to impress people."

"You're just saying that."

He deadpans. "Have I ever been known to bullshit anybody?"

I guess he has a point. "Well ... thanks."

He just nods his head. Before I can say anything else, my phone buzzes in my pocket. I excuse myself and study the unknown number across the screen before answering.

"Hello?"

"River?" It's a woman's voice.

"Yes?"

"It's me. I-It's your mom."

I freeze mid-step. Steph looks up and notices my stricken expression, coming over and brushing my arm with her hand.

"How did you get this number?"

"I have my ways, just like you." There's something off about her voice, but I can't pinpoint it. It sounds shaky, like she's nervous or ... I don't want to think of what else. "Baby, I just wanted to talk to you. They won't tell me where you are. Where did you go? Don't you want to see me?"

Steph's eyes pin me down, silently asking who it is.

"Who won't tell you where I am?" I force myself to ask, worried that I left my *real* family in the dark about her presence in Bridgeport.

I was stupid to think I could pretend she didn't exist, like she wasn't there. But she wants something, or she wouldn't keep reaching out.

She huffs out in disgruntlement. "The people who think they have a right to claim you. You're part of a very important family, River, but you're still my daughter. Don't forget that."

"I am *not* your daughter." My voice cracks and leaves Steph gaping at me, then quickly taking my hand in comfort. "The James' are good people. They took care of me and loved me when nobody else would. They're

393

my family, which means they have every right to claim me."

Briggs comes over when he hears me raise my voice. He studies Steph and me but keeps an eye on my watery gaze.

"I just want to get to know you like they do, baby. Is that so hard to believe?"

"Why now?" I whisper.

"When I heard your new daddy's people were looking for me, I decided to check out the man who spent all that money to find one little person." She laughs, but it's distant and chaotic, and I know there's something not right. "You have money now, River. But trust me, people like that can easily throw you out when they get tired of you."

Nausea sweeps through me. "The James' would never do that to me. Just because people like them hurt you in the past doesn't mean I'll suffer the same way."

"Don't be stupid," she snaps. "I may not have raised you, but I refuse to be related to somebody who's *that* naïve. We're not that different, baby. You and I come from the same background. We do what we need to in order to survive. Those people—"

"Stop calling them that!"

"Tell me where you are," she says, suddenly sounding desperate. "I didn't travel all this way for you to leave me. *You* wanted to see *me*, remember? You had people snooping around me and it ruined everything. I can't leave without getting something in return. Payback."

My eyes widen. "Payback for what?"

"I've been surviving just fine in the dark until those uppity men came sniffing around. The people they found me with aren't too happy with me, River. That's your fault. So now, you need to help your mommy out. I know your family has money."

I stop breathing.

I stop thinking.

I just … stop.

The woman who I broke down in front of Robert over is everything I feared she was. Heartless. Manipulative. Foster kids like to pretend their biological parents are royalty when they have no clue where they come from. But the reality is usually always the same. My mother is no princess, she's the witch.

Steph uses my shocked stature to peel the cell out of my hand. "Listen here and listen good. I don't care who you are, you have no right to call River out of the blue like this. If you reach out one more time, there will be consequences. Leave River, and the James family, alone."

She hangs up and then slides the phone into her purse. I'm vaguely aware of Briggs and her asking if I'm all right. I think I nod, but I'm not sure.

Disappointment drowns out the contentment I was feeling when the party started. I've felt it before when I thought about my mother but could never figure out why. I never knew her; never knew she could be so cold. I only ever had the things Jill told me about her to go off of.

"So that was your mom?"

My jaw ticks. "That was the woman who gave birth to me," I correct. Bridgette is my mom. There's a very obvious difference. "I'm sorry, guys. I'm not in a party mood right now."

She loops her arm around mine. "Okay."

I frown. Mason is still hanging around a group of his actor buddies. "You and Mason were planning on staying out. You don't have to come home with me. I'll just call a cab."

She waves her hand. "Mase is going to some bar with his friends. I want to be with you and make sure you're okay."

Briggs gestures toward the exit. "I can drive you two home. I've about had all the celebrating I can stomach. Need some real beer."

Steph snorts. "You know, you're not so bad, Briggs. And here I thought you were an asshole all of this time."

He gruffs and throws out the Styrofoam cup with the remnants of poorly made coffee in the trash bin by the door. "Don't let that get out. It'll ruin my reputation."

That makes me laugh, which causes Steph to join in. Briggs just shakes his head as we wave goodbye to Mason, following Briggs to his giant pickup.

When we're safely tucked inside Steph's place, pajama-clad with slippers and bathrobes, I expect to cry while Steph tells me it's okay.

But I don't shed one tear for that woman.

For the first time in my life, I realize that some people aren't worth the pain.

"Steph?" I ask quietly.

"Hmm?"

"Can we go shopping again tomorrow?" I shift on the couch, where my legs are draped across her lap. "There's a bookstore we passed the other day that I want to check out."

She grins. "We'll make a day of it."

And the following day, it took one book purchase to make me realize that everything was going to be okay.

FORTY-ONE

Everett / 27

Saturday morning, I walk into town for something to drink at Landmark Café after a five-mile run. My shirt is slick with sweat and clinging to my body, so I fan it out before heading into the tiny establishment.

People tend to leave me alone when I'm out and about. I don't pay them much attention when they lean in to each other and whisper, because caring takes too much energy. What's done is done, and I can't change anybody's opinions of me.

Summer is almost over, and the August temperatures have been insanely bi-polar. Being holed up in the cabin has left me stir crazy, so I run any chance I can or hang out by the lake when the sun sets and read.

But today I needed to come into town and be around people, despite their reactions. Half the town doesn't care anymore. Bigger news has spread across Bridgeport between business deals going awry at competitive companies and the death of a rival businessman.

When I walk past Painter's Choice and glance in the window, I notice a small group of kids surrounding two tables in the center of the room. Melanie is pointing at one of their paintings and smiling, then turning to help another one out with their project.

I jump when a hand hits the window I'm standing next to. A little girl with earbuds plugged into an iPod stares at me, then gestures toward the bag I'm holding. It has an old-fashioned donut and chocolate scone. To be honest, I'm not sure why I bought the scone. There's only one person I know who eats them, and she's not around. It just happened to be the last one, and my stomach had an odd craving for chocolate.

Not just for chocolate.

The little girl glances between me and the bag, making me chuckle. Melanie's attention is captured when I enter the studio, so I shoot her a quick wave. She smiles and walks over to me, noting my messy appearance, then the bag of pastries.

"Isn't that kind of counterproductive?"

The little girl pops up beside me. "It's for me, Mel. Right, dude?"

Melanie's brows raise as the girl takes the bag from me and plops back down into the chair in the corner.

"Save one for me," I tell her, not caring which one she chooses. Landmark makes great old-fashioned pastries, and they're best when they're fresh. But I've been needing something that reminds me of River, some inkling of hope, even if it's in scone-form.

Melanie laughs at the girl. "Charlie, take your time with that. I don't want you getting sick before you leave."

The girl, presumably Charlie, peers up at us from the half-eaten donut in her hands. There are crumbs scattered everywhere.

"No worries, Mel. I've got another thirty minutes to let it settle." She pats her stomach and digs into the remaining half.

Chuckling, I turn to Melanie. She's smiling at me, but it doesn't quite reach her eyes. "She isn't back yet."

Wetting my bottom lip, I nod. "I know. I just wanted to stop by. Needed some clarity, I guess."

Charlie snorts. "How are you going to get that here? It's a paint shop."

Melanie scolds her. "What did we just talk about, Charlie? You need to be respectful of people."

She sinks into her seat. "I'm just saying, it's weird for him to come here for clarity. I mean, don't people go to church for that?"

The spitfire in this kid amuses me. "I'm not really a church-goer, but I suppose you're right. Sometimes clarity just comes in places that reminds us of people."

Melanie squeezes my arm. "She left behind some paintings, if you'd like to look at them. Something tells me she had specific inspiration behind them."

"Aren't you mad at her?" Charlie blurts.

I turn to her. "Why would I be mad?"

She shrugs. "She left us all behind, didn't she? It seems like all of us have reasons to be mad at her. I don't care if she says she'll come back. Most people who say that never do."

Melanie kneels next to her. "River is going to come back, Charlie. You have to believe in people once in a while, even if you're used to it not working out. Okay?"

Charlie's expression doesn't change from the doubtful snare it casts.

"I can't be mad at River," I tell her softly, catching her attention. "How can I fault her for leaving to figure things out? To come back a better version of herself? Sometimes we all need that."

Melanie smiles up at me.

"She promised she'd be here for us," the girl whispers, playing with the brown takeout bag in her hands.

I doubt this kid cares what I think, but I tell her anyway. "I've known River for a long time now. There's always a reason for why she does things, and it always works out in the end. If she says she'll be here for you, she will. Being here and teaching you guys is important to her."

Charlie doesn't say anything, so I don't know if she believes it or not. Her lack of argument paired with the indifference on her face tells me maybe she's considering it.

Melanie gently takes the bag with the remaining scone in it and passes it to me. "I probably shouldn't tell you this, but I heard from a red-haired birdy that she's coming home tomorrow. Her flight lands around four."

My mouth dries. "She is?"

A small smile plays on her lips. "Like I said, she's

coming back soon. She loves too much about this place to stay away for too long."

"Did she ... does she sound okay?"

Sympathy lightens her eyes. "Honestly, Everett, she sounds better than I've ever heard. I think California did her good."

"Good," my voice cracks. "That's ..."

She pats my arm. "Like you said," she tells me gently, "it always works out in the end."

I find myself nodding and shoving a hand through my damp hair.

River is coming home.

Tomorrow.

It's been almost three months since she left, but it feels longer. Is her hair still purple? Is her milky skin the same creamy tone or tanned from the west coast sun?

"I'll take a raincheck on seeing those paintings," I tell her, backing toward the door.

Melanie grins. "I'm sure River would be better at showing them to you anyway."

My attention shifts toward Charlie. "Remember not to give up on her. Sometimes distance is hope in disguise."

FORTY-TWO

River / 23

Bridgeport hasn't changed at all since I left. The trees are a darker shade of green preparing for autumn, the air is blissfully cooler, and the sun isn't violent against my skin. I know coming back means facing a lot of wrath, but I'm ready for it. Sort of.

Mom and Dad take me out to an early dinner after picking me up from the airport, and we go to Underground East. They offer to go to the diner because of how much I love their burgers and milkshakes, but I want a spot that doesn't remind me of Everett—a spot I can talk to my family about everything that's happened without memories of him. Just for one more day.

After ordering, we sit around the small table in comfortable silence while our waitress sets down our drinks. I smile when I see Dad order coffee, no cream and sugar, and Mom order tea with milk and honey. I don't drink coffee or tea often but did occasionally in Cali when I missed them.

Mom sips her tea and then brushes a short strand of

hair behind my ear. "Your hair looks so good, sweetie. I bet it felt better in the dry heat."

Dad chuckles. "Nothing feels good in that dry heat. Right, River?"

I forgot he went to college in California. When I was looking into colleges the summer before my senior year of high school, he showed me his Stanford University yearbook and all the things he did on different sports teams and clubs. I think he was disappointed when I didn't apply, and even tried using Steph's interest in UCLA to get me to consider California. In the end, I think he's happy I chose to stay close to home.

If I had moved away so soon after high school, I would have missed out on a lot. Like getting a permanent job at Painter's Choice, seeing Dad's company expand, and watching Mom flourish in her own endeavors in the party planning business. When I first came to Bridgeport, she took time off from her business to focus on me. I didn't realize what a big deal that was at the time until she went back to work and struggled to find clients with all the new competitive companies that had started up in her absence.

"Having a family means sacrifice sometimes," she tells me. "But it's a sacrifice I will make one hundred times over to have you in my life, sweetie."

They've always made sacrifices for me, and what have I done? Acted on feelings I had no right having and risking everything they've built. JT Corporation is the foundation of Bridgeport's economy, and any type of scandal could make or break them just like Mom's business did when she cared for me.

"How was your time there?" Mom asks, leaning forward and resting her arms on the table. Her elbows, of course, are off the tabletop, which makes me force mine away too.

I think of Steph and Mason, who both hugged me and wished me well when they saw me off. Steph cried and reminded me not to eat all the fancy chocolate she stuffed in my bag as a going-away present, and Mason told me to come back anytime I wanted. I even saw Briggs before going to L.A.X. To my surprise, he hugged me and introduced me to his wife and daughter, who were both beautiful and witty, with sarcasm a lot like Briggs. He asked if I would be okay, so I assured him I would be and told him I found reasons to go back home. He didn't pry, just wished me well and passed me a peanut butter sandwich, crust off, for the journey to the airport.

Smiling, I tell my parents about everything I've done. I mention the movie set I worked on and the people I met, and the places Steph and Mason took me to. Their eyes get big when I show them a few pictures of me that Steph took when I had purple hair and laugh when they try telling me they love it.

They're not very good liars, like me.

What they do seem to be genuinely happy about is how much fun I had while working on set, even though Dad kept telling me he wished I would have just had fun some other way. But the distraction working for Briggs offered me is why I felt like I could come back. Plus, if I didn't get a job on set, I wouldn't have met Briggs or listened to his advice.

When our food arrives, our conversation eases as we dig into the food in front of us. It doesn't stop me from saying what I need to though.

"About Everett ..." Clearing my throat, I poke at the eggplant lasagna with my fork. "I have been struggling with my feelings for him for a long time. Sometimes I would try to convince myself that I only liked him because he was the one person outside of the family that paid me any attention even when he didn't have to. Like maybe I could tell myself it was a silly crush based on nothing other than friendly affection.

"But that wasn't it. The older I got, the more I realized that it wasn't that simple. I kept reminding myself that how I felt didn't matter because he had Isabel, but when he started paying more attention to me than he used to, it felt like ..." I take a deep breath. "It felt like there was finally a chance for us, even though she was still in the picture. I know that makes me sound, well, not like a very good person, but all I could think about was how the feelings didn't seem so one-sided anymore."

I sneak a peek at them both through my lashes, noting their unreadable expressions. Neither of them looks angry at me, not like I expect them to. We never had a heart-to-heart before I got on the airplane, because they thought it'd be better if I had time to sort through everything away from the influences of Bridgeport. While I did think about Everett at night when I tried hard not to, I forced myself not to dwell on it during the day when there were other things to be done. It didn't stop me from thinking about all the times Everett was there for me, all the times I knew he and Isabel fought, and how we stood a chance because he chose me in ways I shouldn't be proud of, but my heart took as a victory anyway.

He kissed me with the type of raw passion that jump-starts every piece of me, like he was trying to revive me from death. And, in some ways, he was. I existed for years, walking around Bridgeport with both physical and emotional scars that tied me to my past. I would hide behind my hair to stay unnoticed, keep quiet in classes to be left alone, and float through every day like a ghost.

Everett Tucker breathed life back into me when I didn't even believe that I deserved it. Every foster parent who told me I wasn't worth it, every foster sibling who would rat me out because they thought I was the weakest link, even my own biological mother made me feel like I didn't deserve the type of happy ending that happens in fairytales.

With a single touch, Everett blows apart those cemented thoughts until their shards are nothing but dust coating the naysayers.

Robert sets down his silverware and locks eyes with me. His eyes are light but serious, like what he's about to tell me is something I'm going to need to listen to.

"I'm going to tell you what I told Everett when he spoke to me about the situation," he begins, voice firm and fatherly. I never thought fatherly had a tone before, but Robert's voice is the epitome of it. "You two need to figure out exactly how you're going to handle the situation. Just because people haven't been talking about it doesn't mean it isn't on their minds. If they see you together—"

"Why would they see us together? I saw the ring. I know about the ... the baby." I whisper the last word, because it still hurts to say, even though Steph said it can't be true. When I told her about the confrontation, she started stalking Isabel's Instagram account, which is full of selfies and pictures of her with her friends drinking, dancing, and all very much slim and toned as always. Someone even took a live video of Isabel at some club doing shots, which Steph said means she lied about the baby, unless she didn't care about its wellbeing, but we both agreed not even Isabel Allen was that cruel.

The engagement though ... well, none of the pictures disproved that. In fact, she didn't have any images of her hand that would show a ring on it or not, which Steph said could be a good sign.

But I can't rely on signs.

It's Mom who reaches out and takes my hand with hers. Her skin is warm and soft, probably from the cherry blossom lotion I know she loves using. "Sweetheart, Everett and Isabel haven't been together in months. They ended things before you left."

My eyes widen.

Dad tips his head once. "And as for the baby, that's a bit complicated. It's also not our story to tell, but I can assure you there is no baby. The challenges you two face are strictly your own at this point."

I'm not sure what to say, so Mom squeezes my hand once and leans back into her chair. She takes Robert's hand and they smile at each other for a moment then glance back at me.

Mom says, "We've always wanted you to be happy, River. Your life hasn't been easy, so you deserve to find happiness. We just wish you would have done things a little differently, is all. Everett is a good boy, a good *man*. One who we've always considered family. You both have pasts that made you grow up too fast, so if there's anyone who truly understands what you've gone through, it's him. I'm a firm believer that things happen for a reason, and maybe Jill brought you to us, so we could bring you to him."

Robert squeezes the hand that's holding hers, but their image blurs when tears well in my eyes. My heart flutters in a different way than when I'm around Everett. It's full, like Jill knew that these two kind-hearted people would change my life in more than one way. And the tears that sting my eyes are the kind that trickle when I'm so overwhelmed with gratefulness that I can't help but let some of the bad pieces of me escape through the salty liquid.

Pushing past the pressure of emotions building in my

ribcage, I blow out a steady breath. "There's something else I have to tell you guys. Shortly before I left, my birthmother came up to me. She ... she didn't say much because I wouldn't let her, but I knew without a doubt she wasn't lying about who she was."

Mom's eyes glaze over with more tears as she takes my hand with her free one. "We know, River. She's stuck around Bridgeport. In fact, we've been wanting to talk to you about her, but we weren't sure you were ready."

Guilt nips at my insides. "I should have told you about her sooner, but I didn't want to deal with it. And then ... things happened with Isabel and I just couldn't stay."

Dad clears his throat. "I've had her looked into, River. Savannah Scott has multiple charges against her for possession and drug use, as well as DUI's that she's been running from. I never heard back from the private investigator I hired all those years ago because she'd been hiding and didn't want to be found."

Mom nods slightly. "She came up to me about a week or two after you went to California. I was doing some grocery shopping when I saw a woman who looked a lot like you, and a part of me knew then and there who she was. But, sweetie, she wasn't well. She approached me and accused me of stealing you away, and when the police were called after she refused to calm down, she ran. There were marks on her arms that the police recognized as needle marks from drug use. The security tapes explain her behaviors. She's still using, River."

The few times Jill answered my questions about my birth mother, she wouldn't give me many details. Looking back now, I think it's because she wanted to protect me from the truth. Nobody wants to accept that their parent chose drugs over their own child.

"She called me," I whisper.

A small gasp escapes Mom.

I play around with my food some more, not very hungry all of a sudden. "I knew something wasn't right with her, because she acted like she was fine one second and then would go off the next. And I knew that it was probably drugs, because Jill told me that she struggled with addiction. But I thought after all these years, maybe she was better. It's why I wanted to find out about her. And knowing that she hasn't gotten the help she needs just makes it worse."

Filling them in on what she told me is probably a bad way to go about our dinner. It's not a light topic, especially when I admit that she practically threatened me for money. Dad goes rigid and red-faced, and Mom covers her mouth with her hands as tears slip down her cheeks.

But unlike all the other times I blame myself for what they feel, I acknowledge that this isn't my fault. I am not my birth mother. I share her blood, but nothing more. And it makes me angry knowing that what she's doing impacts the only parents I've ever known, ever loved, because I know she won't stop.

Mom dabs the cloth napkin against her damp cheeks

after I finish talking. Dad tells us to finish eating and that we'll figure out what to do tomorrow.

"We shouldn't let her ruin your first night back," he tells us, gesturing toward our barely-touched plates. The food is probably cold, but none of us cares. "We're just glad you're back with us, River. We'll make sure she gets the help she needs."

But I know more than anyone that people only accept help when they admit they have a problem. I don't know Savannah Scott, but she doesn't seem like the type of person who will accept anything but money. And knowing Robert James, he won't be willing to settle.

For the night, I try pushing through every truth I've finally spoken aloud to enjoy a meal with my family. My *real* family. And I manage to crack through the barrier of unknowns that hold me back to realize that this is right where I belong.

River James.

Daughter of Robert and Bridgette.

Sister of Oliver.

Best friends with Stephanie.

And in love with Everett Tucker.

FORTY-THREE

Everett / 27

The sound of my phone going off a little past one in the morning has me groggily answering in a less than pleased tone.

"This better be important."

"There's a fire," Gordy rushes out. "You need to get to Painter's Choice ASAP. Chief has been trying to get ahold of you but we couldn't wait any longer."

Bolting out of bed, I find a pair of pants that are on the floor and slide them on. "What the fuck, why didn't you lead with that?"

My apartment still has the scanner that would alert me to get to the station. The cabin is isolated enough where things like that don't work as well here, the frequency gets lost.

"Just get here. It doesn't look good."

My heart is hammering with adrenaline as I run across the room for the rest of my clothes, slide into the closest pair of shoes, and hurdle past furniture with keys in hand toward my car. "What's happening? Fuck, Gordy. What is going on?"

I break about three different traffic laws getting to the station where the first crew is already gone. Gordy tells me the smoke was noticed a little after twelve thirty, and the flames soon spread after that. He stays on the phone with me until I get into my gear and haul ass over to the studio. Even from the station you can see black smoke filling the sky and the glow of flashing lights from first responders. Gold and yellow lights glimmer against blue and red, and I wonder what I'll be walking into.

My heart feels like thousands of needles are being shoved into it while I'm still awake, like I'm being cut open without anesthesia. I haven't had a chance to see River yet, because she only got back two days ago. I was going to see her once I got my shit together, once I figured out what to say.

I love you doesn't seem like enough.

I need you doesn't cover what I feel.

But thinking that I could walk into a situation where I won't ever be able to tell her either of those things, along with the array of speeches I want to shower her with, completely fucking ruins me.

I'm fueled with desperation and adrenaline when I get there. Frantically searching for River in the massive crowd of first responders and bystanders, I'm suddenly choking on air and smoke, on things unsaid.

When Gordy sees me, he comes rushing over with fear loitering his blue eyes. "I tried to stop her, man. She said she needed to go back in to—"

"What?" I growl, shoving past him violently and rushing toward the entrance without a second thought.

Chief tells me to stand down until they can get the flames down—that there's already one person inside going after River. But I refuse to stand here and watch the building fill with flames while I sit back and do nothing.

For the first time ever, I disobey Chief and rush into the flames. My mind is on River, just River, not the heat or the smoke or the chance I won't make it out. It's her I'm worried about. I've had training, and unlike anyone else Chief sends in here, I know the building.

I see Fred's fleeting form in the back office of the studio and tell him to get out.

"Chief said—"

"I know this place better than anyone," I snap, shoving him toward the door. He shakes his head, about to argue with me, when cracking wood sounds from above us. Pushing Fred out of the way of the breaking beam, I move a second before it lands on me.

"Fuck!" Adrenaline has me running toward the stairs, which thankfully, doesn't hold as much smoke. But when I get upstairs and see River's door cracked open, I notice the thick gray fog filling the main room.

Crawling on the floor, I make my way around the room, feeling for River. From her room, I hear a raspy cough, and immediately make my way toward the sound. I move faster than I ever have during training exercises, suddenly realizing everything I have to lose. River is curled on her side on her floor, clasping something tight in her arms. I can't tell what it is, a book maybe, but she's holding onto it like her life depends on it.

If she came in here for a fucking book, then I'm going to have some serious words with her when we're outside.

"River?" I'm hovering over her now, seeing the soot on her face and sweat coating her barely covered body. She's in a pair of sleep shorts and a tight tank. One of her thighs and forearms are burned, and when she opens her eyes, they're red and drained of life.

Scooping her up and cradling her close to my body, I quickly make my way toward the front of the apartment. She doesn't say a word. Maybe she doesn't realize it's even me that's holding her like this, but there's no time for pleasantries.

Another crack echoes in the building and something behind us falls. There's breaking glass, so I assume a window busted. I don't stay long enough to find out whether it's from the heat or the place falling apart. I'm halfway down the stairs when my foot goes through the weakened wood and another beam falls in the main studio. River flinches into me, so I hold her tighter.

"It's okay," I tell her. "It's okay, Riv."

Her face burrows into my chest as another wrack of coughs takes over. She's inhaled too much smoke and I can see her getting weaker. The beam that just fell is blocking part of the way out, so I need to carefully side-step it to get us closer to the front door.

What I don't expect is the sudden blast coming from the back of the downstairs office, blowing me out of the way and falling with River still latched in my arms. I try taking the brunt of the fall, but we both land on our sides onto sharp glass that came from a shattered window. My gear protects me from getting cut, but River is bleeding.

Quickly sitting up and examining her cuts, I graze her face with my covered hand to get her to look at me. "Baby? I need you to stand up. Can you do that for me?"

She's still holding onto whatever item she came in to save, but her body is weak as it lays there. Blood pools from behind her and I start to panic thinking the glass cut something important.

"River, look at me," I demand firmly, hovering over her to try blocking out the elements that surrounds us. "You need to get up and walk out of here. Bridgette, Robert, and Oliver need you to find that strength." Voice cracking, I brush her defeated, tired face. "Baby, *I* need you to find that strength. Don't you dare leave before we get our chance at happiness."

I'm choking on words and emotions as I stare at her beat-up body. Her hand is shaky as it unwinds from the book and brushes my arm. Her cough is choked, but she manages to nod. I help her sit up, then stand, and guide us to the door, avoiding the fallen debris, glass, and other dangers that threaten us.

She makes it to the door, but before I can follow her, another beam breaks off the ceiling and barrels toward me. I'm not quick enough when I bolt back, and the beam shoves me down and traps my right leg with a sickening snap. Pain shoots through my leg as I try shoving the beam off my body, knowing damn well my leg is broken, but it's too heavy.

My name is being yelled from outside, but the sound of the crackling flames around me drowns them out like they're miles away. I hear one of the voices and know it's River. She's screaming for me, and I want to tell her it'll be all right. The ache spreading through my leg worsens when I try moving the beam again, making me curse and lay back down to catch my breath.

I feel too warm in my suit as I try fighting my way out from under the wood pinning me to the dirty floor and hear more creaking like another is about to fall.

Swallowing past my sudden fear, I think about River. If she can make it out of here, so can I. The guys will find a way—I'll find a way.

Don't you dare leave before we get our chance at happiness.

I wonder if she got up because of me or her family. Her family means the world to her, it's why she kept pushing me away when I tried telling her how I feel. I wouldn't mind if that's what it was, the reason she survived. But knowing even a small part of her conscience was standing for me, waiting for me, makes me need to get out of here.

Before I can muster another maneuver, something hard smacks into my helmet and everything goes black. The last thing I remember is seeing River's young, thirteen-year-old terrified face when she saw me for the first time.

I wonder if she'll look the same when they carry my body out.

FORTY-FOUR

River / 23

The hospital is too quiet. There aren't any monitors or conversations that dull the wandering thoughts bouncing around in my aching head.

When I wake up, I find Mom and Dad sleeping in chairs beside my bed. Their bodies are in weird contorted angles that will probably give them both back-aches later, but I doubt they care. They're holding hands and their chests rise and fall at steady rates, which calms me from the memories of what happened.

The blinds on the windows are closed, but it looks dark out still, and when the nurse comes in to see if I'm awake, she quickly asks how I'm feeling.

"Wh-what time is it?" My voice is hoarse from my scratchy throat. When I drag in a small breath, my chest burns.

"Just after six in the morning."

She pours me a glass of water from the pitcher on the tiny table next to my bed. Putting a straw in it, she holds it up for me to take a sip. My dry lips crack when they wrap around the end, but I manage to take a few sips before leaning back into the firm mattress.

"Your voice is going to be like that for a while," she explains softly, setting my glass down but keeping it in reach for me. "When they first brought you in, we had you wear an oxygen mask. I'm not sure if you remember. You were in and out of it, but you're in good hands with Dr. Woodrow. On a pain scale of one to ten, how are you feeling?"

Dad stirs awake first, quickly waking Mom when he sees me.

Sitting up and wincing over the pain shooting down my back, I wet my bottom lip. "I guess a six or seven."

Her smile is sympathetic. "I'll get you some pain medicine, okay? The doctor will be in to check on you shortly."

She exits, leaving me with my worried parents. They quickly surround me, both being careful not to hug me too tight or tug on the wires I'm attached to. It isn't until I return their embraces that I notice white gauze wrapped around my right arm.

"You have second degree burns on your left leg, right arm, and both your feet," Mom says, brushing her thumb across my cheek. "There are a few cuts on your back and shoulders from where you landed on some glass, but none of them needed stitches."

"One cut did need to be glued," Dad adds, squeezing one of my hands between both of his. "When we got the call that there was a fire, we didn't know ..." He chokes up, tears watering his dark eyes. "They didn't know if you could get out. It wasn't until Everett went in that we had any hope."

"E-Everett?" My hoarse voice is ugly, and it makes me want to down the entire pitcher of water hoping it'll help.

"Don't you remember?" Mom asks, sitting on the small space next to my leg. "Everett is the one who got you out."

Suddenly, I'm all too aware of what happened, and I try getting out of bed. The blanket is tangled around my legs and the wires and needles I'm hooked to aren't easy to maneuver. "He was t-trapped. There w-were pieces of the ceiling falling everywhere. He said—"

It's Dad who eases me back down. "The chief managed to get in and pull him out. Last I heard, he's in surgery, but he's going to be okay."

Tears well in my eyes over the thought of him dying because of me. I'd gotten out when the smoke first started filling my small apartment, but I couldn't leave my book or pictures behind. So, I ran back inside despite the entire fire department yelling at me to stay back. They couldn't catch me before I ran upstairs to get the first edition copy of *The Scarlet Letter* I found while I was at an old antique bookstore in Cali. I couldn't lose it. The bookmark I used while I finished reading it was the picture of me and my birth mother.

After seeing her at the restaurant when I was out with David, I couldn't look at her the same. But it was her phone call that made me take the image of us out of the frame. I'm not sure why, because she didn't really do anything to me that I didn't expect. But having her in the frame where she looked at me every night ... it was too much.

I didn't walk away from Everett and the scandal. I left because of her and the truth. I've wanted to know where I came from for years, but having the option is something I told myself not to anticipate. In fact, I accepted never knowing who my mother is or why she gave me up. Realizing I'll probably never see her or how much we look alike or the things we have in common is easier, especially now that I know she hasn't really changed from the stories Jill told me of her giving me up. She's had twenty-three years to change and she chose not to.

"H-He could have died because of me."

Tears stream down my face that Mom quickly wipes away. "He's a firefighter, baby. This is what they do and risk. But he's fine, you *both* are. That's what's important."

Trying to swallow, I wince. Reaching for the water, Dad quickly passes it to me, positioning the straw where I can easily sip.

"Do they know what happened?" I manage to ask when my throat feels a little better. The water is a little cooler than room temperature, so it soothes my sore throat enough to make it hurt less.

Mom runs her fingers through my hair like she always does when she wants to comfort me. She started doing it after I got the flu when I was fifteen. It was the day after my birthday and I had a high fever, so she sat in my room and combed my hair with her fingers and read to me from a poetry book that I'd gotten out of the library at school.

It's her who fills me in on developments of the fire. "The police would like to speak to you, just to get an idea of what you might know. But Chief Anderson went in when they said it was clear to look around and see where it started. We haven't heard more than that because we've been here."

Dad tells me to try getting some more rest because it's early. I manage to sleep for about twenty minutes before the doctor comes in to check on me. He explains my injuries and how important it is to keep them clean and says there are two police officers outside who need to get some information from me.

Mom steps out so we can talk, but Dad refuses. He holds my hand as I tell them what happened, not that it's much. I woke up at midnight when I heard a fire alarm downstairs go off. By the time I went to investigate, there was smoke and flames coming from the back office by the heater. I tell them it was probably the heater that started the fire—it has been broken for a while and kicks on whenever it wants. They say they'll check it out.

I get reprimanded for running back inside, which Dad doesn't know about until now. Then he scolds me until I explain to both him and the officers that I needed my book.

"Was a book really worth your life?" Dad doubts,

shaking his head. "Possessions mean nothing compared to your life, River. For the sake of my sanity, never do something as reckless as that again."

He wouldn't understand and I couldn't explain it to him. The book is the first thing that tied me to Everett, and I wanted to know if Hester got her happy ending. I could have just looked it up online and spoiled it, but when I dragged Steph into the bookstore, it was the first book I found. It seemed like a sign, just like Briggs told me about.

I didn't believe Briggs until the store clerk told me the book was a first edition. It's in rough shape, so he gave me a discount despite its rarity. Steph told me I was crazy to spend so much money on a "silly book" but she doesn't get the significance of it. It was my ticket home, the very thing I needed to see to realize I was ready to face Everett and my family.

Staring down at my folded hands in my lap, I ignore the disapproving look on Dad's face. "I believe that some possessions are worth the risk."

The police tell me they'll be in touch.

Dad inhales a little and sits back down in his chair, our hands still linked. "I'll always be thankful for Everett saving your life, but a part of me worries that he'll still hurt you. Then what is risking your life worth?"

That's why they're called risks.

"It's worth everything."

. . .

THE NEXT TIME I WAKE UP, IT'S ALMOST TWELVE IN THE afternoon. Dad is speaking in low murmurs with the doctor in the corner, and Mom is right next to my bed with a book in her hand. When she notices I'm awake, she smiles and gets the others attention.

Dr. Woodrow has a nurse come in and show us how to change the bandages on my wounds. They emphasize the importance of keeping it clean so nothing becomes infected, which Dad assures them will not be an issue.

When it's just the three of us again, Mom asks how I'm feeling. But I don't want to talk about the ache of my body or sting in my lungs.

"Who's with Everett?"

Dad's brows pinch.

Before they can answer, I reposition myself in bed. "I'm lucky enough to have both of you, but who does he have? Is he okay? Do you know anything about his condition?"

Mom hushes me. "We've both been in to see him, sweetheart. And Margaret, a family friend of Everett's, has come in to see him. He had to have a steel rod placed in his leg because of the break, but he's going to be just fine. I promise he's not alone."

Sucking in a short breath to calm myself down, I nod. "Can I see him? Dr. Woodrow says it's important I try moving around."

"But your feet ..."

The pads of my feet are burnt and numb from the gel they put on it. Right now, I can't feel them, but putting any type of pressure on them before they're healed won't do them any good.

"Please," I whisper, grabbing Mom's hand. She glances at Dad and they share a short, understanding look.

Dad goes to get a nurse to bring a wheelchair in for me. When help arrives, they manage to mobilize the IV bags onto a pole that's attached to the chair.

"The book." I search the room for the one thing I got out of my apartment. I don't know what the condition of the building is, much less what's salvageable. Most of it is just stuff, things I won't really lose sleep over. But the book is something I need to show Everett.

Mom grabs the worn novel from her bag on the counter and passes it to me. Neither she nor Dad asks why I need it, they just wheel me to Everett's room across the recovery unit. My lap is covered in a thin scratchy white blanket that only really helps hide the hideous blue geometric gown I'm wearing. The book rests on the blanket, face down, as we enter Everett's room.

He's sitting up in bed with his leg elevated. When he sees me, his chest seems to deflate like he's been holding his breath all this time. A relieved look washes over his tense features, and a small smile tugs on the corners of his lips.

Everett looks ... good. He always does, but there's a lot different about him since I last saw him, which also happens to be that night in the studio when I finally became brave enough to walk away. His hair is shorter than usual, but still flops over in dirty blond tresses on the top of his head, and his sharp jaw is lined with days-old stubble. I know he likes having facial hair, but Isabel preferred him clean-shaven. I wonder if he'll shave when he's released or if he'll keep it and grow it out.

When his minty eyes lock with mine, something inside me clicks. It's not a flutter or summersault, but the type of feeling that connects us. Maybe it's because he saved my life. Or maybe the feeling is something so much bigger than can be explained.

"River," he breathes, reaching out to me.

I peer over my shoulder at my parents, who are looking between us. "Can I talk to him alone, please?"

They both nod, and Dad kind of eyes Everett in silent warning. When I look back at Everett, he just tips his head as if to say, *I understand.* And he probably does, because he knows Robert better than most people do.

When the door clicks shut behind them, I reach out and touch his extended hand. "You broke your leg."

"It's nothing," he assures me. His eyes dance around my body, which doesn't reveal much of anything between the gown and blanket. "Are you okay? The wheelchair—"

"I'm not allowed to walk because of the burns on my feet." Shifting in the chair, I raise my arm to show him the gauze. "The rest of me is fine for the most part."

His jaw ticks. "*For the most part*," he mutters, shaking his head.

"Hey," I scold, frowning. "You saved my life, Everett.

It could have been a lot worse. You're hurt more than I am, and it's all my fault. I'm so—"

His face hardens. "Don't you dare apologize to me, River. You weren't the one who set that fire."

I toy with the book. "But I shouldn't have gone back in. I just ..." Swallowing, I pick up the book and hand it to him. "I wanted you to have this. Maybe it's stupid, but I saw it in California and just felt like it meant everything was going to be okay when I got home. Home to Bridgette and Robert and ... home to *you*."

His fingers brush the cover. "Nothing you do is ever stupid, River." His head tilts as he glowers at me. "Except walking into a burning building. That was pretty dumb."

My cheeks heat.

He glances back down. "But I get why you did it. *The Scarlet Letter*, huh?"

I crack a small smile. "I lied before when I said I finished it. I thought it was dry and boring, and I honestly didn't understand what was going on. But I kept wondering what happened to Hester because ..."

His voice his quiet. "Because why?"

"Because *I'm* Hester." My voice isn't as hoarse as it was, but it's still raspy and fragile. The topic certainly doesn't help. "I thought if Hester got her happy ending then I would too, but she really doesn't. I mean, the story is depressing. Her lover dies after admitting what happened and she just disappears with Pearl."

When I dare to look up at him, he's watching me

with wide eyes full of wonder. "I never wanted you to feel like Hester. You shouldn't have ever felt like that."

The blanket is all I have to fidget with, so I play with the hem of it. "But I am. I might as well wear a red A on my chest. But that's not really the point. It's a book, a story. And whether it's based on something true or not is debatable, but I don't want it to be *our* story. You told me not to give up on us before we had our happy ending, and I ... I want that. I don't want to be like Hester or the Reverend."

"Baby," he rasps, "that's not us."

Baby. He's called me that more than once. The first time it killed me to hear, because it was like a last-ditch effort to keep me in arms reach while he stayed fully committed to another woman. When he called me baby in the studio with every chance of losing each other for good, it tore me apart in a different way. Like I wouldn't be able to hear him say it ever again.

Especially when he didn't make it out.

My chest hurts. "The book is like a weird sign for us. Bridgette ... Mom told me that I should wait until I was ready to come back, and I didn't know when I'd know. Then someone I met in California told me I'd only know when I was ready when I finally opened my eyes to the things I care about most. It didn't make a lot of sense to me at first. But then I found the book, and everything clicked."

"Was this someone you met a man?"

Confused, I nod slowly.

His jaw ticks. "Remind me to go to California and kick his ass when I'm better."

I giggle. "Briggs is almost Robert's age, and he's married with a kid. He was like a father figure in some ways. Plus, I might not have gone out and found this book if it wasn't for him."

He sighs. "I guess he's fine then."

The mood lightens as he sets down the book on his lap. He watches me with eased eyes, like he's looking for something. I'm not sure what, so I squirm under his gaze.

"What?"

"Can you grab that jacket right there?"

He points toward a jacket draped on the counter next to the sink. I reach over and pluck it off, passing it to him. He digs in the side pocket and pulls something out, a crinkled piece of aged paper.

"I've been trying to figure out how to prove to you that you've been the biggest part of my life for years," he began, staring down at the paper he grasps, "but didn't know how. How could I, when I've been stuck in my head and on old promises? I ..."

He pauses, wetting his lips. "When I was young, I lost both of my parents in a car accident. Honestly, I didn't really know them enough or understand what happened, but I knew when I woke up in the hospital with my grandparents there, something bad had happened. My grandfather used to always promise to take care of me— that Tuckers never break their promises. After years of hearing that, I knew any promise I made had to be kept.

I stayed with Isabel because I promised her she wouldn't lose me. I know she told you we were having a baby, but it's not ..." His voice cracks. "Shit, it's not what you think. When we were younger, Isabel got pregnant but miscarried. She was heartbroken, we both were, so I promised her she'd never lose me like she did the baby.

"It wasn't really love that we felt for each other, even though we tried. I stayed with her because I made a promise that I wanted to make my family proud for keeping, and she stayed with me because she thought it was a way out of her father's control. But it destroyed us. I'm not saying that's any excuse for what I did, how I acted, but it's my truth. We were stuck in a relationship that neither of us wanted to try taming or breaking apart because of our own reasons. I shouldn't have gone after you until I was ready to accept the consequences of dissolving my promise to her, but the thought of letting my parents down, my grandparents, it killed me. Your father made me realize that promises don't really mean anything if they're not supported by commitment."

I'm silent throughout his tale, wanting to hug him, to tell him how sorry I am for the loss of his parents. He's lost so many people in his life, and I knew that something tragic had happened to his parents, because Steph told me as much when we were younger. But to lose his parents so young, to experience so much loss, I get that better than anyone.

My eyes travel to the long scar lining his neck, and

suddenly it makes sense. We're both scarred from our past.

I don't fault him for wanting to make his parents proud, whether they're around to praise him for it or not. If anybody understands the need to please someone, it's me. But we both went the wrong way about it, and we both acknowledge that.

"I don't expect you to forgive me," he finally says, letting out a shallow breath. "But I do hope you understand that, for me, it has always been you."

He holds out the paper to me. Hesitantly, I take it, unsure if I should read it now or later. I'm afraid of what it'll say, but also yearning to know how this plays into whatever we share between us.

It has always been you.

That must mean something.

Setting it on my lap, I close my eyes and take a deep breath. "The scars on my back, everywhere really, don't come with a pretty story either. The first time Jill, my social worker, saw them, they were fresh and needed stitches and a lot of medication for the pain and infection. When Bridgette saw them, she cried. When Steph saw them ... she told me she thought they made me look badass. And I thought for the first time, maybe they were something I should be proud of because I survived the abuse."

"River," he cuts me off hoarsely, "you don't have to—"

"At the diner, you said that you'd only tell me about why you stayed with Isabel if I told you about my scars."

I let a few tears pass the barriers that hold them back, because I deserve to feel this. Not the pain, but the relief of finally being able to tell someone. "I was going to tell you anyway, because I want us to be the couple that shares everything with each other. I want our love to be truthful and honest even when it hurts us the most. I know, then, that you'll truly be there for me, scars and all. Past and all."

His eyes glaze over into an olive tone.

Lips pressed tightly together, I inhale through my nose and exhale through my mouth. It helps me fight off the anxiety that wants to bubble from the memories I want nothing more than to finally wave goodbye to. They'll always linger but won't dictate who I am anymore.

And for the next hour, I tell him everything. He hears all the gritty details and brutal truths. I tell him about how I received every scar, the cigarette burns, the butter knives, the backhanded strikes to the face, the belts to the back.

It's hardest to talk about the belt whippings, because it was the one time in foster care that I wanted to give up on everything ... to let the belt bleed me out on the floor where I took the attack. I remember my torn shirt clinging to me with my own blood as another strike would slash my skin. I remember the tears that drowned my cheeks and the hoarseness of my voice cutting out my desperate pleas.

I wanted to die that day. I wanted Jill to find my body

on the hardwood floor, surrounded by blood and tears and freedom. I just wanted it to end. Everything. All of it.

By the time I admit how close I was to begging for death, Everett's face is wet from tears as he rasps my name and holds my hand, squeezing my wrist because I'm here. I'm here and he's here and we survived.

We survived loss.

We survived pain.

We survived for each other.

Death never claimed me even when I begged for it, because there was always something more for me out there; love of all kinds that I used to believe I didn't deserve.

When Mom and Dad come back in, it's because the nurse needs to check on Everett and mine needs to check on me. When my parents see our tear-stricken faces and clasped hands, they both brush my arm in comfort. Dad squeezes Everett's arm once, tips his head, and starts to wheel me out of the room.

"The letter," he blurts suddenly, almost desperately. "Just ... read it."

Holding onto the letter like it's my lifeline, I manage to nod. When the door closes behind us, separating me and Everett, I suck in a much-needed breath.

Mom looks at me with worry shadowing her eyes. "Are you okay, sweetie?"

For the first time, I don't lie. "Yes."

FORTY-FIVE

Everett / 27

Chief visits me at the hospital the day they release me, three days after I was brought in. He lectures me like I expect him to, and I take the scolding as I deserve. He tells me if I ever disobey him again, I'm off the squad. Honestly, I expected worse.

What I don't expect him to tell me is that the fire wasn't accidental, but arson. River told the police she was sure the heater was what caused it, but the investigation showed evidence that someone purposefully ignited the downstairs studio. My first initial thought is to see how River is. Hearing news that the studio she loves so much was set on fire on purpose is hard to handle.

Chief tells me she took it as well as she could, but not when they told her what they found. Turns out, the investigation didn't need to be drawn out for very long, because paraphernalia was found with DNA evidence that matched one Savannah Scott. Between the previous warrants she has against her on top of hard proof that she was there the night of the fire, it isn't looking good for her.

I know he shouldn't be telling me this because it's not public knowledge, but despite Chief's disgruntlement over me disobeying orders, he knows how much I care for River.

I told her I would talk to her after I got out, that way she wouldn't need to bother Bridgette or Robert for a ride to the hospital. Plus, I want her to read the letter and think about it. It doesn't prove a lot, just that she's been more to me for longer than she might think.

I've always been yours, River.

You were never mine.

She really has no idea.

She's been mine since the day she asked me to take her virginity. She's been mine since the day I punched Asher fucking Wilks for bragging about sleeping with her. She's been mine for years, she just hasn't known it.

But the letter … I hope she realizes how serious I am. Not just about her, but about us. About her family and what part they play in the grand scheme of things. I want them to know how much I love their daughter.

I want them to know how much I love her smile, the way her nose scrunches when she doesn't like something, and the way her brown eyes turn golden when emotion takes over.

The promise I made to Isabel may have been broken under the circumstances I first made them, but I know my parents are still proud. And, really, Isabel will always have me in some way. She has our memories, and my friendship if she ever wants it. She has my well wishes and my pride, because she's strong. Stronger than she thinks, even against her father.

Chief drives me to the James' where River is staying, helping me out of his car and passing me my crutches. My leg is covered by a blue cast—the same color my arm cast was when I was five—and tells me to call him if I need anything.

I don't even ring the doorbell before the door opens and River appears in front of me. She's still in a wheel-chair, but as soon as she sees me standing there, she pushes up and winces before throwing herself into my arms.

Somehow, I manage to keep us upright as I tighten my arm around her tiny waist. I'm about to tell her to sit back down before she hurts her feet when she draws back and presses her lips firmly against mine.

It's the first time she's ever initiated a kiss, and it takes me by surprise. It isn't long before I take over, guiding her lips open and slipping my tongue inside her mouth to taste her. She moans when our tongues twist and I deepen the kiss, my fingertips digging into her fleshy waist.

When my cock twitches in my jeans, I pull back and force myself to take a deep breath. Neither of us are in any condition to follow through on what I'm sure both our bodies are telling us to do next.

"I love you, too," she blurts, eyes glassy as they lock with mine.

"You read the letter," I whisper, ghosting my fingers

over her face. I never want to stop touching her. This is the first time in almost ten years I've been able to touch her the way I want. To feel her, hold her, love her.

She nods, her straight white teeth digging into her bottom lip and nudging the scar there.

Guiding her back down into the wheelchair, I give her a relieved smile. "I love you, River James. I've loved you for a long time."

She sniffs back tears. "Longer than the letter indicates? I was seventeen when you wrote this. That's a long time."

I chuckle, wanting nothing more than to lean down and brush her hair behind her ear. To caress her face. To kiss her lips. "If my professor had told us to write down our feelings sooner, I probably would have admitted them long before that point."

She blushes.

Bridgette appears behind her. "Oh, Everett! Robert and I were just talking about you. Oliver is coming home tonight to check in on River. Are you staying for dinner?"

The last time I saw Oliver, he pretty much told me he'd castrate me with rusty knives if I did anything to hurt River. Maybe if I stay and lay it all on the table for them tonight, they'll know I have no intention of seeing her hurt again.

"I'd love to," I tell her.

River and I stay in the living room propped up on the couch next to each other while Bridgette and Robert go off to plan dinner. At least, that's what they told us. I know Bridgette better than that. Dinner has probably been planned for a day now, regardless of me agreeing to join them.

"How are you doing after what they found out about the fire?" I don't say her mother's name, because I don't know how she feels about her.

"I'm ..." She pauses, snuggling in to the side of my body. My arm is draped over her shoulder, hugging her close to me. Having her curled up against my body, not having to be ashamed for wanting to hold her, is more than I ever dared to believe could happen. "I'm not sure how I feel, to be honest. Robert tried finding out where she was staying and talked to the police about her drug use and past, but they couldn't find where she was until the fire. They found her squatting in an abandoned house not far from the studio. They think she's been watching me for a while, which is how she knew where I work. And how ... how she first found me. We just want to help her, Everett. But to think that she burned down the studio ..." She buries her face into my chest and when I feel the wetness of her tears soak into my shirt, it breaks me. She whispers, "Did she know I was in there? Did my mother *willingly* set the building on fire knowing her own daughter was upstairs?"

"Oh, baby." I stroke her hair and shush her tears, wiping some away from the pad of my thumb. "Your mother is sick, River. I've seen drugs do some nasty things to people. They can't think straight. Either way, she's not going to be able to hurt you again. If she's using, they'll find traces of drugs in her system and get her help. And depending on if the evidence of what she's done sticks, or if she confesses, she'll have to face jail time on top of the charges she's already been running from."

River hiccups. "You know about the warrants?"

Wincing at the information I shouldn't know, I nod. "Chief and I go way back. I won't say anything, River. I just want you to know that she can't hurt you anymore. She's going away for a long time to face what she's done."

We both know it isn't that easy, but it offers some comfort in a situation that's heavier than anyone can handle.

"I love you," I whisper.

She curls in closer to me, one of her arms looping over my midsection. "I didn't think I'd ever hear you say that to me."

Kissing the top of her head, I rest my chin on the crown of her skull. "I'm going to be saying that for a long time, baby. We've got lost time to make up for. Which means a lot of *I love yous,* plenty of kisses, and you bet your pretty little ass there will be lots of touching."

I don't see her face, but I'm sure it's red.

"You can't say things like that," she hisses, swatting my side. "My parents are in the other room."

I laugh, my chest rumbling and shaking her body until she peels herself off me. She looks lost, her brows pinched together like I'm crazy for finding her amusing right now.

It makes me feel youthful to know that at twenty-seven, I still have to be worried about parents catching me cuddling and dirty-talking their daughter. I like it. "It's been a long time since I've had to worry about being caught, but I don't mind playing teenager again. Suppose it could be like role play."

That thought *definitely* makes me happy, and I'm sure River can feel my cock turning to granite under her arm. In fact, the small inhale she sucks in tells me as much.

We'll get there, eventually.

"I'm going to take you out," I whisper, brushing my lips against her jaw, and trailing them toward her lips. "I'm going to buy you dinner, flowers, hold your hand, everything you deserve and then some." My lips graze hers in a barely-there kiss. She shivers, making me smile against her lips, before pressing a little harder against them until she opens up.

Exploring her mouth is like searching for lost treasure, except I'm not searching for long before I find it. She tastes like hot chocolate and peppermint candy, which makes me wonder if she just had one of Landmark Café's specialty cocoas they've been advertising in preparation of fall weather.

My hand cups her face to tilt her head at a different angle when a throat clears at the archway of the room.

River makes a little squeaking noise that reminds me an awful lot of a mouse, which makes me fight off a grin.

Robert is standing with his hands in his pockets next to Oliver, who's shaking his head at the two of us on the couch.

River tries pulling away, but I don't let her. Instead, my arm wraps around her waist as I pull her closer, not ashamed of having her as mine finally. The whole world needs to know it sooner rather than later. River James is mine, now, tomorrow, forever. One day I'm going to get down on one knee and ask her to be my wife, then she'll be River Tucker. Fuck, I love the sound of that.

She clears her throat. "I thought your flight wasn't coming in until tonight?"

"Figured I'd surprise everyone."

Robert chuckles. "Surprise."

River's blush deepens.

Oliver sighs and turns his focus to me. "I already warned you, so I won't bother threatening you again. Just remember what Peter York's face looked like."

His brow raises as if to make his point.

River straightens. "You *hit* Peter York?"

Robert clasps Oliver's shoulder, like he's saying, *thatta boy.*

"Don't you know by now, River? We'd do anything to protect you. And if that means throwing a few punches," he shrugs, "that's what big brothers are for, isn't it?"

The tears in River's eyes aren't sad ones, and her brown hues turn that golden shade I love so much. It gives her pale skin color, a glow that's all mine to love, cherish, and appreciate every damn day for the rest of our lives.

"This is what it's like, River." I kiss her cheek, and she

doesn't flinch away this time despite her family's watching eyes.

Bridgette walks in and wraps an arm around Robert's midsection, smiling at the people surrounding the room.

"What?" River asks.

"To have a family."

EPILOGUE

Everett / 28

The Wedding

The white lace dress clings to River's body as Robert guides her down the long aisle with her arm wrapped around the crook of his elbow. The dress is long, tapered in to accentuate her every curve, and the veil covering her face doesn't hide her curled red hair or red lips split into a big smile when she sees me standing in front of the altar.

This goddess wrapped in white is mine, and the thought alone nearly brings me to my knees. The feeling of absolute completion consumes me when Robert places her hand in my outreached one. His eyes are full of tears that match my own as he nods his head once as if to silently say, *welcome to the family, son.*

Our closest friends and family are watching us from the white foldout chairs placed in two separate sections. River invited Steph and Mason, who got engaged not long before I finally popped the question, as well as Melanie, her social worker Jillian, and of course her family. Steph and Bridgette stand behind River in long, mint green gowns holding white bouquets in their hands. Oliver and Robert stand behind me, both in black suits and matching green ties.

The crowd is small. There are only a few of our close friends from high school watching one of the best days of our lives unfold in front of them. I'd like to believe my own family is watching from the sky, kissing us with a gentle breeze of praise and compassion. Margaret passed away just after Christmas last year, but she gave me her old wedding bands to give to River when I was ready. We were engaged by New Year.

The ceremony takes place in the James' backyard, an intimate setup of white, greens, and pinks. It complements the early summer setting with the sun caressing us as we say our vows.

"I, Everett Tucker, take you, River James, to be my wedded wife, to have and to hold from this day forward, for better, for worse, for richer, for poorer, in sickness and health, through every fight, disagreement, and argument, because I think we both know I say stupid things sometimes—" People laugh as I hold onto River's soft hands tighter. "—as long as we both shall live."

I choke up by the last few words, tears sliding down my cheeks as I watch the love of my life say the vows back to me, her own eyes filling with happy tears that turn her brown eyes golden.

"Ethereal," I whisper. "Mine."

I'm told I can kiss my bride, and I don't waste time before my lips are tenderly pressing against hers. One kiss will never be enough for us. She takes my breath away when her arms wrap around my neck, drawing me closer. Our lips nip and suck each other's until someone behind me clears their throat.

I think it's Oliver.

The crowd laughs again as I draw back, just enough to press my forehead against hers, her green apple scent grounding me. Our noses touch as we catch our breath. Her eyes close for a moment before they reopen and lock with mine.

My hand cups her face, my thumb stroking her cheekbone. "I love you more than words, baby. So much. Every day."

"As long as we both shall live," she whispers back. When she pulls away, I swipe the pads of my thumb against her damp cheeks.

We face the crowd hand in hand,

The priest announces us as Mister and Missus Everett Tucker, and the overpowering feeling of love consumes us as the breeze picks up the flower petals from the ground and blows them around us in a gentle dance. We walk down the aisle as people clap and cheer, and I can't help but stop just before we go into the house to change and pick up my wife.

My wife.

Fuck, that won't get old.

She squeals when I lift her into my arms, cradling her close to me and kiss her again before stepping into the entryway.

"You look beautiful, River." I nuzzle my nose against her cheek, my lips grazing one side of her face until our tongues are tangling together and our breaths become one. I withdraw first, setting her down on her feet. "But you know what would look even better?"

Her breath catches. "What?"

My hands skim her sides in a slow, sensual fashion. "Nothing but skin."

THE RECEPTION LASTS UNTIL AFTER SUNSET, AND breaks apart when I sweep River away to the hotel room I booked for the night. As soon as we're locked away in the honeymoon suite with a *do not disturb* sign hanging on the door, I prowl toward River, hungry.

We've become well acquainted with each other's bodies over the past year. Finding new ways to make her come has become my favorite pastime. River still has shy moments over her exposed body, but I always make sure to wash away any doubt she has. There is nothing about River that I don't love.

Her heart is pure.

Her laugh is intoxicating.

And her body brings me to my knees.

She's not the innocent sixteen-year-old who asked me to take her virginity. She's dangerous now.

She doesn't stop me from cupping the sides of her face and bending down to kiss her, my lips desperately seeking entrance until she gasps and gives in. I back us up until the back of her legs are against the edge of the king size bed, her fingertips digging into my biceps until she abruptly pulls away.

My brows pinch. "River? Wha—"

She slowly sinks to her knees, hands fumbling with the button and zipper of my black dress pants. I groan when the air hits my suffocating erection.

"Baby, what are you doing?"

She doesn't answer as she draws my pants down my toned thighs, her eyes sparking with an amber glow when she realizes I'm not wearing boxers underneath. My fingers itch to grab ahold of myself, because I'm so fucking turned on it physically hurts. Instead, I watch in awe as River shifts closer and blows on my tip.

"Shit. Fuck. River—" I'm cut short when her hot mouth wraps around my cock, wet and tight, taking me in as far as she can. My hands go to her head, not moving her but threading my fingers in her hair as she runs her tongue over me.

I moan when she draws back and takes me in all the way again, sucking me off in the most torturous slow manner.

"That feels so fucking good, baby." My hips jerk forward which makes her gasp, the vibration on my cock making my eyes roll into the back of my head.

She picks up the pace with her mouth the same time

she starts fondling my sack, rolling it in her hand until my legs fucking shake.

I try pulling her away, but she doesn't let me, my hips match her rhythm thrust for thrust. "Fuck, River. If you keep doing that, I'm going to come in that pretty little mouth of yours."

I never expect oral from River, so the few times she's gone down on me, I let her set the pace. Usually, I pull out right before I come, painting her naked body with my seed like my own type of masterpiece. But this time she isn't giving me a choice, and it's when she applies pressure just under the tip of my cock that I explode in her mouth, moaning her name the whole time I come down from the high.

When she finally pulls away, her face is flushed. She stares up at me until I help her stand, kissing her with such fervor that it makes her stumble backwards onto the bed. Quickly stepping out of my pants and ripping off my shirt, I work on disposing of the dress Steph made her wear to the reception, until she's in nothing but sexy as sin white lace lingerie.

It doesn't take long before the skimpy panty set is off her body and she's exposed completely to me. Hovering over her, my lips trail down the front of her body until my nose nuzzles her inner thigh. She writhes under me, hips arching when I start playing with her clit, and moaning my name when I lick one long line from her entrance to her sensitive bud.

I hold her thighs open as she squirms, tasting her

sweet juice on my lips and probing her with my tongue as I finger her clit. Her movements are jerky, and I know she's about to unravel when she yanks on my shoulders.

"Please, Everett. Please."

I come up for air and look up at her through my lashes. I'm ravenous, needing to taste her orgasm on my tongue. "What is it, baby?"

"I need you. All of you. Everywhere."

My brow raises. "Everywhere?"

She lets out a tiny breath. "Please? I need to feel you everywhere. I want you to have all of me."

Is she saying ...?

"Babe, I'm going to need you to be really specific," I press, rising over her. I have every intention of making her come using my mouth but need to know what exactly she's asking me to do right now.

Her face turns red as I wait for a response, my cock swelling with need and ready to take her however she wants me to.

The palm of her hand comes up and brushes my face gently as she sits up. Her nipples are pebbled and I can't wait to feel the weight of her breasts in my hands again, but she doesn't give me the opportunity to play before turning onto her hands and knees.

I'm on my knees in an instant, my cock very much interested in the direction this is going. I've never pressured her into anything, never asked for what she's suggesting.

"Baby," my voice is raspy. "We don't have to do this. If

you think I'm not happy with burying myself in your pussy, you're wrong."

She glances over her shoulder, teeth biting into her bottom lip. "I want to feel you where nobody else has been. You're my husband, my best friend, the person I want every experience with. You didn't get the first that mattered, so take this. I-I'm letting you have it."

My palms reach out and brush her sides, my dick begging to gain entrance inside her. She squirms as my hands make their way to her chest, playing with her nipples and palming her breasts. She moans my name in a barely-there whisper. Her ass arches back, my tip brushing against her as I groan and tighten my fingers into her fleshy hips.

"Baby, fuck," I growl. My fingers find the moisture between her legs, dipping inside her and moving in a slow rhythm. "I need to prep you first, okay? It's going to hurt either way, but I want it to feel good for you."

She shifts back into me again. "I want you to feel good."

My chuckle is deep and husky. "Oh, sweetheart. You don't have to worry about that. My cock's favorite place to be is inside you, no matter what hole."

"Everett!"

I pull my fingers out and she moans again, squirming as I coat her puckered hole with her arousal. She's soaked, which will make this easier. Positioning her in front of me, I slide my dick into her pussy to coat myself. She gasps then leans forward, biting her arm. Her ass is in the air, so fucking beautiful.

So fucking mine.

My thumb circles her tight hole as I slide in and out of her pussy. The same time I pump into her with my cock, I ease my finger into her with gentle strokes. She gasps again, wiggling to try getting used to the feeling.

"Stay still, baby." I barely recognize my own voice as I watch myself take her in two different ways. It's the sexiest fucking thing I'll ever witness, the best gift she could give me besides herself—her love.

After working her over with my finger, I add a second one, quickening my pace. Her head tilts until her hair falls off her shoulder, and I'm dying to know what it feels like to be inside her ass for real.

"Are you ready for me, River?" I'll stop if she changes her mind. We have the rest of our lives to experiment.

But she nods her head, bucking into me again and wiggling her ass. "I need you inside of me, Everett."

Pulling out of her pussy, I reposition so my cock is at her back entrance. I hear her inhale when I first probe her, my length slick with her arousal as it slowly slides into her. She freezes, her body trying to defend itself against this intrusion, so I lean forward and start playing with her clit again until she loosens up.

"That's it, baby," I whisper, kissing down her back. I slide in deeper, biting back the groan of her squeezing me. This feels so damn good that I'm trying not to blow my load before giving her an orgasm.

My fingers slide into her heat again, her clit gaining my special attention, as I take myself all the way inside her.

"Oh, *God*," she groans, her ass pressed against my groin.

"Do you need me to stop?" Worry etches my tone as I brush my free hand through her hair, hoping to dull her pain.

"*No*. Don't you dare."

Chuckling, I begin moving inside her. The sensation is nothing like I've ever felt before, and based on the sounds she's making, it feels good for her too. I match the speed of my cock and fingers, diving into her until she's shaking under me and repeating my name in a husky, sexy voice.

"Everett. Yes. Like that." She moves her hips back, and the sound of our slapping skin is like music to my fucking ears. Her breathing becomes ragged, and her thighs start quivering.

"You're so beautiful, River." I kiss her lower back, my lips caressing one of her many scars, and I hook my fingers inside her until she's coming, her pussy pulsing around me as I drive into her a few more times. I come hot and heavy, my free hand gripping her hips to keep her from collapsing.

When our orgasms calm down, I slowly pull out of her and tuck her into my side on top of the comforter. The soft sound of her breathing lulls my speeding heart-beat. A smile spreads on my lips.

"That was ..."

She nods. "I know."

I kiss her shoulder. "I love you, River."

She turns around, wetness in her eyes as our hands interlock. "I love you, too. And I'm ... I'm just really happy."

Kissing her tears away, I brush my fingers through her hair. "Get used to it, Riv. We're going to be happy for a very long time. Our story is just beginning."

"No," she whispers, fingers stroking what little hair rests on my chest. "It started ten years ago. I wouldn't have it any other way."

Me either, baby.

Me either.

EPILOGUE TWO

Charlie / 13

The Adoption

My hands sweat profusely as I wait for Amy, my social worker, to come out of the office she's been closed in since ten this morning. Mrs. White, the woman who works the front desk at the agency, said Amy has been talking to two very important people about me.

It's almost noon.

I've been sitting in the uncomfortable floral armchair for almost an hour, and it has given me time to come up with a reasonable excuse about why I was kicked out of my last home. Amy told me I had to stop getting into trouble or I would be moved to a group home permanently until I hit eighteen.

But one of the girls I had to share a room with in my current home kept stealing my iPod. Just because I stole it doesn't mean somebody else can. All the music I've grown to love is on there—it calms me down on the days

I think I may never get out. And when I yanked on Jasmine's hair after finding her red handed with the device, it was me who got in trouble.

Violence is grounds for removal.

The fight happened yesterday and now I'm here. Even though Ms. Finch, the woman in charge of the group home, never mentioned anything about me being kicked out, it had to be the reason I'm here.

My eyes go to the bulge in my right pocket where the iPod is. I itch to take it out, to let it ease my worries, but I know it won't help right now.

I freeze when Amy's office door opens, and her familiar face appears. The corners of her brown eyes wrinkle from the wide smile on her face, which confuses me considering the circumstances.

"Charlie!" She claps her hands together once like she's happy to see me. There's no way she knows about the fight or she would greet me with her usual disapproving frown.

"Um ... hi?"

She chuckles over my obvious confusion and waves me to come into her office. When I walk forward, I notice a tan arm resting against one of the chairs across from her desk.

Nerves bubble inside me as I rub my lips together and stop halfway there. "It looks like you're busy. I can wait until you're done."

Her features lighten. "Don't be silly, Charlie. Come in. I promise everything is going to be fine."

I hate when she tells me that. Nobody can promise that foster kids will be fine, because they don't know the places they send us to. Not enough to guarantee our safety.

Despite my uncertainty, I nod and continue forward in small steps. Taking a deep breath, I walk around her ushering hand until my lips part in shock.

"River?" My voice is barely a whisper when I see my art teacher sitting next to her husband Everett. I know them both from Painter's Choice, where River teaches an art program to foster kids.

She stands and gestures for me to take her seat, but I look at her husband nervously. I like him, but I don't understand what's going on.

Amy walks around her desk and takes a seat in her chair. "Sit down, Charlie. We'd all like to talk to you about something important."

Everett stands and motions to his seat, then guides River back to the one she occupied. Taking a deep breath, I sit down and watch as River does the same next to me.

"What's going on?"

Amy looks at River expectantly, causing me to shift with suspicious eyes at River. "I know we don't know each other very well, but there's something that Everett and I would like to ask you. We hope that you'll consider it and say yes, but there's no pressure if you decide you don't want to. Okay?"

If it were possible, my heart would stop.

River's hand extends to me, palm up, as if she's offering me to take it. I don't and she doesn't get offended. "Charlie, Everett and I would like to adopt you, to make you part of our family. We were wondering if that was okay with you. Would you like that?"

I blink.

Amy covers her mouth like she's trying to hide a big grin, but I know she's smiling because of her wrinkled eyes.

River wants to adopt me?

"Why?" I whisper.

River's head tilts, her red hair falling over her shoulder. "I was your age when I was adopted by the James family. They saw something in me that they were willing to take a chance on, to love. I understand what that feels like, because I've seen the same thing in you. But neither of us wants to do anything you're uncomfortable with. So, if you'll let us, we'd love to welcome you into our family."

Tears blur her image that I can't blink away before they're falling down my cheeks. She reaches out and squeezes my hand in comfort, and all I can think is to squeeze hers back.

Going to Painter's Choice is my favorite part of the week. It's the one place I feel safe, even if I don't paint or draw like everyone else. River lets me listen to music or help Melanie clean up the studio. Two weeks ago, River brought in different pamphlets on music classes that the Community Center holds once a week. She told me if I was interested, to let her know and she'd help me get into one of them.

Lips wavering, I ask, "You really want me?"

River nods. "More than anything, Charlie. Our home is yours if you want it. We can get you enrolled in any school you want, in music programs, whatever will make you happy. You deserve the world. We all believe it."

The tears don't stop as I nod and push off the chair until I'm in her arms. She holds me tight and rubs my back and stays quiet as I use her like a human tissue.

When I pull back, I wipe my cheeks using my shirt sleeve, and turn to Everett. "Can we get donuts to celebrate?"

He chuckles. "Is that a yes then?"

"Yes."

Amy claps. "Oh, this is wonderful!" She turns to River. "Jill has always been so invested in you, sweetie. As soon as she heard you were interested in adopting, she knew you would be a wonderful mother."

Emotion floods River's face as she squeezes my hand again. Everett comes over and messes up my hair, something he's done a few times when he visits River at the studio. He would always bring everyone donuts from the café down the street, which I made sure to get at least two of every time.

Glancing at River and Everett, I take in their wide smiles and the soft tone of their eyes as they share a look. My eyes share the same blurry glaze as they turn their focus on me.

Amy sighs happily. "Let's get started on the paper-work. Charlie, I'm so happy for you. These two are going to help you flourish like I know you can."

Smiling, I sniff back more tears. "You're just saying that because you're happy I can't get into trouble again. Like pulling Jasmine's hair and getting yelled at by Finch."

She deadpans. "You did what?"

I wince. I guess Ms. Finch didn't call her after all. "Nothing. It doesn't matter. But see? You won't have to deal with me anymore."

She pinches the bridge of her nose.

Everett laughs and nudges me lightly with his elbow. "Something tells me you're going to keep us on the edge of our seats, kid."

I grin. They have no idea.

A WEEK AFTER SETTLING INTO RIVER AND EVERETT'S two-story house not far from Painter's Choice, there's a small barbecue to celebrate my adoption. I'm nervous to meet River's family, because I know how much they mean to her.

What if they don't see the same potential in me like they did her?

Rubbing my palms against my blue jeans, I peek out the back window. Everett is laughing with an older man with white hair wearing expensive clothing, and a woman dressed to the nines. Glancing down at my jeans and zip-up hoodie, I realize I may be underdressed.

"What are you looking at?"

Shoulders tensing, I glance behind me to find a tall man with dark hair and eyes watching me with a friendly smile. He doesn't look dressed to impress like the others. Like me, he's wearing jeans that fit his long legs and a plaid button-down that shows a white tank underneath. The first few buttons are undone, and the sleeves are rolled up to his elbows.

"Um..." My throat dries.

"You're Charlotte, right?" His voice is deep but light, and his eyes remind me of the brown frosting on the Boston Cream donuts I love eating from Landmark Café.

"Charlie," I murmur, brushing strands of my long blonde hair behind my ear.

He nods. "I'm Oliver. River's brother."

Playing with the string on my hoodie, I glance between him and the older couple outside. He shares their complexion, and I'm sure some of their features if I were closer to inspect them. "Are those your parents?"

He walks over to me and leans his shoulder against the window. "Yeah. That's Robert and Bridgette. They're excited to meet you."

Tugging on my hoodie, I nudge the floor with my shoe. Looking down at them, I realize they match his. "We're wearing the same Converse."

He chuckles. "We have great taste." Our eyes meet and my cheeks heat. "There's no need to be nervous. My parents are very welcoming people, and they're happy for River and Everett to have found you."

"But I don't ... look like them." I point towards my clothing. River brought me shopping and told me I could pick out whatever I wanted. I asked if we could go to thrift stores, so we spent a few days wandering around Bridgeport window shopping. My attire consists of jeans, leggings, hoodies, and t-shirts. I'm not a dress kind of girl.

He shrugs. "So?"

Swallowing, I point to his mom. "So ... they wear fancy stuff. I'm not a girly girl, I don't wear stuff like that."

"Hey," he comforts, "they're going to love you, Charlie. It doesn't matter what you wear. River will tell you the same thing. Are you comfortable?"

I don't answer.

He kneels. "Are you?" he presses.

Taking a deep breath, I nod.

He playfully nudges me. "That's all that matters then. Are you ready? We can go find River and Everett before we head out."

He offers me his arm, which I look at with wide eyes. He wants to escort me? He's twice my size, both in height and weight. I'd look like a shrimp next to him.

But I link my arm around the crook of his elbow and find myself staring up at him. Biting my lower lip, I fight off the blush as he shoots me a big smile.

I don't usually let strangers touch me, but I don't mind it now.

As we walk to find River, I can't help but wonder if she found this comfort in someone so soon after her adoption.

When I find her and Everett holding hands in the kitchen, smiling lovingly at each other like they've known each other for ages, I feel like I find my answer.

Sneak Peek

Coming August 2nd
The Truth About Tomorrow

I'm woken when my body is pulled into a firm chest and hold my breath when the arm hooked around my midsection tightens. Listening to Ollie's even breathing, I realize he's sleeping. He doesn't know he's cuddling me right now.

Wetting my bottom lip, I debate on what to do. If he wakes up when we're in this position, he'll freak out. I know Ollie. Even though I don't mind this, him holding me, I know he'll feel differently.

Carefully trying to wiggle my way out of his grasp, I start slowly lifting his arm, only to suck in a sharp breath when it tightens around me. The same time his palm flattens against my stomach, his hips roll until something hard presses against my butt.

Oh my God.

The palm on my stomach doesn't rest there, but ever so slowly slides down until it's at the hem of my pajama pants. Biting hard on my lip, I feel the heat between my legs as one of his fingers slips under the elastic. He's still sleeping, still not realizing what he's doing.

I tell myself to wake him up, but the need building inside me clamps my lips closed.

Ollie's fingers dip under the waistband of my pants until they meet bare skin. I bite back a moan as he rolls his hips again, arousal fogging my judgement.

We shouldn't be doing this.

But that doesn't stop me from parting my legs ever so slightly as his hand moves lower. One of his fingers brushes my sex and my lips part in a silent moan. I'm wet already just from these little caresses and fist the sheets when he makes another pass.

His hips roll and a guttural groan escapes him, which only turns me on more. I can't help but put my hand on his and guide him further down until he's cupping me.

My legs shake as one finger enters me, his thumb playing with the bundle of nerves that seek attention. His pace is slow, matching the thrust of his hips. The thrust of his fingers paired with his erection behind me makes me pant until I'm on fire. When a second finger enters me, I gasp his name until all his movements freeze.

Oh no.

In a nanosecond, his fingers are gone and he's out of

bed like it's on fire. "Jesus Christ. I'm so fucking sorry. I thought I was just dreaming."

His frantic eyes search mine in the dim morning light and his hands weave through his hair as he backs farther away from me.

His lips are drawn into a flat line as torture darkens his features. "Are you ... did I hurt you? Fuck, of course I hurt you. What I did—"

"Stop," I command. Pushing the blankets away from me, I meet his eyes. "You didn't hurt me, Ollie. I promise. I ..."

He's silent, studying, worrying.

"I didn't mind at all," I whisper.

He makes a choking sound. "Charlie ..."

He turns, punches a hole into the wall, and growls out a *fuck* before leaving me alone in his bed.

Acknowledgments

This book is an emotional roller coaster that started as an assignment in grad school. My professor told me it wouldn't sell, my peers told me there wouldn't be enough to write about, and so many people said there was no market for it. But I know better than that, because I'm an avid reader of forbidden romance—cheating and all.

I want to thank Micalea and Kellen for believing in me as a writer. Not just for this book, though neither of you doubted it would be my best because of the challenge, but because you believe in my drive. My passion. Thank you for being my best friends, my sisters.

Cassie, you helped me break into this genre when I had no idea what to do. It's nerve wracking entering a new world of writing without a single clue. You made me confident that I could accomplish anything, and I cherish our friendship.

To Letitia Hasser for making a stunning book cover, I

have heard nothing but amazing things about your talents and am so happy I was able to work with you on this special project.

To my betas Melissa and Raquel, you ladies have had my back for a few releases now. Your support in making these books shine mean the world to me.

And a forever thank you to my readers.

You guys are the best—old and new.

About the Author

B. Celeste is the alter ego of Barbara C. Doyle.

Her obsession with forbidden romance enabled her to pave a path into a new world of love, sex, sin, and angst.

Her debut novel is *The Truth about Heartbreak*.